FLIGHT TO DESTRUCTION

THE CREATORS PART 2

FLIGHT TO DESTRUCTION

J M Collin

J.M. COLLIN

Matador
9 Priory Business Park,
Wistow Road, Kibworth Beauchamp,
Leicestershire. LE8 0RX
Tel: 0116 279 2299
Email: books@troubador.co.uk
Web: www.troubador.co.uk/matador
Twitter: @matadorbooks

ISBN 978 1788033 114

British Library Cataloguing in Publication Data.
A catalogue record for this book is available from the British Library.

Printed by TJ International Ltd, Padstow, Cornwall
Typeset in 11pt Minion Pro by Troubador Publishing Ltd, Leicester, UK

Matador is an imprint of Troubador Publishing Ltd

To all those who have made our country better placed to face uncertainty than it was fifty years ago.

Flight to Destruction follows *Road to Nowhere* and precedes *The Turnaround* in telling the story of a group of young people during the turbulent 'long 1970s'. They build their lives and begin to build a world-beating business, while making a difference in some of the greatest crises of the time. The three novels are complete in themselves but form a whole.

J.M. Collin is the pen name of a man who lived through the times described and has many recollections.

CONTENTS

PRINCIPAL CHARACTERS IN 'FLIGHT TO DESTRUCTION'

NAME	AGE	DESCRIPTION
Pete BRIDFORD (*narrator*)	27	Now working for International Electronics plc.
Steph COOLIDGE	34	New Yorker. Senior analyst at New Hampshire Realty Bank.
Ana GUZMAN	23	Daughter of Spanish noble and banking family.
Carol MILVERTON	25	(formerly Gibson) Now married to Paul and working for Labour Party Research Department.
Paul MILVERTON	25	Has just completed his Ph.D. at the London School of Economics.
Morag NEWLANDS	28	Now a lecturer in maths at King's College, London.
Sir Pat O'DONNELL	62	Chief Executive of International Electronics plc, the company he founded in 1938.
Liz PARTINGTON	28	Now working at the London head office of the National Coal Board.
Dick SINCLAIR	28	Now completing a three-year postdoctoral contract at the University of Reading.

NAME	AGE	DESCRIPTION
Jenny SINCLAIR	25	(formerly Wingham) Now married to Dick and mother of David (2). Newly qualified chartered accountant.
Brian SMITHAM	24	Now working for Universal Assurance; married to Susie.
Roberta STRUTT	62	Aunt of Pete Bridford, living in south London.
Harry TAMFIELD	26	Now Chief Executive of Tamfield Investments, a property company.
Greg WOOLLEY	30	Electrical engineer, who knows Liz Partington through a hockey club.
Sheila YATES	31	Lecturer in maths at Queen Mary College, London. Partner of Morag Newlands.

BOOK III
THE CRISIS LOOMS

1. SATURDAY, 7TH JULY, 1973

We stopped dead as we came back into the square and saw the two newly arrived Mercedes'. They were parked outside the *Parador* where we were staying, next to my anonymous-looking Spanish-registered Renault.

"That's the Egyptian Ambassador's private car," said Ana.

"That's Professor Kraftlein's car. I recognise the number. You remember, I told you about him," I replied.

"Time for the bulls," said Ana, firmly.

We entered a small bar. It was full of men, and a few women, who were watching a blurry black and white television picture of the bullfighting at Pamplona. We were not too interested in that, since the next evening we would be seeing it from the best seats in the ring. We settled down in a dark corner, from where we could see out into the sunlit square, but no one outside would notice us. Ana got out her camera and attached a long telephoto lens.

Few people in the bar paid us much attention, though the men behind the counter had jumped to serve us as soon as we came in. Ana, or to quote her full name, Doña Ana Guzman de Leon y Vasquez, was of a noble family. In small-town Spain under Franco, that counted for a lot. Since childhood, she had been accustomed to carry herself in a way which gave no scope for error amongst people who wanted to stay out of trouble. They spotted that, even if they had never met her before. She worked for her father's bank, and was responsible for several important private accounts, including that of the Egyptian Ambassador. The green colour of his Mercedes made it distinctive.

The car I recognised was rather older and its dark red colour was somewhat obscured by the dust of a long drive. I had seen it when it was quite new, parked outside the Statistics Department in Cambridge five years before. Then, I had reminded its owner of the significance of its registration, S-PI 729.[1] He was a brilliant mathematician and former committed Nazi, whose appointment to a chair at Cambridge had caused great controversy.

It would have been unusual enough to have seen either car in the square. To see both at once was a remarkable coincidence. We were looking forward to a rest before dinner, but the puzzle attracted us both.

"It may not be Kraftlein's car any more," I said. "Once he was in Cambridge, he might have sold it and bought a right-hand-drive car. He was quite attached to the Mercedes, though. He said that he liked long drives on the Continent. If he used it in England for several years, he'd have had to re-register it. Perhaps he's left it in Stuttgart, and picks it up when he wants it."

"They're probably inside now, being shown to their rooms. Someone will come out to collect luggage soon."

We settled down to wait, glancing round at the TV and joining in some of the shouts of the crowd. Outside, the square was quiet. As the sun lowered, the battered facade of the cathedral to our right took on a reddish tinge. That matched its memorial plaque to Nationalist dead, topped as always then by José-Antonio Primo de Rivera. We were in the centre of

---

1 See *Road to Nowhere*, Chapter 13.

Santo Domingo de la Calzada, near Burgos and not too far from the ancient boundaries between Castile, Navarre, the Basque country, and Aragón. At the start of the Civil War, we would not have been too far from the front, since that war had been effectively amongst those old kingdoms, with an ideological topping.

After five minutes or so, four people appeared outside the *Parador*. Ana raised her camera. The Mercedes' were opened up, and bags passed to a hotel porter. They all went in again.

"Got you all, three times."

She put the camera down again before anyone in the bar noticed. The current bullfight was nearing the kill, and the audience had plenty of ideas about what the matador should be doing.

"The one on the right *is* Kraftlein. Do you have any ideas on the other two?"

"They look Egyptian. They were talking to your professor. Why should they be doing that?"

"Kraftlein has always had a sideline working for the military. He did so for the Nazis, and then for the Americans. A few years ago, he was on a NATO study group. Someone who was also on the group told me that the work was basically about the capability of air defence systems. How do you best deploy your aircraft and missiles to meet a threat which might arrive any time, and from several possible directions? If you're planning an attack, what deployment and timing gives you the best chance of overcoming defences? It must be quite a complicated mathematical problem."

"So he could be telling these Egyptians how to resist air attack from Israel better than they did six years ago."

"Or how to deploy their attack, so as to have the best chance of getting through the Israeli air defences."

"Does our government know of this meeting?"

"Does NATO?"

3

"Look, they have come out onto the balcony of that first-floor room. It is below my room. I think that we might be able to hear what they are saying. They will probably be talking in English. There are no British cars here. They will not expect to be overheard."

"The Egyptians won't recognise you, Ana. Go in normally, and leave the door of your room slightly open. Kraftlein might recognise me. I'll keep in the shade, and go round the back of the cathedral. I can reach the hotel entrance that way, without being seen from that balcony."

A few minutes later I entered Ana's room, very quietly. She was lying on the floor, by the window, wearing just her underclothes. For visits to monasteries that day, she had been properly dressed, rather than wearing the thin trousers and top she preferred for our excursions in hot weather. Now, she had stripped off her skirt and blouse, to avoid dirtying them on the dusty floor. I took off my shirt and lay down beside her. She put her arm round my waist and pulled me closer.

The *Parador* was built around an old hostel for pilgrims. In the Middle Ages, it had been on an established walking route which led to Santiago de Compostela in the far north-west of Spain. The part we were in was new, though in an old style. As package tourists of the time knew only too well, new often meant flimsily built. Here, a drainpipe running down from the roof had been recessed into the wall, so that it was not so noticeable on the facade. That had left a very thin wall behind it; in fact, there was a hole fully two inches across just above the floor of Ana's room. Through the hole, we could hear clearly the voices a few feet below. As she had guessed, they were using their only common language, which meant that they spoke slowly, and sometimes repeated phrases. This created good listening conditions.

Kraftlein was talking. "I will need to look carefully at your information on the Yid defences, but I warn you now, that from what you have just told me and what I know from other sources, I do not believe there is any strategy which gives you a high chance of penetrating them and inflicting significant damage on their air force. Therefore, your land operations will be conducted facing enemy air superiority. I think that you should encourage your planners to consider things differently. As in 1967, you should provoke the Israelis in some way, and go on doing so until they attack. This time, you can be ready for them. The Russian radar systems that you have now are vastly superior to what you had then, and so are your aircraft and missiles. You will have enough warning of attack to inflict big losses, provided your radar operators are awake. You should tell them that anyone caught asleep on duty will be executed."

One of the Egyptians replied. "In tactical terms, you would be right. We can prevent another 1967. But in strategic terms, we would not recover the territories we lost then. The Jews would still occupy all of Sinai, and the Americans would put no more pressure on them to leave. Gamal Abdel Nasser of blessed memory – he gave us our independence, and with American help he humiliated the British, but then he lost Sinai. Anwar Sadat, he has realised that to recover Sinai, *he must humiliate the Americans.*"

"How can he possibly do that?"

"The Americans drive their big cars. They need Arab oil. We must stop them from obtaining it. If the Americans know that they will receive no Arab oil while the Jews occupy Sinai, and also Palestinian and Syrian territory, they will force the Jews to leave."

"So you need to persuade the Arab states that produce oil, in particular Saudi Arabia, Kuwait and Iraq, and also now Libya, to stop supplies to the USA. Why do you need a war to do that?"

"Without a war, those states will not be persuaded. Their rulers fear that unless they supply America, they will be invaded. The Russians would protest, but could do nothing to help them. Our plan is this. On the date I have told you, we cross the Suez Canal with as many armoured divisions as possible. We will not reach Israel, but with surprise, we will get some way across Sinai. We will lose many men and much equipment, but so will the Jews. They, and their friends in America, will be frightened. The Americans will send aid to Israel. We calculate that after a week, perhaps ten days, the Jews will be able to push our forces back, maybe even across the Suez Canal. That would happen even if there was no American aid, but the Arabs will think that it is happening because of American aid. They will see an American-Jewish invasion of Egypt. They will dare to stop selling oil to America, or to anyone else who supports Israel."

The other Egyptian came in. "Think of the plan as like that of your General Manstein, which in 1940 achieved in six weeks what your First World War generals failed to achieve in four years. Our attack draws the Americans to react wrongly, just as your initial attack drew the British and French into Belgium. Then the real attack is from the Arab oil states. It catches the Americans off guard, just as your attack in the Ardennes caught the British and French off guard."

"That was a very great success. I was in Berlin then, working for the Luftwaffe. I can remember cheering as our troops came back. It did not win us the war, though."

"No, because your Führer did not limit his objectives. Once he was at war with the whole world, he could not win. Anwar Sadat believes, like your Clausewitz, in war as an extension of diplomacy. He has already offered peace with an Israel returning to its boundaries of 1948 to 1967, which are larger than the boundaries first given in the partition of Palestine. The Jews have rejected that offer. *We must force the Americans to make them accept it.*"

"The Americans will know that your attack can be repulsed without their help. Why should they rush to support Israel? If they do not, your plan will have failed completely."

"President Nixon is fighting for his political life because of Watergate. He has only just avoided being impeached. He still hopes he can survive, but knows that his position is very weak. He needs every scrap of support that he can find. The date that we have selected for the attack will increase the pressures on him from the Jewish lobby. Also, a foreign crisis will divert attention from Watergate."

"I like your plan, now I understand it. I think the Führer would have liked it, too. He would certainly have agreed with your choice of date. Time is short. I will change my arrangements. I can be in Cairo by July 24th. I will be pleased to help you work out the air strategy that gives you the best chance of penetrating well into Sinai and holding it for two weeks."

"We should not have told you the date. When you reach Cairo, please tell no one that you know it."

"I have not written it down in the notes I have made, even though I shall keep these on my person at all times. I can remember the date easily. The days of Yid occupation will form the smallest number with five different prime factors. Now, gentlemen, it is nearly twenty hours. As a concession to us humble tourists, here they begin to serve dinner then. I suggest we go down, for afterwards I will retire early. Tomorrow evening I am to be in Paris, over one thousand kilometres away. I must leave at seven hours."

There were sounds of people getting up, a clink of glasses being taken in, and a couple of thumps as the doors to the balcony were closed, with a little difficulty. Then there were muffled sounds from the room below, followed by the door of that closing, and quiet apart from a few passers-by in the square and birds flying to their nests. The cathedral clock struck eight.

I helped Ana up. For a half minute or so, we sat on the bed in silence, while the implications of what we had heard sank in. It was like being in a book by John Buchan, or Ian Fleming. Eventually, I found something to say.

"So, Siegmund Kraftlein hasn't changed his spots."

"Before we talk, let us write down as much as possible of what we have heard."

There were pencil and paper to hand. We sat together in the warm room. I wrote, she corrected me, and pointed out phrases that I had forgotten. After forty minutes, we had a record. She put it into her handbag.

"This will remain with me until we reach Pamplona. Can you understand what he was saying about the date, Pete?"

"Kraftlein was showing off. I wonder what the Egyptians made of it. I think I understand. The smallest number with five different prime factors is $2\times3\times5\times7\times11$, which equals, let me see, 2,310. 2,310 days is rather more than six years. That takes you back to 1967 and the 'Six-Day War'. When was that war, exactly? Ah yes, it broke out on the Monday after my final degree examinations at Cambridge. That was Monday, 5th June 1967. Fighting stopped on Saturday, 10th June 1967."[2]

"So that was when 'occupation' started. What date is 2,310 'days of occupation' from then?"

I made a few scribbled calculations. "It's Saturday, 6th October. That fits in well with what they were saying about Hitler approving. He always took the initiative at weekends."

Ana pulled a diary out of her handbag and looked in it. "It is also a big Jewish festival, called Yom Kippur. An attack on Israel that day will be seen as unfair, and that will increase the pressure on Nixon to give support."

I put my arm round her. "Ana, you're brilliant, to spot that we could listen as we did!"

"I had noticed the drainpipe, and guessed how the place would be built."

"You used your observant eye that helps you take such great photos!"

"Even during the festival in Pamplona, we will be able to have processed those I took from the bar. Also, we can talk over

---

2 The formal ceasefire took effect the next day

with Father what we should do. He will know who to tell. There is nothing more for us to do now. It seems your professor will be back in his room by twenty-two hours. We can dine then, without any risk of you being recognised. So, we have time for our last rest together, Pete."

"Yes, this is the last, I know, Ana," I said.

She turned her back to me, so that I could unclip her bra. Then she sat astride me, and it was a couple of minutes before she replied.

"It is not the end of our friendship, Pete. When I sort my photos, and prepare my book, I shall think much of the happy times we have had together. I hope that in England you will find the right woman, and that Carlos and I will be able to welcome you both to our home."

"You'll have time to settle down before that happens."

"Ah, there is Liz, who you took to Marbella. She is not yet married, I believe."

"Don't remind me of that stupid trip! I should have known it would be a disaster. Liz and I could never live together for long. Of course I will look out, back home. I hope I'll be as happy there as I have been with you, Ana. We knew it would come to an end. It's lucky that's happening for both of us at the same time."

After another little pause, she undid my trousers' belt and found what was inside. I slid her out of her pants.

Before going out for our walk round town we had put a bottle of Catalan champagne into the 'minibar'. It was nicely cool now as we opened it, and began our established 'rest' routine. She placed a folded towel on my lap, put pillows each side, and stretched out across me, face up. I took my time to fondle her slight figure gently. I teased a bit, saving until later the places she particularly liked. After a while, she turned over, to lie face down as my hands ran through her flowing dark hair, and worked on her back and bottom.

"Feeling you through the towel is making me wet, it is lovely," she murmured. "The towel is dry though, don't worry... Ah, that is blissful… Aaahh… *Aaahhh!* I will miss you so much, Pete. I have been able to trust you, and to learn from you so many things the nuns never told me. Your gentleness means that I will meet Carlos as a virgin who knows what to expect from a man. Father trusts you, too. He knows how you have helped me."

"Will Carlos let you wait?"

"Once we are betrothed Carlos will want me. If he did not want me, there would be something wrong with him, as there was with Don Ottavio! He will not be used to holding back. That is the way it is in Spain. Men do it, but nice women do not. I must be sure that he has not caught anything in Argentina. You have made it easier for us to wait, Pete. We can do what you and I have done. I hope our fathers will not make us wait too long, though. I think much of how it will be with Carlos. He *is* a handsome man."

"I'm so pleased that you really want him. It's not just what your families plan."

"I am worried that he, and his family, are too much the old Falangists. This is 1973, but they behave as if it is 1943, or perhaps 1953."

"You'll be good at persuading him to be a progressive Francoist."

"I will try."

She turned on to her back again. Now I worked harder, but still carefully so as to leave no sign.

"I am ready," she whispered after a few minutes.

"So am I."

I knelt on the floor, and she crouched before me. There was a soft squelching as I reached over her back to finger her, and she took me in her mouth. A few minutes later, we were two very satisfied people. So it was somewhere in between John Buchan and Ian Fleming.

After we had calmed down, I returned to my room to clean up and change. I knew that for our last dinner on our own, Ana would want to take time about looking good.

But for Ana, so much would be different for me, and for International Electronics (IE), the company which I had joined five years before, after leaving Cambridge suddenly. Now, because of her, we knew that so much could be different for our countries. She had gained us advance notice of the next war.

Three points stood out. First, any action by the Arab oil producers couldn't easily be directed only at the USA. Oil travelled in giant tankers, which since 1967 had had to take the long way round the Cape of Good Hope. It took over a month to reach its destination, which often wasn't settled when it left the oilfields. The UK and Western Europe depended far more on Arab oil than did the USA. A stoppage could hit us harder.

Secondly, a stoppage would lead to higher oil prices. Those would be relished by the important non-Arab oil producers, such as Venezuela and Iran (then ruled by the Shah), to say nothing of the USA's own oil companies. The impact would continue, even after any stoppage had ended.

Lastly, prospects for the UK's own North Sea oil would be transformed. Over the previous two years, discoveries had established the scale of reserves, but it was clear that much of these would not be economic unless oil prices rose significantly. Now, that would happen. For companies able to deliver the right equipment, the potential market would be much larger. A month before, Sir Pat O'Donnell, IE's Chief Executive, had asked me what the next market priority for the company should be. Even then, I had had little doubt. Now, I had no doubt.

There was a lot to do from tomorrow onwards, though not tonight. Ana's father, Don Pedro Guzman de Leon y Jiminez, would certainly be interested in our story. So would Pat.

I had first met Ana more than two years before, after arriving in Madrid to open a Spanish office. My move there happened in the way things often did in IE. The company's founder still ran it autocratically despite being 'Pat' to all, even after he had become Sir Pat on account of his donations to various educational institutions. He had hunches, which usually worked out well.

After some two years at the semiconductor factory in Sunderland into which he dropped me, I thought I had just about mastered the art of production management. Then, at the end of October 1970, the factory manager called me in to say, in a rather resigned tone, that the Chief Executive wanted me for unspecified duties at the head office, beginning the Monday after next. So that Monday, I reported to Pat. He told me that I was temporarily attached to his office for three months. There would be some short-term assignments, but my main task was to learn Spanish and sort a work visa out before going to Madrid.

He had noticed that industry in Spain was growing very fast, though the Franco Government maintained tight restrictions on the amounts of imported materials and components that could be used. Now, that government wanted to see export industries develop, the Spanish consumer wanted to buy goods comparable to what were available in other countries, and the millions of tourists visiting Spain wanted to have facilities comparable to what they would have at home. All this would happen only if there were factories in Spain producing, to high quality, all sorts of components used in larger items like cars and household equipment.

IE's main business was in the manufacture of electrical and electronic components, rather than of finished consumer goods. Pat wanted us to form partnerships with local companies, to develop the component industry that Spain needed. We could sell our expertise, and profit from royalties. That had been the challenge. On a bleak day in February 1971, I arrived in Madrid with very little idea of how to meet it.

I quickly found out that the equity market hardly existed. Industry was almost wholly financed by banks. These were stuffy institutions, located in grandiose buildings occupied by large numbers of men who seemed to do very little, as customers wanting service found out to their cost. Somewhere at the top of the grandiose buildings were rather mysterious men who were directors. Most of them had long and impressive names prefaced by Don, which implied at least some connection with an ancient family owning an estate somewhere, maybe even a castle. Many of the senior jobs appeared to be hereditary. To get anywhere, I had to speak to some of these men.

I wrote many letters, and received few responses. Even those responses were merely rather verbose acknowledgements, with promises of further consideration. I tried calling, and wasted a great deal of time in reception rooms. The British Embassy had a commercial department, but was unable to help. I flew back to London for a few days and talked to the banks with which IE dealt, but they had no contacts.

Three months in, I had got nowhere. It wouldn't be long before I would have to close the office and admit to Pat that I had failed. Then, I had a stroke of luck.

I went along to *Don Giovanni* at the Teatro Real, taking an odd seat in the stalls at the last minute. I found myself sitting next to a young woman with the typical Spanish good looks of dark hair over a thin face. She was accompanying a distinguished looking older man, and they were enjoying the opera greatly. This became very clear during applause after a scene between Donna Anna and her fiancé Don Ottavio, who arrives too late to save her father from being killed. Donna Anna says that the only reason she allowed a mysterious man into her bedroom is that she had thought it was him! My neighbour was sceptical. 'He's such a *wet*, I bet she was really hoping it was someone else!' is a fair translation of what she said.

I had nothing to lose. At the interval, I remarked to her that in the last scene of Act I, Don Ottavio had shown more verve. They were clearly surprised that I had reasonable Spanish, and we began to chat. To my saying that they seemed to have a particular liking for the opera, she explained that her name was Ana and her father was Don Pedro, which is also the name of the now dead 'Commendatore'.

At the end, we had to collect our coats, for the nights were still cold at the beginning of May. Whilst waiting at the cloakroom, we talked more about how Mozart's music described all the characters. Ana commented that when Donna Anna tells Don Ottavio that he will have to wait through a year's mourning before marrying her, she is perhaps expressing her hope that during that time somebody better will turn up. A wealthy heiress should have plenty of choice. Her father had taken this perhaps insensitive comment in good part. With a hint from her, he invited me to join them for supper. It was not yet midnight, quite early for Madrid.

So, we talked on, all on formal terms, using '*usted*' rather than '*tu*' for 'you'. By the end of the meal, I had found out that Don Pedro was a big man in Pamplona. Also, he was a director of the Banco Navarrese, one of the largest Spanish banks, whose head office was there. He was visiting the Madrid office, and meeting his daughter. She was in her last year at the University of Madrid, studying economics. I told him a little of what I was trying to do. He gave me his card, with the name of someone at the bank's head office. When he returned to Pamplona, he would tell them to receive me.

At last, I was started. Only two weeks later, which was quick for Spain then, I visited Pamplona for an extensive discussion, and was thenceforward very much on the books of the Banco Navarrese. Over the next year, partnerships with the fledgling IE España came into being, as I brought managers in production divisions out to meet opposite numbers in the Spanish companies that the bank financed. This was 'technology transfer' in modern jargon. Fees, prospective royalties, and some direct sales began to build up sufficiently that IE's divisional Directors said that I was being useful, and that another of Pat's hunches was working out.

For some time, I had no further opportunity to speak to Ana. In the autumn, at a Banco Navarrese reception, I saw her across the room, with a very handsome man of the kind I would expect her to know. In February 1972, I arranged a reception for my widening range of contacts, on a date when I knew Don Pedro was visiting Madrid. He arrived with Ana, and there was no sign of her friend, so we had a few polite words about how happy had been the chance of that meeting at the opera.

A few weeks later, his bank had held another reception, and again Don Pedro had arrived with Ana. He left her rather on her own as he worked the room. I also needed to spend time with contacts, but towards the end I caught up with her. Quite quickly, she mentioned that her father was taking some guests off to a private dinner, and she was at a loose end that evening. These were still times of formal relationships, and she was the daughter of a man upon whom much of my business depended. So it was with a little trepidation that I invited her out.

Over dinner we found out more about each other. She was a few years younger than me. She had finished university the previous summer, and was now working for the bank. Like her operatic namesake, she was an only child, whose mother had died a few years before. Her father's principal residence was a very large house, in substantial grounds a few miles outside Pamplona. She denied that it was a castle, but admitted that parts of it dated back to the 1300s and had met the security standards of that time. He also owned town houses in Pamplona and Madrid.

We talked about how everyone was preparing for the handover of power, including elections, after Franco died. 'Everyone' included Franco. The story was going round that the young Prince Juan Carlos had asked to work with the ageing Generalissimo. He had argued that as Franco's designated successor, he needed to learn how to do things the right way. Franco had replied that there was no point, since to survive as king, Juan Carlos would have to do things quite differently. Many years later, King Juan Carlos repeated that story on TV, after we had seen its truth amply borne out.

Ana's family had been strongly Nationalist, though like most in Navarre, conservative monarchist rather than fascist. However, they knew that change had to continue. They supported 'progressive Francoism', of the kind then propounded by Manuel Fraga, the man behind the creation of Spain's huge tourist industry.

Talk of change led to talk of how in a few years' time the old Spain that Ana had grown up in would be gone. She asked me how much I had seen of it. I admitted that I had not seen much. Most of my visits had been to large cities, around which industry was taking off. She offered to show me what I had missed. She was a keen photographer. Her father had given her a top of the line Nikon outfit as a graduation present. She wanted to record as much of the old Spain as possible, before it vanished. Doing that would be much easier with me than as a lone woman. I had a car, and she knew where to go. By the end of the meal, we were comrades in an enterprise. We had dropped the 'Doña' and 'Señor', and were using the informal 'tu'.

We began with day trips to places not far from Madrid, but Ana wanted to visit places a hundred or more miles away, which on the roads of the time dictated at least a weekend. She set an energetic pace. On a typical day away we started early, bumping our way along narrow, often unmade roads where cars were infrequent. First, we might visit a small town full of Romanesque churches, unchanged since first built nine hundred years before, at the time of reconquest from Moslem rule. Often there would also be a few magnificent though decrepit buildings in the grand style of the 1500s, when for a while gold and silver poured in from Mexico and Peru. Next, we might see a huge castle perched on a peak, followed by a monastery or pilgrimage church in a remote location. There would be stops in villages where people and animals mingled in picturesque squalor. We would reach another town, and look round before staying the night, perhaps at a comfortable state-run *Parador*, but very possibly at somewhere much more modest. Before dinner, she always dusted and checked her photographic equipment.

Ana was very unusual for her class, as I had realised that first evening at the opera. At that time in Spain, daughters of aristocratic families did not go to university. They stayed at home until married to a suitable man, very likely someone whom their parents had selected. She had broken out of that custom, but had not made many friends at university, because she remained a Nationalist. She was only in the job she was in now because she was her father's daughter. There was no other woman in any kind of responsible position at the bank. Therefore, she wasn't liked or trusted by the other staff. Her father and I were unusual in being prepared to treat her as an intelligent person.

We became close friends, and her English and my Spanish improved greatly. However, our relationship remained tightly bounded. The man I had seen her with was a second cousin, a little older than me and thus several years older than her. His parents owned large estates not far from Pamplona. Her mother's dying wish had been that she should marry him; since then, she had been informally betrothed. He also worked for the bank, and was currently posted to Buenos Aires. It was assumed by all that when he returned, the betrothal would become formal. The expectation was that she would walk up to the altar a virgin. In Madrid, she lived quietly at her father's house, and she could not be seen going out with men. That was another reason to get out of town with a companion.

All this was made plain to me on our second weekend trip, when I gave her a tentative kiss. She was a perfectly normal woman. Her intended was thousands of miles away, and was probably enjoying himself lots with girls out there. She would like to enjoy herself with me, but she had to be able to trust me not to go too far. I observed that my name wasn't John, and expressed hope that her intended's name wasn't Octavian. She told me that it was Carlos. That concluded an awkward conversation with a laugh together, and a friendly kiss back.

The fact that I depended on her father's goodwill certainly built her trust. I needed to work within that, but friendship and comradeship built affection, and interest.

At a small hotel on our fourth trip, only her room had a shower. She invited me to use it, and didn't leave the bathroom whilst I did so. Instead, as I stepped out she looked over me, nervously and intently, before passing me a towel. So when she used the shower, I did the same, rather apprehensively.

We said nothing until we were both dressed again. Then she put her arm round me, and started to talk, hesitantly. It was the first time that she had seen a man naked, or been seen naked by a man. She asked how many women I had seen naked, and I replied that I had so seen three women. She asked me to tell her more about them, and what we had done together. That took the rest of the evening. Fortunately, it was unlikely that anyone else in the dining room spoke English.

Nothing further happened on that trip, but gradually we moved on. By August, when Madrid emptied in the heat, it had become part of our routine to pleasure each other safely during a 'rest' before the late Spanish dinner. I did not return to England for a break, since in June my parents had visited me during a touring holiday of their own. They had been pleased to meet Ana, and relieved to be made aware that she would never be any more than a good friend, but they had declined to join one of our excursions as it seemed to be rather energetic.

In the autumn of 1972 came dramatic intelligence. Ford were planning to build a huge new car factory on the outskirts of Valencia. To go ahead, they would need assurance that local suppliers would be available. IE were ahead of the game in creating such suppliers of electrical components. Now, we needed to grab a large share of the new business. I received two assistants from the UK, and recruited several more local staff. Things were very hectic, and the winter cold. It was March before weekends became possible again.

Just after Easter, Ana and I were very respectable when we visited friends of her family who lived in Seville. We enjoyed the great spring festival, the *Feria*, as well as exploring in and around the small palace in which we were staying. That was in the Santa Cruz quarter, the scene of the action in the play on which *Don Giovanni* is based. So it set off happy memories of our first meeting, as has done any performance of the opera since then. One of the best produced of the thirty or so that I have seen was at the English National Opera in the late seventies. It picked up the Santa Cruz setting.

The last evening away, Ana told me that Carlos was due back early in July, during Pamplona's Festival of St Firmin. Her betrothal would be announced and celebrated at the end of the festival. However, she and her father very much wanted me to be their guest for a short time early in the festival, before Carlos arrived. Their town house had a balcony from which the famous 'bull running' could be observed safely. The bullfights were rivalled only by those we had seen in Seville.

Officially, this was a business invitation, but it was also to show their gratitude for the help I had given on her explorations, which had yielded a crop of thousands of photographs. As soon as she was formally betrothed, she would have to give up her job with the bank, and retire to Pamplona. There, she would prepare a book of them and seek a publisher.

By then I was shuttling back and forth between Madrid and London, arguing the case for investing in key suppliers. Benefits to IE from the Ford Valencia plant would be even greater if we did so, but interest rates were rising, there were exchange control problems, and other contenders within IE for the funds available. I would probably have to be content with half a loaf. Or rather, others would have to be content.

During my most recent visit, Pat called me in to ask about the next priority, and went on to say that whatever the decision on investment, my task in Spain was complete. He suggested that Doug Gilbert, the more senior of my assistants, could take on my job. I agreed, and said that I could hand over to Doug and return permanently by mid-August.

Meanwhile, though, he wanted me to attend the annual IE Corporate Meeting, which was to take place from 12th to 14th July. He said, rather mysteriously, that at the meeting would be someone whom I knew already, and would be interested to meet again.

So that morning, Ana and I had set off early from Madrid on our last journey together. My car was less heavily laden than it might have been. The week before, Don Pedro had stood us a very good lunch for his and my joint name-day.[3] Ana pointed out how large was his car, and suggested that if he could take to Pamplona some of what I wanted to move back to the UK, there would be room for her and her luggage in my car.

Our first stop of the day was at the magnificent Romanesque double cloister of Santo Domingo de Silos. We had been there before, but this time, Ana's connections had secured us permission to visit the private upper level to enhance her photo collection. Then an arduous drive over rough roads, with a picnic on the way whilst the car radiator cooled, took us to the monasteries of San Millan de la Cogolla, where the celebrations of a thousand years since construction were already being trailed for four years hence. It was not far from there to the Santo Domingo at which we were now staying.

We would arrive in Pamplona for lunch the next day. Before I left, I would see two afternoons of bullfights and two mornings of bull running. Carlos would arrive late on Tuesday afternoon,

---

3 St Peter's Day, 29th June – a public holiday in Spain.

at about the same time as I was sailing out of Bilbao on the Swedish Lloyd ferry *Patricia*.

Ana and I had done so much for each other. My first few months in Spain had been frustrating from the point of view of work, and lonely in personal terms. There had followed times which were very rewarding and very busy, but still lonely. The last year had been so much better personally, and my work had not been impaired.

At Cambridge, my life had improved in the same way after Liz Partington had prised me from my academic shell. More than anyone else, she had made me the man I was. I owed her a great deal. She was the daughter of the Master of my College, Waterhouse, and an only child, as was I. My relationship with her had gained empathy on that account; we had become the sister and brother neither of us had.

Though Ana was very different from Liz, I had some of the same empathy with her. I had been someone who met Ana's needs, but whom she could trust not to go too far. I had put off any unwelcome advances from others, as well as being the driver and equipment carrier for our excursions. I had shown her how she could have a relationship based on mutual respect, rather than domination. Her father too had known how valuable it was for her to have me around. Neither of them had suffered the fate of their operatic namesakes.

We could not have gone further. I could not have become a Spanish grandee, a Roman Catholic living on an estate. Nor could she have come back to the UK with me. Her plans were set, and though they seemed very old fashioned, they were what she wanted and accepted.

I wondered how Liz was getting on. My life with her had started one evening during my fourth term in Cambridge when, on returning to my room with two mugs of coffee made in the staircase kitchen, I had found her ready and waiting in my bed. A year or so later, our very different interests had led us to revert to being 'best friends plus' – like brother and sister, but with occasional incest. After she had rightly broken off what had seemed to be a glittering engagement, and I had become a production manager rather than a promising academic, she had been able to take a job with the National Coal Board and follow me to the North East. Initially we had seen much of each other, but Liz's interest in sport soon led her to friendships and more. For some while, what little time I had left after work was spent mostly on writing up my Cambridge research for publication.

Then I moved to Spain, and shortly afterwards Liz moved to a job at the Coal Board's London headquarters. I met her sometimes when back on business, and that had led us to have another go at being together. In the spring of 1972, we tried a holiday in the south of Spain. It was good for a few days and nights, but soon the problems of our relationship had reappeared. She wanted to be by the pool or water sporting all day, and at discos much of the night. I had my car and wanted to visit some of the interesting towns of the south. By the end, we were holidaying almost separately, particularly once she met some like-minded men. Soon after that, my relationship with Ana had taken off. Sometimes I would call Liz to say that I was visiting London, but her diary had always been full.

So, I had been quite surprised, as well as pleased, when a call to Liz to tell of my latest plans led to an invitation to stay over the weekend following the IE Corporate Meeting. That would work out well; before catching the boat back to Spain, I could go on to spend a few days with my parents in Dorset.

I was interrupted in these thoughts by a knock at the door. I gasped at what I saw when I opened it. Ana's crimson dress and necklace set off her dark skin superbly. She smiled and explained.

"On Tuesday, when Carlos sits beside me for the bulls, I will be wearing this. Then, it will be a clear sign. I wanted you to see it, Pete. Tomorrow and on Monday, I will be plainer, and you will be three places along from me. Now, I have heard Professor Kraftlein return to his room."

She took my arm, and we went down for the best dinner the *Parador* could provide.

2. THURSDAY, 12ᵀᴴ JULY, 1973

"You're blooming marvellous, Jenny. That's about both what you've done and how you look now. I'm very happy it's all working out so well."

"It's not been easy, Pete. I made the right choice of firm. Plenders have a written policy that women should have the same opportunities as men. That doesn't help when you're out on a job in an audit team, though. Apart from the lads who assume that you're fair game when you're working away from home, there are the managers who assume that you won't concentrate on your work because you're worrying about your family. I've made my number, now. I'm finishing at Reading in three weeks' time, but from next summer there's a three-day-a-week job at the Brighton office."

We were leaning on the rail of the *Patricia* as it nosed up Southampton Water. Jenny Sinclair was six months gone with her second. As a proud mother to be, she was just as attractive as when, some five years before, she had been my girlfriend. A suntan set off her blonde hair, and shorts showed her fine, long legs.

"When are you moving?"

"By the beginning of September, I hope. We've an offer on our flat in Reading. Before going home today we'll drive along to Brighton. The market there's now distinctly in favour of buyers. We'll also call in at the hospital and make sure they know I'll be there."

"From what I've read, you did well to buy rather than rent when you went to Reading."

"That's very right, Pete. At the time, we were lucky to get the mortgage. Dick had a three year postdoctoral contract to wave, and I made clear I was going on in accountancy. No one dared to ask about family plans, and it was far too early for there to be any sign of David. Now, our offer is for double what we paid. We need a little house near Brighton, which I reckon we can do. My salary is more bankable now, Dick has a two-year contract at Sussex, I've still got something from Mum and Dad, and I think Dick's parents will help too. What are *you* going to do, though? By going abroad, you missed out on the property boom."

"I've something saved. The overseas allowance isn't bad. First, I must find out where Pat O'Donnell wants me to go next."

"If you want any advice, give me a call, and that reminds me, perhaps you can give *me* some advice. I bought last Sunday's *Telegraph* at the shop here, and noticed this in the share column."

She pulled a cutting out of her handbag.

'Tamfield Investments

At the age of 26, Harry Tamfield continues to be the most audacious of the young buccaneers who have taken the property world by storm during the last two years. Early investors have every reason to be pleased. Can he go on pleasing investors, now? The market clearly believes he can, with the issue to finance last April's takeover of Cardinal Properties being three times oversubscribed and going away at a 20% premium.

But the takeover makes him very dependent on the success of a few big projects, notably the Bishop's Park development of over 800 houses and flats in south London. Harry Tamfield's initial success was in small developments and property conversions. He was right to take on Cardinal at the price, but now, as credit becomes more difficult, he faces as big risks as he took three years ago when credit began to ease and he expanded so aggressively.

Recommendation: HOLD, watchfully. BUY as a high risk element of a balanced portfolio.'

"I'm glad Harry's doing so well," I said. "Your Uncle Archie must be grateful for the tip I gave him. I think he put in £10,000 of his own money."

"Harry Tamfield must think he's doing well. The day before we came away, this arrived."

She showed me a rather expensively produced and ornate invitation to a celebration of Tamfield Investments' acquisition of Cardinal Properties. This was to take place on the coming Sunday afternoon and evening, at a country house near Maidenhead. At the bottom was a handwritten note from Harry.

'This isn't far away from you. I do hope you can come.'

"That's good of Harry, to remember you all. I hope the weather stays fine. I expect there are pleasant gardens. Will you take David?"

"You've been away, Pete, so you wouldn't know. That place is a club. It's mentioned from time to time in the newspapers. It stays just the right side of the law. Those who go will know what to expect. There'll be good-looking young men and women, who aren't there because they took part in the acquisition."

"Oh, so it's another angle on Harry being a high-risk player. Some of those he's invited will like the idea. Others may be curious enough to go along, but he risks offending important contacts, or at least their wives."

"Not so many will be offended, now. Things have changed a lot in three years, Pete. The message these days is to enjoy yourself before it all falls apart. I wouldn't take David near that place; and even if we could get him looked after, I wouldn't enjoy it myself. Harry Tamfield is a nasty man, just as I said after that one time I met him. There's been a lot in the papers about how he's made his money. I'm not Labour, but the way people like him work isn't proper business."

We were passing the Fawley Oil Refinery, alongside which a huge tanker was unloading. How many more of those would arrive, later in the year? The message to enjoy yourself before it all fell apart seemed to me very appropriate as I replied.

"So you're not going, then."

"That's the problem between us. Dick wants to go, but I don't. Dick said that perhaps he should go on his own. He can't use the car without me, but it's not far from Maidenhead Station. When I asked him why he wanted to go, he wasn't very clear. That was all before we left home, and we haven't talked about it while we've been away. Now, we need to sort it out. You know why I'm worried, Pete."

"Yes I do, Jenny, but I don't think you should be. Harry is showing to the world that he's made it, and he wants his friends to join in celebrating that. Hey, that gives me an idea. Harry has my office address in Madrid. An invitation has probably been sent there. It hadn't arrived last Friday, but you know what the Spanish post is like. I need to call in tomorrow, so I'll check. I'm curious enough. On Sunday afternoon and evening, Liz is going to the guest day at Brian Smitham's firm's sports club. It's up to me whether I go with her. When Dick asks you again, say that I may also have been invited to the celebration, and suggest that on Saturday evening he calls me at Liz's place to find out if I'm going. We could arrange to meet at Maidenhead, and I could keep an eye."

"Oh Pete, that would be a relief. It's great too that Liz wants to meet you again. She's working very hard, and sounded to be in rather a state when I called her a couple of weeks ago."

"She seemed cheerful enough when I called. She's planning a dinner party for the Saturday evening, and wants me there by six o'clock, so that I can help cook."

Dick Sinclair joined us, along with a handsome blond boy taking after both his parents.

"Has Daddy taken you for a nice walk round, David?"

"Yes, Mummy. When will we be home?"

"First, we're going to see where we'll be moving for Daddy's new job. If you're good, we'll buy you some rock. That's a nice sweet, to lick. Now, come back to the cabin with me. I must change, and I know what you may need. It's lovely to have met you again, Pete, and to hear that you're coming back to England. Dick, why don't you stay with Pete until we're called to the cars?"

"It's great to meet you all again, especially on your anniversary. Happy twenty-fifth birthday to come, Jenny."

Jenny and David left, and Dick continued.

"It's great to have met you again, Pete. You've clearly had a good time in Spain, what with Ana as well as your work. We would have let you know our plans if we'd made them earlier. Jenny wanted to celebrate her examination results as well as our third anniversary. She remembered your tip about how good northern Spain is and how easy it is to get there. There was just room on here, and Swedish Lloyd fixed up the hotels. It's good value too, and they make you feel welcome. Last year we went to France at this time, just after the pound was floated. That made it more expensive, but even worse, a lot of banks weren't changing travellers' cheques and people in hotels didn't want to know you unless they saw your money, in francs. It wasn't the way to have a pleasant holiday."

We chatted on until we were called. As I waited to disembark, I thought of the contrast between Dick and Jenny.

As I had expected, once married they had got on with it; but Jenny had returned to her accountancy firm, Plender Luckhurst. Early in June, her long hours of evening study had borne fruit with success in the examinations to become a qualified chartered accountant. She had knocked around, shown the force of her character and escaped from her rather sheltered upbringing.

Dick was still the tall and handsome man I had known, but he was beginning to sound older than his twenty-eight years. He had recovered from the setback in his research that had driven him to take an overdose of sleeping tablets, but it had taken him nearly four years to complete his Ph.D., even with extensive help from Geoff Frampton, the brilliant biochemist who was his research supervisor and Liz's erstwhile fiancé. Dick had yet to secure a permanent academic post. He had found another two years of research funding at the University of Sussex, perhaps because the professor there was related to Sir Archibald Frampton, who was Geoff's father, Jenny's uncle, and a Cambridge grandee.

Jenny led the marriage, though she was three years younger than Dick. She was also bringing in the money. They travelled in her company car. It would be her career that determined where they went in the future. He might end up at home, looking after the children. All this is not so unusual now. It was very unusual then.

Jenny had been more vehement about Harry and his invitation than I might have expected. She was not at all averse to harmless and suggestive fun, and her interest in financial numbers had been awakened through an argument with Harry that one time she had met him. I knew why she was worried, though. Until Harry had entered Waterhouse College, Liz had been Dick's girlfriend. Then, Harry and Dick had been together for nearly two years, leaving Liz to take me in hand. Jenny had known all this when she went with Dick rather than with me, and all had been well so far. But could Harry and Dick now be interested in each other again? This little ripple could be the sign of a greater, unseen disturbance.

I remembered Ana's amazement when I had told her about Dick and Harry. That had been in response to her asking me whether I had ever met a homosexual. In Spain, homosexuality was strongly repressed, and a more liberal approach wasn't high on the agenda of 'progressive Francoism'. I had told Ana that to me the most important thing was that my friendship with both Jenny and Dick had survived, whilst Harry was doing well on his own.

We had kept up by letter, but I had not seen Jenny or Dick since being Dick's Best Man three years before – to this day, the only occasion other than the investiture on which I have worn morning dress. Only at lunchtime the day before had I spotted that they were on board. After we sailed on Tuesday evening, I had dined in the later sitting, being by now a confirmed Spaniard in my eating habits. With David, they had naturally taken the earlier sitting.

Joining in anniversary celebrations had given me a rather sleepless night, with my mind going back just over five years. After a long and happy weekend at Jenny's home in Cambridge, I had left seemingly without a cloud, and was looking forward to end of term jollifications. A week later, she had been with Dick, helping him to recover from the overdose, and I had been beginning my first day with IE in Sunderland. Just as with Liz, our relationship wouldn't have worked out, but its sudden end had been quite a wrench.

Eventually, I explained my heavily laden Spanish car sufficiently to the Customs, and found my way to my parents' Dorset home. My mother greeted me with a pleasant surprise.

"Pete, Roberta's staying with us until the weekend. She's pleased you're here."

This was a surprise, because my mother was on cool terms with her older sister, and my father positively disliked her. It was a pleasant surprise, because once I had made my own contact with Roberta some years before, she and I had come to get on very well. I had seen the intelligence and force beneath her rather cantankerous nature. Though now widowed, she continued to live in a large house in Bellinghame, a pleasant south London suburb. When working at the IE head office before going to Spain, I had stayed there for three months. Now,

I would probably be based in London again for a while, so the opportunity for another stay would be very welcome.

I impressed them both by saying that I needed to call Spain, and unloaded most of my luggage whilst waiting for the call to be placed. Fortunately, I was through quite quickly. Over lunch, I told them something about Spain. My mother was pleased to hear how useful my friendship with Ana had been, but was clearly relieved at confirmation that it would go no further. My aunt had heard about Ana in letters. She nodded, but I sensed that she wasn't listening; certainly she looked worried.

Over coffee, my mother came to the point.

"Pete, I think Roberta needs your help. Roberta, you'd better tell Pete what you've told me."

"You remember that behind my house there was a school with a lot of grounds, and an old hospital. When you stayed, we knew that both were closing. Also, we knew that houses would be built on the sites."

"Yes, I remember that."

"Early last year the school and hospital were demolished and they started to build. I'd not taken much notice. It was all behind the hedge at the end of the garden. It was better to have something done with the land than to leave it waste. It looked as if there would be some space between the nearest houses and my boundary. Also, for several months nothing happened at all because the building workers went on strike. In May, work began again, and now, some of the houses, and one block of flats, look almost finished. There's a notice outside saying that the Sales Office and show houses and flats open on Monday. But, a month ago, I had this letter from the company that's taken over the firm who began the work."

She showed me a letter from a Mr Percival of Tamfield Investments, which explained that following their takeover of Cardinal Properties they were now the developers of the Bishop's Park site. It said also that she would be aware that the planning permission for the development, granted on 22nd April, 1971, required the demolition of her house to allow an access road to be constructed. He would call at her earliest convenience, to discuss arrangements for the purchase of the property, on which the company was ready to move to rapid completion. She would wish to consult her solicitor, whose reasonable fees the company would pay.

"I'd no idea that any of this might happen. I contacted Frank Booth, the solicitor who dealt with Herbert's will and holds the deeds. He checked with the Borough Council offices. Apparently, I should have been sent a letter, asking for my comments on the planning application. I never saw it. That was around the time you went off to Spain, when the postmen were on strike for six weeks.[4] Maybe the letter got lost."

"Why is another access road needed? The school and the hospital had access from the main road your road leads into. Presumably the construction traffic uses that access now, and so will visitors to the Sales Office. What's wrong with it?"

"The main road is busy. The Council doesn't want a lot of traffic coming on to it there. They want most of the traffic to use our road, which is quite wide, and already has a roundabout where it meets the main road. The way through my house needs to be ready, before most of the houses are sold."

"There won't be any way through your house unless you agree to sell. It's perfectly possible for a council to give planning permission to A in respect of B's land, though they should tell B about it. That doesn't give A any right to the land, though."

"That's what Frank said. I was very firm when we met Mr Percival. It's my house. I'm not going to be pushed out, particularly when I've never heard of any of this before. He was apologetic and explained that his firm had only recently taken over. Cardinal should have approached me much earlier. He would see what they could do, and write again. That seemed

---

4 Between 20th January and 8th March, 1971

sensible enough. I could move if I had the right offer, including something for the disturbance."

"Tamfield Investments must sell these houses fast, to bring their borrowings down now house prices have stopped rising and interest rates are going up. Before they can do that, they need to get you out and complete the new access road. What's your house worth?"

"Other houses of the same size in the road have been advertised for around £30,000, recently."

"An extra £5,000 or even £10,000 for you is money well spent for Tamfield Investments. What happened next?"

"For over a fortnight, nothing except that over the back hedge I could see the access road being built, heading straight for the middle of my house. Then two weeks ago, I received *this*."

The second letter from Mr Percival said that Tamfield Investments were ready to purchase the property, at an independent valuation plus £5,000. If the offer were not accepted by 5th July, the Council would be asked to begin procedures for compulsory purchase, for which the terms were likely to be less good. Roberta continued, firmly:

"A valuation would be low. In that very wet weather we had in the autumn of 1968, a lot of water got into the roof. We should have had it repaired properly, but we didn't, because by then Herbert was very ill and we couldn't face the trouble. After that, I never got round to it. Now, there's some rotten timber."

"This is very heavy handed," I replied. "The Council could begin procedures in the public interest. Perhaps they could argue that completing the development and people moving in benefitted the area as a whole. You would have right of appeal. It would take at least six months. Tamfield Investments can't afford that delay."

"Yes, that's what Frank said too, so I didn't reply. At half past eight last Friday morning, the 6th, my phone rang. I answered, but there was no one there. That happened several times during the day. After I'd gone to bed, there was a crash of breaking glass from the front. I went downstairs. A brick had been thrown through the dining room window. I couldn't sleep the rest of the night. In the morning, I found that some of the roses in the front garden had been trampled on and broken. During Saturday, there were more of the phone calls. On Saturday night it seemed quiet, and I drifted off to sleep. Then on Sunday morning I found – oh dear, it was horrible."

Roberta paused, obviously upset, and my mother continued.

"There was excrement on the doorstep. Roberta spoke to Gerald, who moved in on Sunday. He kept a lookout in the evening, and chased some people away. On Monday, he rang me to say that Roberta was finding it difficult to be there, because she didn't know what would happen next. He's staying there at nights, and has had the window repaired."

"Has anything else happened?" I asked.

"Some more plants have been uprooted. He says the front garden is now a mess. There may have been more phone calls, though he doesn't know, since he isn't there during the day. He's contacted the police, and the telephone people, but there isn't much that can be done about any of this. He's being very helpful, but he can't leave his wife and family for ever. Pete, I know that you were planning to be here from Monday. You're very welcome of course, but if instead you could stay at Roberta's house until you go back to Spain, that would give Gerald some relief. You could meet Roberta at Waterloo on Monday afternoon, and take her home from there."

"I can stay until Thursday night. I've the last cabin on Friday's boat. I'm expecting to be back permanently by mid-August, and probably working in London for a while. I would be pleased and grateful to stay with you then, Roberta."

My mother and Roberta both looked relieved, and Roberta found her voice.

"Oh, that is good, Pete. Gerald is away on holiday from about then. Joan, I know I must go back soon, though it's been lovely of you and Ben to look after me."

"Meanwhile, there's something else I can do," I continued. "Harry Tamfield was at the same College as me. I've not met him since, but I knew him quite well. I went to Hungary and Czechoslovakia with him."

"So he *is* the man you told me about, whose concert was wrecked," said Roberta.

"That's right. I'll try to see him early next week. His firm must have only just realised that they have this access problem. Some of his people are going much too far. They'll deny it of course, so there's no point in paying Frank Booth to write letters. Harry needs to call them to order, very fast, and have them make a sensible deal with you."

I extricated myself soon after, for time was beginning to press. The IE Corporate Meeting was at a hotel outside Worcester, and I wanted to be there in good time for the 6.30 pm start. Whilst heading north on country roads, I had plenty of time to reflect.

I had last seen Harry on the evening when Jenny had encountered him for the only time, some months after he left Waterhouse without a degree. He had been intending to follow his success in managing the Cambridge University Baroque Society orchestra with a career in musical administration. Then, one of the society's concerts had been smashed up, ostensibly by left-wing protestors. He had changed his plans, and gone into the property business. Jenny's argument with him, and her current view of him, reflected his statement that those who didn't co-operate in his schemes for improving and selling their accommodation had a 'rather disturbing time'. It seemed that Roberta was now having such a time.

When Jenny had shown me the *Telegraph* article, I had not recalled that Bishop's Park Hospital and School had lain behind Roberta's house. The total sale proceeds for 800 houses and flats there would be about £15 million, all of which would go to reduce borrowings on which Tamfield Investments would be paying at least 10% interest, about £4,000 *a day*.[5] That was with things as they were. I knew that things were going to get worse – much worse. Tamfield Investments needed to make sales as soon as possible.

I hoped that I would find that I had been invited to Harry's party. I wouldn't raise Roberta's predicament there, but I could speak to someone about fixing a meeting at Tamfield Investments' offices.

It was annoying but understandable that Roberta couldn't call on much local support. Though she had friends through her hobbies of bridge and gardening, her forthright manner meant that she didn't get on well with her neighbours, especially with the perfectly respectable 'coloured' family that had progressed to one of the houses next door. Her son, Gerald, lived near her and would be doing his best in his own rather stodgy way, but his wife would be telling him where his prime duty lay.

I could easily visualise the Roberta of thirty-five years before, making big-sisterly comments to my mother that this young man of hers simply would not do for a daughter of the town's draper. He might be working at the bank they used, but his father was a farm labourer living in a hovel. It had made things worse that my mother's indiscretion with an American officer had left no alternative when my father returned from the War[6].

By tradition, Roberta should have married the son of one of the other better class tradespeople in the town. Instead, she had gone with Herbert Strutt, who she had met through a shared intrest in amateur light opera productions and whose private income had made him seem a more attractive prospect than his rather humdrum job merited. After the War, she had stirred

---

5 Multiply this and other sums of money mentioned in this Part by ten to give an estimate of current (2017) equivalents.

6 Throughout this account, I adopt the universal usage of my generation, learnt from our parents; 'the War' means the 1939-45 conflict.

him into securing a slightly better job in London. They hadn't attended my parents' wedding.

Right through my childhood, I had heard only the vaguest news of the Strutts. I met them only at the funerals of my mother's parents. That hadn't bothered me overmuch, until I was old enough to put in some relief employment at the family store and thus to realise why the dividends weren't allowing us as good summer holidays as had been possible a few years earlier. The business was not responding to the fact that more and more of its customers had cars, and could easily travel elsewhere to obtain a wider choice of fabrics and better service. That was the fault of Edward, my uncle, who ran it and owned 60%, with each sister owning 20%. To secure change, the two sisters needed to act together.

All this had come up in a long conversation with Pat O'Donnell, on the first occasion that I met him. At his prompting I had called in on Roberta and Herbert, on my way home from Cambridge at the end of 1967. The visit had been overshadowed by worries about Herbert's health, news of which had persuaded my mother to make contact.

A year later, we all attended Herbert's funeral. However, there had been no progress in improving the family business. My parents' latest excuse for inaction was that my father was the manager of the branch where it banked, and couldn't have any conflict with his professional role. I could think of plenty of ways round that, but basically they didn't want to be involved. They wanted a quiet life.

Once through Bristol, out of my West Country homeland and onto the M5,[7] I put family concerns out of my mind. My car was responding well to a lighter load and a fill of better petrol than was then available in Spain. As I overtook most other traffic at 65 mph, I reflected on the couple of days ahead.

The IE Corporate Meeting was held every July. Pat invited about thirty people in all, comprising IE's Board of directors and

---

7 Not then open south of Bristol.

a selection of staff who reported directly to a divisional Director. So, though I had no definite information about any change to my grading, and IE was not a rigid hierarchy, I was now being regarded as at two levels above where I had started, five years before. I was certainly achieving the progress that Pat had suggested I could achieve, though it had been very hard work.

I pulled up in the hotel car park at five to six, and by twenty past was tidied up and talking fairly respectfully to people outside the conference room. I saw no one who fitted the description 'someone I knew already, and would be interested to meet again'. As was the practice, none of us had a programme. Pat didn't want people to work out in advance what to say. He wanted their immediate reactions to the questions he put. All we knew was that before dinner there was to be a presentation on the economic climate by IE's recently appointed Chief Economist. Comments flew around such as 'Wonder why Pat thinks we need one of them? He flies this outfit by the seat of his pants and usually gets it right', and 'we know what it is, bloody awful'.

Pat appeared, and we moved into the room. My puzzlement was resolved by the handout before us, the summary of which is opposite. Then its author entered.

Paul Milverton had entered Waterhouse College in October 1967. Within six months, he had shown impressive political grip and had been elected President of the undergraduates' club, the Junior Combination Room (JCR). In June 1968, he was attacked by persons unknown and quite seriously injured. Fortunately, he had recovered fully by the start of the next term and went on to play a big part in university student politics, representing left-wing views but believing in organised, peaceful protest. That hadn't distracted him from getting a first in economics, to which subject he had switched after a year of studying maths. He had moved to the London School of Economics to do research for a doctorate.

UK, EUROPE AND WORLD ECONOMIC PROSPECTS, 1973 – 1983

Dr Paul Milverton, Chief Economist.

SUMMARY OF KEY POINTS

In 1971, the government removed many controls on lending and credit. Their aim was good. The controls rationed credit artificially;

However, removal was too abrupt. The money supply was vastly increased, with no corresponding increase in goods available. The inevitable consequences have been inflation, first in property and then through the economy, and also an increasing balance of payments deficit as imports are sucked in;

The flotation of the pound in June 1972 was also good in principle, but falls in the exchange rate have caused more inflation and cannot benefit exports quickly, since there is no short-term capacity to produce more;

Rapid inflation has made it more worthwhile for workers to strike for pay increases. They might get several per cent extra, which within a year would recoup the cost of a two-week strike;

The government's response of wage and price controls has made things worse. Underpaid productive or essential jobs are not being filled. Controls on prices of home-produced goods are making shops push imports, on which they can make more profit;

So we have moved, willy-nilly, from one set of controls to another. There are now so many contradictions in the way the economy is being run that a crash of some kind is inevitable;

There is one big ray of hope. North Sea oil can be the basis of a huge new industry, as well as a benefit to the balance of payments. However, the technology needed is way beyond anything attempted anywhere else. Benefits will take several years to come through. Oil prices are uncertain. The higher they go, the larger will be the programme, costs, and benefits;

Our Continental neighbours are overtaking us in standard of living. West Germany did so several years ago. Now France, Belgium, and the Netherlands are doing so, too. Consequently, companies are moving towards supplying the UK from factories within their larger markets, on the Continent; and

The UK has entered the EEC[8] on terms which impose very large costs. There will be sufficient benefit to outweigh these only if we can develop industries capable of dominating the European market, and competing worldwide.

---

8 The European Economic Community, often referred to as the 'Common Market'. It and two other communities were the predecessors of the European Union. The UK had joined on 1st January, 1973, at the third attempt.

That was Paul's life, as known to many. I knew rather more, and Paul knew I knew.

Paul had never looked particularly scruffy, but his smart suit and short, well-groomed black hair were certainly a transformation from the man I had known before. He had also learnt more about putting things over clearly and concisely. After an hour of presentation and discussion, Pat concluded.

"Thanks, Paul. I'm particularly taken with your analogy between the way Heath and Barber[9] are running the economy and flying an airliner with only the engines on one side running. It's possible for a while, but it can't be kept up for long. It's a flight to destruction. Thanks also for the comments around the room about how the position is affecting us. Our first session tomorrow, at 8.30, runs until ten o'clock. I'm expecting two minutes from each of you on specific things we should be doing to get through the next few years and come out stronger. I'm hoping the UK can somehow do that too, despite what Paul says. Paul will note what you say, and produce a summary which we'll take away with us on Saturday."

Over drinks and dinner, I caught up with some colleagues who were not too much older than me. I was feeling rather the same as I had felt just after being elected a Fellow of Waterhouse at the age of twenty-one. I didn't want to push in too hard, though I reminded myself that too much diffidence had been a mistake then; I had allowed things to happen which I could have prevented.

In the 'Bar Lounge' afterwards, I noticed Paul working the room. Eventually, he joined the group I was in, and was greeted as 'the marker', though that may have been a euphemism for 'the nark'. His being at this senior meeting, though not part of it, was helpfully distracting people from wondering why I was there. Eventually, others drifted away, saying that they needed time to prepare for their two minutes, and we settled down.

---

9 Anthony Barber, Chancellor of the Exchequer in the Conservative Government headed by Ted Heath that had taken office in 1970.

"Welcome to the team, Paul. Congratulations also on actually getting a PhD, in very good time. What was it on?"

"The development of oil futures trading, 1859 –1910."

I gulped momentarily, before continuing. "How did you end up here, then?"

"It was rather a surprise. The post wasn't advertised. Two months ago, I had a letter from Sir Pat's office asking if I could come and see him. I did, and he said that he knew of me and was offering me a job. I'm an applied economist, and there was no decent postdoctoral job to hand, so I said yes. It was all over in five minutes. Is he always like that?"

"It was much the same with me, except that I had to start less than a week later."

"I remember Carol telling me you'd left. I was still in hospital, then."

Paul said that rather warily, which was understandable. After a short silence I replied. "How's Carol doing?"

"She's very busy, off to various international conferences over the summer. I'm going with her to one in Rome. She's also looking for a first try seat, where she can attract attention and reduce the majority. Her real problem will come at the election after next. She'll be after a winnable seat where they're ready to run a woman candidate."

"What does she think of your moving to the capitalist world?"

"She can put up with it. After all, she put up with *you*."

Paul was quite right to say that. I had last seen him five years before, when he was being carried into hospital on a stretcher. Since then, though, I had seen much of Carol.

She was aiming at front-line politics, whereas he was a backroom organiser. That reflected their different personalities. Though they had grown up as neighbours in Manchester, and had been together 'since it was legal', she was more highly sexed than him. At Cambridge, she began a discreet additional relationship with me. It ended when Jenny and I became close, but events had led us to renew it just before I left, and to continue it whilst I worked in Sunderland. During Cambridge vacations, we met when I visited an IE factory near Manchester. During terms, if I had business in London the next day, I would travel down on an evening train which called at Hitchin. She would be on the platform, and nearby there was a late-opening Indian restaurant and a decent hotel.

The arrangement had suited all. Liz had moved on, the hours I was putting in didn't allow me much time to try for girls, and there were few around locally who were unattached and worth knowing. Someone I already knew and liked, and who was pleased to offer full satisfaction, was ideal. To all but a very few, Paul was Carol's settled boyfriend. He knew that Carol's roving eye would look no further than me. Carol's parents had had to cope with the bad end to an earlier roving, and saw me as helping to avoid a repetition. From about my third Manchester visit they welcomed me into their home, where politics was under almost continuous discussion. The knowledge about planning and compulsory purchase that I had shown earlier in the day came from Carol's father, Councillor Bert Gibson, chairman of the Manchester Corporation housing committee.

Carol may have said to Paul that she had to buy my silence about what he had done. The pleasure of anticipation was enhanced by imagining her saying that. However, I made no such condition. I wouldn't have enjoyed her if I had done so.

The 1968 disturbances in Paris led to the fall of President de Gaulle and opened the way to our third application to join the EEC. They also forced a devaluation which had temporarily made it easier to visit France within the foreign currency allowance, which had been reduced to £50 following our devaluation in 1967. So, early in September 1970, I took Carol there on holiday. By then, she had left Cambridge with a first in history, and was to take a job in the Labour Party Research Department. Paul was about to start at the LSE. On our last night, she had told me that he wanted her to move in with him permanently. I had told her to go for it. They were right for each other, whilst she and I could remember our good times together.

This end had been timely. Within a few months, I was out in Spain. Last year, I had sent best wishes and a cheque for their registry office wedding. Now, I changed the subject.

"Your talk was very monetarist, Paul. Some of it reminded me of a speech by Enoch Powell that I read about two months ago."

"I've been inspired by Bill Letwin. I've been invited to some of his discussion groups. Keynes was right for his time, but that's not our time. People like Frank Hahn don't recognise that. It's quite possible to reconcile monetarism with socialism."

"I thought the last man who tried that was Philip Snowden. Hey, we're wanted!"

Pat O'Donnell was motioning in our direction as he left the lounge. After a slight pause, we followed to his room. I was glad that Pat realised that for the two of us to be seen with him would at once arouse suspicion and resentment. Once he had poured us whiskies, he began firmly.

"I've a few things to say to the two of you. First, you're both on my team now. You work together for the team. What's in the past stays in the past. Is that agreed?"

We nodded, and he went on.

"Secondly, something that's not for quoting, though it stands out a mile from your talk, Paul. There'll be a general election later next year or early the year after. Whoever forms the next government will have a very difficult time indeed. They'll pay the price at the election after next, round about 1979. Provided the development of North Sea oil isn't completely messed up, things will be improving for business by then. What government do I want to be elected in 1979? So, what government do I want after the next election? Just remember that. Thirdly, Pete, you'll be first on tomorrow, as the youngest. Give me an advance of what you're going to say. I assume it will be a repeat of what you told me last month."

"Yes. As Paul says, there's going to be huge investment in North Sea oil. Lots of it will be on things we don't make, such as offshore platform structures, drilling gear, and pipelines. However, there'll also be lots of investment on control gear and electrical equipment for the platforms, which are the kind of things that we do make. We need to have a lot of our bits on those platforms. Bits out there have to be tough. They mustn't go wrong often. When they do go wrong, they need to be replaceable quickly, by semi-skilled labour; pull out the old and slot in the new, with the shortest possible stop in production. We need a specialist outfit, which finds out what's wanted and makes sure we develop and supply it – fast."

"Right. Your next job is to get that outfit going. You'll be reporting to Terry. He knows that. Speak to him later tomorrow about a sensible timetable, but I want things happening by next March. Paul, you'll provide Pete with a market assessment by the time he's back from Spain permanently, say 10th August. I'll tell Terry that you need to draw on his people for data."

This was good. Terry McAvitt was the Director of the Instrumentation Division, which was likely to have the biggest share of North Sea business within IE. Terry and I already had a good working relationship, based on the Spanish business I had brought him. Any suspicions that he had of me as a too bright young thing were well past.

"To give you the best assessment, I'll need to buy in some work from brokers," said Paul.

"Once Pete's signed a few things in the office next week, he'll be able to authorise that. So, there's an official job for you, Paul. Now, fourthly, there's an unofficial job for you. Pete, tell Paul what you told Terry in May."

As I began my account, I tried not to be distracted by Pat's oblique confirmation that I was being formally promoted to senior manager. That was the grade normally held by those in IE who reported to directors, and also the grade at which significant unusual expenditures had to be authorised in a company which prided itself on tight financial controls.

Two months before, I had visited a city in Belgium, where was located the European head office of an American company which was setting up a manufacturing operation in Spain. I gave the usual message about no-hassle local supply of various components. After lunch in a good restaurant, I walked away with the likelihood of substantial contracts, which had indeed materialised. I had an hour or so to spare before leaving for Brussels Airport, and strolled round the picturesque old town. Then, as now, it was full of bars and restaurants. Then, not as now, most of them had signs in Flemish and French meaning 'TURKS AND ALGERIANS NOT ADMITTED' or similar kindnesses. I thought of this as just distasteful and was glad that there was no such sign where we had eaten, though the prices may have made it unnecessary. In the UK, such overt discrimination had been illegal for several years.

In London for other meetings the next day, I met Terry McAvitt and told him of my success. He replied that the Belgian city was not his favourite place just now. A competitor's factory, located there, was getting too much of the business. He knew that it was staffed largely by 'guest workers', and wondered why we couldn't make the product at the right price, whilst they could. My rather flippant response was to describe what I had seen and to suggest that the workforce should be encouraged to go on strike about not being allowed in the bars and restaurants. Evidently, Terry had told Pat of this suggestion.

At the end of my account, Pat handed Paul a sheet with details of our competitor.

"So, Paul, we need some trouble over there, particularly involving the workforce at this factory. I know that you can deliver trouble when you want. You'll be striking a blow for racial equality, of course. You can draw funds from this account, which we've set up in a Belgian bank. Pete, on this Paul reports to you. You report to me."

Pat handed over another sheet, with the account details. Paul looked surprised, but perhaps not too surprised. He must have realised that there was more than one reason why he had been specially recruited.

Pat certainly knew a fair amount about Paul's capabilities, through seeing a diary kept by Andrew Grover, who had been Bursar of Waterhouse College. That was enough to explain why Pat had taken him on, but I wondered just how much more Pat knew about what had happened during my last year in Cambridge. Sir Arthur Gulliver, the Vice-Master of Waterhouse, might have told Pat the full story, though I couldn't see why he should have done so.

Paul's College room key, adapted to allow him to plant false evidence, had by chance come into my possession. That had allowed me to discover that Sir Archibald Frampton had used Paul to further his scheme to divert Pat's donation of £1 million from Waterhouse to Carmarthen College, of which he was Master. The wrecking of the Baroque Society concert had been part of the scheme, as had been the setback in Dick's research. I had told only four people of my discovery, each of them for a clear purpose. As the price of my silence, Sir Archibald had to set things right for those who were hurt as a result of his scheme. Liz and Arthur had to make sure that he did so. Carol had to ensure that Paul recalled nothing of his attackers.

When Carol and I parted, I had given her the key to return to Paul. That had been a sign that to me, this was all in the past.

Now was clearly the moment to tell my story from Spain, including further news which Ana had given me when I called at lunchtime. Her photographs had enabled an intelligence office in Madrid to identify the two men speaking with Kraftlein as high ranking Egyptian Air Force officers. Officially, they had been staying with the Ambassador, a personal friend. They had checked in at the *Parador* on false passports, giving civilian names. I concluded by saying that the full note Ana and I had made was now in a safe at the Banco Navarrese head office in Pamplona.

As the implications sank in, there was silence. Pat poured another round of drinks, and eventually spoke.

"So, what does that mean for the rest of us?"

"Paul can answer that. He's the economist."

"It means a further big increase in oil prices. It strengthens what's in my presentation about the next few years, and further ahead. It certainly strengthens the case for your specialist outfit, Pete."

"It also strengthens what I said just now, about elections and governments," said Pat.

"It raises an immediate opportunity for us, too," I said. "Paul, you did research on the oil futures market. Tell us about it."

"You can buy an option to buy oil at some time in the future, usually three months ahead, at a specified price. So, if on 1st September you paid 25¢ a barrel for an option to purchase on 1st December at the current price, say $3 a barrel, and by 1st December the price was up to $6 a barrel, then you would have a straight profit of $2.75 a barrel. If on the other hand the price had fallen to $2 a barrel, you wouldn't take the option up and you would have lost your 25¢."

"If Pete's right, an option sounds a good bet," said Pat. "But surely others will find out about this – Mossad and the CIA, for starters. Then either it won't happen, and the price won't change much, or people will guess the same as you, and the option price will shoot up."

"It all depends on how good the Egyptians are at keeping this quiet," said Paul. "If it leaks out, we'll see the three-month price moving up sharply. If it doesn't do that by September, then a punt on the oil price will look very good indeed."

"Needless to say, when we arrived in Pamplona we went through all that," I said. "Ana's father is Don Pedro Guzman, a director of the Banco Navarrese. They're our lead business partner in Spain, Paul."

"Do the Banco Navarrese have any experience in oil options trading?" Paul asked. "It's not a game for amateurs. Plenty of people have found that out the hard way."

"No, they haven't any experience. They know that they'll need to form a partnership with an experienced trader. They're going to look at various possibilities. When I'm back in Spain on Monday week, they want me to tell them whether IE is in principle interested in joining in. If so, they'll discuss with us who to approach. They accept that the information to be used is half ours."

"We can be interested in principle, but it's not our business. George's latest report makes clear how short of capital we are."

Pat sounded doubtful as he referred to George Armstrong, IE's Finance Director, but I persisted.

"What's our problem in Spain right now, Pat? If we had a billion pesetas, that's about £7 million, we could buy into the key growing companies and IE España would be right in pole position for the big league when Ford commit to Valencia. George is clear that we don't have £7 million, but we do have £1 million. If we go in with Banco Navarrese, we could turn £1 million into £7 million, discreetly, in Spain."

"How would all this be recorded? I'm sure George would point out snags on foreign exchange and tax. Apart from that, we don't want to be seen to profit from what would be one hell of a problem for everybody."

"Spanish accounting practices are less well developed than ours. I'm sure there's a way that all this needn't feature much in group accounts, until the companies we buy begin to deliver profits. Then our gains could be lost in those."

Paul came in, helpfully. "Given the value of the information, I think Banco Navarrese, and ourselves, if we went in, ought to be able to find a trader who would carry some of our interest.

That is, the trader takes some of the risk for us, which would reduce the stake we need to put in for a particular return."

"Both of you, talk to George next week. Pete, subject to any immediate blocks that he raises, you can tell Banco Navarrese that we're interested in principle. Paul, give Pete as good an assessment as you can of possible oil trading partners, to take back to Spain. Both of you, by the end of August put together a proposal to me through George. Paul, there's a separate task for you, also by the end of August. Make an assessment of what a sudden increase in the oil price would mean for IE and its customers, and what we can do to minimise the hit. Meanwhile, no one other than George is to be told, inside or outside the company, without my specific agreement. Got that, both of you?"

Pat was looking hard at Paul, doubtless with Carol in mind. I made a suggestion.

"It's being kept very tight in Banco Navarrese, too. At the risk of sounding melodramatic, can I suggest that we have some code word that I can use if I need to call either of you from Spain."

"How about 'Crafty'?" Paul suggested.

"That's a good idea, being a little joke no one else will understand, Pat. I'm told that at Cambridge, Professor Kraftlein rapidly became known as 'Old Crafty'. He certainly lived up to that."

"I remember hearing about both of you being involved with him. It's a good thing that he didn't spot you, Pete, but you and your friend seem to have managed things with your typical resource."

"His spelling out the date of the attack through a mathematical puzzle almost suggests he knew that someone like you was listening," said Paul.

"It would have been a pretty odd thing to do, but I did wonder. On Sunday morning, Ana went to early Mass in the cathedral. That gave me a chance to check around, after Kraftlein had left. There's no way he could have known that I was staying at the hotel, let alone that I was listening. The desk doesn't leave passports or records of people lying about. He was just showing off."

"Shouldn't we be warning someone in our government about this?" asked Pat.

"Don Pedro was clear that as this meeting happened in Spain, the first report should be to their government. He's making that through his contacts, discreetly. Then, there'll be something via embassies. The fact is, though, that no one will believe it. Don't forget that in 1941 UK intelligence knew of the impending German attack on Russia.[10] Churchill warned Stalin, who ignored it. Intelligence services discount anything found out by anyone else."

"All right, but one other thing, Pete. Before we sign up to anything – *if* we do – I'll want to meet your namesake Don and someone senior at whatever trader is brought in. Say that very clearly. For a deal like this, you have to have looked right into their eyes. In September I ought to come out to Spain, whether or not 'Crafty' goes ahead. You've managed the relationship with Banco Navarrese very well, but it would be unfair to Doug not to have some support from here initially. Speak to my office about the arrangements, and to Doug when you get back, but not to bring them in on 'Crafty'. If a trip is pre-arranged for another purpose, it's easier to keep the real purpose quiet. Well, that's enough for tonight. Tomorrow will be a long day. Pete, you've given us lots to think about. Both of you, just remember that if you take big risks, it has to be for big prizes."

---

10 My statement reflected what was widely known then. When the story of the Enigma decrypts became public, we understood why the warnings were very guarded as to source, though very explicit and exact as to date.

3. SUNDAY, 15ᵀᴴ JULY, 1973

I stirred to see Liz pulling on running kit.

"Back in half an hour. Get some coffee made." With a kiss, she was off.

I got up gradually, and looked out of the living room window. Jenny and Dick might have done well with their property, but Liz had done still better. On moving to London, she had supplemented her savings with help from the Coal Board, and doubtless her father chipped in too. This had allowed her to buy a flat on the top floor of an elegant early-Victorian terrace. It was a trek up four flights of stairs, but there was a very pleasant, quiet view over private gardens to a similar terrace opposite. Gloucester Road Underground Station was only a few minutes' walk, and there was easy parking outside at weekends. Over dinner the evening before, Liz had pointed out proudly that similar flats were now on sale for well over double what she had paid. That, of course, was just a start. Ordinary people can't buy there any more.[11]

At the IE meeting, I had already found that property prices were a feature of almost any social chat of the time. Their doubling in two years had been the most spectacular result of the decontrol of credit.

In 1968, Liz and I had moved to Durham. Jenny had put us in touch with an estate agent who had found us both pleasant and

---

11 As I write this, typical prices for such flats are *over one hundred* times what Liz had paid – in real terms, about nine times higher. This is now the remaining legacy of Mr Heath and Mr Barber.

inexpensive rented flats. These were far better for us than living in lodgings, as single people were then meant to do. Neither of us wanted some officious landlady trying to rule our lives. After about a year, I had considered buying, but was told that though I could easily afford the repayments on a mortgage, as a single man I was at the back of the queue. As a single woman, Liz had been even further back.[12] When everything changed, she had gone for broke, before everyone else did. In the property race, she was a winner. Those who hesitated or had been out of the game, like me, were losers.

Property prices had not been the main topic at dinner, though. The other guests were a Coal Board office colleague of Liz and his girlfriend, a single man Liz knew through her hockey club and who worked for the London Electricity Board, and also Morag Newlands, whom we had both known at Cambridge, was now a lecturer at King's College, London, and remained a true daughter of Red Clydeside. Unsurprisingly, therefore, we touched on how the Coal Board was to handle the National Union of Mineworkers (NUM) during the next few months.

The year before, the first national miners' strike since 1926 had ended in total humiliation for the Coal Board and the government, and had given the public an enduring memory of domestic power cuts and blackouts. One item of salvage from the wreckage had been a pay deal lasting for sixteen months. That moved the settlement date from November to March, and in principle reduced the opportunity for disputes to disrupt supplies during the winter. However, ten days before, the NUM's Annual Conference had passed a motion demanding a large pay rise from November. Higher inflation was their excuse, if they needed one. What was more, Mick McGahey, the communist Vice-President of the NUM, had said they should be trying

---

12 The message was clearest in the logo of one of the largest building societies, the Abbey National (now part of Santander Bank). This showed a man in a suit accompanied by a woman in a skirt. The man was holding a roof-shaped umbrella.

to smash the Heath Government or any other Conservative government.

We had not come to any answer. Morag said how difficult and dangerous miners' work was, as shown by a serious accident, apparently caused by Coal Board negligence, a few months before. After a few drinks, Liz's colleague said that the then Chairman of the Coal Board, Sir Derek Ezra, was simply not strong enough to handle the NUM. His predecessor, Lord Robens, had shown his strength when confronted by unofficial disputes. He had been a front-rank Labour politician when appointed by Harold Macmillan's Conservative Government. Unfortunately, Ted Heath had not allowed Robens to continue. Fortunately, we were diverted from any further indiscretion by Morag saying that Robens was as much a traitor to the left as Ramsay Macdonald had been. The electricity man said that the government were too much involved in what was a matter between the Coal Board and the union. There were even rumours of a secret meeting to take place between Heath and Joe Gormley, the NUM President whose aims appeared to be less political than those of McGahey. He wondered how the Board could negotiate effectively in these circumstances. I agreed with him, and suggested that the Board should stand firm on the March settlement date, though I admitted that all I knew was what I had read in the last three days' papers. Liz kept fairly quiet through all this, whilst giving the impression that she knew a fair amount.

I had arrived rather later than I should have done, because of traffic down from Worcester. Liz was in a rush, after being at the office most of the day. There was just time for me to give the help she needed, and for her to tell me to play along with what she said. Then, she introduced me to the three I had not met as 'my boyfriend, back from over two years in Spain'. At the same time, she put on an attractive pout that I knew of old. I responded suitably. Morag had perhaps also been prompted; later, she took the lead in saying they must leave us to it. However, after tidying up we were both feeling very tired. All explanations and action were postponed, though we both found it comforting not to be alone.

Over coffee and toast, Liz was still in no hurry. Indeed, she seemed rather nervous.

"So, what's up today? What did Dick want to speak to you about?"

She had taken Dick's message for me to call, which I had done as soon as all guests had arrived. I explained why I was expecting his call. On Friday, my office in Madrid had confirmed that I too was invited to Harry Tamfield's party. Dick and I were to meet at Maidenhead Station.

"You're obviously still fond of Jenny, and ready to help her keep an eye on Dick."

"I'm fond of her, just as I'm fond of you, Carol, and Ana. I want to meet Harry again, too. He's getting on fast, perhaps too fast. His company needs to buy my aunt's house in a hurry. They're trying to pressurise her. They don't know she's my aunt."

That led to more explanation, before Liz came back to her point.

"Jenny still thinks the world of you. She knows what you did for her. She said so when I was down with them in April. Rather like you, I got to chat while Dick looked after David. I was the first to know she was expecting again, even before her parents. I admire her, though she does want things her way. I hope Dick goes on putting up with that. If he doesn't, she's in real trouble, with two small kids."

"He's no alternative to her way. He isn't doing well in academic life, even with Frampton backing. Looking after the kids is part of his future."

"Mmm, yes. Now, Pete, tell me all about Ana. She's the daughter of that big shot you met at the opera, isn't she? Jenny said you were going around with her a lot."

She grinned in anticipation. I told, giving plenty of the graphic detail that I knew Liz would like. We were back to being brother and sister, without many secrets from each other. Then, we moved on. She gave me a luscious kiss.

"So, you had lots of fun together, but she's still intact goods with a happy Dad. Good for you, Pete. It began when you both had a shower. So, we'll have a shower, and then you can give me the Ana treatment, to start."

We had always liked soaping each other in the shower. Liz particularly liked having her ample breasts caressed and bounced. So, we were there for some time. Afterwards, the only difference from Ana was that we did not bother with a towel between us as she lay across me, turning over from time to time. First gently and then more firmly, I found all the places where she was tense, particularly in her belly, and felt her relaxing as she purred. Then I stroked her all over.

"Lovely, Pete. You're still so good at this. Time to rub harder, or I'll fall asleep."

"It's lovely to see and feel you relaxing, Liz, and you're so fit."

She had lost a few pounds in weight without being at all skinny, and the muscles in her torso and legs showed well in the sunlight coming through the windows. My finger found its way through her thick 'jungle' of dark brown hair.

"Mmmm… that's great…Down just a little bit… Aaah, harder… *Aaaah*… Lucky Ana. Now, to finish properly."

I lay down on a rug. Gentle squelching turned to the slapping sound of buttocks meeting groin as she rode me hard and athletically, her breasts and hair flying around. Then panting turned to mutual screams of pleasure. She was as good as ever at tightening round me to squeeze the last little bit out.

We disconnected gradually. She lay on me, her head on my shoulder, nuzzling me as I ran my hand gently through her hair and over her back and bottom. We dozed contentedly for some time, for the morning was already warm. We each knew what the other had wanted, and had provided it. It was my first 'proper finish' since early in our holiday together. I sensed that for her, it was a break from frustration. Eventually, she found something to say.

"Am I forgiven for being so rotten to you, on that holiday and since?"

"Of course, provided you stop avoiding telling me what you're up to now."

"We'd better get dressed, first."

We dressed, and made more coffee. She lit a cigarette and began.

"I've been rather mixed up since I moved here, and before that really. You know I had some good times with men up north, but nothing came to anything. Here, it's been the same. Morag helped, but the best times I have are on my social therapy."

"What's that?"

"I organise a lot of the top-level meetings of the Coal Board. The people who come to them are big men from the coalfields, Area Directors or the level immediately below. They're usually big men physically, as well as in what they run. Most of them didn't start off as miners, but they've had years of running mines before getting to where they are. You don't go into a job like that without having the build and strength of a miner. Most of them married young, and by now their children are grown up. They're left with their wives, who may have had something in the past but don't give much now and are pretty limited as people. So, they start looking."

"And they find you, ready and willing?"

"Yes, the message goes quietly round. It's good for all. They have what they need, without causing problems in their area or with their wives. You can see it in them. At meetings, the day after, they show just that extra bit of edge. I get lots of nice dinners and enjoyment. There's definitely something about being held by a really hefty, strong man. I liked that with Brian.

I need to wind it down, now, though. The man I work for isn't well. I've been doing more and more of his job, as well as my own. He'll have to retire before long. Then, I want his job. A bit on the side is no problem for that, but it mustn't be the main thing I'm known for."

"So, you need someone else, visible."

"At twenty-eight, I need someone anyway. Last autumn, Greg joined the hockey club when he moved down here from Leeds. What do you think of him?"

She asked with a look in her eye. Greg Woolley was the man from the London Electricity Board. He was fit and handsome, with dark hair like Liz, but unlike her he was quite tall. He was a little older than her, judging by what he said about his life since he had gained a first in electrical engineering at Leeds University.

"I'd better say quite a lot, hadn't I, Liz? But that's true, in fact. Everything he said last night was thoughtful. To be frank, my only worry would be that he's rather serious for you. He may be too much like me."

"He's another only child. His father is a Baptist minister in Yorkshire. He goes to his local Baptist church in Hendon. That can make him serious, though not like you. He likes parties and suchlike, and he's a good dancer, unlike you. There's something of you in him, but there's something of Brian, too."

"So, how goes it? He was clearly unsettled by my being here and in possession. I assume that was your plan."

"Yes. He wants me, wants me lots and lots. That's shown, and it's made him even more embarrassed and inhibited. He's never had a serious girlfriend. He's nearly thirty, and a virgin. I hate to think how he's feeling, now. Probably he didn't sleep a wink."

"Aren't I going to put him off even more?"

"Yes, if you stay around, but if you throw me over, I think I can make him sorry enough for me that he'll do it."

"So, what do you want from me?"

"Ideally, you should go with another woman. The Ana story gives me plenty to say, though. Having enjoyed me for a couple of nights, you told me about this daughter of a Spanish duke or whatever. I can be tearful. I don't need to mention Carlos."

"So, you'll want me to keep away for a while. I'm back in Spain for a few weeks, but I don't want to be out of touch with you for ever, Liz. Nor do I want Greg coming after me with a horsewhip."

"You won't be out of touch, Pete. I want Greg to know you, and Brian, and Dick. Once he's on board we'll all be friends, I promise you. He just needs to be brought over the edge. He also needs to be convinced that he should stay in London. He's not sure. He's let his flat in Leeds, and lives in a furnished bedsit down here."

"I understand. We've all rubbed off on you. To understand you, he has to know all of us."

"Talking of all of us, you can meet Brian before you go off to meet Dick. He's booked a tennis court for Morag and me from two o'clock, but we're meeting first for lunch. Afterwards, you can pick up your train at Ealing Broadway."

"So, that's why last night Morag said she would meet you today."

"Were you wondering something else then?"

"You said she'd helped you."

"Last autumn, we slept together for a while. It was rather like those three months when I was still in Cambridge after you left – mostly about feeling there's someone with you at the darkest time of the night, rather than about doing anything physical. This time, that went for her as well as for me. We both felt lonely. I wasn't really going on my social therapy. Morag had just moved to London, but couldn't find anywhere decent to live that she could afford. Her father died earlier last year, and she's sending money to her mother, who's not well herself. Angela had decided that she wanted to try a man she'd met, though their time together had been good."

"Has Morag moved on, now?"

"Yes, she's met another les academic. That's a good thing for me as well as for her. Last night, Sheila was tied up on the voluntary work they do, but she'll be along today. She particularly wants to meet you."

"I'll be sorry to miss the game. You and Morag are such well-matched opponents. You're faster and have the verve, whilst she has the height and style."

Liz smiled a sisterly smile. My mind flashed back to a week before I left Cambridge. Jenny and I had watched the two of them going for each other, hard. The sun had been out, and we hadn't seemed to have a care in the world.

"Yes, it's evens which of us wins. That's rather like the argument you and she had about Franco last night."

"Yes, I think we both enjoyed that." Morag had berated my support for 'fascist Spain', and was well enough informed to give me a good run when I quoted figures about the economic progress of the last ten years.

"We must be going soon. Before I forget, my regards to Dick. In a fortnight, I'm visiting them, for Jenny's twenty-fifth birthday. I'll remember he doesn't know she talked to you about the party. Oh, and you remember Morag is not yet on the telling Greg list."

On our way to the Underground, I voiced another thought.

"I hope Brian doesn't start more talk about coal. I thought your colleague was unwise to say what he did last night, though from what I've heard I agree with him."

"We all agree with him, but you're right, and it's not the first time. He wasn't trained at Waterhouse in what to say, or not to say. Nor did he start in an area office, as I did. Quite apart from being near you, that was a good move. Most of my work there was in co-ordinating announcements about pit closures, of which there were plenty then. I learnt that anyone you met outside might be involved and have strong opinions. You kept your mouth shut. Between us also, what you and Greg said about pay negotiations is quite right. However, some of the Area Directors want their local problems to be taken over at national level. They want to pass the buck. That just encourages the local union militants."

"Maybe more of the directors need a session with you, to give them more edge."

"The Chairman is good at passing the buck to the government, too. It's not looking good. If you want more background to how we got here, I'll lend you Robens' book.[13] It came out last year, just as the strike was beginning. There was a programme on the radio to discuss it, with Robens, Roy Mason who had been a miner and then Minister of Power, and Lawrence Daly of the NUM. Daly sensibly kept quiet, the interviewer barely got a word in, and by the end Robens and Mason were about to have a fight! Really, just for you, Gormley meets Heath tomorrow. Robens wouldn't have stood for that. It's why I was at work for most of yesterday."

Brian Smitham worked in computing services for Universal Assurance. Their ample sports ground was not far from Ealing Common Station. We arrived to find Brian already changed for cricket. With him was his wife, Susie, who didn't say much.

"Hi, Liz – and Pete, we've not seen you since five years back, the day of the overbump! Wasn't that a great day, and it really started something! Now, you two, are you together again?"

"Let's say we're still very good friends, Brian." Liz showed that with a nice long kiss.

We bought drinks and snacks, and sat down outside the clubhouse, to enjoy the sun. Brian's remark took my mind back to that fine sunny day by the river, just before I had left Cambridge. Then, the storm had broken around us. Today, all seemed calm, but what Liz had been saying about coal just added to my premonitions.

---

13 *Ten Year Stint*. This also explains the circumstances of his departure (*q.v.*)

Morag arrived soon afterwards, with Sheila Yates, a stocky but handsome woman who appeared to be in her early thirties. On hearing her name, I knew why she wanted to meet me. Six years before, I had looked at two of her first research papers. Now, she was a lecturer at Queen Mary College, and her research interest remained close to my work in Cambridge. I was *the* Peter Bridford who had written one important paper, and then disappeared.

Somehow, I mentioned Professor Kraftlein's name. Sheila stiffened, and explained that she had refused to attend any meeting at which he was present. Her mother was Jewish, but had escaped. Her grandparents had not escaped. However, she was no longer faced with this issue. The year before, Kraftlein had also disappeared; he had not found Cambridge to his liking. After a while, Liz interrupted.

"Hey, you two, stop ignoring the rest of us. Morag and I must change for our game. What's happening for you, Brian?"

"We're batting, and I'm the Ken Barrington[14] of the team." He waved towards the pitch, where the scoreboard showed 21 for 0.

"So, you'll be waiting around, like you do in cricket. Pete needs to go in twenty minutes, so why don't you two talk?" With another kiss, she and the others left.

"Same old Liz, cricket is a bore," said Brian. "She just don't understand it, and nor does Susie – women. So, where's you off to, Pete, when yer'e only just back?"

"Do you remember Harry Tamfield, whose concert we thought we had saved, but hadn't? He's big in property now. He's giving a party out near Maidenhead, to celebrate a deal he's done. He's invited the Sinclairs too, though in Jenny's present state only Dick will be there. I met them last week, on the boat back from Spain."

---

14 An un-showy but effective cricketer of a few years before, renowned for batting some way down the order and rescuing the situation after a collapse.

"We've not seen Jenny and Dick since the spring. How's Jenny looking now?"

"As I told her, she looks blooming marvellous. I remember reading out your message at their wedding reception. How did you come to know them so well?"

"It happened because I'd not found digs for my second year, as I was sure I would fail. Then I got a second, thanks to your help, Pete. You could have bowled me out."

"My help was worthwhile. You'd had a bad time, but you had it in you to do well, as you've done since."

"Susie had the answer for digs. Her aunt lives off the Mill Road. She'd let for Churchill College, but they'd just finished a new block and no one had taken her room. So, I took it. It was a nice big room, officially just for me; actually, for me and Susie. A week into term, I spotted Jenny walking along our road. Who could miss *her*? She and Dick were just round the corner, and she knew Morag, who'd set up not far away with Gill Watkinson. Nick Castle had brought Morag in to do the supervision work you would have done, and she was taking me for pure maths. We all chummed up. Mind you, Susie *was* a bit shocked to find that Morag and Gill weren't just friends!" Brian gave a grin.

"So, there was quite a social club, down the Mill Road."

"Yup, once or twice a week we would meet up at one or other of our places or in the local. It was more like what I was used to than I'd found in College. I stayed there for my third year, rather than try to get back in."

"That night you and I first met Pat O'Donnell, he said to me that I should take a look at the other side of Cambridge, the side deliberately kept poor. Doing that was an eye-opener for me."

"It was an eye-opener for Jenny too, a change from her people's big houses. She said it had been nice there, but she weren't going anywhere. She needed a real life."

"She's certainly going places now."

"She sure is. We've all kept in touch. Jenny and Dick came to our wedding, and Morag too, with Angela by then. I guess you've heard how *that* happened."

I smiled. "Liz told me all, in *some* detail. I was sorry to miss your wedding. I'd been in Spain for about three months."

"Your message was great, Pete."

"I have been rather out of your way while you all got to know each other. I was working jolly hard up in Sunderland, and then in Spain."

"You may have been out of our way, Pete, but you left another great message for us all. Jenny took down what you said at the May Bump Supper.[15] It was as famous for that as for what she and Liz had just done! I worked, and now I'm in a good job. Lots at Waterhouse did the same, when they knew how they'd been put down by Carmarthen and wanted to fight back. With Jim Smythe as JCR Secretary, even Paul Milverton had the message. We found we could get along. Paul and Carol dropped in on our group sometimes, and now they're part of the Cambridge chums, as we call ourselves. They live in Tooting, not far from us in West Norwood, though they're still renting, mark you. Susie and I keep up with them. We're not Labour, so we argue, but that's good fun. Paul has just joined IE. You'll be meeting him, I guess."

"I met him on Thursday. He thinks that being with IE is quite consistent with being Labour. How do you get on with the rest of your family, not being Labour yourself?"

"No problem. Don't believe this crap about miners wanting to throw the government out. My dad is now Branch Secretary at his pit, but four years back, he led some of the unofficial strikes. They didn't want to throw the government out; it was Labour then. They wanted more money. They could see people

15 The traditional drunken celebration on the Saturday evening at the end of the summer inter-college boat races, the May Bumps. These are held during 'May Week', which is early in June and includes many other celebrations, culminating in May Balls.

in cushy jobs catching up with what they were getting for nasty, dangerous work. It's the same now. The Yorkshire men didn't elect Arthur Scargill for his leftie talk.[16] First, they elected him because he's the best at getting them compensation for injuries, and then, they elected him because he'll be best at getting them more money. Now, 'nuff of that. You'll need to be off for yer train soon. My best to Dick, and have him pass that to Jenny. Cor, she's a great girl, but 'course you know that. Sorry, Pete."

"Yes, I know that, Brian."

"She knows what she wants, and how to get it. Sometimes she can seem a bit prissy, other times, well quite a surprise, like at the Bump Supper, and at her hen party. Did Liz tell you about what she did to her brother's girl, Amanda?"

"Yes, and about what they all did to her!"

"'Twas good Susie went to the party, 'cos we'd already booked a holiday over the wedding date. She was a tad scared about going. She knew Morag would be there, and was on the prowl as Gill had gone away. But she came back right on for a darned good fuck, and told a great story. I'd not known that *Carol* once had a bit on the side with you, Pete."

"That was a long time back, very soon after she arrived in Cambridge."

"Talking of parties, have a good time with Harry Tamfield, but watch yer back. Last year, his company bought the place some friends of ours were renting, wanted them out, and nasty things started to happen. It was sticky for them, though in the end they were bought out with enough for a deposit on where they are now."

"It's sticky for my aunt, right now. I hope that at the party I can fix to meet someone senior enough that I can arrange a sensible deal."

---

16 Although he had achieved national attention as leader of pickets during the 1972 strike, his first full-time union post was Compensation Agent, to which he was elected later in 1972. He was elected Yorkshire Area President in May 1973.

I gave a few details. Brian was forthright.

"Bloody 'ell, that sounds rough for 'er. Serious, Pete, if you need help dealing with this mob, call me. I owe you lots. Our friends would join in."

There were shouts and cheers from the pitch. A man was walking, and the scoreboard was moving from 45 for 1 to 45 for 2.

"Bugger. I'd better go; one more down and it's me. Pete, when Liz told me you was around the next week, I spoke to me boss. There's something he and I would like to talk to you about. Not about IE; to do with the maths you know. Is there any chance of you coming in? We'll do lunch."

"Yes, though I'm pretty rusty on maths. Talking with Sheila earlier was some effort. I'll be around, as I'm looking after my aunt at nights after tomorrow until Thursday."

We arranged to meet on Tuesday morning. That fitted with the progress review I had arranged with Paul for the afternoon, before we both met with George Armstrong on Wednesday morning. I headed for Ealing Broadway Station and was soon rattling along, putting up with noise and diesel smoke for the sake of a cooling breeze from an open window. I reflected on what Brian had said, and what he had not said.

It was good to see how the feckless student I had known was now on his way. I was sure Susie had much to do with that. She would have been telling him not to throw away his advantages. My only misgiving I also put down to her. The little she had spoken was in a rather false, 'cultured' accent. Brian too was trying to speak in more received English than he had been used to at home. He still relapsed sometimes. It was all or nothing.

I had given Brian a chance to retrieve himself. Rather than failing his first-year exams, he had done quite well under the terms of the deal I had struck with Sir Archibald Frampton. Separately, I had told Carol that Paul must have no recollection of who had attacked him, and that he must bury the hatchet with Brian, though he might want to do that in any case. Liz had told Brian that the police were unlikely to trouble him further, and that he too needed to bury the hatchet.

I had encouraged people at Waterhouse to view being tricked by Carmarthen College as a challenge, and to fight back together. Jim Smythe had led the first response, by coxing the College First Boat through to a sensational result. Then, as another part of my deal, Carmarthen had contested the result in a way which was seen throughout Waterhouse as unfair and therefore had galvanised the wider response I wanted. Jim had taken a hand in that, as I had hoped he would.

Brian had referred to Jim, but not to the oarsman who had made the biggest effort for Waterhouse. This all suggested that I was right about what had happened when Paul was attacked.

I had visited Cambridge just twice since leaving; the first, soon afterwards for Jenny's twentieth birthday party and to collect the rest of my luggage; the second for Jenny and Dick's wedding. Both visits were out of term, and I had stayed with Liz at the Master's Lodge. I had wanted to keep out of the way and let people get on with the lives to which I had, mostly unwittingly, caused such disturbance. It seemed that they had done so.

Brian had summed up Jenny very well. He knew that she had been my girlfriend, but I wondered if he knew just how close we had been. She hadn't been around the College with me very much. Nor had Carol ever been noticed with me. She had told the hen party only about what had happened before my time with Jenny.

I spent the rest of the journey in pleasurable imagination of Jenny's hen party. I had heard about it from Liz during the course of Jenny's wedding night. Carol's account, given whilst on our holiday in France, had filled in a few gaps, and fully earned her the spanking that turned her right on. So, I had known how the ladies had bonded, but I had not realised the full extent to which the 'Cambridge chums' had brought together people whom I had known separately, but hardly knew each other.

Dick was on the platform when I arrived at Maidenhead. He was looking very smart in a way already rather old fashioned – blazer, shirt with cravat, and flannel trousers. I had done my best with what I had with me. We set off in the sunshine.

"It's great that you can come to this, Pete. Jenny suggested I should ask you."

"Something has come up that makes it doubly good for me. Harry is still behaving like a little piranha fish, though gobbling up Cardinal has put him into the big league." For the third time that day, I described Roberta's problems.

The party was well under way when we arrived. At the reception desk was a handsome young man who wore a badge numbered 1, as did his female colleague. He greeted us with a knowing look, and asked for a name. I have always had the useful knack of reading papers upside down, so I pointed out that my name was on the first page of the guest list before him, whilst my friend's name would be quite near the end. As he turned over the pages to tick off Dick's name, I noticed that the list included several MPs and peers. One of their names, Sir Reginald Emerson, seemed vaguely familiar. His name and a few others on the list bore an asterisk.

We moved through to a large terrace, overlooking a swimming pool and gardens. It was very warm in the sunshine, since trees around gave shelter. In the middle of the terrace was a raised platform about sixty-foot long and six-foot wide, with spots numbered 1 to 12 on each side of a central spot with a microphone. We picked up champagne at the bar, and sat down to look at leaflets the young man had given us.

These encouraged us to consider now our votes for Round One (dressed) of the three-round Body Beautiful contest. We could judge from amongst the six men and six women hosts, who were at our service for the evening. Also, up to six men and six women guests could take part in the contest, by claiming numbers 7 to 12 at the reception desk. There were tear-off voting slips for the best man and woman in each round, and a ballot box at the bar. Following the contest, the pool (heated, water temperature 75°F/24°C) would be open to all, and towels would be provided. Afterwards, there would be a buffet. We were enjoined to 'enjoy the evening in the house and gardens', but 'strictly no photography, please'.

Hosts wearing badges numbered 2 to 6 were mingling with guests. They wore the same elegant outfits as the two on the desk. Two women with badges 7 and 8 passed by, chatting away in American accents. Number 7 looked to be in her thirties and was very neatly turned out in summer top and skirt, whilst Number 8 was about my age, and looked muscular and athletic, with well-tanned head and shoulders.

"What do you think are my chances, Pete?" asked Dick.

I looked at him. "Not bad. You know what you'll have to do in Round Three."

"Yes, and I've an advantage there."

He made off to the desk, and was very cheerful when he returned a few minutes later, wearing badge number 12.

"It looks like you just got in, Dick."

"That's right. The bloke in front of me was asking, but he was with his wife. When told about Round Three he looked rather sheepishly at her and turned away."

We got up and circulated. Dick's badge created interest. Soon we were talking to an older couple, the man distinguished looking, the wife short and rather wizened. We introduced ourselves as friends of Harry from Cambridge.

"I've heard that he was rather unhappy there," the man said.

"Not really, but he thought that there were better things he could do with his time. He seems to have been proved right," I replied, looking around.

"Yes, indeed. What have you been doing since you left Cambridge?"

I explained that I worked for International Electronics, and had been in Spain for the last two and a half years. This led to his pumping me for information about developments there. Dick looked restive, as he wanted more people to see him. Fortunately, after a few minutes Harry joined us.

"Ambrose, Martha, how splendid that you're here. This couldn't have happened without you."

"Thank you, Harry. It's very kind of you to invite us. It shows that you're committed to our prosperity together. We are both looking forward very much to voting in your entertaining and stimulating contest. Now, can you excuse us until a little later? I need to speak with my friends."

As they moved off, Martha gave Dick a further look up and down. Harry smiled.

"Thanks for joining in, Dick. I'm looking forward to voting, too. It's good you've made it, Pete."

"Thanks, Harry. Your invitation was well timed. I'm over here for a week, though next month I'll be back in the UK for good."

"Trust you to spot the most important people here. Ambrose is boss of National Amalgamated, the lead of the consortium that financed the takeover of Cardinal. He's joined the other bankers at that table. I wonder what they're cooking up. It was visiting Ambrose and Martha's very swish house that gave the idea for today. The pictures there are, shall we say, in the style of Rubens. Much of the conversation at dinner, with the ladies, was about whom of those portrayed looked best. Now, there's a couple just arrived whom I must welcome."

We moved on around. The desire to give Dick the once-over brought us into more groups. Other numbered hosts and guests were attracting similar attention. This was certainly a way of breaking the ice amongst strangers and creating an animated party. Jenny had been right about people wanting to enjoy themselves.

After a while, Harry took position on the platform centre spot, and addressed the crowd of nearly two hundred.

"I'll say to you all together what I've tried to say to you all separately, though apologies to those I've missed so far. Welcome, thanks for all you've done to bring Tamfield Investments to where it is now, thanks for coming today, and enjoy! Now, it's men contestants to the left facing me, and women to the right. For everyone else, Round One votes are needed in the box in five minutes. Take a last look at the contestants as they are now. You'll have longer in Round Two, and even longer in Round Three, when you'll have most to view. In all rounds, no touching or photography, please."

In those days, photography meant carrying and showing a substantial and obvious film camera, so this admonition could be enforced. The contestants took position on the platform. Amongst men, I had no reason not to choose Dick. His spot placed him next to Harry, who was asking after Jenny and hearing about the growing family. Amongst women, I picked the well-dressed older American numbered 7, who carried herself well on the platform and looked very cheerful. There was a pleasant sense of anticipation.

After a few minutes the contestants filed into changing rooms in the house. The rest of us cast our votes, chatted and recharged glasses, until Harry welcomed the contestants back for Round Two. The men now wore matching swimming trunks, and the women wore matching, good quality one-piece swimsuits of the kind then seen in 'Miss World' contests. We all wandered round the stand and made our selections. I noticed the woman called Martha looking particularly intently at both men and women and almost licking her lips in anticipation. This time I picked the woman host numbered 6, who looked rather like Jenny and was particularly sleek in her swimsuit. The buzz of conversation suggested that she was a front-runner. Amongst the men, it was easy to stay with Dick. The male hosts had looked well enough fully dressed, but were now seen to be either rather skinny or muscular in an unattractive 'bodybuilder' style. Some of the male guests now seemed apprehensive.

The contestants went inside briefly, and reappeared for Round Three. Gasps of feigned surprise were followed by applause as they took their positions again, standing with legs a little apart, and hands on hips. Harry welcomed them, and encouraged us to take our time in deciding. We did so, particularly the banking contingent who walked round the stand three times, with lots of pauses and discussions. They at least were impassive. Some younger men in the audience were visibly excited, as I would have been myself, but for how I had spent the morning.

The male hosts were all well-endowed, and had plenty of attention on that account, but could not compete with Dick. Unlike other male guests, he posed in a relaxed way, and was clearly enjoying himself. His advantage was revealed – an all-over suntan which set off his blond hair and made him look very handsome indeed.

The women's contest was concentrated in the middle of their row. Number 6, though very attractive, was now revealed as probably a redhead, rather than a natural blonde. I was tempted to vote again for Number 7, who chatted cheerfully to those inspecting her. She was as elegant and tidy unclothed as clothed, sporting a neatly trimmed triangle which matched her brown hair, and allowed a distinct view of what was beneath. However, I eventually plumped for her friend, Number 8. Her muscular body had seemed rather ungainly in the borrowed swimsuit, but was now very striking, a taller and lighter-haired version of Liz, and like Dick well bronzed all over.

Harry gave all the men a careful inspection, particularly Dick. He was also polite enough to pay some attention to the women. Then he spotted me, and we had a brief exchange before he took his place for another announcement.

"We have here today an old friend of mine, who was top of his year in maths at Cambridge University. You can't do better than that. So, I've asked him to supervise the count. We will bring you the result as soon as we can. Meanwhile, the pool is open. I'm sure the contestants, and some of you, will want to *cool down*."

To the sound of splashes and laughter, I went inside with the ballot box. There were over a thousand slips inside, to be sorted amongst the twenty-four contestants. With two staff to assist me, I had a first count in ten minutes. The men's order was clear, but the women's order was closer. I left the others to check that, and told Harry that in five minutes he could announce the result. So, he asked the contestants to return.

By now there were about forty people disporting themselves in the pool. I saw Dick bouncing a ball at Number 7. They emerged, and towelled themselves. Number 8, who had been doing steady lengths, called to me in a strong Midwest accent.

"Hey, Brains, grab a towel and help me out... Mmmm, I like your hands. Pat me down, go on, a bit more. Yes, there, don't be shy. What are my chances, then?"

"Fair. I'll be back soon."

I collected the results sheet and walked slowly out, past the contestants who were lined up again. The bankers' party was now in the front row of the expectant crowd, and was discussing what attributes were most important as they pointed at one contestant or another. I passed the sheet to Harry, trying hard to look very serious. The women's order was 6, 8, 7. After announcing that, and the two male hosts who took second and third places, he concluded cheerfully.

"And the winning man, with over twice as many votes as any other male contestant, is another old friend of mine, right here next to me at Number 12. But all the contestants have given us a most entertaining and exciting time. Please show your appreciation again. The buffet will be served in twenty minutes. Meanwhile, the bar and pool remain open. You may want also to explore the house and gardens, though you can leave that until later."

The applause died away, and Number 8 strode over to us, the muscles rippling in her body as she moved. Her direct approach bade for no dispute.

"So, Harry, that gives you time to come in with us. And you, bright boy with the nice hands, and you, blondie, again of course."

When I returned with Harry into the warm sunshine, I was less self-conscious than I had feared I might be. In the company, all seemed quite normal. Number 7 greeted us, and at the same time eyed me up and down, carefully.

"Wow, Harry, you look every inch the hungry predator, waiting to pounce."

Harry had been wearing a slick Italian business suit. Now, his slim figure, topped by short blond hair, looked hard and tough. He and Dick maintained commendable control as they gazed at each other.

In a less crowded pool, Number 7 splashed around with Dick and me, while Harry pounded up and down with Number 8. After ten minutes, we saw that the wooden components of the platform had been stacked, cloths laid over all, and the buffet brought out. Harry and I climbed out, and eventually reached the changing room, after being spotted by Martha and asked to allow her a closer look.

Harry dressed quickly, and went to join the bankers. I emerged with Dick, to find the two Americans waiting for us. Number 7 was as neatly dressed as before, and had preserved the style of her brown hair, whilst Number 8's hair now had that swimmer's look I knew from Carol. By now, most tables on the nearby lawn were occupied, with only those for couples left.

"You take blondie, Gail, I'll take brainy," said Number 7.

"Dick has a Cambridge doctorate. I have only a first degree," I observed.

We went to the excellent and certainly expensive buffet, and settled down to eat and drink. My companion had plenty to say.

"Wow, all this is a surprise, but much more fun than the usual corporate bash. Gail dared me to enter. I'm glad I did, and glad you all had the taste to score me well. The girl who won did look great in the swimsuit. Gail has a very fine body. She spends lots of time in the gym, and she uses the solarium."

"I voted for the three of you in the three rounds. You first, because you looked the best when dressed, just as you do now."

"Thanks. Sure, that'll be the way the women here voted, but I guess the guys were all imagining what they were gonna see."

"Perhaps they were, but my impression was that the women here, both contestants and audience, were enjoying it more than some of the men. Apart from Dick, the men guest contestants all looked embarrassed, and some of the younger men in the audience were, too. Not so the older men, though. The banking crowd loved it; so did their wives, particularly the one called Martha."

"You're right. Younger men can't be excited without showing it, even if they're dressed. Women can be excited without showing it, even if they're nude. It's OK too for a woman to look over and appreciate another woman's body. On the stand, I was mighty excited. I had good views on each side of me. I was enjoying the looks I was getting from men like you, and from women too, even from old Martha, who just wanted to push a finger up the girls and grab the men. Wow, she was taken with the winning girl. She was just licking her chops until Ambrose moved her on. Even from along the line, I could see your pal Dick was enjoying it, too. He's got such poise. I spotted you and him talking to Harry earlier. He liked it lots when Harry stripped off. At Cambridge, were they lovers? Whatever, I thought I'd better be the graceful older woman and leave Dick to Gail. She does like a good body."

"You're very perceptive, and you've done the better deal. Dick and Harry were together, but Dick went back. Now, he's married, with a second child on the way. That's why his wife didn't come. She could have seen off the lot of you. I know that well, because once she was my girlfriend. In the end, she preferred Dick, but she's still a good friend of mine. She knows about Harry, of course."

"So, you're on your own?"

"Yes and no. I've been out in Spain, and had a girl there. Last night, I slept with another ex. She's athletic, like Gail, and would also have done well, but she was already fixed up when my invitation reached me. I'm still friends with my exes."

"That's more than I am with some. It sounds like you have a great life. I find London a bit lonesome at times. Wow, here we are, you've seen all over my naked body, I like the look of yours, we're having all this talk, and we don't even know each other. Bit topsy-turvy, but this party's made it like that. Well, me to say first. I'm Steph Coolidge, no relation[17] as you'll have guessed by now, a New Yorker, aged thirty-four, divorced and unattached, no kids and don't want any. I'm Senior Analyst, Europe for New Hampshire Realty, the US member of the group that's financed Tamfield's takeover of Cardinal. The head of our London office and his current wife are over there, with Martha, Ambrose and Harry. Gail Morton is on my staff."

Over the next hour, I heard plenty about Steph, and she a little about me. Gail and Dick followed the example of the host contestants by going into the pool again. Harry moved round several groups of older people, perhaps including the MPs and peers. I noticed him looking pleasurably at and speaking to the male host who had been a distant second to Dick. Suddenly, Steph looked at her watch.

"Wow, our car back to Town is in forty minutes. I like you, Pete. You're younger than me, but act up. You didn't sit around at Cambridge, you're going places. You've that something guys have who get on in the States. Not enough Brits have it – certainly, not enough in the City. Plenty there who think it's some kind of gentlemen's club. Are you on? There are cabins in the garden,

---

17 Of J. Calvin Coolidge (President 1923-29), a man of famously few words.

and rooms in the house, with nice comfortable couches. We can go find one, and slide the catch to 'OCCUPIED'."

"I like you too, Steph. You definitely have that something for me, but after last night, I could well disappoint you. Can we meet one evening this week?"

"Good thinking, Pete. You'll find out I'm a hustler. Tuesday is fine, if nothing comes up. Call me at the office between eight and nine. I know that's early for a Brit, but meetings begin at nine. Hey, you two, don't miss us out. You look real great."

Steph waved to Gail and Dick, who had emerged from the pool. They were walking around to dry in the warm evening and to show themselves off again, as the very well-matched pair of winning guests. The last of the sun glinted on the drops of water remaining on their tanned bodies, and caused Gail's muscles to cast shadows, in ways that would have excited many artists and certainly excited me.

The pair circled our table slowly, and then pulled up chairs, to make a less misogynistic version of Manet's most famous painting. After a few minutes, Dick went to have a shower and dress, and Gail picked up a wrap, for it was beginning to cool.

The three of us talked of the economic situation. Steph and Gail had similar views to Paul, but were rather pessimistic about the prospects for North Sea oil, because New Hampshire Realty's oil trading group didn't believe that a further big increase in the oil price was likely for some years. They pointed out that the doubling of the price that had occurred since 1970 was largely concealed from the British public, because so much of the price of petrol here was tax and duty. In the USA, it was encouraging a move to 'compact cars' of only three-litre engine capacity rather than six.

The party was thinning out. Only a few tables were still occupied nearby, and there was less noise from the pool. Gail looked over to the bankers' table, which Harry had rejoined.

"Steph, they're breaking up over there. I need to dress, and we need to collect our prizes."

Steph passed me her card, and after goodbyes I was left alone in the fading sun. I was wondering where Dick was, for we needed to head for the station before long. Then I heard the end of a heated conversation.

"Yes, Ambrose, I can assure you on that. The Bishop's Park Sales Office opens tomorrow. We'll have three quarters of the properties sold by December, and the rest by March. You have the projections for cash flow, and can see what they mean for your exposure."

"But Harry, when will you solve the access road problem? You said before that you would solve it by 6th July. It is now 15th July, and you haven't solved it. Every day you don't solve it increases our exposure. You are approaching the agreed limit."

"I've said before, don't *worry*, Ambrose. There's a silly old woman who thinks she needn't accept our generous offer for her tatty old house. She's going to realise just how wrong she is, very fast indeed. We'll be through there well before anyone is ready to move in."

"I hope so, I hope so very much, Harry. I'm sure my colleagues feel the same. Like all bankers, I worry about exposure. Thank you, Harry, for organising a most pleasant entertainment, based indeed on exposure of a different kind. We all enjoyed it very much, particularly the contributions of your university friend and of two of our own staff, and also the little bonus that you yourself gave us. I am sure that you will ensure that this remains a wholly private event. Here come our drivers, and here are those travelling with us. It is, therefore, *au revoir*."

I waved to Steph and Gail as they left, leaving the terrace empty apart from Harry and me. Dick had not returned, but I was concentrating on what Harry had said.

"Phew, that was hard work," said Harry. "I need a drink, before I really unwind."

"Were you expecting to strip off yourself?"

"No, but as you may have heard just now it went down very well with the bankers, and their wives. It also gave me a few minutes out, which I needed."

"I don't remember you being as strong a swimmer as you are now."

"I've worked it up. When you're in the game I'm in, and my type, you need to do something physical. I'm up to a good standard on skiing, too. I try for a couple of breaks in the winter. Now, let's see."

At the bar, he picked up a drink and also a note for him, marked 'CONFIDENTIAL'. He opened it and smiled, viciously.

"Ah, good, only Reg has taken. Andy and Julian are left for me. I'll start with Andy, then sleep with Julian, and take him in the morning. When I'm finished, they'll both have very sore backsides, but that's what they're paid to have."

"What's that all about?" I asked.

"Special guests can stay the night with a host if they want. For them, the contest was an aid to selection. Three of the men hosts suit men, and the other three suit women. The women hosts suit either. Ambrose and Martha had first pick and have *both* selected women. The winner is for Martha."

"I thought the Dugdales had left for home."

"Once out of sight of the other bankers' cars, theirs will return. I don't want any jealousy. You've been helpful, Pete. Woman Number 3 is free."

"I'm staying with Liz, so no thanks Harry, but very many thanks again for inviting me. You were lucky with the St Swithin's Day weather."

"When you're back for good, we must meet up. I want to hear how Spain has changed since I was there. Now, I must go."

"Harry, there's something I didn't mean to raise with you tonight, but sorting it is clearly very urgent for your company. The 'silly old woman' you mentioned is actually my aunt. Your people are harassing her. I'm sure that you don't know what they're doing. Provided that it stops, there's a fair price for an urgent sale."

After a pause, Harry turned to me with gritted teeth.

"Pete, go to hell. *Go to hell.*"

"What do you mean?"

"Just that. We've made a perfectly good offer. Now, you're trying to screw us. Your aunt knew of the access plan two years ago."

"No, she didn't."

"We can prove she was sent a letter about it."

"Look, Harry, we can move fast. Your people have her solicitor's details. Have them contact him first thing tomorrow. I'll tell him to expect a call."

"I've no more to say, Pete. You think you're being clever. You'll soon realise that you're not being at all clever. Goodnight."

Harry marched off into the house. Clearly, he was under more pressure than I had realised, and this was unbalancing him. Perhaps he thought that I was behind Roberta's failure to co-operate.

I went to look for Dick. The men's changing room was quiet, but I could hear a gentle thumping sound from an open cubicle, and then his voice.

"Marvellous Andy, marvellous."

Dick was face down, being massaged by the host to whom Harry had spoken. The bulge in the host's trunks showed that he was finding his task very enjoyable.

"Now Dick, think of who you love most."

Andy slid a pillow under Dick. His left hand set to work between Dick's legs, whilst his right hand stroked Dick's bottom. After about half a minute, Andy's finger was into Dick's rectum.

"Aah – *aaah – aaaaaahh!*"

Dick's golden buttocks thrashed up and down, as he pumped into the pillow. Andy grinned with delight and dropped his trunks. The sight revealed was very fine, though out of proportion to his rather skinny body. I too was excited by the spectacle, which recalled good times with Carol. Now, though, it was time to cough. Andy glowered at me, subsided, pulled his trunks up again and forced a smile. After a few seconds, Dick turned over.

"That was lovely, Andy. I felt both your hands right through me. Hi, Pete, this is my special reward from Harry for winning by so much. I'll clean up before we go."

"I will tell Mr Tamfield that you liked my service," said Andy, slyly.

Dick made off to the showers. I spoke forcefully. "Mr Tamfield is very stressed and annoyed. I know what service he'll have from *you*."

I smiled while Andy slunk away, shuddering in anticipation, just as I wanted.

A few minutes later Dick and I were hurrying along to the station, not too much slowed by the magnum of champagne Dick was carrying.

"It's great you could come, Pete. We'll put this in stock. We're not doing much for Jenny's birthday, but we're thinking of a party for our old friends once we're settled in Brighton and the baby has appeared. It will probably be in mid-November. You'll be around then, won't you?"

"I certainly will be. Tell Jenny that it was a great suggestion that we should come to this together. I guess you won't be saying what happened right at the end."

"I have to admit that the way I was, I would have enjoyed the moment with Andy, but I would be sorry now. So, thanks for the rescue."

"Harry asked him to bring you on. Think about why."

"Yes, I know, Pete. Jenny will like the rest of the story, if she's in the right mood. She's liked some fun in the past. I'm sure you've heard about her hen party."

"I certainly have."

"Expecting has made her less interested. It's like that for some women, I'm told. She knows I feel a bit frustrated, so she'll be pleased to hear I had some treatment for that. I won't tell her though that when Andy fingered my bottom, I thought of Harry. Seeing him naked did bring back some happy memories."

"Harry wasn't expecting Gail to be so persuasive, but none of us was expecting any of this. You've a super tan, and you were so relaxed."

"I was relaxed because of how I got the tan. The other blokes weren't used to being naked in public. I am, because of Jenny. Maybe going with Liz at that Bump Supper started her off. Next there were the sunbaths with John, and then with Amanda too."

"You obviously enjoyed those! I remember what you said to warm us up after Jenny and I followed Liz and you into that freezing cold lake."

"It was hot when we stayed the weekend with some second cousins of Jenny's, two months before we were married. Their house turned out to have a swimming pool. We hadn't brought kit, but Jenny had everyone joining in, including some other visitors. On our honeymoon in Yugoslavia, there was a naturist beach not far from our hotel. Jenny liked being eyed there. She *is* proud of her body."

"To my recollection, she's right to be proud. Just now you should be proud of your body, too, Dick. How did you manage in Spain? Not that long ago, the mayor of Benidorm had to petition Franco to allow women to wear two-piece swimsuits."

"We stayed in San Vicente for a few days. It's a charming town, and nearby there's a superb beach about three miles long with occasional parking. Even with David we could have no one within a quarter of a mile, so there was no risk of arrest, and Jenny didn't have to find a suit that fitted her. We just had to use lots of suncream."

"Tell Jenny from me that if she'd been able to enter, she would have won by as much as you did. I told Steph that, when she was regretting leaving you to Gail."

"It was good being with Gail."

"You were a really splendid sight together."

"Showing off gave both of us a lift. Together, we did what we couldn't have done separately. She doesn't relate to people easily. This evening, I was enjoying people appreciating me, for myself. Being with Jenny is marvellous, but she does organise me, in the loveliest sort of way. You know that very well, Pete."

"Yes, I do."

"I'm glad you hit it off with Steph."

"We may see more of each other. She came over eighteen months ago, partly to get away from a pretty horrid ending. She's not settled with anyone here."

From Maidenhead Station, we went our separate ways. As my train rattled through the gathering twilight, I had plenty to think about. By the time I reached Liz's flat, I had a plan.

Liz had returned not long before me. She was tired but excited, having won her match with Morag 7-5, 6-8, 13-11, with an audience including the people who had booked the court but were quite prepared to wait and watch them battle it out. That had been followed by well-earned mutual reminiscence under the shower. Brian had come in at 58 for 3 and scored 62 not out, in a total of 165. The other team had been going strong at 141 for 4 before crashing to defeat by six runs in the evening light. So, there had been much to celebrate. My account excited her further, hearing about Steph cheered her even more, and she was receptive to my plan.

"It sounds fun, and smart if you can bring it off. It does depend on Harry reacting in the way you think he will. I can't judge that, but I don't know him."

"From my memories of him, and what he said tonight, I can guess how he'll react. If I'm right, he'll have the lesson he needs."

"I'm sorry I can't join in myself, but I'm booked tomorrow for social therapy. Call Brian in ten minutes, and I'll call Morag. They should all be back by then."

"Do you think Morag will be interested in helping?"

"She's no supporter of people like Harry. More to the point, she's a supporter of yours, and always has been. She told me today how great it was to meet you again. I hope she'll rope Sheila in, too."

"At lunchtime, Sheila was rather monopolising me. She's quite a pushy type."

"You can talk, Pete. If Sheila wasn't a pushy type, she wouldn't have done what she's done for victims."

Liz told me more about the voluntary work Sheila led. Then, both our calls had positive results. After that, it was a quiet night before early starts, hers to deal with last-minute briefing, mine to drive to Roberta's house in time to collect the keys from Gerald before he went off to work. Liz had the last word, before we dropped off to sleep, each for the second time comforted by being with someone we knew so well.

"You're a really super brother, Pete. It's great that you're back."

4. TUESDAY, 17TH JULY, 1973

Midnight had come and gone, the traffic on the main road had thinned out, and there were few pedestrians. I had parked my rather noticeable Spanish-registered car in the next side road along from Roberta's, and asked my four passengers to stay in it. That was not an unwelcome request, since there was a slight drizzle. So as to appear less obvious, I was strolling up and down near the roundabout at which Roberta's road joined the main road.

I began to wonder whether my plan was going to be fruitless, but whoever was trying to get Roberta out would now be under big pressure from Harry to deliver. I had some idea of what might happen. I just had to wait.

At twenty to one, a small car turned into Roberta's road, followed by a builders' lorry carrying ladders. I noted the numbers of both vehicles. Two minutes later, my car was about fifty yards from the roundabout and two hundred yards from Roberta's house, parked broadside-on between a tree and a lamp post. Though the road was fairly wide, nothing could get past. The five of us spread across the road. Owing to its curve, we were not visible from outside the house.

Now, we waited again, for what seemed a long time but was only about five minutes. It was quiet, though we could occasionally hear faint tinkling sounds of something being dropped. I hoped that no late returnee would disturb us, though that didn't seem likely in Bellinghame, after midnight. Nothing else had turned into the road for half an hour.

Suddenly, there were whistles through the night air, and wavering lights as our other party used their torches. We heard running, a slamming door, and a car start. A moment later it came round the corner, and screeched to a halt. My trap was sprung.

The driver jumped out, and saw two men and three women barring his way. He tried to butt his way past the women. That was a mistake, for they were Morag, Sheila, and Carol. In a moment, he was firmly in their grip.

"Take your hands off me. What the hell are you doing, blocking my way?"

"Relax," I said. "You'll wake the road. Let's go back to my Aunt Roberta's house and see what's been going on. Paul, take those keys out of his hand."

The other four marched him along. I moved both cars to the side of the road, and followed.

It was much as I had expected. Four men had alighted from the lorry, and ladders were against the darkened house. Two men were still on the roof, having already removed and thrown down quite a number of tiles, mostly on to an old mattress that had been spread on the ground to muffle the sound of their falling. Some had already been removed from the mattress, to make room for more. Within a few hours, they would have stripped the roof, thus making the house uninhabitable.

The men descended from the roof, I opened the house up, and all were escorted indoors. I stayed behind for a moment to apologise to and reassure some disturbed neighbours, one of whom fortunately remembered me from when I had stayed nearly three years before. When I came in, Gerald was ringing off.

"Frank Booth is bringing Mother over. They'll be here in five minutes, Pete."

"Great. Thanks Gerald, Brian and all of you who've helped bag this lot. I'm sorry you're all rather damp. If a couple of you go to the kitchen, you'll find that this morning I put out kit for making coffee. Milk is in the fridge."

One of the men from the builders' lorry interjected.

"Honest, guv, we won't to know it won't this bloke's 'ouse. 'E sez 'e owns it, wants it down, but some cove might get a preservation order. So, we woz ter take the roof off in the night."

"Do you know who this bloke is?"

I pointed to the very miserable looking driver of the car. He was a man of about my age, whom in the light I recognised. I might have seen him from a distance, as he walked past the house the previous morning. More definitely, on Sunday he had been one of the less impressive guest contestants. He looked much more naked now than he had done then.

"Not seen 'im before this morning. 'E finds us in the caff, tells us wot 'e wants, gives us a hundred quid for starters, meets us 'alf an hour ago and brings us 'ere. Then when yer pals comes along, 'e does a runner. We're glad you nabbed 'im. Why don't yer let us take 'im round the back for a little friendly talk, eh?"

"I think we need his story, first."

The driver now looked more scared than miserable. The question of his identity was solved by Roberta's exclamation, on her arrival with Frank Booth.

"Well, well, we meet again, Mr Percival."

There wasn't much more to do. Frank had brought a typewriter with him, and in ten minutes there was a note for Mr Percival to sign. This admitted that he, being an employee of Tamfield Investments, had attempted to coerce Roberta into selling her house to them by making various specified threats and causing various specified actions amounting to criminal damage. I passed it to him.

"Right, sign that or we'll let your friends here have that talk they're suggesting."

He signed. I handed him a carbon copy, and continued.

"At ten o'clock sharp, I'll call at your head office. I know what deal for sale of this house is acceptable, and I'll expect to see someone who can settle the matter quickly. If there's no settlement, this goes to the police. Here are your car keys. Brian, Jack, could you show Mr Percival out, please?"

The sound of two hefty feet kicking Mr Percival down the front path amused all, particularly the builders. They promised that two of them would come back during the day and put a tarpaulin over the damage to prevent immediate wet inside. To them, I was a 'gent'. They were doubtless pleased to get away, £100 up. Soon afterwards, Gerald and his friends departed. Roberta, Frank and I briefly updated our dinnertime conversation about terms. Then Roberta and Frank exchanged friendly kisses before he left with the original signed confession, and she excused herself as really very tired but most grateful.

Brian's party decided to stay, rather than disturb their homes. We spread around Roberta's lounge, too excited to sleep. My litre bottle of brandy from Spain seemed just the right thing. Geraldine Foster took the lead. She was one of the couple Brian had told me about on Sunday.

"To you, Pete, for your great plan. It's stopped Tamfield in its tracks."

"To you all, for dropping everything to help."

"What made you think that they might try something tonight?" Brian asked.

"On Sunday I told Harry that what was happening wasn't acceptable. I said that I was sure he didn't know about it, and that I could come into his office and discuss a deal I could put to Roberta. He didn't react well."

Jack Unwin asked the obvious question. I remembered him from Cambridge days, and was interested that Brian had roped him in.

"Do you think he knew what would happen, or even that he ordered it?"

"Mr Percival was at Harry's party. Harry could have spoken to him after he spoke to me. Perhaps he gave the impression that he expected something to happen fast, and left it at that."

"So, this is 'Tamfieldgate'. That's very topical," said Carol.

"It's an old, old story. Around Christmas 1170, Henry II asked 'Will anyone rid me of this turbulent priest?' and landed up to his neck in trouble."[18]

"Yes, and so were his successors over the next 350 years. I can say that as someone who took several courses on medieval history. To be let off, Henry had to sign up to far less control over church revenues than other monarchs had. Six Henrys later, over a quarter of the land in England was owned by monasteries and suchlike. Twelve thousand monks and nuns, less than half a percent of the population, lived the life of Riley on the proceeds."

"I bet we were paying a lot more than most to Rome, too," said Brian.

"We certainly were."

"Ted Heath has signed up to begin that all over again, without being involved in any murder."[19]

The discussion moved on. Before Carol and Paul left home, they had heard on the ten o'clock news of the first revelation that conversations and telephone calls in President Nixon's office had been recorded. The battle in the US courts and Congressional committees would now be about obtaining transcripts covering the period just after the Watergate break-in.[20] Morag observed that Nixon would be desperate to secure diversions. I tried to avoid looking at Paul. We knew that others had already made that calculation.

It was beginning to get light when I showed the ladies to the beds I had made up. The rest of us made ourselves as comfortable

18 A reference to the murder of Thomas Becket.
19 A reference to the terms on which the UK had entered the EEC.
20 It was a long battle. The first transcripts, full of 'expletives deleted', would not appear until April 1974, and the damning transcript that sealed Nixon's fate not until August 1974.

as possible. I dozed, reflecting that it had indeed been a great plan, but it seemed a long time ago that I had pulled up outside Roberta's house to meet Gerald before he left for work...

Nothing more had happened over the weekend. Gerald harrumphed over my plan, but had nothing better to suggest and could bring in some friends. We found some empty suitcases. He took a while to load some of them into his car, and then set off.

I set off myself on foot. About three hundred yards on from the house, Roberta's road came to a dead end, and a footpath led to the local shopping centre where Frank Booth had his office. Fortunately, he was in, and unengaged. He had heard nothing further from Tamfield Investments. We talked for half an hour. Then I did a little shopping before returning to the house.

I spent some time visibly pottering around in the garden, before locking up and driving off, with some more empty suitcases placed in my car. Any watcher could have gained the impression that the house was being left unoccupied. As day turned to night, their impression would be reinforced. They might also notice that the occupants of the houses on either side appeared to be away, leaving the coast clearer.

The Borough Library had files of newspapers going back a year. After an hour there, I was clearer on how Cardinal Properties had become bankrupt, through their incompetence in managing the Bishop's Park development and the long construction strike. Cardinal's bankers had invited Tamfield Investments to take it over. In modern parlance, the takeover was highly leveraged. Despite the stock issue, the margin of equity below debt was slim. It was not surprising that the bankers were worried about exposure. Everything depended on completing and selling properties fast, particularly as prices had now levelled out and interest rates were rising.

As I left the library, I was confronted by the name which on Sunday had seemed vaguely familiar. A notice giving details of constituency surgeries was headed 'Meet your MP, Sir Reg Emerson.' He was the politician with an asterisk, and I could guess what the asterisk meant.

After a quick lunch, I met Roberta at Waterloo, and had explained my plan during our drive back to Bellinghame. She went with it, though it would require her to move fast. She was showing the qualities of thought and decision that she, and only she, had inherited from her father and grandfather. Inheritance is a chancy matter.

We visited a teashop, and then called at the Bishop's Park Sales Office, which was daringly open until 7 pm. I was sure that whoever was causing trouble would not be there, since the letters to Roberta had come from Tamfield Investments' head office in Islington. We looked at a three-bedroomed bungalow, which was quite spacious and had a reasonably sized garden, and was available from mid-August for £17,995; two years before, it would have cost less than £10,000. Roberta was taken with it, as providing her with what she now needed whilst keeping her near her bridge club and gardening society. She identified the plot that she wanted, but hadn't given her name to reserve at this stage.

Next, we met Frank Booth for dinner at a steak house near where he lived. We made plans, and I told them about Spain. Roberta prompted Frank to reminisce about his fine war record in the RAF, comprising nine kills and a DFC. His greying moustache helped him to look the part. He also admitted to a less successful part of his record; a spur-of-the-moment marriage, which had not long survived peace but had hit his finances hard. He and Roberta seemed to like talking to each other.

We were back at Frank's maisonette as it began to get dark. Whilst Roberta had admired the roses in his small garden, I settled down to phone. Gerald and Brian had both recruited full carloads. They were to wear dark clothing, bring whistles and torches, and meet me at the shopping centre car park at 11.30 pm. Brian had another message for me: he had spoken to Carol, and she and Paul were ready to join in. This was good news in more than one way. After more phone calls, I had a full load to pick up at East Croydon Station.

The meeting at the car park was brief. Gerald's and Brian's parties were to use the footpath and wait about a hundred yards along the road from Roberta's house, out of vision of the headlights of any vehicle driving up the road. They were to move in quietly once it was clear that something was going on, but not before. They should use torches and whistles only when seen.

And so, it had happened…

By half past six, I had the smell of bacon and eggs wafting through the house. By half past seven, I had dropped my carload back at East Croydon. At ten past eight, I rang Steph at her office.

"Wow, you sound sleepy, Brit boy. Are you still in bed?"

"No, I've not been to bed. I'll tell you more tonight."

"Great, you're on, really *on*, I mean?"

"Definitely. I've been invited to a business lunch, so I won't need a big meal."

"That suits me. I've a lunch today as well. Say, are you at the IE office this afternoon?"

"Yes."

"I live not far from there. I'll call in at reception; when, six thirty?"

"That sounds fine to me."

"I've been thinking of you lots, but I must concentrate on my work. I'll be seeing you."

The prospect of being 'seen' again by Steph woke me up. I took a cup of tea to Roberta, promised to call, and tidied the kitchen. I was on my way before nine o'clock.

Luckily, the train I was aiming to catch actually ran. At Victoria, the departures board showed that about one third of the local suburban trains were cancelled 'because of staff shortages', though there was no current industrial dispute. The day before it had been the same at Waterloo, and I had been waiting for some time at East Croydon before all of my passengers arrived. The government's wage controls were making it impossible to retain enough staff to run the scheduled service. I had already had Gerald's views on this. Whatever the pros and cons of the privatisation of train operations in the 1990s, it did take away from the Treasury the decision about how much to pay railway guards.[21]

The then new Victoria Line took me to the Islington offices of Tamfield Investments. These were full to bursting, since those headquarters' staff of Cardinal Properties who were retained after the takeover had found themselves unceremoniously moved from their plush offices in Mayfair. Disposal of those had been welcomed in the financial columns, and doubtless by Sir Ambrose Dugdale and his colleagues. I found myself in an alcove with a jovial man in his forties, who introduced himself as Joe Aspinall, Construction Director. He took the only sensible approach in the circumstances.

"God, this is a right pig's ear. I can only apologise. I was at another big site near Derby all day yesterday. I went up on Sunday night, and missed the party which sounds as if it was great, though the wife wouldn't have liked it. I got back late, shagged out – that site's as big a balls-up as Bishop's Park was when I joined the company and had to settle the strike. Then at six this morning, the Boss calls about all this. I'm told you know him."

I made vaguely sympathetic noises, said that I had been involved in managing a factory, and acknowledged that things didn't always go right. Then I showed him a copy of Mr Percival's confession, which he had already seen, and moved quickly to state terms.

Roberta was ready to buy the £17,995 bungalow whose plot number I gave. If the documents could be made ready, her

---

21 The recent troubles on routes served by Southern Railway give some indication of the quality of service throughout the rail system when it was state run.

solicitor could exchange contracts today on the basis of swapping her house for the bungalow, plus £30,000 and costs. If Tamfield Investments arranged for a company to send packers tomorrow and remove furniture and effects to store on Thursday, she could be out early on Friday and completion on the house could take place immediately thereafter. Thus Harry could tell his bankers that the access road works could begin on Friday. Also, they would have sold another plot, and Roberta could move in as soon as the bungalow was ready.

We had a little negotiation, more for the principle than anything, and settled on swap plus £27,005, thus putting the house into Tamfield Investments' books as purchased for £45,000. I had authority to conclude at a balance of £25,000 up, so that was fine.

In parting on friendly terms, I gave him a useful idea. Roberta's front and back gardens both had attractive herbaceous borders along the sides. Mr Percival's antics had caused only superficial damage. There was plenty of room to retain the borders and construct the road, provided the contractors took care. If maintained, the borders would still look attractive when the road was finished and prospective buyers as well as those moving in were using it.

I borrowed a phone and called Roberta, who was particularly charmed at the prospect of still being able to see some of her garden. It would be a talking point with her new neighbours. I said that I wasn't expecting to be back that evening. She was a knowing and amused aunt at that news, but grateful that I would be down by lunchtime the next day to help sort out what she wanted to take with her. Disposal of what she didn't want would be Tamfield Investments' problem.

Next I called Frank Booth, who congratulated me and certainly seemed keen to help Roberta. My most difficult call was to my mother, with first the good news, and then the message that I would be dropping Roberta back with them before catching the boat on Friday.

Even though I said that I would suggest to Roberta that given the deal I had struck she should regard herself as a paying guest, my mother sounded apprehensive at this news. That didn't surprise me. The previous Thursday, my father had been conspicuous by his absence. He worked only half a mile away and quite often returned home for lunch. I could imagine his reaction to the news that Roberta would be with them for another month.

However, I was on a high, and now was the chance to press that home at home. Roberta couldn't stay with Gerald, who had a growing son and daughter and only three bedrooms in his house. Margaret, Roberta's daughter, lived with her family near Liverpool and Gerald had told me that they were about to go on holiday. My parents were not going away until September. I saw no reason why Roberta should have to put up in a hotel. The family feud might well have been justified when it began, but thirty years was quite long enough for it to have lasted. I would say to Roberta that she needed to make a real effort with my father. I would also suggest to both my mother and Roberta that they should meet with their brother Edward. At last, there might be an opportunity to do something about the family business.

As I was leaving, Harry appeared, and I greeted him.

"I think we're all on track. That wouldn't have happened if I'd missed your party, so thanks again for your invitation. I'll call about a meet-up once I'm back permanently from Spain."

"I'll like that, Pete, but I meant what I said on Sunday. I won't have people interfering in my company's operations."

I wondered how Joe Aspinall's straightforward business approach matched with Harry's tactics. Indeed, what kind of exchange of views had they had earlier? Joe had implied that the hapless Mr Percival, doubtless now perusing 'situations vacant', had had no instructions from him. However, that was being said by all sorts of eminent people, formerly in President Nixon's cabinet but now facing prosecution. It was unlikely, though, that Harry's 6 am telephone call had been recorded.

At the Holborn offices of Universal Assurance, I updated Brian, thanked him again, and apologised for not having already congratulated him on his innings on Sunday. Then we moved to our business. He showed me the latest in computing – the teletype terminal.

I had not seen a computer during my time in Spain, so my knowledge dated from 1970. Then, doing anything had involved writing a program, putting it onto punched cards or tape, and sending it to the computer room. There it joined a queue to be fed into a reader. After the program had been run, output was printed out and returned to you. Typical turnaround was one or two days. The first few tries were almost always rejected by the computer, because of typing or positioning errors in the instructions. When the program ran, it usually took more tries to get it working correctly. Even for a short program with small amounts of input data and output, obtaining useful results could take several weeks.

Now, one could link directly into a computer from a teletype terminal, through a telephone line. You could sit at the terminal, type in instructions, and the messages pointing out your errors would be typed out within seconds. Before long, you could type RUN, and the terminal would type messages asking for data. Some output would be typed within minutes at most, depending on how many other customers the computer was serving. In one session of an hour or two, you could develop a program which worked correctly. Then you could save it within the computer's electronic storage, and run it with new data when you wanted.

Universal's sales force needed to provide prospective customers quickly with accurate quotes for life insurance. They relied on sets of tables and intuition. The big computers at head office could do the accounts, but couldn't help them out in the field.

Brian showed me a program he had written. The terminal asked you various questions about the client, such as age, sex, medical issues, the sum insured, and what was to be paid on survival to a particular age. Then it told you the premium to be charged. He ran a few examples, before pointing out that the program wasn't directly helpful, unless the salesman had with him a little computer capable of running it and showing the results.

People spoke of 'Moore's Law': owing to developments in chips and circuitry computing power available would double roughly every eighteen months. There was talk of 'suitcase computers' being available within a few years. Exactly when such a computer could run Brian's program depended on how large the program needed to be. If it could be halved in size, it could be usable eighteen months earlier. That would give the company which switched over to it a real advantage over its competitors. He wanted my advice on whether some short cuts could make the program smaller.

As memories of my Cambridge courses came back to me, I made a few suggestions. We thrashed around, scribbling on bits of paper, and eventually concluded that the scope for condensation was limited, and hence the idea was for a few years' time. That was a useful conclusion in itself.

We picked up Brian's boss, who took us to a good lunch for my trouble. In those days, the two-hour, alcoholic lunch was a recognised business tool. As with all tools, it was valuable if used properly, but harmful if abused. We talked about all sorts of things. Like Brian, the boss was not a Labour man, but his views on the 'performance' of the Heath Government were nearly the same as those in Paul's presentation.

Brian and I congratulated each other on keeping awake after our shared short night, but I was glad that I had time to walk the mile or so to the IE head office. The weather was rather dismal and drizzly, but that had me more alert when I arrived.

The meeting had brought home to me how computers were developing in new ways. IE supplied components to several manufacturers of the large machines of the time. What were the prospects for building smaller, portable computers? How would the components market develop? If computers became mass-produced items, should IE assemble them as well as make components? No one had brought any of this up at the Corporate Meeting. I would try to find out more about what was happening.

I called in at the Personnel Office and collected written confirmation that I was now into the senior management structure, at a useful rise in pay, though without the overseas allowance the difference wouldn't be so great. I also had the pleasure of selecting my new car, which could now be a model noticeably better than the average family saloon. I would be passing the Spanish car to Doug.

Paul had had a busy day and a half in the office. Several firms of investment brokers were already producing regular assessments of the North Sea oil market for various capital goods. He proposed to see them during the next week, and select the most suitable to retain. The 10th August was a bit tight for a preliminary report, but I suspected that on return from Spain I would need a day or two to settle Roberta into her new bungalow, so we agreed on a 17th August deadline and a limit on fees. It was nice to be at the management level where I could sign that limit off.

He had found out that in Belgium there were three separate groups campaigning to end discrimination of the kind I had seen, feeling over which was particularly intense in the area where the factory was located. All three groups were disorganised and underfunded. He proposed to identify their leaders, visit each of them as an anonymous well-wisher, offer some funding to each, and let them compete to protest. Any disturbances were likely to be amplified by the attitude of the local police. Many of them were supporters of a Flemish far right party which had backed Germany during the War. There was a good chance of success, and it was very unlikely that we would ever be linked to events. Paul's career record left me confident that he could bring this off.

He moved on to 'Crafty'. "I'm getting together a short list of four or five oil traders. I'll bring it home on Thursday, so you can pop over and collect it."

"Will you be recommending a choice?"

"I'm not absolutely sure yet, but quite likely I'll suggest New Hampshire Realty. They're a big New York bank, who are expanding over here pretty aggressively. For example, I noticed they're involved in financing Tamfield. The analysts rate their oil-trading operation over some more well-known outfits."

"At the party on Sunday, I heard something about them from their senior analyst over here. In fact, I'm meeting her again tonight, if I can keep awake. Thanks to everyone who helped last night, including you and Carol. I'll have some good news for New Hampshire. This morning, I struck the right deal. I've stopped Harry from being silly. 'Tamfieldgate' is closed, and sales at Bishop's Park can go ahead, fast."

Paul tipped his head to one side, always a sign that he was interested.

"We knew you'd have it taped, Pete. It was fun to help. It was useful for Carol, too. The constituency round there, Bellinghame South, is one of those she's applying for. Last time, the votes were Conservative 27,000, Liberal 15,000, Labour 5,000. So there's quite some scope to boost the vote, and have a chance of a better seat next time."

"If she does run and I'm around, I'll help. I'm not joining the Labour Party, but I know what I think of Heath. I'll be following IE policy too, as set last Thursday."

We talked on about what to say to George Armstrong in the morning, until Paul realised that it was half past four and he needed to phone some of the investment brokers concerning North Sea potential. He rose to go, and I took my moment.

"Paul, I'm really pleased that you and Brian have made it up, to the extent that last night he brought you in, as well as Jack Unwin. I must admit that I wasn't totally confident about asking you as well as him directly."

"He knew that Carol was interested in the locality, but it goes further than that, Pete. You've never heard what actually happened that night in Cambridge, though Carol said you might have guessed. I was nearly at New Hall when someone large came up behind me, knocked me about, pulled me down and dragged me into a side road. I caught a glimpse of Fred Perkins' face as he started kicking me. He was right out of control. The last thing I can remember before I went out is Brian pulling him off. Without his help, I would have been much more seriously hurt. That makes a difference between us."

"Carol was right. I've always wondered whether that was what happened. During the last few days, no one has mentioned Fred Perkins to me. That did rather confirm it."

"I wonder where Fred Perkins is now. He was aiming to become a doctor."

"That will have settled him down. As Pat said, all this is in the past."

I settled down to some research in the library, which had a few essential reference books, and a good stock of corporate reports and accounts.

Sir Reginald Emerson was impeccably educated, and had served in the Guards. His marriage to the daughter of an earl had ended in divorce. He was a Parliamentary Under-Secretary at the government department which dealt with housing and local government issues, and also with the construction industry.

The Report and Accounts of National Amalgamated, a leading 'secondary bank' of the time, identified its chairman as

Sir Ambrose Dugdale; looking him up in *Who's Who* identified his wife Martha as daughter of a notable Jewish family.

The Report and Accounts of New Hampshire Realty included photoshots. From Sunday, I recognised Martin R. Steinberg, their Vice-President, Europe. The name and picture raised some interesting questions in my mind. A smaller but more attractive picture was of Stephanie J. Coolidge, Senior Analyst, Europe. She was presented as a valuable strengthening of the bank's analytical team, following her promising earlier career with J. P. Morgan. Also shown was Thomas Y. Sambrook, who ran the oil trading operation from Rotterdam, which was then the centre of the world oil market. Property in New Hampshire and elsewhere was a big part of the bank's business, which presumably explained how they had become involved with Cardinal, and now with Tamfield. Paul would have looked at this and other reports to compile his list. I spotted something at the back which he might have missed. Amongst New Hampshire's 'correspondent banks' was the Banco Navarrese.

By half past six I was in the reception hall of the block in London Wall, two floors of which IE occupied. Steph arrived with her hair uncharacteristically dishevelled.

"Wow, your British weather. Fortunately my office is only over in Gracechurch Street, and we've not far to go. So, what kept you up all night then, Pete?"

"It's good news for you, or at least for your bank. I've solved the Bishop's Park access problem, and I've stopped Harry from imitating Nixon."

I put my umbrella over her and we headed off. By the time my explanation was complete, we had taken the lift to a high floor of the newly completed Cromwell Tower in the Barbican development, and Steph was laughing.

"The grass doesn't grow under your feet, Pete. I can see why you didn't stick in Cambridge. I agree with you about Harry, and about Joe Aspinall. The Cardinal organisation had fallen to bits, and while Harry's outfit had the drive we wanted, it hadn't the expertise needed on big developments. Hopefully, Joe is delivering that. Here we are. This is my little abode as of earlier this year. Like the view? It's better when it's sunny."

"It's spectacular," I replied. Even without sun, in those days one could see right over the City and suburbs to the Downs, with the course of the Thames out past Greenwich also very clear.

"And what about the nearer view?" Steph asked, facing me.

"That's spectacular, too."

"I've been waiting for this for nearly two days. On Sunday you, Brit boy, put me off. You were right to do that, though it left me aching. We're going to take our time now, and really enjoy ourselves. We can have a private rerun of the competition, with the missing bits. First, though, open my winnings – only a single bottle for a place, but that's just right for two."

After a glass she took her shoes off and stood on a coffee table in the centre of the room. "Don't worry, Pete, it won't collapse, I've tried this already. Right, it's Round One. How do I score in City garb?"

"You look great, Steph, really great." That was very true. Her dark red suit over white blouse set off her face and brown hair very well. They radiated professionalism and authority, without the 'power dressing' and padded shoulders of some more recent years.

"I've found a good tailor. That's one thing you people do well. I'll be airfreighting a good collection back to the States. Now for Round Two, so fill our glasses."

She went off to her bedroom, and returned wearing the swimsuit she had worn on Sunday.

"We were able to take these away, and last night I made some little adjustments. I've my own machine. Tailoring is a good relaxation. What do you think?"

"You've done well. The suit fits you now like Number 6's suit fitted her. Bust, waist and hips are all just right. You made some pretty clever adjustments. My mother was in the drapery business, so I can see what you had to do."

I had been using my hands to check the fit, and finished by patting her bottom. She stepped down and kissed me.

"You do know to say the nice things, Pete, and Gail's sure right about your hands. Let's go straight on to Round Three. Unzip me."

She stepped out of the swimsuit and back onto the coffee table, taking the same pose as on Sunday. We chatted away as I looked over her carefully, just as I had done then. There was a difference, though. I was visibly excited.

"Now, we move to Round Four. Martha had made so clear what she wanted to do. When you came along, I just wanted you to do it, and I wanted to see your body. Thanks to Gail, I did see your body. Then yesterday, she said how good your hands felt when you patted her down. That gave me a wakeful night, rubbing myself and thinking of you."

I undressed, she spaced her feet wider, and for a minute or two I ran my hands all over her body, feeling her excitement build.

"Wow, lovely… aah… time to come inside."

My left middle finger found its way through her neat brown triangle, soon followed by the index finger. She was already very wet.

"Ooh… *oooh…* Lovely, Pete, you've found where I like, bit harder now, yes, there too. *Oooooh*, have your sweeties… *Ooooooooh*."

Her 'sweeties' were right in front of my mouth and nicely hard to suck. I had put my right hand round her waist to steady her, and now I slipped it down, with a finger between her buttocks. I found the place and touched gently.

"Mmmm… *mmmm…* go on in."

I dampened the finger from a now ready source and slid it in, very gently. The feeling of a ring round my fingertip hardened me further.

"Oooooooh – *ooooooooooooooh – I'm coming down.*"

She eased herself on to me. My right finger continued its work, whilst I pushed up into her and we kissed quite ferociously, with her tongue further into my mouth than anyone had managed before.

When it was over, we took the rest of the champagne along to her bed and lay in each other's arms, gently kissing. Eventually, Steph broke the silence.

"That's the best since I came over here, Pete. To have you in me all ways made me feel real great. Was it great for you?"

"Mmm, yes. I've been in all ways before, but not when standing up."

"When did you learn to finger arse so well?"

"From a woman called Carol, nearly six years ago. Her husband is now Chief Economist of IE. They both helped me last night."

"Tell me more. I've had bastards, like my husband, say it would be nice. Then they made me real sore. They gratified themselves. Hurting me made them feel powerful."

I recounted earlier times with Carol. That led to talk of Liz, Jenny, and Ana.

"They all sound to be intelligent. You must like intelligent women."

"Yes, I do. I think you'd like them, too."

"There aren't many men who like intelligent women. Not here, nor in the States. My husband didn't, when my career passed his. He wanted to be on top, all ways. Since then, men have been fun at first, but never for long. I've been with some like-minded women, but that doesn't last either."

"Until recently, there haven't been many intelligent, educated women around, and they've been looked on as blue-stocking types, and a put-off. Most of the people I was working with near Durham had married pretty stupid women, who'd never had any real career of their own. Liz has found the same at the Coal Board. There were no women at the IE conference last week, apart from the secretarial and organising team. Jenny has had some tricky times in her firm, though its policies are good on paper. In Spain, Ana has found it even worse."

"At the typical corporate bash with spouses in the States, you end up with a group of men drinking highballs or whatever and talking business or politics, and a group of women drinking tonic or 7-Up and talking about women's things. They don't even know much about women's things, like clothes. If I join the men and they don't know me, sometimes even if they do, they wonder why I'm there. Meanwhile, the women glare at me, wondering who I'm after. Worse still, if I take a guy with me, he's either an outsider with the men or he has to go with the women. It's horrible."

"Sunday night wasn't like that."

"No, people were sure stirred up. I do wonder what some of the guys thought about being eyed by Martha. She's the type that gets Jewish women a bad name."

"Harry told me that the idea for the party came from seeing the Dugdales' art collection. I don't think Martha Dugdale being Jewish has anything to do with it."

"Nasty slip of the tongue, sorry. She reminds me of someone I was misguided enough to go with soon after my break-up, but that's no excuse. Give me a smack on the bottom – ow – *ow*. Oooh, that's nice, just a touch, don't tickle, I'm still very sensitive there – *oooooh!*"

After a couple of minutes I continued. "Your boss is Jewish, or at least he has a name that's often Jewish. Do you have any problems with him?"

"With Mart, none at all! He's from a Jewish family, but doesn't think of himself as Jewish, any more than I think of myself as English, or German, or Dutch, all of which are in me. He likes his bacon with the rest of us. He's positively anti-Zionist. Why should twentieth-century Jews think Palestine is theirs just because some old geezer promised it to their ancestors three thousand years ago? If the effort made to set up Israel had gone into bringing Jews to the States, more of them would be alive and it would be easier for them and other honest Americans to make bucks out of the A-rabs. That's his line. Hell, I'm chatting away again. Just say 'Calvin' to me when this happens."

We kissed and cuddled, and then I yawned.

"I'm sorry, Steph, how rude I am. Last night is catching up with me. It's not yet eight o'clock, and I feel sleepy."

"Don't worry, Pete. You have a rest there. In a little while I'll do us some supper."

I was asleep almost before she bounced out of bed. The next thing I knew it was nearly ten o'clock, and Steph was tapping me on the shoulder, trim in slacks and a top and looking very cheerful.

"Wakies time."

I got up, showered and looked for my clothes. They were on the bed, neatly set out. The shirt had been washed and ironed, and there was a new silk tie.

"Goodness, you've done all this for me."

"No trouble. I spotted the tie this morning. Then I saw you'd not brought a change of shirt. Don't put it on, so it'll be fresh in the morning and you'll be really smart for the office. Wear this wrap for now. Come and have supper."

We sat down to an attractive smoked salmon salad and a glass or two of Chablis. Outside, it was nearly dark, and the sky had cleared. The lights of London were spread out before us.

"You reckon I need looking after," I said, with a chuckle.

"Yup, just a bit, Pete. You've looked after me, lots already. I want us to go on looking after each other so long as we're both in London. Where are you planning to live when you get back from Spain?"

"Probably I'll stay with my aunt, in her new house at Bishop's Park. When I was down here before going to Spain, I stayed in her old house."

"Probably?"

"All this excitement seems to have given her and her solicitor something of an eye for each other. Before long, it might not be so convenient for me to live there."

"Hmm, I bet you've gotten her a nice little nest egg out of all this, Pete. She'll need to be careful if he starts suggesting how to invest it."

"I'll keep an eye, though she's pretty smart."

"I believe you. She's your aunt. Now, look at the view. Enjoy it with me, while you can, Pete. Move in. There's plenty of room here. You'll need to do some jobs, and know how to use the washing machine, but it's five minutes to your office. You won't need to catch trains which run when the loco engineers feel like it."

"You said it yourself, Steph, you're a hustler. Let's give it a try. I'll take a share of the rent and costs. I guess I'm not earning as much as you, but I have just had a good raise."

After a business-like conversation, we moved on to the latest Watergate developments, and then she asked me more about Spain. She was fascinated to hear of the bull running and bullfights in Pamplona, but like me regarded them as a once-in-a-lifetime experience. That led on nicely.

"I did some homework this afternoon. I noticed that your report lists the Banco Navarrese as a correspondent bank. They've been my closest business associates in Spain. Ana's father, with whom I was staying in Pamplona, is a director."

"Wow, you don't say? A tall, distinguished looking guy with a moustache and fair English?"

"It sounds like you've met him."

"Both banks are involved in financing the big ski developments around Formigal, in the Pyrenees. Six months back, there was a meeting there, with opportunities to try out the facilities. I've not met his daughter, though."

"Ana isn't the skiing type. I'm with her on that. Harry has taken it up, though, and is still in one piece. I hope you weren't too smashed up."

A few minutes later, it was Steph's turn to be yawning.

"Last night is catching up with me, too, Pete. I'll just say again, today was better than I possibly imagined. I think I can survive a month without you, but it'll be real hard. Let's cosy up, and see what we can do in the morning."

After my earlier rest, I lay awake for a while, reflecting on an eventful few days. There was enough dim light for me to feast my eyes on Steph's sleeping body, and to anticipate the morning. She had said that she didn't wear pyjamas, at any time of year.

Living together after just two meetings would be something of a leap in the dark, but we had hit it off so quickly, in mind and in body. We could fill a hole in each other's lives. I could hope to leave her with good memories of her time in London. I was going to be working hard. It would be very good to be near the shop. We were a good turn for each other.

The 'Cambridge chums' were largely a circle of friends I had made there. After my sudden departure, they had come to know each other better. I could join them again, and I could introduce Steph. Her vivacity was perhaps a sign of insecurity and loneliness. It might also be a tool, for it led others on. On Sunday, it had led me to say more about Harry than I should have done. Fortunately, that had caused no damage. I would have to say 'Calvin' to myself too, particularly if IE linked up with New Hampshire Realty, though I would be doing a quite separate job within IE.

Chatting away with Steph had made a link-up more likely. When I called Ana on Friday, I had sensed that the Banco Navarrese were uncertain about their choice of a partner experienced in oil trading. My research in the library today had shown me why that was. I could give Don Pedro and Ana some assurance that Mart Steinberg wouldn't be over alarmed by news of a pending attack on Israel. If there were money to be made, he wouldn't spill the beans.

My going with Steph was also good for Liz. It was her style to pull an inexperienced man over the edge. She had pulled Brian over the edge a few days after he had arrived in Cambridge. She had worked hard to pull Geoff Frampton over the edge. Before all that, she had pulled me over the edge. Now she could say to Greg Woolley just what she was hoping to say, and perhaps pull him over the edge.

I had not been untruthful in saying to Steph that I had been in all ways before, but it had happened only once and was not a good precedent, having been at the start of my last weekend with Jenny before she went for Dick. I still had my regrets at the sudden split, but she had made the right decision for us both. We had realised that we both had our own agendas. Had we stayed together, neither of us could have achieved what we had achieved separately over the last five years. Eventually, we would have split, and probably we would no longer be friends.

Instead, we were friends, and a little more. Jenny had known that Liz and I regarded each other as brother and sister, and in each other's total confidence. She had said that we should be the same, though she had a real brother, two years older than her. Indeed, I had met Jenny through John, who was then another maths research student at Cambridge. Only during that last weekend had I realised how close they were. As we prepared for a sunbath in a secluded part of their parents' garden, she had responded to my slight surprise by reminding me that 'He *is* my brother, Pete.'

Now, Jenny and Dick were doing very well together. Dick accepted being organised in the loveliest sort of way, provided he could do his own thing occasionally. He seemed to be relaxed about Jenny's closeness to John, and to the girlfriend she had found for John. On Sunday, Dick's time with Gail had been pleasant and fulfilling but harmless; and he had enjoyed Andy's attention. In the nick of time, I had prevented that from going too far, and Dick was now alerted to Harry's renewed interest. I had again been Jenny's brother.

Other Cambridge chums valued each other in settled relationships: Carol and Paul, Susie and Brian, and it seemed also Morag and Sheila. I hoped that Sheila's forceful approach would allow Morag to assert her personality, but their shared interest in voluntary work would help to keep them together.

I now knew much of what had happened on that terrible night, a few days before I had left Cambridge. I also knew why Carol had never told me. She had known that I didn't want Brian to be in trouble, so she had kept quiet about the extenuating circumstances. If I had any hold over her, she had one over me. Now, we were all frank and disarmed. Perhaps Brian didn't know how much Paul remembered of that night, and therefore was careful to keep on good terms; but it was clear that both Paul and he had learnt their lessons. I didn't know whether Jack Unwin had been involved, but he also seemed to have settled down.

I hoped that today Harry too had learnt his lesson. He had made it to leadership of a substantial company. People with Joe Aspinall's experience referred to him as 'the Boss', which showed that he had the skills and authority required. He needed to behave accordingly. As a person, he needed a settled relationship based on valuing someone. Presently, he valued no one. He had told me how he now obtained physical satisfaction. That wasn't through a shared, pleasurable experience, of the kind he had had with Dick, but through hurtful gratification, of the kind that Steph had suffered from her husband. The wrecking of Harry's earlier ambitions had damaged him more than I had realised, though there was no doubt he was much wealthier than he would ever have become as a musical administrator.

Dick had been thinking of Harry, when Andy fondled him face down. When I had fondled Jenny face down, she had thought of Dick. That had been a step towards her realising that he was her man, so it had turned out well. There was no way in which any renewed relationship between Dick and Harry could turn out well. Fortunately, it was very unlikely that they would meet again soon.

Whatever happened between Roberta and Frank Booth, I had helped her to move on, from being a querulous old woman to showing the intelligence and force that I knew she had in her. I hoped that she would get on better with her new neighbours. I also hoped that she would get on better with both of my parents.

My thoughts drifted back to national events. I wondered what had happened at Ted Heath's meeting with Joe Gormley. Brian was doubtless right that the average miner was more interested in a fatter pay packet than in forcing a change of government. I knew what would strengthen their interest. If oil prices went up, coal would become more valuable. The miners would want their share.

The Labour Party had been split over joining the EEC. There had been a bipartisan response to the deteriorating position in Northern Ireland, which was now leading to terrorist attacks in England. Therefore, Ted Heath's Government had had an easier ride than its appalling performance merited. That easier ride would soon end.

And I knew something about Roberta's MP...

NOTE OF A MEETING HELD ON WEDNESDAY 5th SEPTEMBER
1973 AT THE HOTEL EXCELSIOR, FORMIGAL, SPAIN

Present

BANCO NAVARRESE
Don Pedro Guzman de Leon y Jiminez (PG), Director
(Copy 1)
Don Carlos Casares Gonzales (CC), Senior
Manager-International
Doña Ana Guzman de Leon y Vasquez (AG), Special
Assistant-Policy

NEW HAMPSHIRE REALTY BANK
Martin R. Steinberg (MS), Vice-President,
Europe (Copy 2)
Thomas Y. Sambrook (TS), Vice-President, Oil
Trading (Copy 3)
Stephanie J. Coolidge (SC), Senior Analyst,
Europe

INTERNATIONAL ELECTRONICS plc
Sir Patrick O'Donnell (PO'D), Chief Executive
(Copy 4)
Mr Peter Bridford (PB), Senior Manager-
Development
Dr Paul Milverton (PM), Chief Economist

PB and AG answered questions on their note
(Annex A) concerning an overheard conversation
about future developments in the Middle East,
and its implications for the price of crude
oil. The meeting thanked them for this valuable

112

intelligence. It was noted that since the time of the event they described, no particular rumour of these developments had circulated, though tension in the area remained high.

PG said he had informed appropriate contacts in the Spanish Government, and tabled the note sent to the US Government through its embassy in Madrid (Annex B). MS and PO'D agreed that the sending of this note met reasonable obligations to governments. Its recipients would need to form their own view of it.

It was agreed that a Trading Fund to the value of US$ 25 million would be set up and operated by selected personnel of New Hampshire Realty, under the direct supervision of TS. This amount was considered by TS, SC and PM to be the largest intervention in the market which could be conducted without attracting undue attention. The equity in the fund would be $7 million from each of the participant bodies at this meeting, and $4 million from the combined personal contributions of some present at the meeting and a number of Spanish citizens, listed at Annex C. In recognition of the value of the intelligence provided to them, New Hampshire Realty would fund 80% of the equity of Banco Navarrese and International Electronics by loan, on terms set out in Annex D.

75% of the Fund should be applied by 14th September, to purchase options for 3 months ahead. Subsequent positions could be taken as judged appropriate.

New Hampshire Realty would provide the other

participants with weekly reports on progress. All parties would recognise the sensitivity of these reports and of all other information about these operations, and inform others within their organisations on a strictly 'need to know' basis.

All positions should be closed by 31st December 1973. As soon as possible thereafter, the Fund should be distributed to participants in proportion to equity and to suit their accounting requirements. PO'D said that International Electronics would be looking to receive proceeds up to 1 billion pesetas as distribution in Spain, to fund a programme of acquisitions by its Spanish subsidiary being discussed separately with Banco Navarrese.

Following a break and the preparation of this note in Spanish (Copy 1) and English (Copies 2 – 4) versions, these were agreed and signed as a true record of the discussions.

(signed)
Don Pedro Guzman de Leon y Jiminez
Martin R. Steinberg
Sir Patrick O'Donnell

5th September, 1973

SECRET declassified September 21st 1998

To: Director, Middle East

From: Section Head, Egypt Date: September 12th 1973

Subject: Report received from Spanish Government sources via Madrid Embassy regarding a conversation at location in Spain between senior personnel of the Egyptian Air Force and former NATO consultant Prof. Siegmund R. Kraftlein, suggesting an attack to take place 6th October on Israeli forces occupying Sinai: intention of attack to involve US in confrontation with Arab oil producing states.

Recommendation: No specific action regarding US policies. NATO to be informed that Prof. Kraftlein should not be given further consultancy work or provided with any further classified information. Close monitoring of situation to continue.

Issues

1) Tension in area remains high and outbreak of hostilities during next few months is possible. US policy is clearly stated, that all parties should act to avoid this.

2) Photos with report identify participants as having met. Kraftlein did visit Cairo, ostensibly as a tourist, July 24th – September 4th, but has now returned to Stuttgart, German Federal Republic. He resigned from NATO work in 1970, and no information received by him is any longer of significant value to the USSR. Action against him would cause difficulties with the GFR government, and would air issues of why he was involved in work for US military from 1946, despite having been an active Nazi Party member from 1928 to 1945.

3) This Agency and Mossad could be expected to detect preparations for any attack with at least 2 weeks' notice. There is no current evidence of such preparations. In the event of such evidence the issue for the USA will be to discourage a pre-emptive strike by Israel which (as the reported conversation states and is well enough known to all Agencies) would be unlikely to meet with the same success as in 1967.

4) The reported conversation also reflects the current understanding of all Agencies that an Egyptian attack would achieve some initial success, dependent on the degree of surprise, but could be expected to be repelled within 14 – 21 days. Further US supplies of arms to Israel would NOT be required to achieve this outcome. The advice of this Agency to be given in the event has already been considered. The political factors affecting the Executive, also referred to in the reported conversation, would make it important to persuade other Departments of State to give the same advice.

5) In summary, the report does not add significantly to the existing intelligence picture, which will continue to be monitored closely.

BOOK IV
THE CRISIS BREAKS

5. SATURDAY, 17ᵀᴴ NOVEMBER, 1973

Paul emerged from Pat O'Donnell's office, but there were a couple of letters for Pat to sign, so I paused before going in.

"I must dash, Pete. The selection meeting is at noon and you can't rely on the trains. Bellinghame South is her last chance for the next election. She has the backing of the party centrally, but two local stalwarts are also in the field."

"I can guess who they might be, Paul. She can see them off."

"It comes down to whether the local party wants a woman of twenty-five."

"The best of luck to Carol, and see you later."

I went in to join Pat, and George Armstrong. One of Pat's staff officers was dialling and moving switches on a cabinet to one side of the room. Then we heard Terry McAvitt's voice, from his home near Leeds. We were using the latest IE teleconferencing gear. Up to three groups of people could link in on separate lines to meetings here, and all could hear each other. Apart from being saleable, this gear assisted in Pat's strategy of keeping the head office small. On our two floors were his and George's offices, a conference room with the same equipment as in his office, some desks for visitors and those staff on temporary assignments such as mine, a press and general enquiries unit, the small central Personnel Office, and a library. All other staff were located on various factory sites.

We all knew Pat worked six days a week, and expected senior staff to be available on Saturdays when necessary. However, he began politely.

"Thanks for coming in, Pete, and thanks for your October report. Sorry not to have talked earlier. So, Terry, your views please."

"We went through it when Pete was here on Wednesday. It's well thought out. We need that office, and soon. I'm ready to transfer in six staff, perhaps eight. I hope that other divisional Directors will provide two or three each, as Pete suggests."

Back in August, the broker's report that Paul had commissioned had allowed me to spot items of electrical equipment that were needed offshore in quantity, and were identical or similar to current IE product ranges. I asked a firm of engineering consultants to specify what improvements this equipment needed, so as to be durable enough for use offshore. By the end of September, I had a list of about thirty items which we could produce to the required standard. Then I visited factories, to discuss how we could deliver them quickly, to identify prospective staff for the new office, and to take their views on organisation. Now, I was contacting the key oil company and main contractor personnel involved in buying decisions. Several of these people were already based in Aberdeen. Others would soon be moving there. We needed to be there, too.

After a few questions from him and George, Pat summed up.

"So, Pete, you want to be there from January, and to have a full team from mid-February."

"Yes. Meanwhile, I'll identify work for Staines, to support product development. I'm going there on Thursday."

"Pete should put a paper to next month's Board," said George. "That way, everyone will be committed to it."

"Agreed. On what I've heard, I'll support it. That's a good idea on Staines, Pete. You were spot on about them when we first met here. Thanks, Terry."

'Staines' referred to IE's research laboratories located near that town. Nearly six years before, I had made to Pat the same proposals for getting a refreshed and better focussed effort from them as had been reached after a long discussion at a meeting of IE's Board. That had prompted Pat to suggest that I come to work for IE.

After clicks and whirrs as Terry rang off, Pat continued.

"Pete, I know why you've kept away from 'Crafty'. You've plenty to do without it, but you really have handed over to Paul very well. I can see how he's developed in a few months. Taking him on was a good move of mine."

"He knows plenty about oil trading," I said. "And some years back, I had first-hand experience of his negotiating skills."

"He showed them in handling arrangements with Banco Navarrese and New Hampshire Realty," said George. "Much of our interest is carried, though that doesn't matter any longer. We're already a good £5 million up, just from last month's OPEC[22] price rise. Paul reckons that there's a long way to go yet. Doug will have the money for the chances you spotted, Pete."

"That's one bit of good news to end the week," said Pat. "The only bit, I'd say. Heath's clowns are intent on fighting the wrong battle. Labour are no better."

"Paul did well on that Belgian business, too," said George. In September, 'guest workers' there had rioted, and the local police had reacted violently. A strike at our competitor's factory had followed, and IE had bagged a big order.

---

22 The Organisation of Petroleum Exporting Countries, the cartel which between 1960 and 1986 set prices for oil exports.

I spent an hour clearing paper at the desk I had not seen for three days and wouldn't see again until Wednesday. Just before noon, a phone call from the Barbican flat was the signal to stuff the remaining material into my briefcase. In doing so, I noticed an envelope left at reception late the day before, addressed to me in typescript and marked 'PERSONAL'. Because I was often away, I had enough of my own correspondence at the office for the secretaries to banter along the lines of 'which lady this time, Pete?' A note earlier in the week had justified the banter.

'Pete – Liz tells me you're now with an 'older woman' (her phrase!). I'm looking forward to meeting her on Saturday. Could you arrive a bit early, say about 4? You can help cook, and there's something I need to talk about.
Jenny.'

In reception, Steph was waiting, looking informal but smart in jersey, trousers and coat. After a hug, I picked up her overnight bag, and we headed for Bank Underground.

"It's nice to feel we've most of a weekend off together. I was relieved to be back from Geneva on time this morning. How was your trip?"

"Pretty bloody. After leaving you on Wednesday, I reached Leeds by half past three. I was on site until half past five, and then had an hour with Terry McAvitt. On Thursday, I went on to the place I used to work at, near Sunderland. Then I just made it to Aberdeen, via a very late, bumpy flight from Newcastle. Yesterday, I had four good meetings in Aberdeen, but my plane due to go at twenty past five didn't leave until half past seven. So it was a good thing you weren't around last night, I guess. How was yours?"

"Not as bad. The European Group Conference is rather a jolly. There was a lot about the crisis, of course. I had to be careful not to let anything slip out. Mart, Tom and I had a talk on the side. It is going *rather* well, too well of course from the point of view of everything else."

"Yes, Pat was saying that just now."

Steph and I were enjoying life together, when we were both in London. We had been able to keep our business and personal lives sufficiently apart.

In July, we had parted regretfully after our first night, and early morning, together. That day, Paul and I met with and satisfied George Armstrong, before I had two frantic and very long days of sorting things out and seeing into store what Roberta wanted to keep. I fitted in a call to Jenny and a visit to Paul to collect his shortlist, which indeed recommended New Hampshire Realty. On the Friday, a visit to Frank Booth's office was followed by a hurried drive to Dorset. There was only just time to unload, say hello to my father who arrived shortly after his branch closed at 3.30 pm, and return to Southampton. I slept for much of the way back to Spain.

On the Sunday, I was in Madrid by Spanish lunchtime (4 pm). Much had awaited me, including an invitation to a meeting in the offices of the Banco Navarrese at the remarkably early hour for Spain of 10 am the next day. There I found Don Pedro and Ana, and for the first time met Don Carlos Casares, who was now her fiancé. I said that International Electronics was interested in joining in, but because I was urgently committed to an important new project, the lead would be taken by our Chief Economist, who was expert in the principles of oil trading. Paul was on a plane that evening, and we talked all the next day.

As I had suspected, Banco Navarrese knew that their correspondent bank would be a good choice of partner, but they were worried about Mart Steinberg's possible reaction to our information. I was able to reassure them. In doing so, I had mentioned that it was a good thing for me that Paul was taking over. Don Pedro had remembered Steph from the meeting earlier in the year, and congratulated me.

Later that week, Steph had called me, to explain in guarded terms that Mart Steinberg had talked to her about a new, and very confidential, assignment. She was needed to model the costs and benefits under various scenarios. Was this something to do with me, and was this Paul Milverton Carol's husband? I replied affirmatively to both questions, but much to her relief said that she could tell Mart that I was out of it.

I had flown back to England on Tuesday, 14th August. Steph was in Rotterdam, for her second meeting with Tom Sambrook, Don Pedro, Ana, and Paul. This allowed me time to collect my new car, bring Roberta up from Dorset, and settle her into her new bungalow before a long, energetic, and very pleasurable Thursday night at the Barbican. Steph told me that Paul was driving a pretty hard bargain.

Roberta had been visibly relieved to hear that I would not be staying with her. However, I was visiting her quite often, because if I didn't need my car during the week I left it in her garage, rather than pay the high charges for the Barbican car park. She too had wanted to meet 'my new lady'. So now, we were on our way to lunch with her.

We waited ten minutes for a tube train, owing to 'long intervals because of staff shortage'. At Balham, we picked up a suburban train, and reached Roberta's place without much further delay. Soon afterwards, Frank Booth arrived.

Roberta had taken a lot of trouble to produce a light but attractive lunch. She knew that we were going on elsewhere, and later they were at a dinner of the Rotary Club, in which Frank was a stalwart. Steph had a Rotarian uncle, so that generated quite a lot of conversation. Towards the end of the meal, Steph turned back to Roberta and said how nice it was to sample real English home cooking.

"It's very easy here. The equipment is all new. I expect you know how I moved here. It's turned out very well."

"I'm glad to hear that. I work for a bank that's involved with Tamfield Investments. I hope everyone here is as satisfied as you, and that sales are continuing well."

"I've not heard any complaints from the neighbours I've met. I don't know about the sales, though. Can you say, Frank?"

"The market is slowing right down. That's affecting Tamfield as much as others. My firm has a good share of the conveyancing business from this estate. Through to September, we were taking two or three instructions a week. It's only about one a week now, and the higher mortgage rates following the Minimum Lending Rate going to 13% on Tuesday won't help at all. Tamfield put the prices up nearly 10% for the second phase, which they released late in September. I guess they meant to sell out the first phase by making buyers think they were getting a bargain, but in retrospect it was a mistake. Don't quote me on any of this, but it's what people are saying."

The conversation moved on, and Steph looked thoughtful. After lunch, I pointed out that we had not seen the new entrance drive, having arrived on foot directly from the main road. So we took a stroll.

The demolition and road contractors had indeed taken care. Roberta's herbaceous borders had largely been preserved and would look good again in the summer. Indeed, there was some new planting alongside the part of the drive where her house had been.

We continued round the estate. Near where Roberta lived, most houses and flats were occupied. Further away, some properties appeared to be finished, but unoccupied. The far end was still a large construction site. That, Frank said, was 'Phase Two', which was to have been completed by the end of the year, but was now expected in February. It amounted to about 450 properties, over half of the whole estate.

As we walked back to the house, Steph and Frank were a little ahead and talking away. Roberta dropped back to me and took my arm.

"I do like Steph, Pete. Is there any chance of her being The One?"

"Not really. She goes back to the States early next year. It looks like I'm going to be based in Aberdeen."

"Oh, what a pity. She's a few years older than you, but still young enough to have children. The age difference isn't affecting your lives, just as it isn't affecting Frank and me. I'd better tell you. We're a couple, now."

"That's really marvellous news, Roberta. I'm so pleased."

"That's more than Gerald is, but I'll tell you what I've told him. My money will stay quite separate from Frank's, and any legal work for me will be done by his partner in the firm." For a moment, Roberta sounded rather angry.

"He can't complain, then. What about Margaret?"

"She's taken it in her stride. She's a sensible woman, married to a sensible man. That takes me to Christmas plans. I don't want to go to Gerald and Hilda. Margaret and Ian are going to his people. So I've invited your parents to come here. I do hope you can be here too, and Steph of course, unless she's already arranged to go back to America then. It will be a squeeze, but we can all fit in."

"Yes thanks for me. I'll check with Steph, but as far as I know she has no other plans. I could book us all a show for Boxing Day."

"It's so good that I can speak to your mother and father easily, after all these years. What you said on the way down there in July had me thinking about what to do."

"It was your good idea to contact Edward and offer to help in the shop during staff holidays. Not only did that take you out of the house, it also allowed you to persuade Mum that she and you together should speak out about how the business should be run, and to persuade Dad that he wouldn't be compromised by your doing so. I hope that Edward takes note."

"Maybe he will, maybe he won't. He's set in his ways, and so is his son, like too many people down there. As I found out quickly, the customers are mostly around my age. That's not good for the future of the shop, but it did mean I met all sorts of people I remember from years back."

Soon afterwards, Steph and I set off south in my car. I had filled up before panic-buying really began, so we could feel rather superior as we nosed past queues of cars outside those petrol stations that were still open. One sign that sticks in my memory referred to the latest audio-cassette system of the time.

Closed for petrol – but OPEN for 8-track in-car stereo entertainment.

The Heath-Barber boom was turning to bust very fast.

"Sorry to be pushy," said Steph, "but the number one rule for analysts is, if there's intelligence to grab, you grab. Thanks for suggesting the walk."

"Frank was relaying gossip that will be all round the Rotary dinner tonight. Let's grab some more."

I pulled up outside a newsagent's, and was soon back.

"Here we are, the two local papers. The *Bellinghame Record* comes out on Wednesdays, and supports the Conservatives. The *Bellinghame Advertiser* comes out on Fridays, and is more independent."

As Steph thumbed through them, we joined the Brighton road at Purley. That prompted me to describe how Harry Tamfield had spotted the opportunity to turn to profit an inheritance of three tobacconist's shops there, and hence to realise that he had a talent for the property business. I finished my account as we passed through the M23 motorway construction site at Hooley.[23]

"Look at this bridge to nowhere. Harry's definitely got somewhere since leaving Purley. He's in a different game now, though.'

---

23 Plans to continue the M23 into central London had been abandoned after construction of the 'bridge to nowhere' seen today had begun.

"Yup, and he's heading for big trouble, which means trouble for New Hampshire. In both these papers, there are big adverts for Bishop's Park. 'Phase One – last few remaining at these prices.' It looked like more than a few to me. For you only, Pete, New Hampshire has an opportunity to pull out. Amazingly, National Amalgamated wants to *increase* its stake. We can quit now, at a very modest hit. On Monday, I'll be for just that, 'following a site visit with my guy, whose aunt lives there'. That's enough of work. We're out for a break together. Tell me again about the Cambridge chums."

"There are six couples, plus little Katie and David. Jenny and Dick are our hosts. Then in no particular order, there are Liz and Greg, Susie and Brian, Carol and Paul, Morag and Sheila, and you and me. You've met Liz, and Dick. You've also met Paul, of course, but only he and I know that."

"Jenny must be a super mum, to move house only a month before the birth and to invite us all when Katie is only six weeks old. She'll still be up most nights."

"Jenny *is* well organised. She's had to be, to make it as far as she has. Fortunately, Dick backs her up. We'll need to rally round, to help."

"What are Morag and Sheila like?"

"On the face of it, they're a couple of serious academics, both old-fashioned Labour and with the Scottish dimension for Morag. There's more to them than that, though. Morag has a great deal of sense and always helps out. Sheila had some money from her family. Three years ago, she bought this big old house in Stratford."

"Is that where Shakespeare grew up? I thought it was near Birmingham."

"This Stratford is about four miles east of where we live. Sheila and Morag live on the top floor. The two floors below are used by a charity Sheila supports. It provides refuge for women beaten up by their husbands or boyfriends. That's a big problem around there. The police aren't interested when it's 'just a domestic.'"

"It's the same in New York. Sort it out yourself. They do, with guns."

"Sheila and Morag both help out, two or three evenings a week. I think this very worthwhile hobby holds them together. Morag was the dominant partner with her previous girlfriends. She's even the only person ever to have seduced Liz, though replays have been more equal. I first met Sheila earlier on the day I met you, and saw that she's a dominating type. I wondered, but going on what Liz has told me, it's all absolutely fine, at least for now."

"How do we handle Greg? Is he OK with us?"

"I called Liz last night. I was later than I was expecting, but she was only just in and about as shattered as I was. She's had a frightful week, with Tuesday's announcement and debate. She didn't even get to see anything on Wednesday."

"Oh, what a shame. I'm so glad we both saw something of it. You Brits can still do the ceremonial just grand."

The previous Tuesday, Ted Heath had changed his previously confident tune, and declared a state of emergency. The shortage of oil was compounded by a shortage of coal, resulting from the overtime ban which the NUM had called once it became clear that 'Stage 3' of the government's Incomes Policy[24] would not allow the pay increase they wanted. Wednesday was a public holiday, for the marriage of Princess Anne to Captain Mark Phillips. Steph and I had caught a glimpse of the procession, before she was off to Heathrow and I to King's Cross.

"There's no risk of Greg thumping me for dumping Liz, or you for luring me away. After the event, he was pleased that her tears had nerved him up to do it. Liz thinks that he'll want a talk with me on his own, as part of knowing her better. He's worried about her affairs with senior Coal Board people."

---

24 'Stage 1', introduced in November 1972, had been a total standstill. 'Stage 2', from April 1973, had allowed some increase, enough that the miners then settled. 'Stage 3', announced in October, allowed rather more, but not enough for the NUM given the oil crisis and accelerating inflation.

"Why is she going on with these men, if she wants Greg so much?"

"She doesn't find it easy to end a relationship. That happened before, with Brian whilst she was going for Geoff Frampton. Now, she knows that she helps these men do their jobs. Just now, that's important. I need to get that across to Greg."

"I see Liz's point. That man we met had the smell of power, didn't he?"

Liz usually entertained her clients à deux, but this man liked to talk, and she wanted to meet Steph before Greg did. So about three weeks before, she had cooked for the three of us. What we heard about the mood in the coalfields had made Tuesday's announcement less of a surprise.

"My job is to convince Greg that he can handle Liz. By the way, though Greg knows that Liz has been with Dick, me and Brian, he doesn't know about Morag, yet. Also, incidentally, everyone knows that I've been with Liz and Jenny, and most of them know that I slept with Carol a few times before taking up with Jenny. But only Liz, Paul, and Jenny know how long I went on with Carol. Importantly, Brian doesn't know that. He and Paul are pals now, but he wouldn't be able to resist a matey joke or two. Paul is a serious sort of guy, as you're doubtless finding out. Also, everyone knows about Dick's time with Harry, but don't refer to it. Harry is just an old College friend who's done well. Jenny doesn't like him, though she's only met him once and the row she had with him then changed her life completely. It set her thinking that she could become an accountant, and it made Dick so upset that she wanted to cheer him up."

"Wow, the group dynamics do have something of Noel Coward or Evelyn Waugh. From what you've told me, the girls all like some fun."

"Yes, though they're more settled down now: three married, one long-term partnership, and one hopeful. Tonight's agenda doesn't include a repeat of Jenny's hen party. Greg doesn't yet know about that, either."

We found our way through the suburbs of Brighton to the Sinclairs' house in Moulescoomb, near the University of Sussex campus. Dick answered the door, holding hands with a grumpy looking David. Jenny was on the telephone in the hallway, to the background of yells from above.

"Pete has just arrived. I'm sure he can pick you all up. Does your train stop at Preston Park? ... Well, look at the board... I'll get him to go there, then... Oh, *great*. More to celebrate."

Steph crouched to talk face to face, so that Dick could dash upstairs.

"Why David, I've been looking forward so much to meeting you. I'm Steph, from the United States, a big country far away across the sea..."

Jenny rang off and greeted us.

"The good news is that Carol has the nomination! The bad news is that Brian couldn't buy petrol, so they're coming by train. They're all at East Croydon, and should be at Preston Park at five past five. It'll be much easier for you to pick them up there than at the Brighton terminus, Pete. God, why are we in all this trouble because of an oil embargo which isn't supposed to apply to us? I was relying on you to help me cook. Now, you have to go off."

"I can lend a hand, that's if David here will let me," said Steph. "One of the nice things about living with Pete is that when we're both in, we cook. It's so much more worthwhile cooking for two. I'm less rusty on it than I was, but Pete is the expert. He says he learned to cook when he was up in Durham."

"I was fending for myself, for the first time in my life. It was a change from being at Cambridge," I said.

"Dick and I made the change *at* Cambridge," said Jenny. "But we were pretty impressed when we came to see you."

I brought our luggage in, together with a sister of the magnum of champagne that Dick had won in July. I had brought this back from France, and Roberta had kindly started it to cool. Dick reappeared with six-week-old Katie.

"Not a stinky-poo any more, are you? Here are Auntie Steph and Uncle Pete, the first of lots of nice people come to see you."

After a cup of tea I found Preston Park Station. Carol was very cheerful, Paul contented, and Susie rather quiet. Brian claimed the front seat.

"Nice job this, Pete. Tricky to come by, I'm told. Is it going OK? I've heard there can be problems."

"IE's dealer values our business. It was delivered in five weeks from order, thoroughly checked. So far, it's gone fine."

As Paul had pointed out in his presentation, the Heath Government's policies had caused credit fuelled demand to outstrip supply. That applied particularly to the better British-made cars. Waiting lists of months were common, nearly new models changed hands at well over list price, and makers were tempted to cut corners on quality. Anthony Barber could hardly have done better for Audi, BMW and Mercedes if he had tried.

"You've quite a bit on the clock already."

"I do a lot of my trips up north by train or plane. In September, Steph and I ran it in, over in France." To all but a few, including one of my passengers, that was the whole story.

The 'go/no go' meeting that Pat wanted had been set for the first Wednesday in September in Formigal, the then new ski resort in the Pyrenees where New Hampshire and Banco Navarrese had substantial interests. Pat had asked me to attend, in case there were questions about the overheard conversation and my mathematical deduction.

So, Steph and I had crossed to Le Havre on the overnight boat, spent the weekend exploring the château country, and made a brief stop in the Dordogne. Pat and Paul had flown to Madrid on the Monday, and spent most of Tuesday in meetings with Doug before taking a chauffeured car to Formigal. Others had reached this then remote location, which was very quiet out of season, by a variety of routes.

Pat, Paul and the two New Hampshire vice-presidents had left on the Thursday morning, but Steph and I stayed on for a day with the Banco Navarrese team. After walking in the mountains we returned to a very convivial dinner, at which Ana and Carlos looked very happy following what Ana murmured to me had been a most satisfying 'rest'. Ana was very happy at the 'go' decision – for several reasons, including that she would continue to have something to do, despite having had to leave her job in Madrid.

The next day, Steph and I had been on our way home, travelling faster now 'run in'. It seemed likely that this would be our last break for some time.

Back at Moulescoomb, I introduced Steph to my passengers, including Paul. She and he got into the kind of chat one might expect of two professional economists. Soon afterwards, another cheerful carload arrived. Three of them had been in winning teams – hockey for Greg and Liz, and basketball for Morag. A game of pass the Katie began, which allowed Dick to give David his tea whilst Jenny and Steph carried on in the kitchen. Susie was the clear winner.

Greg seemed nervous in the new company. He riled Brian a little by being rather full of having queued for petrol for over an hour the day before, and then by going into the arrangements he had made for picking his party up at three different Underground stations. I had already noted him as a more formal sort of man than was Brian, but he didn't need to rub it in.

Then, it was goodnight to Katie and David. The two married couples, and 'two single women sharing a room', went off to leave their things at a nearby bed and breakfast. Amongst just the four of us, Greg seemed more relaxed and sure of himself, with no sign of animosity to Steph or me. He gave us the cheerful news that the electricity industry was getting ready to make rota power cuts, of the type imposed during the previous year's coal strike.

Everyone was back by the time Jenny and Dick came downstairs. Jenny asked me to do the honours with the first magnum. I succeeded, without spilling a drop, and Jenny began.

"Now, we Cambridge chums have several things to celebrate. Katie is safely with us. Carol is nominated for Bellinghame South. Whatever party we support, we can all be pleased for her. Pete is with us again too, after years far away. And, we welcome Sheila, Steph and Greg."

There was a slight pause. I was expecting Dick to say something. He didn't, so I did.

"That's not all. In June, Jenny became a chartered accountant, after five years' study on top of a full-time job, whether in the office or as a mother. Let's celebrate that, too, and thank her and Dick in advance for throwing this party ten weeks after moving in here and six weeks after Katie's birth."

Jenny looked delighted, and things got going with a buzz. It wasn't long before I was opening the second magnum. A little later, Steph was pouring her a glass whilst I was returning from the kitchen with more snacks, having started rice to cook.

"Thanks, Steph. I gather you met Pete in a rather unusual way. Do tell us the story."

"Hey, yes, what a night that was. Dick and Pete, I'm sure you agree."

Steph sounded quite surprised at this request, but she was soon into her stride, and gave Dick plenty of compliments in telling of what she saw and did. Most of us laughed, including Morag and Sheila, whom I had thought might regard the event as distastefully exploitative. Paul was amused in an interested sort of way, and Greg was looking rather nervous again. At the end, Jenny thanked Steph.

"What a story that is, from B.K. In this house, that stands for Before Katie. She'll have to get used to being born on 6th October, when so much changed. When we heard the one o'clock news that day, my waters had just broken. It's time to eat, now. Dick and I will put things out in the kitchen, and then you come through and help yourselves. Pete, can you open a few bottles, please. Mum and Dad were here last weekend, and brought down some good stuff from the Pembroke cellar. They just made it back to Cambridge, with the fuel gauge on EMPTY."

Steph and I also remembered that one o'clock news, as no doubt did Paul.

September had moved on to October with no particular hint of trouble brewing in the Middle East. That had kept the option price low, but increased the initial risk. If nothing happened, IE was going to drop a good £250,000, even on the terms Paul had negotiated. New Hampshire would lose much more. At the Barbican, the night of 5th October was restless. There had been nothing on the radio in the morning. Finally, at noon UK time, Egypt and Syria had attacked. Later, it transpired that there were plenty of warnings besides ours, including one delivered on a secret visit to Israel by King Hussein of Jordan. All had been ignored.

A few minutes later I was seated again, with a plate of *boeuf bourguignon* and rice balanced on my knee, and a glass perched on a shelf where I could just reach it. Jenny's remarks had prompted lively discussion of current events. I ate for a while, and then she asked for my views.

"To me, there are several questions. The first is to ask why the USA became involved in resupplying Israel. It must have been clear to the CIA that the Israelis could stop and push back the Egyptians and Syrians with what they had. At the very least, there should have been no resupply until after fighting ended, three weeks ago. The Russians would have had to follow suit. What's the answer, Steph?"

"It's home politics, of course. I come from New York, the city with the world's largest Jewish population. They're influential. Watergate means that Nixon needs any friend he can find. He wouldn't have gotten away with the Saturday night massacre[25] if he hadn't just announced resupply. Incidentally, in the kitchen earlier I heard on the radio news that Nixon's told my people he ain't a crook. Ha, ha, is all I have to say. Like most New Yorkers, I'm a Democrat as you may have guessed."

Greg joined in, and looked happier now the conversation was more serious. "Nixon has sorted out the mess in Vietnam that Kennedy and Johnson left him."

"Yup, and last year because of that I was a Democrat for Nixon, I'm ashamed to say. Now, he's so powerless that Congress may not fund the continuing effort required.[26] The man is such an idiot. He wasn't in control of his staffers. He didn't need any of the Watergate stuff to beat McGovern by a landslide."

"Just as back in July, Harry Tamfield's firm could have bought my aunt's house for thousands less if Mr Percival hadn't mucked around," I said. "Carol, you were right to call that 'Tamfieldgate'. Incidentally, Roberta sends again her thanks – Steph and I met her earlier today, she's thriving in her new place. So, the USA supported Israel, for whatever reason. That takes us to my second question. How have *we* become involved? A common European foreign policy of neutrality seemed to be getting off to a good start. Did anyone here in the UK seriously disagree with it?"

"My mother is Jewish," said Sheila. "But she's realised that Israel wants to retain and colonise the territory conquered in 1967, rather than give it up in return for a guarantee in accord with UN Resolution 242. So, she's not sure who to support."

"That's the point, isn't it?" said Brian. "In '67, most people where I lived thought it was great that the Israelis were duffing up all comers so well, particularly Nasser. It's a pity you lot didn't

---

25 The dismissal on 20th October of Watergate Special Prosecutor Archibald Cox, who had refused to accept a plan to allow a senator friend of President Nixon to review privately the taped conversations in the Oval Office. This also occasioned the resignation of Attorney-General Elliott Richardson.

26 and they didn't, hence the 1975 *débâcle* of people fighting to get onto helicopters out of the US Embassy in Saigon (renamed Ho Chi Minh City, which name continues despite Vietnam now being very capitalist).

allow us to deal with Nasser in '56, Steph. But now, the Israelis want to keep all of Palestine, and more. Why should they do that? Meanwhile, countries like Saudi and Iraq are important to us. There isn't a threat to Western security unless we make one. We need to look to our own interests. By the way, Pete, the first European country to come out with a pro-Arab line was Spain. How did they manage to make up their minds so fast? It was almost as if they knew what was coming."

"They are still pretty much a dictatorship, so they can make decisions quickly if they want. Also, there aren't many Jews in Spain. The most Catholic monarchs were stupid enough to expel them in 1492. The Spaniards did get worried when Gadafi suggested that war on Israel might be a prelude to an Arab reconquest, but it soon became clear that wasn't anyone's official policy."

Others agreed with Brian's key point, though not with his view of the 1956 Suez adventure. That had been disastrous for the UK, though Brian pointed out that it appeared to have had less impact on our French associates. Greg recalled that it had given the USSR an excuse for brutal intervention in Hungary. After a while I brought things back to the present day.

"However, the Dutch started to do their own thing. They allowed American resupply planes to refuel there, and even sent along some supplies of their own. No one has really explained why. It's been suggested that they were continuing their wartime resistance to German persecution of Jews, or perhaps that they were guilty about making things easy for the Germans by providing a handy list of all their Jews, or perhaps that it was both. Whatever their reason, their action prompted the oil embargo which is causing so much trouble here. The government tried to say that the Dutch line isn't our line, but Harold Wilson is taking a more pro-Israeli line. My third question is, why is he doing that, Carol?"

"It was outrageous of the Americans not to consult their allies about putting their forces on alert."

"Yes, I know, that's what Wilson said in Parliament on the 30th October. The alert did make the Russians press Egypt to agree a ceasefire. Anyway, that's over and done with. What reason has he for a pro-Israeli line right now?"

"He's worried that unless the present Israeli Labour Government headed by Golda Meir has some international support, it will be replaced by a more extreme government, maybe even one including Menachem Begin."

"Only an Israeli Government which can't be outflanked can cut a sensible deal,"[27] said Liz. "I think that Labour needs to sort out its policy on this urgently, Carol."

"Quite right," said Greg. "Otherwise, Wilson is vulnerable personally. He does have a lot of Jewish friends. There's nothing at all wrong with that, of course, provided they don't influence him on policy issues. If they were seen to do so there would be a lot of unpleasantness that we certainly don't want here."

"This is great," said Jenny. "But we should take a short break for second helpings and recharging glasses."

After we had done that, she continued. "What's your fourth question, Pete?"

"The oil embargo isn't supposed to be directed at us. Three weeks ago, Ted Heath thought it wouldn't affect us.[28] Now, however, the big oil companies are talking of sharing the available oil 'fairly' and of 'equality of misery'. They have cut supplies to the UK. It's even suggested that the government will now accept a 10% cut in deliveries. Why on earth should they do so, Dick?"

The response to this was predictable. Dick's father had recently retired from a post with a large oil company.

---

27 as indeed happened in 1978 through the 'Camp David Agreement' following which Israel withdrew from Sinai. The members of the Israeli Government which concluded this, including ex-terrorist Begin, survived. Anwar Sadat achieved his objective, but was assassinated at an anniversary parade on 6th October, 1981 (and was replaced by Hosni Mubarrak, President of Egypt until 2011).

28 'We have received firm assurances from important oil-producing countries that they have no wish whatever to damage this country, and that they will take what steps are within their power to prevent that happening.' (*Hansard*, 30th October, 1973)

"The big companies are dependent on markets worldwide. They can't discriminate. If they do, they'll lose out to smaller independent companies."

"That's an issue in the States," said Steph. "Since the spring, the big companies have stopped selling oil to the independents. In the summer, that led to gas shortages, even without any embargo. The US Government has been trying to regulate to sort it out, but as always, business after the buck stays in front."

"Yes, forget the idea that the USA is the land of the free, as far as oil is concerned," said Paul. "It's the most regulated market in the world. But, coming back here, what we have and others haven't is North Sea oil. If the oil companies want to profit from it, they must see us right."

"Quite so," I said. "The government should be twisting arms. I'm now assigned to developing the North Sea market for IE. I'm beginning to meet senior people from oil companies. They all know what their bosses should now promise the UK consumer, to make sure they can stay in the North Sea. So, Heath shouldn't be taking this 'Be British, keep a straight bat, play fair' crap from the top oil company people. If he does, they'll just think he's weak and try to get away with more. That's the normal rules of the game. Wilson hasn't got it right, either. Here's question five, for you again, Carol. He's still saying Labour will nationalise North Sea oil. Why? Has anyone worked out how much that would cost? All the benefits can be obtained by setting up a system of production controls and taxation of profits that leaves the companies with just enough incentive to invest."

"We'll be looking at the policy further," said Carol, rather defensively.

"The companies have legal concessions. If our government interferes with them, you're giving the excuse to other governments," objected Dick.

"Other governments don't need any excuse," said Jenny. "Earlier, it was on the radio that someone called Saddam

Hussein who's now running Iraq has taken it out of the embargo. Instead, he's nationalising remaining oil company assets there."

"There's a Scottish dimension to this," said Morag. "The Scottish Nationalist Party is saying that it's Scotland's oil, and is moving up fast in the polls."

"Certainly we mustn't forget that down here," I replied. "But if Scots want to benefit, they'll need to forget about having a quiet life. From early next year I expect to be based in Aberdeen, the centre for offshore action. People there have to stop pretending that it's a peaceful fishing town. They have to accept that things will happen *on a Sunday.* Nor can they close their airport at ten o'clock sharp. On Thursday my flight in was delayed, and the pilot told us that we had only just made it. Apparently, you can be on the approach at one minute to ten, but the lights are turned out and you're sent away."

After calling another break, for us to collect desserts or cheese, Jenny launched in.

"It's my turn to ask question six. Why isn't Heath accepting that the higher oil price means we'll use more coal, so miners need to be paid more to make sure there are enough of them to produce it? There's an HMSO bookshop in Brighton. When I was there on Thursday, I bought the *Hansard* of Tuesday's debate on the state of emergency. It made me feel for you, Liz. You were there, helping people in the Box[29] to provide detail about the pay rates and allowances for various types of miner. Clearly you can prove almost anything by selecting the right figures, but that's all missing the point."

"Quite right, Jenny," said Brian. "I've said it before to most of you, so I won't go on. My dad is a NUM branch secretary in Yorkshire. His message is that the country needs miners, they need more money, and they're *going* to get it. That's their objective, and their only objective. The miners won't be trying

---

29 The Officials' Box in the Commons Chamber.

to bring the government down, unless stupid people annoy them."

"As Harold Wilson has said, the government's pay policy is unworkable," said Paul. "We need enough miners, just as we need enough people to run the trains, the hospitals, and so on. Even our local supermarket is apologising for long queues at the checkouts, because the policy doesn't allow them to pay enough to keep staff. You can't control prices and incomes, and not credit."

"If the miners are so united and determined, why doesn't the NUM call a ballot?" asked Greg.

"Right now, the NUM Executive Committee thinks it can get what the miners want, without a strike," said Brian. "There's scope for a settlement that fits current facts. If Heath presses for a ballot now, there might be one – on a strike. Is that what he wants?"

The miners' union was then the only union which required a membership ballot before a national strike could be called. However, no ballot was required before an overtime ban.

"It's said that Joe Gormley wants a ballot. Why?" asked Sheila.

"As my dad says, with Joe you don't know. My guess is that it's good for his image to say he wants it, knowing his executive won't agree. What do you think, Liz?"

"I think that's very possibly right," Liz said, guardedly.

"The NUM knows it's negotiating with the government, not with the Coal Board," said Dick. "Ministers and civil servants don't know the industry, and nor do the various MPs who chip in with their own ideas. It's quite ludicrous to think that you can sort out what the right offer is during a debate in Parliament."

"The Coal Board did rather pass the buck," said Jenny. "At the first negotiating meeting, it made the maximum offer permitted under Stage 3. Liz, I don't think we can expect you to say why it did that. A week later, the government picked the buck up, by meeting the NUM."[30]

---

30 On 23rd October.

Greg nodded in agreement. "No one knows any longer who is in charge of pay negotiations. In the electricity industry, the unions, including my own, aren't militant, but represent people who feel left behind in the pay race. For coal, there should be pay negotiations at pit level. Collieries vary hugely in ease of working, type of coal, and so on. Unlike power stations, they're not connected to a grid. They don't operate as a system. They're separate businesses. The most productive pits should be allowed to attract more men and deliver more coal, soon."

This was too much for Morag. "You mean leave the people in the less good pits with low pay, set man against man?"

"No, encourage miners to move to where their skills will be more useful, and they can have better pay, *and* better working conditions."

"Quiet everyone," said Jenny. Her sharp ear had picked up wails from upstairs.

"Katie has woken David," said Dick. "It's because they're both in our room."

Jenny and Dick hurried out. I decided that it was time to sum up.

"Ted Heath has missed a big trick. He was stuck in policies which were so self-contradictory that they just wouldn't work. Paul, I recall you saying that they're like trying to fly an airliner with only the engines on one side running. The Middle East War and the increase in oil prices could have let Heath say that new events need new policies. We need more coal, more people will use the trains because petrol is more expensive, and so on. Therefore, there are key groups who will have to be paid more, and the rest of us will have to accept that they don't set a precedent, though it's for employers, not the government, to negotiate with the unions. He could also have said that the government expects the oil companies to maintain supplies, and those who don't do so will find themselves frozen out of the North Sea. That wouldn't be an easy policy, but it would make sense and I think it would have a lot of public support. It would also wrong-foot Harold Wilson."

Jenny came back with Katie in her arms, and unbuttoned her blouse.

"Dick is reading David another story. Now, sweet, you're hungry, aren't you? Try this side."

Greg looked nervous again at what was then an unusual sight. Then it was a quiet night-night to Katie, again. Liz had served coffee by the time Dick and Jenny came down for the last time. It was Jenny's turn to sum up, between yawns.

"Well, every cloud, as they say. Katie has settled, and on the last week's form there's a fifty-fifty chance that she'll sleep through. It'll be an early call though, so now's our bedtime. Look after yourselves. Drinks are in the sideboard. The forecast for tomorrow is good, so we've scope for a walk along the sea front. Volunteers to push the pushchair will be very welcome. Then we can have fish and chips or whatever at the restaurant on the pier. Afterwards, it's up to individuals, and for Dick and me up to the children, but the Pavilion will be open. That's worth a look, if you've not seen it. Can we aim to leave here soon after ten o'clock?"

We all joined in tidying up, and the B & B contingent departed. Liz and Greg went upstairs. Steph and I paused over a brandy. She was impressed by the evening.

"I'm glad everyone liked my story. I wasn't expecting Jenny to ask me to tell."

"Nor was I, but perhaps it made a fairly innocent substitute for a hen party."

"Then Jenny started off the serious talk, and you kept it going."

"That was in the Cambridge tradition, though we were talking about issues that are actually important. Back there, all the talk was about things happening on the other side of the world, or about issues which in the confines of a College could inflate out of all proportion. The UK's economic problems, or Europe, were a turn-off."

"You've said that was part of being on a road to nowhere."

"It was. It's great that we've all stepped away from that road. A first step for some was to be together in the other half of Cambridge."

"Harry has stepped away, too."

"Yes, though we don't know what road he's on now. Tonight, everyone contributed except Susie. I'm glad that Greg came in so well, particularly the last time, when he took pressure off Liz to say any more. He liked the serious talk, and it made him feel more part of us than he had done earlier on, when he was annoying Brian. There was less of a feeling of two Yorkshiremen in the room."

"It was all good. Jenny was playing you quite something. We and Paul didn't know too much. I didn't know Paul. You handled Brian's question about Spain very neatly."

"I'd thought about what to say, if anyone raised it."

"Carol was taking careful note. There's a message or two, but not for now. I'm getting to know your friends, and through that I'm getting to know you better, Pete."

We sat affectionately on the sofa until we heard the bathroom being vacated. Steph knew what she wanted next.

"Right, you first, then get into that bed and warm it up."

When Steph came in a few minutes later, I was in bed, and certainly felt warmed up, though not in the way she had been requesting. I touched my lips for silence, and enjoyed watching Steph undress whilst we listened to what was happening on the other side of a thin internal wall.

Through sounds and words, we followed Liz instructing Greg, much as she had instructed me during our first few times, some eight years before. She used her hands, and had Greg use his. Next, there were false starts and reinsertions. Finally, she was able to ride him harder and harder, to her loud panting, loud creaking from their bed, and slaps as buttocks met groin.

Our bed was small; this was David's room, as its decoration reminded us. Steph and I soon both felt very warm as we fondled quietly and listened.

After ten minutes or so, gasps, kisses and murmured congratulations told us that Greg had delivered the goods. For us, that was not before time.

"Quick and noisy, I think," I murmured. "We won't wake the children. The staircase and bathroom are between us and them."

"I'm well on, so let's do a 'Carol', but no spanking. It's too cold to be out there for long."

Steph liked it lots of different ways. We had named them from past experiences, for example a 'Liz' had just happened next door. She crouched, I went in from behind and after a few strokes slid a finger through her ring, very gently. Her yells of delight seemed deafening in the small room.

6. SUNDAY, 18TH NOVEMBER, 1973

I awoke to creaks from pipework as the central heating started up. Soon afterwards came creaks from the stairs, and muffled squeals and entreaties to silence. Steph was snoring quietly, not to be disturbed. There was enough light coming around the ill-fitting door to allow me to get dressed. I still felt rather sleepy as I followed Jenny and Katie downstairs, but I was fully awake as soon as I entered the kitchen.

The oil boiler was a typical product of the early sixties. Its poor insulation made the kitchen already warm, but limited what it could do for the rest of the house. Jenny was sitting with her back to it, feeding Katie. The nightdress she had been wearing was on the table beside her. She smiled at my apology and glanced at it.

"You're still my brother, Pete. This is warm, but doesn't unbutton, so off it comes for feeding. Well done for remembering that I wanted to talk to you. It's good to do that now, after Steph's account of Harry Tamfield's party."

"We were both slightly surprised when you asked for that, but it went down well, and it brought her into the group, so thanks."

"Now, my sweet, let's bring up the wind and then you can go on the other side... I'm glad she didn't say anything about Dick's massage."

"She had left before that happened, and I've never told her about it. As I said back then, I'm very sorry that, because I was chatting up Steph, and talking to Harry, I didn't notice soon enough that Dick had been distracted."

"It seemed to have turned out for the best. When you called in July, he had already told me about the massage. I realised that until I was ready again, I could still help him. We've carried that on. I've liked to give him 'an Andy'."

"I'm very glad to hear that."

"Then, two weeks ago, Dick told me that Andy had called, to say he's now coming down to Brighton on Wednesdays, to work in a massage parlour. He liked massaging Dick so much that he's offering to do it again, free of charge. So Dick has been along twice, and is going again this Wednesday."

"I guess that Andy is looking for custom. The state things are now, there won't be as much paying business as his employer was hoping for. Maybe Andy thinks Dick will make recommendations, and more people will come in. He could charge them."

"Yes, but can't you see there's something rather odd about this, Pete?"

The scene before me was rather diverting, despite its similarity to many supposedly religious paintings. I closed my eyes to concentrate for a moment.

"I guess it's by chance that Andy is working near here, but how did he know that Dick was here, and how did he find your telephone number? Your name isn't uncommon."

"So a week ago, I was worried enough to write to you. Then on Thursday there was an opportunity to leave the children down the road for an hour or so whilst I popped into Brighton. I didn't just go to HMSO. I went to the parlour, which didn't look too sleazy and advertised massage services for men and women. I took my rings off and said to the bloke on reception that a man friend had told me there was this wonderful masseur called Andy, here on Wednesdays. I hoped he did women as well as men, as I would like to try him."

"What a great idea, Jenny. You could turn it into a shared experience. Andy would have to be very uninterested in women not to enjoy massaging you."

"The bloke knew nothing about Andy. He said I must be talking about a man who hired a room for an hour to work with a particular client, paying cash in advance. So it's not a question of Andy working at the parlour, finding out somehow that Dick lived nearby and inviting him in. Andy is paying a lot of money to come to Brighton and use the parlour to attract Dick, having found out that we're living here. He's targeting Dick; or rather, somebody is paying him to target Dick."

"There's no prize for guessing who that somebody might be."

"Yes. Dick and I shared the job of sending out change of address notes. Dick would have sent one to Harry Tamfield. I thought over what Dick told me about the party. I had the feeling that he'd left something out. That's why I asked Steph for her story. I was right. He never told me that Harry and you stripped off."

"He didn't seem worried that Steph mentioned it. Perhaps that shows he isn't so interested in Harry. I remember feeling that they both kept commendable control."

Like me right now, I thought, as I made that rather disingenuous remark.

"Perhaps he wanted to put out of mind what he did think. Oh, Pete, what am I to do?"

"I'll talk to Dick during our walk. I'll say that Steph's account brought back memories, and see what happens. I'll let you know later."

I risked putting my hand on her knee. We heard coughing from upstairs.

"Gosh, Liz and Greg will be down soon. They're going for a run. Last night, Greg was shocked enough. What *would* he think, now? You've finished, my sweet, haven't you?"

Jenny stood up and passed Katie to me. I tried to cheer her up.

"Wow, turn round... mmmm, your figure is nearly back."

"Two inches to go at the waist. There are good exercise sessions locally."

"You've still some of the same Spanish tan as helped Dick win, I see."

"Not as much as six weeks ago. The gynaecologist, a lad not much older than me, was clearly impressed, though he was fully professional."

"If you had been there, you would have won by as large a margin as Dick. The winner actually looked rather like you, but the last round showed that she wasn't a natural blonde. I think you would have enjoyed it, too."

"Maybe I would have done, whatever I said before. I do like people admiring my body, especially if they're my brothers and sisters. Remember that stunt with Liz?"

"Remember disposing of Julia and hauling in Amanda?"

"Do you still have the book of photos?"

"Yes. I've not looked at it lately, because it's packed away at my aunt's house, out of Steph's way. I've never shown it to anyone."

"I've never told anyone you have it, not even Dick. It's just between us, Pete."

She was speaking quietly, her hand on my shoulder. There was a moment before I could reply. Jenny had given me this album as our relationship began to develop. When our relationship ended she had asked me to keep it as a memento of our happy times and a sign of her gratitude. It had been commissioned by a former boyfriend who sat in on the sessions. I had helped her to rebuild her self-confidence, after that relationship had ended very badly. Yet it was posing in front of two men that had made her proud of showing off her body.

Eventually, I gave her a brotherly pat on the bottom.

"Now, put that nightdress back on, Jenny!"

The kettle had boiled and tea was ready by the time Liz and Greg came down, in running kit. They gulped down mugs, were directed on a route of five or six miles over the Downs, and dashed off into the bright but frosty dawn. As Liz left, she slapped my wrist.

"Show-off!"

"What was that about?" asked Jenny.

"Last night, we entertained each other," I explained.

"It's good that Greg isn't uptight about you and Steph."

"Liz and he make a fine looking couple, nearly as fine as you and Dick. Liz would have done well in Harry's contest, too. Steph's colleague Gail looked splendid with her tan, but on a same day comparison, Liz has a better body, fit from playing sports rather than from working out in the gym. Greg looks to have what it takes for her, just as Susie and Brian have what it takes for each other. Our talk last night was rather above Susie. How can we involve her today?"

"I'll talk about being a mum, and let her hold Katie again. Brian is doing well and they've bought a house. It's time for them to start a family. Are you and Steph having any thoughts about your future, Pete? How's she taking us?"

"She likes you all. She's been short of friends over here, so it's really good to bring her in, thanks. We're enjoying each other while we can. I'm probably in Aberdeen from January. She goes back to the States in April. She's a woman on her own, who doesn't want kids. Her marriage broke up very nastily. She was racing ahead of her husband, so he took it out on her. You're racing ahead of Dick, but he's not taking it out on you. He wants to do his own thing sometimes, but he's a very nice man who will look after you and the children, provided you go on making clear you value and want him."

"Are you saying that Steph needs somebody like Dick?"

"She's a hustler. She has more in common with Liz than with you. She needs somebody more like Greg, with the strength and calmness to settle her down."

"You are thoughtful, Pete. Now, I must dress and make breakfast. Make some more tea."

She gave me a friendly kiss and went upstairs with Katie, leaving me to reflect on what might have been. To distract myself, I pulled out my briefcase, which I had left behind an armchair. After ten minutes I came to the envelope marked 'PERSONAL'.

Inside was what appeared to be a copy of the minutes of a meeting of Tamfield Investments' Board of directors, held on the previous Thursday, 15th November. The key extract is below. I contemplated it for some time. It was very relevant to a big decision which faced me that morning.

'The Director (Marketing) said that sales at all developments are well below target. At Bishop's Park, 85 completed Phase One properties though reserved await exchange of contracts, and only 39 of the 462 properties on Phase Two have been reserved, with no sales confirmed. There was no possibility whatsoever of selling 75% of all properties by the end of 1973, as the company had committed with its bankers to do.
The Director (Construction) referred to the decision made at the October meeting, to slow the pace of work on Phase Two. Whilst this benefitted short-term cash flow, it would increase total unit costs and hence reduce profits. It was also reducing the confidence of buyers, who hoped to be living on a completed and tidy estate within a short time. Some might fear that the total cessation of work of 12 months ago might be repeated.
The Director (Finance) said that the increase in Minimum Lending Rate to 13% two days before has worsened sales prospects, and has also increased the costs of borrowings. Unless some way of realising assets could be found, the company would run out of cash by late in February. This prospect would become apparent by mid- January, resulting in increasing difficulty in obtaining credit from suppliers and carrying on operations generally. The highly-geared takeover of Cardinal had not anticipated the events of recent months.
The Chief Executive noted that there was a possibility of selling Bishop's Park Phase Two in its entirety to the

Greater London Council, for use in its 'overspill' relocation programme, at a price comparable to the Phase One price for individual units.

The Director (Construction) said that this had to be a last resort. The reaction from those already living on Phase One, from others in the locality, and from the local authority would be very adverse for the reputation of the company and would hinder sales at other developments.

The Chief Executive said that there was no other way the company could survive. He could discuss presentation with Sir Reginald Emerson, the local MP and a junior minister in the government department which dealt with local government and housing. This needed to be taken forward quickly, because the GLC could be in discussion with other developers.

After further discussion, the Board by majority vote empowered the Chief Executive to conclude the best deal possible with the GLC.'

I had just taken the decision, and put the copy back into the envelope, when there was a thump on my shoulder.

"Hey, you snuck off, leaving me all cold, and on my lonesome! Who have you been up to something with, Brit boy?"

"I've been seeing something of Jenny, in fact rather a lot of her. She'd said she wanted to talk to me. I'll tell you all later, but when we're on our walk I'll need some time with Dick on his own."

"Now I know Paul, I want to talk shop, out of earshot. I guess we'll all switch about."

Steph did better than me at entertaining the children whilst Jenny and Dick got breakfast ready. Liz and Greg returned, panting but cheerful, and when they had cleaned up we all crammed around the kitchen table. Afterwards, Jenny asked if someone would like to collect the newspaper, which was not delivered on Sundays. Greg offered and wondered if I would like to go with him. We set off down the hill.

"Liz and you make an energetic pair," I observed. "She told me that you met through hockey."

"Yes, that was about a year ago. You've known her much longer, of course, as have Dick and Brian, too."

"Yes. Dick has known her longest of all."

"Has she always been as unsettled and restless as she is now?"

"Not always, but quite often. She's an only child, as I am. Her mother died when she was seventeen. More or less since then, she's been after Mr Right. At Cambridge we came to know and understand each other very well, well enough to know that it wouldn't be me, because we have such different interests. In that sense she's the sister I never had, whilst I'm the brother she never had."

"You continued your relationship, though."

"Yes, we did when we wanted to, but on the clear understanding that we were both looking elsewhere. Five or so years ago, she seemed to have found the right man, Geoff Frampton. Luckily for her as it turned out, but very unhappily at the time, she then found out just what a selfish and unpleasant man he is. He's not married anyone else."

"Liz told me about that. It still upsets her, though she said how supportive you were. It was all part of a very complicated story which involves almost everyone here today. I didn't really follow it all."

"Don't try. The great thing is that we're over it and value each other as friends."

"The thing that sticks in my mind is that she was running Brian whilst she was going for this man Frampton."

"At first, she did that to wind Geoff up. Then, she found it very difficult to wind Brian down. She and Brian liked each other a great deal. However, Brian couldn't relate fully to a woman who is very intelligent, though not an academic type. He really wanted someone like Susie, and here they are. Greg, you have the interests Brian has and I haven't, and you also accept that Liz has a personality and views worth considering. You *are* the right one for her. You know that, inside you, otherwise, you wouldn't be sleeping with her. I know that was a big decision for you."

"My father is a Baptist minister. Some of that has rubbed off on me. I took a while to realise that I couldn't understand Liz as a person without taking her as a woman."

"That's the way she is. She's coming to understand you, too. Be very clear, she's wanted you for some time."

"In July, she said that you were her boyfriend."

"It was the same as with Brian, really. We hadn't seen each other for well over a year, not since we tried a holiday together and it went badly wrong. She wanted to make up, and to show we were still friends, but she also told me what she felt for you."

"She still sleeps around the Coal Board."

"That's for a reason as well as for pleasure, Greg, as I'm sure she's told you. If she has a better reason, she will stop. You can provide that reason. You want to provide it. She wants you to provide it. So, provide it."

We walked in silence for a minute or so, before Greg continued.

"I wish she would stop smoking. It makes her cough when she runs hard, and in the mornings."

"She's always smoked a little, but more when she's tense, as she is just now because she's under huge pressure in her job. You can deal with that. Caress her breasts. Bounce them up and down gently. She likes that a lot. Then spread her across you. There are some muscles in her belly that get very knotted up. You can feel them. If you rub gently, they relax after a few minutes. Stroke her all over before finding the spots she says are extra special. She'll seem almost asleep, which is the sign she's really enjoying it. Then she'll ask you to finger her inside, and after that she'll be fully ready. By doing all that and taking your time, you're showing that you care for her, and that you get pleasure out of giving her pleasure. She'll respond by doing the same for you. That's what it's all about."

"I see what you say, Pete. It should be an expression of mutual respect, and feeling, of love I suppose, but it should also be a way of bringing children into the world, eventually if not straightaway."

"You know what you can do for that to happen."

We arrived at the newsagent's, and on the way back told each other more about ourselves. Greg was clearly doing well with London Electricity. His own union, the Electrical Power Engineers' Association, had banned overtime working because of the impact of Stage 3 on its members. He felt that professionals had duties and shouldn't take industrial action, but what was the alternative?

Back at the house, Jenny was topping up Katie, and Dick was reading to David. The rest of us divided up the paper. I was scanning the smaller articles in the business section for anything relevant to my work when I noticed an entry in the Construction Diary. I showed it to Steph.

'**Joe Aspinall** has been appointed Director, Major Contracts at Northfield Construction. He will be taking up this post on 1st January.'

"His current employment isn't mentioned, but I hope Ambrose doesn't spot this."

"It's not in a part he would read."

The B & B party arrived, we piled into cars, and followed the Sinclairs down to the east end of the promenade. With a few protests, David was placed in a pushchair. Katie liked to be in a papoose from which she could see her mummy's face, and who could blame her? Jenny shaded her from the sun behind as we set off to walk the two miles to Hove, where coffee would be available.

The little party naturally spread out over fifty yards or so. Steph and I were near Carol and Paul, and Steph was soon talking to Paul a few yards in front. It was time to put my big decision into effect.

"Now you're the candidate, Carol, I've quite a lot to tell you. It's all for very careful handling. First, you need background on Sir Reg. In July, he was at Harry Tamfield's party, and he had an, er, extra benefit."

I explained. Then I showed her the Board minutes.

"Phew, Pete, this needs some taking in."

"Yes, it does."

"If this sticks, it will blow Reg Emerson out of the water. That's no good to me if it happens now, though. He wouldn't run again. I would be up against a fresh new Tory as well as the Lib taking advantage. Can we sit on this until an election is called, so that the Tories are stuck with Emerson? That could be a year away, or it could be much sooner."

"The only explanation of the way Heath is behaving is that he's trying to force a confrontation. He thinks that then he can call an early election, and win it."

"I'll talk to a very few people at Transport House[31] about this. We need to be sure it will stick. For the right money, the guy Reg took would spill. We need to find him."

"There were three men for men. Harry took Andy and Julian for himself. You want the third man."

"Is there anyone else who was at the party, whom we could speak to and might know?"

I mentioned the names of a Labour peer and MP. "They were at the party, though not on the list for anything extra. Emerson might have boasted to them. Someone at the club, or maybe one of the people driving taxis, might have something. The Dugdales left and returned. That was to stop the other bank people from knowing about the extra benefit. Reg Emerson may have done the same."

---

31 Then the headquarters of the Labour Party

"I'll be saying that we need time to work out what to do. Now, how do you think people at Bishop's Park would react to sale of the rest of the estate to the GLC?"

"They'll be very angry indeed, and as Labour control the GLC, some of their anger will be directed at Labour.[32] The typical buyers aren't like Roberta. They're young couples who've pushed themselves to the limit. They may have borrowed 90% of the price they paid. They would see living right next to an overspill council estate as hitting the saleability and value of their property very hard. They would wonder how their new neighbours might behave. That's not very charitable, but it's realistic."

"The people the GLC would move in are presently living in squalid conditions, and are bound to fail where they are."

"I'm sure they need something done for them, but is shifting them out to Bishop's Park the answer? What kind of jobs will they need? Are they available locally?"

"I ought to be able to find out how serious the GLC are about it. If all this reflected badly on Reg as well as on Labour, the main beneficiaries would be the Liberals, especially following Sutton and Cheam."[33]

"I wonder what Harry thinks Reg Emerson might do to help him. Could it be just to prevent the local Conservatives from objecting? Might Reg Emerson's department have any involvement in or control over what the GLC does? Fortunately, you have your own expert to answer that question, Carol."

"I called Dad yesterday with the news. He's over the moon. So is Mum."

"I owe it to Roberta to do something with these minutes, but I'm a busy man. If I hadn't been in the office yesterday, I wouldn't have seen them until Wednesday, at the earliest. Let's talk again, quite soon."

---

32 The Greater London Council had been controlled by Labour since the local elections earlier in 1973.

33 A famous Liberal by-election victory late in 1972, in a nearby constituency.

She looked thoughtfully at me, through her glasses. These weren't as heavy as those I remembered from when I knew her as a student, but were doing the same job for her short sight. Today, she was dressed much as then, but she looked authoritative as well as young.

"Pete, you're a champ. How is it that all these things happen when you're around?"

"I don't know. Jenny said once that trouble seems to find me. That was just after she came back to Gilbert Lodge with Dick, expecting to find me unwell, and found us together! There was a fairly innocent explanation *that* time."

"Ooh yes, don't say more, Pete! It makes me think of other times."

"Talking of those times, I'm glad to see that you've now found a bra that fits you."

"It has some build out, and I've put on a few pounds. These days, I don't have time for as much swimming as I used to do."

"There'll be time for you to pop in, later today. Perhaps Liz would like to join you. You wouldn't be seen, back down there."

We had passed a stretch of beach which sloped down out of sight. A few years later, this was officially designated as a naturist beach, but even then, it apparently had some unofficial status, at least at quieter times.

"Pete – oh, you do like the last line. Look, we're slowing down. Can I find a shop that's open and does copying? I'll catch you all up."

She dashed off with the minutes. Ahead, a fractious David was being lifted from his chair. We continued at toddler pace. Steph was now up with Jenny, and was successfully trying the papoose. I caught up with Dick, who was a little behind them, wheeling an empty pushchair. We paused to look at the sea view, on which I commented.

"The West Pier looks pretty shabby."[34]

---

34 It closed in 1975 and the remains have been increasingly dilapidated by fire.

"They're still looking for someone to renovate it. It used to be quite an entertainment centre."

"Talking of entertainment, Steph's account was a reminder of a fun evening."

"Yes, it was a fun evening. I told Jenny all about it, apart from Andy getting over excited. That led to us talking things through. We couldn't do much together before Katie was born, and we can't do much together whilst she's feeding. Last night, you saw how Jenny gets tired."

"I guess that will pass."

"I should think so. Meanwhile, there's been a lucky break for me."

He gave me the story about Andy that I had already heard. I sounded surprised.

"Gosh, you must have impressed him. What does Jenny think about it?"

"She's happy enough. If I'm less frustrated, there's less risk that I disturb her at night. There are just two things I haven't told her."

"Oh, what are those?"

"The first is that when Andy brings me off I try to think of Jenny, but that picture of Harry when you both came out of the changing room still comes to mind. Andy hasn't tried anything again, though I can see he gets pretty excited. I don't want Andy, but on Wednesday I did feel that if Harry were there, I would want him."

"I should try to think more of Jenny. Quite apart from her personality and sense, she's the best looking woman I've ever met. She'll soon be ready for you again."

"I know you still like her, Pete. She still likes you, too. I don't mind that."

"You should stop these sessions with Andy if they go on having this effect on you."

"They may stop anyway. The other thing I haven't told Jenny is that it's not working out here for Andy. There aren't enough customers. So after this week, he's finishing. He says he'll continue doing me for nothing if I go to the place in London where he does most of his work."

"That doesn't sound easy for you. You need the time at the university, as well as with Jenny and the children."

"Yes, I know. Don't preach at me, Pete. It doesn't help. I know I'm not doing much in my research. It's all rather a dead end. I should have moved on, like you, and like Harry."

"Sorry, Dick, I'm not preaching. It's your life, not mine."

"I know that I should back up Jenny and the children. She has a good job she can return to. She'll get on further. I won't. It's not that easy just to be supportive, though."

"Whether or not you take up Andy's offer is your decision, but talk to Jenny about it. She'll understand. She knows that sometimes you need to do your own thing. Don't forget that five years ago she wanted you and was quite determined to have you. She still wants you. She'll help you work out what's best for you, as well as for her and the children."

"Yes, OK, Pete. Let's drop the subject, now," Dick said, rather wearily.

We caught up with the rest of the party near the Brighton/ Hove boundary. David wanted to be back in his chair, and I took a hand with it, pointing out the Regency terraces to Steph as they came into view. By a quarter past eleven, we were at the coffee stop. Carol slipped the note back to me.

We started back mostly together, though Carol and Steph were chatting away separately. After a little while, David was on foot again. Brian was with Liz and Greg, but Susie joined the lead party, and was a great success with the papoose, attracting some charming smiles from a changed and refreshed Katie.

"Oooh, you are lucky, Jenny, having two such lovely kids. Brian said you were planning to go back to work in April. How *will* you manage?"

"Dick helps a lot; yes, really you do, Dick. It's too easy to forget to say that. I'll be starting off part-time, three days a week. Dick reckons he can work at home on two of those days, when I'll do visits. The other day I'll be in the office, and they're prepared for Katie to be with me at first. So the nursery bills won't be too bad."

Jenny pulled Dick to her, and they kissed.

"You two are a great example to us all," laughed Steph. "In the States, women are more assertive of their 'rights' than they are here, but there's too much shouting, and not enough of the practical organisation that gives real fulfilment."

"Mmm, yes, but some of us will go on being happy with a hubby who's the breadwinner," said Susie. "I've a nice job at Allders in Croydon, but once Brian gets another rise... oh, you *dear*, Katie, you're waving your little hand! I just hope that all the trouble now doesn't get in our way. I'm sorry I didn't say anything in all that talk last night, but I did find it good to hear and I think I took it in. Lots of the girls at work just don't know what's going on, and the telly's no help. It'll be nice if I can tell them tomorrow. It'll help too when we go to Brian's people for Christmas, though I won't say much. The women in Brian's family don't say much – serious talk is for the men. That's if we can get there, of course. I'll have to let Brian get up early to buy petrol. Yesterday I didn't let him, as I had the whole day off."

She giggled as Brian joined us. For a moment, Jenny and I dropped back.

"Well?" she asked, quietly.

"It *may* come to an end soon. Carry on as you've just done. Be interested in him, like just now. He clearly wants to talk to you about where he's going. I'll call you on Thursday or Friday morning. Is about half past ten OK?"

"Yes, make it Friday. On Thursday, I can leave the children again to go out. *Gosh*, this part is tatty."

We were again passing the Grand Hotel. Jenny had raised her voice at the onward view of dereliction whose later replacement even by a brutalist conference centre was an improvement.

"Atlantic City is worse," said Steph, cheerfully. "You *are* doing well, David. What a big boy you're getting. It's only a little bit further to your lunch, just to that pier. Do you see it?"

David grumbled the last two hundred yards, and again when we had to wait a few minutes for our meal. We gathered round two tables moved together.

"Is this your first time with our national dish, Steph?" asked Jenny.

"Sure, yes, but how am I supposed to eat all this?"

"It's not as big as it looks. There's lots of air in the batter."

"National dish? There's only one national dish," said Brian, firmly, to nods from Greg.

"If you mean Yorkshire pudding, forget it. Now a proper Lancashire hotpot, that's something different," Carol contested.

"It's simpler for us Scots," said Morag. "We have haggis, but one wouldn't eat that now. I have to admit I don't like it very much."

"Just let Mummy finish eating her meal, sweetie," said Jenny. "At least here, we can have wine or beer with our lunch, not tea made far too strong."

"That shows it's not a proper fish restaurant, and it's dinner, not lunch."

That chorus from the northerners carried on the discussion. After lunch, we strolled briefly along the pier. David had a first go at 'Try Your Strength', and was rewarded with rock. I joined Morag and Sheila.

"You two have been keeping a little to yourselves," I commented.

"Aye, but we like to be with you," said Morag.

"You're all alike in some ways, and so different in others, but all worth knowing. We both like Steph," said Sheila.

"I did wonder how you might take her account of Harry Tamfield's party."

"It was good to hear that men were posing, too."

"Other than Dick, the men weren't impressive. They included Mr Percival, whom you met just over a day later."

"I liked to hear that you stripped when Steph's friend asked you to," said Morag, in a tone which suggested that she would have liked to see it happen, too.

"I rarely turn down a woman's request to strip. Certainly not when she's naked."

Morag changed the subject before this became too personal for Sheila.

"Brian said that you and he had looked at how soon portable computers might arrive. Someone in the Engineering Department at King's is building one. Brian wants to meet him and see it. Are you interested too, Pete?"

I was interested, though I was often away just now. Morag would find a time. Then it was back to Sheila, who wanted to score another encounter with *the* Peter Bridford.

By two o'clock, we were back at the cars, for the parting of the ways. David and Katie had had enough. Greg wanted to be back for evening service at his church. Steph and I wanted to see the Pavilion. Since we were a car short, others had less choice, especially as Sunday engineering works would have made return by train very tiresome. However, Carol and Paul had lots to do, whilst Susie and Brian were not interested in seeing more, so Greg agreed to drop all of them off on his way.

As part of the goodbyes, Steph had something to say.

"It really has been great to be so welcomed by you all. You like to enjoy yourselves, but you think about what's happening, too. Pete told me you called yourselves the Cambridge chums, but you're not all from Cambridge. You're so determined to make your way, and to create something with your lives. I'm going to think of you as The Creators."

Five of us walked back to the Pavilion. This was less appreciated then than it is now, and was not crowded. I pointed out that it was an iconic building of the Industrial Revolution, when the UK led the world. It was the first building anywhere to allow its privileged inhabitants something like a modern way of life. It had central heating, a first since Roman times. It had adequate provision of flush toilets, whereas in the grand palaces Steph and I had seen in France the custom was to use any out of the way corner. Its kitchens had state-of-the-art equipment, which attracted the best chefs to create new dishes. They were next to the dining room, thus allowing these dishes to be served at their best. The oil-burning uplighters must have seemed from another world to visitors used to places lit by candles. The strange and extravagant decoration was mostly ironwork.

Steph saw in all this the predecessor of the millionaires' palaces of America, whilst Morag and Sheila appreciated the craftsmanship. Liz was quiet. While the others looked at some furniture, she took me aside.

"After talking to you, Greg wants to be on his own for a day or two."

"Good. I'm very pleased that you've brought him so far."

"Yes, you've heard exactly how far."

"Steph and I liked to hear that you were satisfied. We let you know that we were satisfied, too. I hope Greg didn't mind that."

"He did have a grin about it. He can be serious at times."

"I said that when I first met him in July. There is something of me in him, me as I was when we started together. You lightened me up. You can lighten him up. If he had a grin, you are lightening him up. Liz, he's better for you than anyone you've had before."

"He wants me to stop smoking."

"That's a good idea. You are smoking more than you used to. You know the risks."

"I need to unwind. I don't know where I'm going. I can't get much further in the Coal Board. It's a man's world, there."

"Your social therapy must make you more influential than you might be."

"Oh yes, but am I really a courtesan? Well, I know what Greg will do next. You've brought things to a head between us, which is I suppose what I wanted. Thanks, Pete."

She gave me a nervous grin, and we exchanged the kisses of siblings.

"Liz, I owe it to you, after what you've done for me."

"So, I'd better decide how I'll respond. One thing I won't do is put him off. I'm just worried that he's going to be boring. I need an exciting man. When Dick and I broke up, I was beginning to feel he was boring, though I knew nothing about Harry. Dick is certainly boring now, though he's still just who Jenny needs. You and Brian were exciting in different ways, and we've stayed friends. Geoff seemed to be exciting, but then he turned out to be a shit."

"For you, Greg can combine the exciting bits of Brian and me, and he's not a shit."

We followed the others on, and after a call at the pleasant tea room returned to my car through the dusk. I was taking it up to the Barbican, because the next week involved some visits which were best done by car. There was a filling station at the Barbican which was expensive, and perhaps consequently had not run dry. We made good time up the quiet A23. This prompted Morag.

"I've read that not being allowed to drive on Sundays because of the embargo has made Dutch people more aware of what they can do near home, and of their neighbours. It could be a way of encouraging community spirit."

"That's an uplifting thought," replied Liz. "I've read too that all this will bring out the best in us, like in the War, but it won't, because it didn't then. During the War, my father wasn't in Borneo, because the Japs held most of it. He was involved in social observation back here. I've read some of his papers.

People weren't thinking heroically all the time, or even some of the time. They were thinking about how to get on with their lives as well as possible, and preferably just that little bit better than others they knew. That links up with what you were saying last night, Pete. People won't be prepared to make sacrifices if they don't see a clear government policy."

Steph agreed, and quoted several economists with impressive sounding names.

"When the chips are down, the imperative is to look after yourself, your family, and others – in that order."

"I don't know how good the trains and buses are in Holland," I said. "Maybe not driving is more practical there than it is here. The government can scarcely ask us not to drive when the whole message of the last fifteen years, under Labour and Conservatives alike, is that people who don't have cars are a nuisance, to be allowed the most grudging facilities for travel. That's an idea imported from across the Atlantic, I fear, Steph."

"I met a guy from Holland at our conference. Of course, they use bikes. Also, most of them live pretty close to a rail station. There's a decent rail service, even on Sundays. Much of the place runs on natural gas. The north of Holland is sitting on the stuff. Incidentally, Pete, you were saying last night that you didn't know why they've gotten themselves into the embargo. They don't know, either. Various people did their own things, and it ended up that way, just like lots of other things that happen. Sheila, to change the subject, Pete tells me you and Morag live above a place you've created, for women who need help. Tell us about it." By the time we dropped our passengers off, we knew more about the Pankhurst Centre.

We were back at the Barbican soon after seven, and settled on the sofa, feeling like a relaxing evening together. Steph kissed me, slyly.

"Now then, Pete, you were up to lots today. Tell me."

"To begin, I'm relieved that you're already going to advise your bank to get shot of financing Harry."

"That's right. The news about Joe is an extra reason for moving as quickly as possible. Hopefully, we can transact this week. So, why are you relieved?"

"I've been sent these, anonymously. I expect they're genuine. I'm going to pass them to residents at Bishop's Park, without it being clear they've come via me. Don't refer to them before the story breaks."

I showed her the minutes. Unusually for her, Steph was silent for some time. Eventually she spoke.

"Jesus H. Christ. Thanks Pete, I'll say nothing that suggests I've seen them."

"That's the simplest part of the story. Now, first I'll tell you what happened to Dick at the party, after he went to get dressed. I'm glad I didn't tell you about that before, so you had no problems about what not to say yesterday. Then I'll tell you what's happened to Dick since."

It took a while to go through the story. Steph said nothing other than 'wow, she does like her body' when I described my early morning conversation with Jenny. At the end, we again sat in silence as Steph analysed. Eventually she spoke.

"So, Pete, I think I get it. Back in July, Harry wants Dick again, and suspects that Dick may be interested in him, too. Thanks to Gail, quite possibly Dick *is* interested. Harry had this Andy remind Dick of old times. Then, he paid for Andy to go down to Brighton and remind Dick again. Now, the game is to entice Dick up here."

"Yes, but why? Before the party, Harry had shown no interest in Dick since he left Cambridge. Remember he upset Dick by saying he wasn't interested. That prompted Jenny to help Dick. I'm sure that Harry can now pay for whatever he wants. He must have plenty to do right now. His company is in a very tricky position indeed."

"That may make him more determined to have Dick, while

he can. Here's my thinking on how he'll try to do it, based on visits to a few parlors in New York. Some of them have rooms for two. You're both massaged how you like, and then left together to do what you like. My time with Beth began that way. The masseuse brought us on enough to break down our inhibitions, mainly my inhibitions that time, but not so much that we had nothing to do when she left us together. I guess the parlors here are the same. So Dick goes wherever he's told, and finds Harry there too. Andy brings Dick off but not Harry, and then he leaves them to it. What are you going to do about this, Pete?"

"I hope to hear from Jenny that Dick has told her what he told me. I've also encouraged her to be appreciative of him, as she was today. I don't want to be a go-between, and it would antagonise Dick if I tried."

"You're quite right about that, but there's something you can do to stop Harry. Pick up Jenny's first idea. If Jenny tells you that Dick is coming up here, say that you're interested too, as a paying customer of course. I reckon you would enjoy it. You said just now that seeing it happen to Dick gave you a kick."

"Dick is a very handsome man. With the tan he had in July, he looked really great."

"Less than an hour before you saw it happen, you said that Liz had left you with nothing for *me*! Oooh, that feels promising. I'm a bit stiff from that small bed and the walking today. Give me the Ana treatment, to begin."

Steph's hand was on the site of the kick. She unzipped me, and I began by lifting her jersey over her head, taking care not to disturb her hair. For a while we were quiet, apart from murmurs of appreciation.

"So how do I look, compared to Jenny?" Steph continued, eventually.

"That's a tricky question to ask me. You're very smart,

undressed as well as dressed Imagine Jenny as the lady who did win, but not shown up in the last round."

I slid my hand over her neat triangle, and slipped a finger in.

"Mmmm, it's nice to imagine Jenny all sorts of ways, best of all as at her hen party. Being a direct type, this morning I said to her that the story took me to my sorority hazing at Pembroke,[35] and then to how I enjoyed doling out the same to new girls. Mmmm, those are nice thoughts – *mmmmmmm*."

"How did she take that? Liz and Carol both told me that they were all a bit shocked at how far they went. That didn't wear from Carol, and it certainly wasn't right for Morag. It may have been right for Jenny."

"She said she knew they enjoyed doing together what they wouldn't have had the nerve to do separately, and that looking back, it was good to have had one real lesbian experience before getting married. It helped her to understand Dick, and was supportive for her cousins. She's got on with them better since."

"Brian took the story in good part, and it seems Dick did, too. Back in July, he mentioned it as an example of how Jenny liked some fun. Mmm, you're really squelchy."

"Oooh... *Ooooh* – harder, yes there, *harder* – oooooooooh! Thinking of the hen party makes me want 'Beth plus'. It will put you in practice for Andy."

Beth had been the best of Steph's relationships with women, and their favoured style explained Steph's neatly trimmed triangle of hair. We had added 'plus'. She spread herself over me, and took me in her mouth. Her muffled yells grew louder and louder as my tongue found its way in through her triangle. Then I lifted my legs, and we each felt the other's ring. We were a very good fit for each other, all ways.

Rather later, over supper, Steph was direct again.

---

35 The women's college associated with Brown University, Rhode Island. It merged fully with Brown in 1971.

"Do you actually want Dick and Jenny to stay together?"

"They're a very well-matched pair. Anything else would be terrible."

"For whom would it be terrible?"

"Certainly for Jenny and the children, and where would it lead for Dick?"

"That's very decent of you. I guess you're right, Pete, but I'll say just one thing, which was obvious to me, and must be to Dick, too. Jenny likes having you around again. She must have been mighty pleased that you came downstairs this morning."

"She gets a kick from people admiring her body, particularly if they're real or honorary brothers. Dick knows that. He's rather the same, though being a man he has to be careful about showing the kick. At Harry's party, he was pleased to be in the contest, and he said to me something like what Jenny said to you earlier. When he and Gail did their victory parade, they were doing together what they couldn't have done separately."

"That's also when Dick said that Jenny likes organising people in the loveliest sort of way. This morning, she was certainly organising you."

"I'll be helping Jenny as her friend, brother if you like, but I agree, she enjoys using her body to get her way. As soon as she had sorted out her own love life, she sorted out her real brother's love life. John had this rather stupid girlfriend, Julia. She wasn't losing interest, and he was too nice to dump her. A month after I left Cambridge, Jenny's parents went away for their summer holiday, and Dick moved in. The next Sunday was fine, and there was a repeat of what had happened with me. John came over, and suggested sunbathing in a secluded part of the garden. Jenny pointed out to Dick that John *was* her brother. Afterwards, she suggested that during the next weekend, they could top up their tans further. John reminded her of what she already knew: Julia was to be in Cambridge then. Jenny asked whether she might like to join them."

"What was the response to that?"

"John looked worried, and Jenny knew why. He had met Julia in the south of France. Some other girls she was staying with had joked about her always wearing her swimsuit at their pool. So on the next Saturday, Dick had a problem in the lab, and John could remind Julia that Jenny *was* his sister. Once settled on the lawn, Jenny asked John to oil her, just as she had done the week before and indeed with me. She didn't disguise her enjoyment of John's hands, and John failed rather spectacularly to disguise his enjoyment of using them on her. Perhaps he was encouraged by Dick's absence. Julia didn't look happy, but Jenny laughed and said that the next day, Dick would be there, so each couple could do their own oiling. However, on the next day John arrived alone, saying that Julia had been called in for an evening show at the art gallery in London where she worked. That was the beginning of the end."

"How did Dick take to John?"

"Well, as far as I know. John is a handsome man. I'd found it exciting to watch him oil Jenny. I compared them to Eros and Venus. Dick may have found it even more exciting. Jenny's next step was to fix John up with Amanda Farquhar, the nurse who gave such great support after Dick's suicide attempt. Once Jenny and Dick had their own flat, they invited her to a 'thank you' dinner, and included John. Things then happened fast, for a reason which became clear the next summer. Jenny's father went off to a vacation job in the States, taking his wife with him. So, the house and garden were left for the children to look after, trash, and in particular to sunbathe."

"Did Amanda take to that better than Julia?"

"Not half. She recalled some unprofessional enjoyment when helping Dick to use the shower, and welcomed an off-duty repeat look. But she couldn't take her eyes off Jenny, and the expression on her face said it all. Jenny liked to see her ache."

"Did John and Dick like seeing her ache, too?"

"John did. He and Jenny are very close. Dick knew Jenny's purpose, and he took it in good part. Later in that 1969 summer, they came up to Durham for a long weekend. By then, Liz was with a hefty cop who played rugby for her sports club, but on the Sunday he was on duty, so the four of us went out in the hills. At a quiet spot by a lake, Liz said last one in's a cissy. Dick, ever decent, followed her, so Jenny and I had no choice. As we dried off, Dick said that none of us four was seeing anything new, and got talking about the new foursome, and how he liked to watch the nurse who'd stripped him strip herself. Then he described their celebration of Apollo 11."

"How did Jenny take him talking about all that?" asked Steph, after I had elaborated.

"You're right to ask. She scowled at Liz, and said her hair was wet and she was cold. I was cold, too – it was windy, and the water had been freezing. Then she went quiet. It was as if she wanted John and Amanda to be in a separate box in her life from Liz, me and the others you've met. She didn't bring them into the Cambridge chums, so they're not Creators. At the hen party, Amanda talked, but then Jenny made absolutely clear who was in charge."

"Jenny didn't mention Amanda when we talked about the hen party."

"I don't know how they relate now. Jenny gets a lot just out of being admired. There won't have been much chance for sunbathing since Jenny and Dick moved away from Cambridge."

"Are John and Amanda still together?"

"It's a low-key romance. Amanda is doing specialist training and lives in several nights a week. I think they'll be marrying next year, once she finishes that and can join John in Sheffield. Perhaps with some prompting from Jenny, she made him apply for a permanent job at the university there, and buy a house, rather than sit around for too long as a Fellow of King's. Amanda is a very determined woman. She's good for John, who is rather easy-going. That's all as I've been told, mostly when I met Jenny and Dick on the boat back from Spain. I've met Amanda only twice, and both times very briefly. The first was when Dick was in hospital and the second was at the wedding. She's about the same age as John, or Liz. She's fairly short, and quite stout. She looks very strong, very much the hospital nurse."

"So nowadays Amanda, and through her John, are more of the people who Jenny has under her little finger. She knows what she wants, and she's not afraid to use her body to get it, even if nothing physical happens. You wouldn't always have given her what she wanted. You wouldn't be under her little finger. That's why we're here."

"It's me she asks for help, not John or Amanda."

"That's because you're not just her honorary brother, Pete. I woke up today to hear her coming upstairs and leaving Katie with Dick. Then she went into the bathroom, and was there for a long time, though she didn't have a bath. I was feeling real uncomfortable, desperate for a pee. I reckon she lay down on the mat, thought of you and brought herself off. Mothers of six weeks aren't usually up for that, but I bet she was aching for it. Harry ain't the only man destabilising that marriage."

I responded to that rather testily.

"The last time I saw Jenny was in July, and the time before was three years earlier, at her wedding. From January, I should be nearly as far away from her as I was in Spain. I won't see her very often. That's probably a good thing. I won't have much opportunity to destabilise anything."

"I know you won't, and I shan't be around from soon after," Steph sighed. "We need to talk more about us, but not now. We both have tough weeks ahead. It's been great to meet your friends, Pete. They're quite a crowd. They were good to me, too. Don't think I've got it in for Jenny. She's doing very well in her job, while being a super mother too, and she certainly tries to support Dick. Carol is very smart indeed, as well as having a very fine butt. Paul has done well there, and so did you. Liz is under pressure, and is worried that she'll pass her sell-by date, though she's well younger than me."

"She also feels hard pressed in her job. She wonders where it's going."

"I know that. I like Liz. We're both children of the Pill. For ten years, we've both had precious few weeks without a fuck. I do hope things work out between her and Greg. He's very hot for her, but feels guilty about it."

"I may have forced the pace." I described my conversations with Greg and Liz. Then Steph moved on.

"Brian's smart too, but Susie delivers what he wants. She made clear enough what *she* wants. Then there are Morag and Sheila. It was great to hear about the women's centre. Clearly they're very bound up in it. They all add up to a bunch who are gonna make things happen, as I said."

"Yes, 'The Creators' is a good name for us. Years ago, Liz said that what drives people forward is the desire to achieve and make a difference, some for themselves and some for others. I guess that's what gives people determination and resolve, and it sums up most of us."

"With Ana and Roberta too, I've met all the other women in your life, Pete, bar your mum. They're all very much worth knowing, and I'm sure she is, too."

That gave me the chance to suggest a visit to my parents the next Sunday, and also to mention the Christmas invitation. After some consequent telephone calls, I found Steph perusing the business section of the Sunday newspaper she took, and expressing relief that there was no mention in it of Joe Aspinall. We browsed for a while, and were beginning to yawn. Then Steph sat up, with a start.

"Look at this. You were saying you wondered how Bill Latham was doing."

She passed me the arts section, open at 'Concert Announcements'. On Thursday, 13th December, the former leader of the Baroque Society Orchestra was playing the Beethoven Violin Concerto in an early evening concert at a church in the City.

"Goodness, we must try to go."

"In July, Harry suggested meeting up with you. Why not invite him? You could suggest he comes on to dinner here afterwards, and say we both owe it him for getting us introduced."

"I wonder what he'll make of our being together. Might he think that's why New Hampshire is leaving his banking consortium?"

"He can think that, if he wants. It's New Hampshire's decision, and doesn't affect him. You're going to make sure the leak of the minutes doesn't link to you."

I was right to make the point, but also glad that Steph had fobbed it off. Worries about my relationship with his bankers could distract Harry from recalling that he had referred to 'Reg'.

Soon I had a letter written, and soon after that, we were in bed. My sleep was not long delayed by a sudden realisation that Steph's idea for helping Dick might lead me to the answer Carol needed, or by any worries as to whether my decision to talk to Carol had been the right one. I was taking forward IE policy as defined by Pat. I liked making things happen, even though I was rather like the Dutch in not knowing to what they might lead.

7. WEDNESDAY, 28ᵗʰ NOVEMBER, 1973

"So you're sure that all Harry said to you was that 'only Reg has taken'. He didn't refer to Sir Reg, or Reg Emerson?"

"I'm quite sure on that. All our conversation was about the Dugdales both taking women, and therefore how Harry could enjoy two men. I linked Emerson with what Harry said only because I'd noticed his name, asterisked, on the invitee list."

"Have you told *anyone* else about this?"

"No. I showed Steph the minutes, after she told me that New Hampshire Realty was likely to sell. I said nothing at all about Reg or other politicians being at the party, or about the Dugdales' extra benefit. I wouldn't want Mart Steinberg to feel left out, though I recall his wife as being rather younger than Martha."

"Steph might guess that Reg was at the party, as he's mentioned in the minutes."

"She might. She hasn't asked me about him. If she does, I'll say, quite truthfully, that I don't recall seeing him there. I suppose that she could find a picture of him and try to recall whether she had seen him herself."

"Good. I'm sorry to seem rather firm, and that I've taken so long to get back to you, but this has gone right up the line – really right up the line, and very need to know. I have to give clear answers to those questions, and now I can. Thanks, Pete."

Carol and I were in a restaurant not far from Smith Square. It wasn't very expensive, but the Labour Party was paying. We were in an alcove where we couldn't be overheard. She looked very businesslike and pleased with herself. She wasn't just another rookie candidate any more. I too was enjoying my first political lunch.

"How are you doing on getting proof?"

"Not very well, so far. Your two names sang like canaries when their Chief Whips applied the thumbscrews, but only confirmed Steph's account of the party. They knew nothing about anything else happening. The Commons Chief has enough gen on Reg to make the story credible, but no more. We had some discreet enquiries made at the club, but hit a very solid brick wall. Their clients' affairs are private. We'll keep trying."

"You don't want the answer too quickly."

"That's right. Heath won't call an election before Christmas, so we've more time. The plan would be to blow this open immediately nominations close. We would go earlier only if Tamfield falls apart or the story breaks some other way. That could happen if Ambrose's bank goes under. The place is full of rumours that one of these fringe banks is in big difficulties.[36] Where one goes, others follow."

"The financial columns yesterday were saying that National Amalgamated increasing their stake shows continuing confidence in Tamfield, despite any short-term difficulties. Recommendations are still 'HOLD'. It's amazing that Joe Aspinall's move hasn't been picked up. What about the GLC?"

"Party contacts confirm that their bid is serious, though they're still negotiating on price. They have the money and don't need formal consent from anyone. We didn't get more, because relations between Transport House and the GLC are rather strained. Dad did better with an old chum. The GLC wants an estate with low running costs, and in an area of low unemployment. Dad had to explain his interest, of course, and that led straight to the key point. The GLC knows that this will be unpopular with local people, and with the Borough, but

---

36 The problems of London and County Securities became public the next day.

Harry Tamfield has assured them that Reg Emerson will stop the issue from becoming party political. He says that Emerson has a big majority, and can afford to lose a few votes by not doing as much to oppose the deal as a Conservative MP might do."

"To which your response is…"

"Like hell he can. You need to tip off the residents now, without leaving a track back to me. Can you do that, Pete?"

"Yes. I stayed Monday night with Roberta, and noticed a circular from a residents' association, with the address of its secretary. Here's a typed, stamped addressed envelope, containing a copy of the minutes. All I have to do is put it in the post."

"Great. It will take a week or two for a row to brew, and that will make the GLC pause. The other thing Dad picked up is that they're not in too much of a hurry anyway. They would rather finalise when Phase Two is finished. Can you keep in touch with your aunt and let me know as soon as the message gets around?"

"Yes. Her friend Frank the solicitor will be involved, pretty quickly."

"The association will probably call a residents' meeting. They'll invite the GLC, the Borough, and also Reg and the Liberal candidate. They may not even think to invite me. Make sure they do, but not in a way that suggests I have a special involvement."

"What will you say, Carol? Like it or not, people are going to see this as action by a Labour controlled body that will reduce the value of their properties and lower the tone of the neighbourhood."

"I have a line approved, already. I understand their concerns. They have bought houses and flats for nearly double the price of two years ago. I'll fight to stop Tamfield from profiting again at their expense. Equally, I hope they understand that there are people still living in squalid conditions who could do much better in Bellinghame. I might bring along a few photos of how these people live now. There needs to be time to find the right solution for all."

"There isn't much time. Once this is known, two things will happen. First, any remaining uncommitted buyers will drop out, feeling that they've had a lucky escape. Second, Tamfield's financial problems will become more public. Their suppliers of bricks, timber, concrete, windows, baths and other bits of houses will want cash on the nail. The problem predicted for mid-January will arrive sooner."

"This is important enough that big names at Transport House will press the GLC to advance money to keep Tamfield going, pending a deal."

"Good, but if local people don't see something better for them settled by the time of any election, you'll be shown right up. You could still be £150 poorer,[37] whatever happens to Reg."

"I know this is high risk, Pete, but it's my best chance to attract attention for next time. Just following the national swing won't get me anywhere. What do you know about housing associations?"

"Not much."

"They've been around for nearly a hundred years and used to be an important way of housing the less well-off decently. Their time is coming again. The days of the vast council estate are passing. There are already developments being shared between private buyers and associations, with no indication of any detriment to the value of the private properties. I'll get details, for use later."

"What will your local party's line be?"

"I'll have to stop them from saying anything stupid. Most of them are from the council estate at the other end of the constituency."

"I'm one of your voters. I've registered at Roberta's address, since I don't know where I'll be living from January. Here's a

---

37 Then the level of the deposit lost by a candidate failing to achieve 12.5% of votes cast.

different point for Labour. On Sunday, Steph and I made a belated Thanksgiving visit to my parents, looking at Stonehenge and Salisbury Cathedral on the way. On Monday, I put her on the train at Southampton and went on to meetings at IE's factories near Portsmouth."

"What's the point?"

"We were able to travel by car, confidently. My father had told me that there's no shortage of petrol in south Dorset, because the 10% reduction in deliveries is from the levels of August. In November, that's not a cut for a holiday area. Conversely, for London, and for other cities, it's a larger cut than 10% from present demand. The oil companies are giving the impression of a bigger crisis than there actually is, so that they can divert supplies to countries whose governments are more prepared to stand up to them. Do Heath's crowd even know that they're the fall guys? When will Harold Wilson show them up?"

This provoked the kind of ding-dong argument we both liked. After ten minutes it was time to go. Carol signalled for the bill, and was ignored by the waiter, who was idling in a corner. She glared, signalled again, and was still ignored. She went over to him and said some forthright words. That produced the bill. She did not leave a tip.

"Well done, Carol," I said, as we went out.

"Steph told me about the good example you set in France."

"I learnt how to do it in Hall at Waterhouse. The day I first met Paul and you, Harry Tamfield, Dick and I had stuck our ground whilst the waiters were trying to clear everyone out. It was a bad habit of theirs. If you let people kick you about, they go on doing it, and enjoy doing it. If only Mr Heath knew that."

"See you this evening. It's such marvellous news. I hope it works out, this time."

"I was grateful for the message from Paul yesterday. That was my first news, because I was away over the weekend and

Monday. Keep your fingers crossed. We're all a little older and wiser these days."

I said that in a slightly more serious tone. Carol replied after a slight pause.

"Yes. Paul won't be there. He rang just as I was leaving for here. He has to go to Holland at short notice, for a meeting tomorrow."

"Gosh, it must have been short notice. He didn't mention it when I saw him earlier today. Steph is away, too. On Monday evening, she set off for various meetings at New Hampshire's European offices. She won't be back until Friday."

I met Carol's interested look with a grin and a shake of the head, as if to repeat that we were a little older and wiser. I posted my envelope in the first pillar box I passed.

Liz was handling all the Coal Board's briefing for Mr Heath's meeting with the NUM today, because her boss was ill again. So I had not been able to congratulate her on becoming engaged to Greg until late the previous evening. They wanted to celebrate first with as many as possible of the people who were in Brighton with them. It had to be tonight, for the next evening they were seeing the Minister at Greg's church, and on Friday evening they were to call on her father, on their way to a weekend with Greg's parents in Yorkshire. So all available Creators were to meet at a pub in Kensington which unusually for then served good food in the evenings, and offered a glass of white wine at something like the right temperature. They hoped that I could be there, since I had pushed Greg over the edge.

This would be much less grand than the celebration of Liz's previous engagement, to Geoff Frampton. However, that had lasted for only three weeks. For a really grand event, I would need to wait until the spring. On the Underground train, I pulled out of my pocket another personal letter whose envelope with unfamiliar writing had caused amusement amongst the secretaries at the office.

'Dear Pete,

I hope you and Steph are well. Our ventures are certainly prospering! Father is saying how Paul is very smart. What is so special about Waterhouse College?

Formal invitations will be sent at the proper time, but I tell you now that Carlos and I are to be married by the Archbishop in Pamplona Cathedral on Easter Monday – 15th April. It is a long time to wait, but you showed me how to make that easier for us both. Before Lent, the weather would be very cold.

We both hope very much that you can attend. Father is planning some very fine festivities, including a whole afternoon of bullfights in my honour. He can certainly afford them now! There will be absolutely no difficulty in Steph accompanying you, if she has not by then returned to America. She has earned her place, and Father enjoys meeting her (look out, Pete!).

Work on my book must wait until 'Crafty' is completed.

Lots of love and fond memories, Ana.'

It was certainly cold here, now. The evening papers were picking this up as adding to the grim prospects for fuel supplies. Supply voltage was already being reduced at times of peak demand. The main story was, however, a meeting between Ted Heath and the NUM's National Executive Committee of over twenty local leaders, including such figures as Arthur Scargill.

Everyone in IE whose job included handling trades unions thought that this meeting would do nothing but harm. Once again it cut out the employer, and politicised an industrial dispute requiring realistic settlement. It encouraged anyone who might be thinking of a concerted effort to bring down the government. It was absurd to suggest that the meeting might encourage the NUM 'moderates' to take a more conciliatory line. They could do that only in private, not in the full glare of publicity. That applied most to Joe Gormley. Who was advising Heath to take this further disastrous step, and why? If he thought that he could 'win' a confrontation, he was crazy. Even if a general election were to return him with an increased majority, what would he then *do*? Elections didn't make miners dig coal.

To cheer myself up, I recalled just how well my visit home at the weekend had gone. I had wondered how my parents would take to an American, in view of my mother's wartime experience, but all had been smiles and friendship. They had even avoided asking whether Steph was 'the One', perhaps because Roberta had passed on what I had told her. The prospects for a snug Christmas in Bellinghame were good. The thirty-year feud was over.

I also thought back to the good example Carol had mentioned. On the way to Spain, we had stayed in the château country for two nights, at an hotel near to a Michelin-starred restaurant. Dining there was Steph's treat, using her fully convertible dollars. The food was very good, but on the first evening the waiter had smirked at the older American paying for a younger Briton. Eventually, she persuaded him to accept her order for wine. When he brought it, late, he opened it clumsily and corked it. Steph asked him to bring another bottle. He returned with what I recognised as the same bottle on account of a mark on its label; evidently he had topped it up with water. Then he poured ostentatiously, and splashed wine on to her food. At that point I called over the Head Waiter, and showed that my French was good enough to detail events and make clear that unless the service matched the food and the price thenceforward, messrs Michelin would be informed. The Head's dismissive glance following a taste of the wine had said it all. He served us himself for the rest of that evening, and provided an excellent brandy on the house. The next evening, the offending waiter had not been seen.

I was back at IE to an urgent message from Pat's office, summoning me to a meeting with him and George Armstrong at four o'clock. To anyone senior in IE, such a message was unnerving. The five operating divisions were very much their own businesses, but management accounting was good and any falling behind financial targets came quickly to George's attention. If it was serious, those responsible found themselves in front of Pat and him. No sufficient explanation, no job.

I told myself that as yet I had no agreed financial targets. I had completed my visits, and was finalising my plan for a North Sea sales office. Initially there would be about thirty staff, mainly people transferred within IE. I had already spoken to most of those I wanted. I thought it realistic to aim for additional turnover (in 1973 prices) of £5 million by 1976 and £20 million by 1980, with profits of £500,000 and £3 million in those years. The 1972/73 profits of IE were a respectable £41 million on turnover of some £300 million, so this looked to be good business.

Like my activities in Spain, my proposal marked a change from IE's normal policy of divisions marketing separately. I knew that Terry and George would support it. Pat himself was sympathetic. My paper to IE's Board would have to convince its other members. If I succeeded, I would move to Aberdeen immediately after the New Year. There, the pace was accelerating to frantic as the full importance of North Sea oil was realised. I wanted to be picking up business, as soon as possible.

The meeting wasn't about this, and to my relief Pat was smiling as he began.

"Well, Pete, you've given us a problem – a problem of success, to quote our exalted Prime Minister only a few months ago,[38] but in this case a genuine success. Paul has been called urgently to a meeting this evening and tomorrow at New Hampshire's Rotterdam offices. Perhaps your lady friend has told you why."

"No, she hasn't. We don't talk about 'Crafty' at home. This week, Steph is away for several meetings on the Continent. The weekend before last, we were away with friends. She officially met Paul and had a long talk, without attracting any attention. I guess that was about 'Crafty'."

"Yes, it was," said George. "Paul has made his name with these traders. He came up with an idea for repackaging the options, effectively selling out in advance and rebuying to increase leverage. They went ahead on the basis that only the excess profit above expectations would be put at risk. They've hit the jackpot. It now looks as if total profits could be over £60 million, and IE's share nearly £20 million."

"Well done, Paul," I said. And well done, me and Ana, I thought.

"So now our problem is, *what do we do with our winnings?*" said Pat.

"We moved £1 million to IE España, ostensibly to fund acquisitions," said George. "That's what everyone in my team thinks, that's what appears in the half-year statement, and that's what we told the exchange control people at the Bank of England. Now as you said back in July, Pete, Spanish accounting practices will allow plenty of scope for disguising that somehow the £1 million has financed £7 million worth of acquisitions, particularly if Banco Navarrese speaks to the right people over there. No one over here need know, so there shouldn't be any exchange or tax problems, or arguments about what we were up to making money out of everyone else.

---

38 In the summer, Ted Heath had stated that 'Our problems are those of success', a comment which was by this time entering the same league as Neville Chamberlain's 'Hitler has missed the bus' of early April 1940.

Now, though, we have much more than £7 million coming our way."

"Perhaps Doug and Banco Navarrese can suggest more acquisitions in Spain," I said. "Ford's Valencia project is now better defined. Some ideas which seemed too speculative a few months ago could be very worthwhile now."

"Doug reckons there's scope for £10 million, but not £20 million," said George, to whom my former team in Spain reported.

"So, Pete, you're the ideas man and they've all been good so far," said Pat. "From opportunities to girls, you spot them. What do you spot now? How can we spend another £10 million plus without drawing attention to ourselves? There are some decisions about placing proceeds to be made very soon, which is why New Hampshire has called an urgent meeting. Paul will phone George as soon as he reaches their offices in Rotterdam, probably in about an hour. Any guidance we can give him would be very helpful."

I paused before answering.

"With everything that's going on and the pound falling, we want to hold that money out of harm's way, perhaps in a Swiss account in the name of IE España, and bring it back over several years, ostensibly as profits of ventures in Spain and with Spanish tax paid. Banco Navarrese can tell us how to do that."

"If we keep the money out of the 1973/74 Accounts, we would be understating group profits as well as violating exchange controls," objected George.

"Is there any other way?" asked Pat. "Plenty of people have come to grief for *overstating* profits, but very few for *understating* profits. Really, we would be spreading profits forward, and paying tax properly, assuming there aren't double taxation problems which I'm sure you'll check, George. Pete, I think we need you in on this again, because you know the people in Spain."

"I don't want to leave out Doug. He needs to build his contacts. Local knowledge goes out of date very fast."

"You won't leave him out," said George. "He has a full job on developing the markets. This is separate from that, and from what Paul is doing. Nor does it involve New Hampshire Realty. I'll ask Paul to say to Banco Navarrese that we need to see them, preferably in Madrid rather than Pamplona. We'll see Doug separately. Arrange it, Pete. I've nothing in my diary for next week that can't move."

"Good," said Pat. "No doubt you'll sort out too how we bring our personal winnings back here. I'm not interested in buying a villa in Torremolinos."

Selected individuals had been allowed to stake their own money in the trading operation. This had been intended to smooth the way with various high personages in Spain, but Paul had arranged that others 'in the know' could join in. I had staked £3,000 worth of pesetas saved in Spain. On what I had just heard, I stood to get the best part of £25,000 back. I needed some of that money soon, if I were to commit to buying a flat in a block under construction in Aberdeen. It would have the lot – a large living room, super kitchen, and balcony with harbour views. It would be the place to live and to entertain. My neighbours would be some of the people I needed to know. So I wanted it, and so I had already worked out an answer to Pat's question.

"We can receive it in Spain as commission, related to our expert input. That will mean it's income, on which their tax isn't very high. It can come back here, free of further tax. Banco Navarrese can help to arrange all that, too."

"Good, fix it. Any problem has a solution, I always say."

Half an hour later, I left the office for Islington. Before the gathering for Liz and Greg, there was a new experience for me.

The previous Friday, Jenny had relayed Dick's news about Andy offering services in a London parlour, rather than in Brighton. He didn't know what to do. It was a long way to go, and he wasn't sure where it might lead, but he did find the massages very pleasurable. I told Jenny that I had found it very pleasurable to watch. So if Dick did decide to go, and called me, I would say I was interested in joining him.

The previous evening, I had hardly rung off from Liz when Dick had called, to say he was coming to Liz's celebration. Did I agree that as the Creator who had known her for longest, he should say a few words? I did agree, and then he mentioned that he had arranged for a massage with Andy beforehand. I said that I was always up for something new, and Steph was away, so could I join him? He welcomed that suggestion, and said that it would make Jenny happier, too. So that morning I had called up a receptionist named Gloria with a strong East End accent, and was told that there was no problem at all about a 'double'. The charge was £5 for standard service, or £8 for full service, including VAT.[39]

I had not been surprised to find that the parlour was near the offices of Tamfield Investments. One of the laudatory press articles of earlier in the year had noted that despite his success Harry still lived modestly and almost 'above the shop'. This was his home territory, and was beginning to smarten up. Whatever Harry had done, he was contributing to that.

The parlour was advertised to contain state-of-the-art solarium, sauna and massage facilities for both men and women. It was in a new extension to an older looking swimming pool and gymnasium. I found Dick talking animatedly to the women's winner at Harry's party, Number 6, who had looked so sensuous in a swimsuit and later on entertained Martha, Lady Dugdale.

"Here's Pete, now, Gloria. Do you remember him? He counted our votes."

"Yes, what a splendid evening that was, particularly for both of you. Gosh, do all of you who hosted at that party work here?"

"Just Andy and me. Sm'others at that club where that party was, rest round the place. Smash to meet yer both again. Andy's

---

39 The clarification that was always being given then – VAT had been introduced in April 1973 following our joining the EEC.

sorry, he's runnin' late. Two of his clients wanted things *extra* special. Yer've just got time for the sauna if you want, no one else there, no extra charge. Be out in forty and Andy'll be ready. Now then, Pete, der yer want standard or full service?"

"Oh, full, definitely."

"Andy gives yer a *very* nice time. S'yer later."

"You do a long day here, Gloria."

"I doos mainly women, in the day. Andy doos reception then. His're in the evening, after work. I did recep this morning 'cos Andy was in late, after a *very* nice overnight job with someone *very* important round here – guess who!"

Both Dick and Gloria had looked a little surprised that I wanted full service. As we set off, I murmured to Dick that I had a reason. We made our way to the sauna, and as quickly as advisable to a room which was quite warm enough for both of us. We stretched out on benches. Dick did look good, even with less of the Spanish tan than in July. It would have been like this at the start of Jenny's hen party, three years before. My mind moved to the accounts I had heard...

Some weeks before the wedding, Jenny had phoned Liz, full of woe about having to invite her cousins, Angela and Penelope Frampton, to some kind of celebration. Liz recalled her 'little hen party' of two years before. Clorinda and Tisbe needed to be livened up, so what about some 'girlie fun'? Jenny said that Morag had been to a new sauna, which could be booked for private use. Two weeks before the wedding, Carol and Susie would be in Cambridge, because degree ceremonies took place in the morning. Liz needed to visit at about that time, for the fitting of her dress. So Jenny had sent out invitations. Morag and Carol were very pleased to come along. Susie was a little apprehensive. Jenny knew why Amanda wanted to come, though she had said that she wanted to meet more of Jenny's friends. Angela said it sounded good, and Penelope – Penny – tagged along.

Late on a hot and oppressive Saturday afternoon, Jenny and her seven guests headed for the sauna. Most of them were nearly there when caught by the unexpected and spectacular downpour that broke a glorious spell of weather through May Week. As Liz had said, that didn't matter too much. Before going into the heat, they spread out their clothes to dry.

At first, Angela, Penny and Susie kept towels bashfully around themselves, but Amanda was quick to join those who stretched out luxuriously on the benches and chatted. As at least some had hoped, physical bareness led to emotional bareness and frankness. Admiration of Jenny's body moved on to detailed anatomical comparisons, to which Amanda contributed various medical terms. Then there were lengthy reminiscences of partners, and favoured positions.

Liz talked about me and prompted Jenny and Carol to do so. Fortunately, Carol confined her remarks to the early days in Cambridge. Morag seemed to be interested.

Jenny and Liz compared notes about Dick, and then a knowing prompt from Liz brought Amanda in. Once started on reminiscences of foursome sunbaths, she didn't stop. The four had seen the first Moon walk on live TV at the Wingham house. The next day was a Monday, but nothing was happening at Jenny's office, so on a baking hot afternoon they were all back in the quiet garden. First Jenny had asked John to oil her, and three had enjoyed seeing him becoming very excited as he did so. Then they had reverted to their normal pairs, and had all become very excited. On a brotherly dare to Jenny, they had carried on to a finish. Amanda had been ecstatic to ride John, to the sight of Jenny's long legs over Dick's shoulders as he drove down into her.

Liz's disparaging remarks about Geoff Frampton had his sisters laughing, though they still remained covered. However, her account of Brian prompted Susie to drop her towel, and to compare him favourably with a series of earlier partners.

Then it was Morag's turn to describe life with her last boyfriend at Edinburgh, her first attempts with girls there, what she described as a near miss with me, occasions with Liz, and her longer time with Gill Watkinson, which had ended through Gill's recent departure from Cambridge. Morag also confided that the other single Fellows of Newnham didn't look to be as good prospects as she had hoped for when elected earlier in the year...

Harry came in, removed his swimming trunks and stretched out on a third bench.

"Dick, it's great to see you again. Andy told me you were coming here. And you too, Pete."

He was clearly surprised to see me. Dick was pleased to see him.

"It's great to see you, too, Harry. You look fit."

Harry did look fit, though even more the lean predator. Maybe I was imagining it, but he looked as if cornered in a hunt, and ready to strike out viciously.

"Welcome to what's really my club. It's open to the paying public, but I and a few others have put in enough to tidy up the pool and install these new facilities. We're not losing on the venture, and I'm well treated here. I try to do half an hour in the pool every day. I need it after business."

We all lay there, without saying much. Dick and Harry just looked at each other. More would doubtless have been said if I hadn't been there. My mind drifted back to what Liz and Carol had told me of the party...

Morag's mention of Gill had its intended impact. Angela's laughter turned to grimacing, and then she exclaimed tearfully how a week before she had been dumped by her boyfriend, who was Gill's cousin. She asked for reassurance that she wasn't that bad looking. Liz invited her to stand up, drop her towel, place her hands on the back of her head, and turn round slowly, keeping her legs a little apart. She was then assured that she had a fine body. Morag was particularly attentive and complementary. Then Penny received similar attention and assurance.

They emerged from the warm shower as eight bosom friends, with Liz's ample breasts well bounced, Jenny's nipples well fingered, Carol's flat chest well stroked, Morag's cleavage well investigated, and each of the others caressed in the ways it turned out that they liked best. Morag had made Angela feel particularly good…

After ten minutes, Harry thanked me for the invitation to the concert and left us. Dick and I cooled off, dried and continued to the massage room. There, Andy was already noticeably excited inside his white trunks. He did not seem displeased to see me, despite our earlier encounter. I hoped that he was not too sore after his hard night.

He was certainly an expert at his job. He moved back and forth between us, working more intimately each time. To see him work on Dick, before he did the same to me, fitted with my imagination…

The changing room was warm, it had comfortable seats and a couch, and Jenny had brought in an icebox full of champagne. No one wanted to put on clothes that were mostly still rather damp. The chatter was more and more excited, until Penny suddenly became mournful. Her current boyfriend wanted to take her from behind, but that left her cold. He was saying that she was frigid. Carol said that as a bottom girl herself, she wasn't surprised that the boyfriend was turned on by Penny's rear. She could show what worked for her, but she hadn't three hands and would need help. So Penny crouched in front of Liz, who supported and caressed her breasts, whilst from behind Carol fingered, stroked and gently smacked. After a little while, Carol produced her pot of Vaseline, greased another finger and felt Penny's ring round it. The result was spectacular…

Andy washed his hands and moved over to me for the last time.

"You have liked watching your friend. You liked watching before," I remember," he murmured.

I nodded. The combination of actuality, imagination and expectation did not leave him very much to do. I turned on to my front and spread my legs. He slid a pillow under me, then his left hand, and held and squeezed in a way which both stimulated and restrained. His right hand stroked my bottom gently, and then a finger moved in. The need for release grew almost unbearable.

"Are you thinking of who you love?" he asked.

I murmured assent, and he released his left hand's grip. As I thrashed up and down, he controlled me with his finger…

Jenny was well recovered from the quiet spell that had followed Amanda's account. She lay back at the end of the couch, with legs spread, and invited them to pleasure the Bride. Liz commenced her duties as Maid of Honour, by directing how they should do so.

Morag kissed deeply, whilst running a hand through Jenny's hair. Amanda and Susie fondled a breast each. Angela and Penny each had one hand raising a leg, the other stroking a buttock. In between them, Carol lay on her front, with Liz kneeling astride her bottom. Liz fingered harder and harder, and at a nod Carol's washed and newly greased finger slid gently through Jenny's rectum…

I pumped into the pillow to a vision of Jenny's writhing and yelling. After Andy left, we lay silent for a while…

An appreciative Jenny invited others to take turns on the couch. Morag took Angela's hand, gave her a very long kiss, and led her to it, for the 'Beth' that had begun their two-year relationship. Carol and Liz had an entertaining close-up from where they stayed in pleasurable body contact, and were very ready to try the same, with Liz's greased finger providing 'plus' to Carol. Susie gently fingered herself as she watched, and was next on the couch, with Penny.

Then the expression on Amanda's face changed from adoration to 'pure worship' as a smiling Jenny settled her onto the couch and moved her legs apart. Jenny licked her lips with relish as her hands felt Amanda's total submission, and with still more relish as the gentlest fingering drew the loudest yells of the day. She remained standing by the couch, and did not kiss Amanda. She had no need to do so.

All their clothes were well dry by the time they dressed…

Eventually, I was able to say something to Dick.

"I'm glad you liked the idea of my joining you."

"Harry didn't want you here."

"He's shown his hand. All this business with Andy has been to bring you here. If I hadn't come along, he would have watched Andy do you, and then taken you. Would you have wanted that?"

"I don't know, Pete. I really don't know what I would have wanted."

"It would have happened, whether you wanted it or not."

"I know that, but I need to make my own decisions. You do, and Jenny does, so why shouldn't I? Sometimes I think that the last decision I made myself was to take those pills."

I left Dick in this rather maudlin state, showered and dressed quickly, and returned to reception. Gloria looked very different from an hour before. She had been crying, and there was a red mark on her face.

"Hey, what's wrong, Gloria?" I asked.

"Aw, jest I'm done with here. No prob, we move round. There's a nice place in Soho where I'se known. I cin start there tomorrer and take several good regular payers wimme. But I donts like it this way. Howm' I ter know people're playin' games if they donts tell me?"

"You're better out of here. I can guess what happened. I'm sorry I caused it."

"Yer ain't caused it. Mind, I thought when yer comes in, odd, yer don't look queer. Then yer both takes full service, don't usually happen with two blokes. Wannit you chattin' up that smart older Yank? She was great. We both liked lookin' at each other."

"Yes, it was. We're together now, but she's away this week. I'll try anything once, or twice. When Dick suggested I join in, I was up for it. You were right. Andy gave us both a nice time. Mind you, I was hoping that Andy would be the man I was most taken with at that party. I don't know his name."

"T'would be Julian, or Robin. They was the other two for men there."

"I heard one of the others being called Julian, so it must be Robin. Do you know how I could contact him?"

"Yeah, got his card 'ere. Clients like changes, and we get kickbacks. Cin I give 'im yer name? E'll give you a harder time than Andy. Clients who want that go for 'im."

"Great, that's the man. Here's something instead of my name. I'm going away soon, so I may not catch up with him for a while. Good luck at your new place."

A fiver (with no VAT) bought a card showing the muscular man who had been third in July, and giving the address of a parlour in Richmond. The transaction helped to recover Gloria's spirits. You had to take these knocks in her trade, I guessed.

Dick appeared, and we set off for the Underground. I explained what had happened to Gloria, though not about Robin. Deliberately, I sounded rather uncaring as I concluded.

"It was lucky for Andy, as well as for us, that Gloria was on reception when I rang. He was doing very nicely out of both servicing Harry and being paid to work on you. He didn't want to succeed in enticing you. He's looking to go on with Harry, and he was able to put on to Gloria the blame for my being there. If when I rang he'd been on reception rather than with Harry, he'd have had to put me off."

"Harry's behaviour to Gloria has decided me, Pete. I won't come up here again. I'm sure that Jenny and you will be pleased about that."

"It's the right decision, Dick. If Harry or Andy contacts you, don't mention Gloria. We don't want her to be in more trouble."

"I'd have been interested in coming to the concert with you and Harry, but not now."

Dick's public school education had had a great emphasis on 'decency'. On this occasion it was serving him well, however much harm it had done to him otherwise. He had finally realised that Harry was not a gentleman.

We arrived at the pub to find everyone who was expected, except for Liz. Greg was nervous, but knew why she could be delayed.

"I heard on the radio that after the NUM had met Heath, they held their own meeting at No. 10. They've decided to continue the overtime ban, without calling a ballot."

"So, Heath has achieved nothing but to confirm that he's on the ropes," said Carol.

"He's been seen to 'Do Something', which is the basic aim of most politicians faced with a crisis," I said.

"The government has done something else," said Greg. "It's introduced an emergency Bill to control fuel supplies. It's not asked for advice on drafting from anyone who knows anything of the subject. If the Bill is needed, it will have to be completely rewritten to deliver any effective result at all."[40]

We agreed that thenceforward, anyone who mentioned coal, oil, electricity, miners or related subjects had to buy a round.

"So, can anyone think of *anything* good that Heath has done?" asked Morag, in a tone that indicated her answer.

"He's got us into the EEC, at last," said Dick.

"The rest knew he was desperate to get in," replied Brian, scornfully. "They knew they could screw us. They saw him coming, and skinned him alive."

---

40 As was said in Parliament the next day (29th November) by Arthur Palmer, the only MP who had technical knowledge of the electricity industry.

"There'll need to be a renegotiation, and a referendum," said Carol, once we had all laughed at the vision of portly Ted Heath being skinned.

"Maybe the new talks will lead to Northern Ireland settling down and an end to terrorism,"[41] said Sheila.

"I'm sure we all hope so. Any bets?" asked Greg.

There were none. I tried a mischievous change of subject.

"Carol, I'm sure you're pleased that Heath and his Education Secretary, Margaret Thatcher, are abolishing more grammar schools than Wilson and Crosland ever did."

"They're not abolishing them. Local education authorities are abolishing them – Conservative-controlled authorities like Surrey, as well as Labour and Liberal authorities. They're doing that because it's the right policy."

Dick's parents lived in Surrey, so he chipped in. "The people who run Surrey don't send their children to state schools, so they don't care about state schools. They're doing it because they think it's popular."

"I'm afraid that's right," I said. "IE's research labs are in Surrey, and I've talked to some of the people there. They've mostly benefitted themselves from going to grammar schools, but now they say that not selecting is much less stress for the kids, and for them. Their kids will stay with their friends, at a nice school since they're in a nice area. Basically, they're saying that they want a quiet life."

"It's all right for them," said Brian. "I had to get away from my friends, or end up down the pit. Bugger – my round."

Whilst he attended to that, I had a moment with Carol.

"You'll need to work out your line. Bellinghame used to be in Surrey, but it isn't now. It's staying selective. That has widespread support. The difference from Surrey is that lots of people aim to use the grammar schools."

---

41 These led to the 'Sunningdale Agreement', which had some similarities to the 'Good Friday Agreement' eventually reached in 1998, but included provision for a 'Council of Ireland', which was totally unacceptable to most Protestants. It collapsed in June 1974.

"I can emphasise local decision."

I lowered my voice and passed over the card.

"I posted the note, and here's the man your people need to talk to."

Carol's eyes widened. "Oh, *Pete*, how did you, what can I do…?"

"Through a lot of luck, and nothing tonight after how I did it, if that's what you're still thinking about. I'll tell you more, another time."

Brian and Susie returned with drinks, and we ordered food. There was still no Liz. Greg was rather silent and worried looking. Brian didn't help, by giving him a matey slap on the back and saying that he would get used to it. Susie did help, by continuing the conversation.

"Don't forget that Heath abolished Retail Price Maintenance.[42] That's been hard for small shops, but I'm sure it was right. I would say that, wouldn't I? I work in a big shop." She giggled.

"That's all very well," said Morag. "If the small shops go, how are people who don't live near a big shop going to be able to buy what they need?"

"Small shops can survive if they provide good service," I said. "If they don't, they won't, and why should they? People used my mother's family business, a drapery store, when the alternative was to take an hour's bus ride to Dorchester. Now, the combination of no RPM, more people having cars, and dozy management by my Uncle Edward looks like curtains for curtains in our town. It needn't have been like that, though. Most of you have met Roberta. She has far more intelligence and drive than Edward. She would have made a go of it. Coming back to Edward Heath, didn't I hear that he had a go at conducting the London Symphony Orchestra?"

"That was two years ago," said Dick. "Jenny and I were on our first evening out since David was born. In a pub near the theatre we heard an American voice. 'Yeah, he conducted Elgar's Overture *Cockaigne*. No, that's not about drugs.'"

---

42 The power which manufacturers had to impose a minimum selling price for goods. It was abolished in 1964.

"Steph wouldn't have made that mistake."

We carried on like this. Greg looked more and more anxious. Finally, at nearly nine o'clock, Liz arrived. She looked stressed, was full of apologies, and did not dispute others' suggestions that she had been held up on the Underground. Greg took her in his arms as we cheered. Susie admired her ring, and I collected the champagne I had ordered.

"Smoked salmon sandwich?" I murmured to Liz as I poured.

"Oh, *yes*. I've had nothing since lunch."

I had ordered it with my food, and it was behind the bar. I knew how tense Liz would feel inside. Pending the right treatment from Greg later, this was a substitute. Dick launched in.

"Liz, to those of us who've known you for so long, it really is marvellous that you have now found the right man. Greg, we've not known you for so long, but welcome and heartfelt congratulations on a very wise choice."

From that rather pompous start, the occasion bubbled on. To myself, I recalled the grand party of five years before. Then, I had headed Brian off from making a drunken fool of himself. That had led to Jenny becoming attracted to Dick, and had given Carol a chance to try her luck with me.

Soon after ten o'clock Dick made to leave, because he had furthest to travel, but first he had a message of another happy event.

"You're all invited to Katie's christening, which will be in Pembroke College Chapel on Sunday, 3rd March. There's a degree ceremony the day before, so those of you due for MAs can take them then, and dine at Waterhouse High Table in the evening, or in New Hall, for you of course, Carol."[43]

"New Hall will be dead on a Saturday. I hope Paul can take me into Waterhouse."

"Yes, he'll be able to do that," I confirmed.

---

43 At Cambridge, one is eligible for the Master of Arts (MA) degree ten terms after graduation, so those who went up in 1967 and graduated in 1970 were to be eligible from the start of 1974.

Jenny's parents weren't at all religious, but her mother liked to do the right thing, and her father was a Fellow of Pembroke. I could see Jenny's practical hand in selecting the date.

Sheila handed round invitations and location maps, in connection with another message.

"On 22nd December, the Saturday before Christmas, come over at about six o'clock to see what we do for women victims at the Pankhurst Centre. Bring a bottle. Donations are invited, of course, even if you can't come."

Susie and Brian left also. Whilst Greg was talking to Sheila and Morag, I found myself with Liz.

"Pete, thanks again so much for your help in getting us this far. I may need to talk to you more. I didn't give the real reason why I was late. I was with the Coal Board team that briefed Heath. He's just like how you see him on TV. Then only I stayed, since we aren't part of the process any more. I was in a side room during the meeting."

"How on earth does Ezra think that he can continue, when he's treated like this?"

"He knows what he wants. Heath is paying for not keeping Robens. Anyway, I had to stay around during the NUM 's own meeting. You know the result of that. Then there were a lot of press and TV people outside, and I kept out of the way. So, it wasn't until much later that I came out into Downing Street. Some of the NUM people were still talking to each other or to reporters, but it was breaking up. Then, he spotted me and said, gosh he needed a drink – not with them, but not alone, and where we wouldn't be bothered."

"Who spotted you?"

She mentioned the name of a very senior man in the NUM.

"At several meetings over the last few months, I've noticed him smiling at me, and I suppose I smiled back. We went off to what seemed to be a kind of small club over near St James's Square. The drink went to several. He was soon telling me loads about where others in the NUM were on the negotiations, and about Heath. A lot of it I knew or had guessed. Heath more or less promised him in July that there would be a special payment to miners for 'unsocial hours' that then turned out to be available for everyone under Stage 3. Today's meeting had been quite useless, and had ended any chance that the NUM would call off the overtime ban. There was plenty that I didn't know, though. Tomorrow, I'll have quite a lot to write up."

"That sounds really worth being late for. I thought something important must have happened. You've always been punctual, but you had a special reason tonight."

"You haven't heard it all yet, Pete. He noticed that my ring was new, and congratulated me. That allowed me to say I needed to get away. He apologised for keeping me, and said he had been hoping that I could have dinner with him there. He suggested that perhaps we could find another night, soon. He wanted to talk about whether I would be interested in taking over from someone on the NUM's office staff who retires in the summer. The job would be to organise briefing for meetings of the National Executive, and statements for them to sign off. He had seen me in action, and so had some of his colleagues. They didn't agree on everything, but they did agree that I was someone who could do the job and wasn't linked to any faction. He gave me his private number."

"Wow. That would be an interesting move for you, Liz. It wouldn't happen until the summer, by which time all this will presumably be over, one way or another. Your boss being sick gives you the opening to go straight to his boss."

"That's the Board's Secretary."

"He'll have to move you up, or let you go. Meanwhile, you've opened up a new informal line of communication with the NUM. We certainly need that, right now."

"Why is this happening, Pete?"

"You're being talent-spotted."

"It's more than that. The place we went to is very discreet. We were in a quiet corner of the bar, but I saw several older men, one or two of whom I recognised. Their companions were mostly women of around my age. There are private dining rooms, rather than a restaurant, and you can go upstairs afterwards."

"He knows that you've a good reason for not going upstairs."

"How good a reason is it, as seen by this man? In coal, men run things and have what they want. One of the Area Directors must have told him about me. I'll be OK whilst I'm engaged. When I'm a married woman, I'll be fair game. Meanwhile, what do I do? If I tell Greg what I've told you, he'll be all uptight."

"Start by telling him about meeting Heath, the drinks, and the possibility of a job. He'll know that's important. There can't be any conditions on the job. Now, I see Morag and Sheila picking up their coats, and coming over. You must say goodbye."

8. WEDNESDAY, 12TH DECEMBER, 1973

"Bugger." Brian was not happy when he finally arrived, just before ten o'clock.

"Let me make you a coffee," said Morag, solicitously.

"When I heard there were no trains, I thought I could catch a bus most of the way here. But could I get on one? Eventually I caught one going the other way, and stayed on it when it turned round. That was a good move. Some of the people in front of me at my stop were still there when I passed it. It's no surprise that ASLEF has put the boot in, I guess. Heath is on the floor. He's such a tempting target. He represents Bexley, where people are totally dependent on the trains to get to work."

Morag made tut-tutting noises, but was less full of socialist solidarity than usual. This was perhaps out of deference to Tony Higgins, whose dim view of the train drivers' union had already been expressed.

For an hour, she and I had been sitting in his office, viewing a suitcase-sized box full of electronics, linked to a teletype machine and a cassette tape recorder. An electric fan was blowing to keep it all cool. At the heart of the set-up was an object which resembled a large centipede with golden legs. This was an Intel 8008 microprocessor, the latest model, capable of handling 16,384 bytes of memory. Over the previous three months, Tony had built the system around it. It was nearer to the 'suitcase computer' than anything I had seen before.

Over an early breakfast before Steph set off for a meeting in Rotterdam, she and I had heard on the radio that ASLEF had found a way to intensify the effect of the overtime ban and work to rule that they began that morning in pursuit of a pay claim that breached Stage 3. The electric trains used for local services in south London never went very fast. A few years before, someone in management had concluded that there was no evidence that the drivers actually used the fitted speedometers, rather than judging their speed by eye. Therefore, the speedometers had been removed, in order to economise on maintenance costs. So, the trains were technically defective, and unfit to drive. So now no local trains were running, whilst the drivers sat at the depots drawing full basic pay for doing nothing. The Underground was not involved in the dispute, but did not go anywhere near Bexley.

Brian carried on, once we had settled him down.

"It's ridiculous. The rail management has said that the petrol shortage means fare revenue is up enough to cover the cost of a pay increase that should allow them to retain enough staff to actually run the full timetable. Heath has ignored that, saying it's all for this damn Pay Board he's set up.[44] Who *is* in charge?"

"Clearly, not the management," said Tony. "They've copped out, like the Coal Board management. They've given the clear message that ASLEF, like the NUM, is fighting the government, not them. They haven't sacked the man who decided to remove the speedometers."

"The management of the railways is good at copping out," I said. "It's been so committed to making services unattractive to use and then closing them that it's no good at spotting fast-growing markets, for example travel to and from Aberdeen. The flights are pretty unreliable. You have to travel the day before and stay over if you want to be sure of a meeting in the morning. I've tried the night sleeper train. I'm told it used to be very good. You left after work, had dinner on the train, and were there early the next morning. Then as an economy measure the

---

44 A feature of Stage 3.

restaurant car was taken off. The sleeping cars are now so old and ill maintained that you can't sleep. A new train with proper service could charge high fares and make a profit. The railways management should speak to people hanging around waiting for planes. Anyway, whilst hanging around waiting for planes I've read magazines for computer enthusiasts, but I've never seen their work for real, so let's carry on, Tony."

Tony would now be described as a 'geek'. He looked the part, being a shortish man in his thirties with heavy glasses and long dark hair. His talk was peppered with names later to become world famous, and other names which have been forgotten. He had acquired the 8008 whilst on a visit to California in the summer. He was clearly pleased that Morag had introduced him to me and Brian, as we represented an electronics manufacturer and a large potential user.

He had shown me details of construction and components. Now, he showed Brian what the machine could do. First, he played a tape cassette into the computer.

"Type *TYPE. The asterisk indicates that this is an instruction. Then type some words."

Brian sat at the teletype machine and did so.

"Make a mistake, and go on typing."

Brian misspelt a word, and typed three more words.

"Now type *CORRECT 3, the right word, and then *PRINT."

Brian did all that, and the teletype repeated what he had typed, with the correction made three words back. It was all in capitals and in no fancy font, but represented a start towards the word processor I'm using now. There were also *SAVE and *LOAD commands, for whose use you changed the tape cassette to one used to store data.

Tony played another tape in, and we were invited to type instructions in the fairly well known BASIC computer language. I wrote a simple program, corrected it, and obtained results.

"This doesn't feel very different from working at the terminal in your office, Brian," I said. "That's linked by phone to a full-size computer, Tony. Let me see how much more I can do."

I tried expanding the size of the data until the teletype churned out a message that the computer had run out of space. Then, Brian produced two sheets of instructions.

"Here's my program about insurance risks, as it was after our talk in the summer, Pete. Tony, do you think you could run this?"

"We'll have a try. How long have you all got?"

"Until a quarter past twelve," I replied. "Could I make a couple of local phone calls?"

"Yes, use the office next door. The bloke there is out today."

Tony began to type. Morag had to leave us to give a lecture. I called the office, to say that I would be in after lunch, and then Carol, to confirm arrangements for the evening. I asked her a question.

"What will you say about ASLEF? Tonight, you'll meet a lot of annoyed people."

"I'll repeat Harold Wilson's quote for the evening papers. This is an unnecessary dispute, created by the government's inflexible and unrealistic policies."

"Fine, we all know that, but why is it happening just *now*? The rail pay settlement date is April, and always has been. I think your man should put that in his pipe and smoke on it, thoughtfully. Does he want to be in charge of the Opposition?"

"We'll talk later. I'll be ready, Pete."

"I've booked a spot in the Barbican garage, because on Friday afternoon I need to be out at Chelmsford. I'll drive up tonight, and can drop you off on the way."

I returned to Tony's office, where input was nearly complete. After twenty minutes of tries, the program ran.

"Great. That's the right answer. Try this data," said Brian.

The answer was right, again. Then the computer stopped.

"Damn, it's overheating," said Tony. "We'll need to let it cool down, for an hour or so."

The room was very warm, despite the efforts of the fan. I pointed to a large transformer and rectifier which were delivering a low voltage supply.

"How much power does it use?"

"Nearly a kilowatt, plus what the teletype uses. That's the problem about making all this small enough to be carried around, which I know is what prospective customers like Brian need. If the components are more spread out, the heat can be carried away more easily."

"You need parts that do the same work as the present parts, but are smaller and use a lot less power. I suggest a maximum of about 100 watts. You also need a small keyboard and printer. Then it can all be boxed up, and cooled by a fan in the casing. Have you a list of the parts you've used?"

"Yes." He pulled from the drawer several well-thumbed sheets.

"Do you know of our research labs near Staines?"

"Yes, a couple of students of mine have found jobs there."

"Good. I think people there would like to see this set-up. Also, they can look at your list, and say if there are alternative components already available which use less power. If there aren't, then they can work out the specification that's needed. It's important to IE to know what we'll need to make."

"With a few days' notice, I can put all this in my car and set it up down there. It's transportable, if not portable."

"Good. How much did that 8008 cost you?"

"$100. I just avoided paying import duty on it. The price will come down, and the product will get better."

"My guess, and this is a guess, is that if the right parts were available for a reasonable price, and allowing for labour costs and overheads, then given a decent production run a finished product could be on the market for about £3,000."

"That's a lot," said Brian. "We have over a thousand sales people. We haven't £3 million to spend."

"It won't happen like that," said Tony. "By the time anything came to the market, it would be obsolete."

We talked on, until I realised that it was twenty past twelve. I took a copy of the parts list and promised to be in touch shortly.

Liz had asked me to meet her in a pub opposite St James's Park Underground. This was not too far from the Coal Board offices, but far enough away not to be used by colleagues of hers. Also, it was then fairly quiet, because the nearby government offices which had generated most of its business were being demolished, to make way for the hideous building which would become the headquarters of the Home Office.[45] She arrived just after me, and once we were settled, began breathlessly.

"I must be back at half past one. All the morning I've been on last-minute briefing for this afternoon's Statement renewing the state of emergency. There may be a further call from you know where, any time from then till it's made. Well, I talked to the Secretary. He was all in favour of my meeting the man again. He said that he knew I had the sense to handle it, and that just now we need any information we can get. He asked me to keep him in touch. He's also had me temporarily upgraded, so now I'm as senior as any other woman in the Board."

"What about Greg?"

"He seemed pretty impressed, and realised it's important. He wondered how long I expected to work after we married, but he didn't press it. I called the private number, and said that I was interested, but I was quite tied up in the evenings. I asked if we could meet for lunch."

"That was a good idea, Liz. You gave a gentle and respectful message. 'I know what *you're* up to, but let's keep this professional'. So, what happened?"

"We lunched last Friday, at the same place as he took me before. It was a long and good lunch, but however busy it is in our

---

45 It is now the headquarters of the Ministry of Justice.

industry from Monday to Thursday, nothing happens on Friday. The union doesn't stint on expenses for their senior people. I paced myself on the drink whilst making it clear that I can take it. He asked me what I was getting from the Board. I gave him the figure including the upgrade, and he said that the job is mine from June, on £500 more. During the union's Annual Conference early in July, I would overlap with the current holder. I said that there should be no problem with my moving then, assuming the current dispute was resolved. He smiled and said he was sure it would be. I said I was grateful to him for the offer, and was ready to accept it, if confirmed in writing. It fitted in well with my personal plans. I would leave the Board at the end of April, just before being married. We're planning that for 4th May."

"This sounds great, Liz. Very well done."

We had finished eating. Before continuing, Liz lit a cigarette. This was perfectly normal behaviour then, and did not bother me, though I've never smoked myself.

"That's what I thought, but the meal wasn't over, not at all over. He told me all his woes. You can imagine who featured in *them*. He said more about the talks with Heath, stuff that no one in the Board knew. That certainly earned me my time out of the office when I reported back. Then he came on to his personal life, saying what he missed, and what he needed. In a perfectly gentlemanly way, he made it clear I featured in that. I picked my words carefully. It was very kind of him to think so well of me. I'd respected him from the first time I met him. Now I liked him, too. I looked forward to the opportunity he was offering me. I would make my own decisions, *after* I had taken the job. I would not accept the job on *any* precondition. He said he understood me, indeed he thought better of me for it."

"So do I, Liz. You've the toughness to work with him, and the others there. I knew that already. Now he knows it, too. He and you know where the other is. He'll respect that. He may have left school at fourteen, but he's not stupid. He clearly understands people very well. By the time that you arrive with a nice new wedding ring, he may well have found someone else."

"Perhaps – that's what worries me, perhaps."

"What do you mean?"

"As I sat there looking at him, a strong and handsome man though much older than me, I began to realise that *actually, I wanted him.* I think I showed it in my eyes. That's how he understood me. He doesn't *need* to make any precondition. He can wait for my decision. That's why I need your help, Pete. You're the brother I never had. You've known me for a long time, and I think you understand me better than anyone else. I worked to land Greg. I know he's right for me. I want to settle down with him, and to raise a family with him, *but I want this man, too.* It's the same as when I wanted to make a go with Geoff, but I couldn't let go of Brian. If I'm working for the union, I'll be torn apart."

"Perhaps you'd better not go there, then, Liz. Your happiness is the most important thing of all."

"My happiness isn't just about being with Greg. I want to fulfil myself. Look at it this way, Pete. Your career is going very well. In fifteen years or so, you could be running International Electronics, or something similar. You've justified leaving Cambridge. Whatever we say about Harry Tamfield, he's also justified leaving. He's taken risks and trampled on people, but he's already head of a big property company. Jenny has pushed on while raising a family. In ten years, she could be a partner in her firm. Well, I left Cambridge, too. I didn't put up with Geoff and join the Frampton gang. What have I done, since?"

"You're doing a pretty important job, right now."

"The job is hard work, and I mustn't make mistakes, but there's no scope to make a difference, and no opportunity to progress further from what I'm effectively doing now. So, it's not really important. The way things are going, the job I've been offered could be very important. On that union's National Executive Committee, there are all sorts of different views. They need to be brought together in a way that all will accept, and which gets the best result possible for the members. That will be important for us all during the next few years, whatever happens during the next few months."

"I understand that. Have you talked to Greg about this?"

"We've talked, and talked, and talked, right through the weekend, and on Monday evening. He knows a lot more about me now – including about Morag, and about Jenny's hen party. Yesterday, neither of us had time. I've been as frank with him as I've been with you. I can't do something that he doesn't accept."

"What you want him to accept is that he should marry you, whilst knowing that he *may* not be your only man. That's quite a tall order for Greg, especially with his background."

"I know. Greg wants me, and I want Greg. We suit each other, physically and in our interests. You said to both of us that we're a good match. You're right, Pete, but I want this job, too."

"And, as you've said, you may want this man, too."

"Yes. I'm asking Greg to be rather like Paul, who accepted that he had to share Carol with you."

"As you know, Liz, there were some reasons. There came the time when he wanted her solo, and that was the right time for me, too. Soon afterwards, I went off to Spain. Nothing has happened since then."

"She still likes you being around."

"We've had some things to talk about. There's another rumpus involving Harry's company and the estate where my aunt lives. Tonight, I'm taking her to a meeting there. Let's return to the point. You're asking Greg to risk being a compliant husband, right from the start."

"Yes, because I think I can make a difference, as well as because that's me."

"How could you have a family if this were going on?"

"I've said to Greg that then, I'll leave the job. It will have to be within five years. If I can't make a difference in that time, I never will. I've also said that there's one thing he can be sure of. This will not be public. Apart from my man, no one but you and Greg will know."

"Why have you told me?"

"Greg suggested that I should. He thinks you'll knock some sense into me."

"I don't know what course *is* sense for you, and for him. It's nearly quarter past one. You need to be getting back. Have you received a written offer?"

"It arrived yesterday, with a personal note at the bottom, saying that it stays open until the current dispute is settled."

"So, you don't need to make a decision, yet. What do you want me to do?"

"Talk to Greg, as soon as possible, and persuade him that he should agree. Can I say that you'll meet him here, at the same time tomorrow? His office isn't far away."

"I'll do my best for you, Liz. You're the sister I never had, I owe you a great deal, and I want to see you fulfilled and happy. I'm not a marriage guidance consultant, though, and I don't know Greg very well. I don't want to make things worse."

"You won't. I trust you, Pete. You're my brother."

She leaned over and kissed me, and then she was away, in time to provide any more briefing that was needed. She looked less tense for being able to talk things through.

I couldn't see what I could do to help her and Greg, but perhaps talking it through would help him, as well. They were another couple facing the then largely new issues of reconciling partnership with individual aims. Despite not being a marriage guidance consultant, perhaps I could do as well for them as, by luck, I had done for the Sinclairs.

Jenny had given me a cheerful call. Dick was shocked at what had happened to Gloria, and at the change in Harry that it showed, but pleased that he had found that out by acting for himself, and by making his own decisions. So, he could be his own man, *and* be with her. That was bringing them closer. He was working all hours, mostly at home, on an idea in his research.

Ana and Carlos were doing well, too. In Madrid, I had heard more plans for their wedding. On my return, I had mentioned their invitation to Steph. She liked the idea of attending, but wasn't sure when she would be going back to the USA. I had got rid of Ana's rather imaginative note. Although I could not actually envisage Steph becoming a member of the Spanish aristocracy, I hadn't wanted her to find it when tidying up my suit.

Back at the office, typing of the final version of my paper for IE's Board on the North Sea sales office was going well. The few mistakes were mostly treatable with correction fluid. Only one page would need to be retyped, and by luck that was the only page on which I had noticed a few extra words which could with advantage go in. This was going to be worth some nice Christmas presents, especially as following the computer demonstration I would have another tricky technical note for typing. I spent most of the afternoon working on that.

I was nearing the end of two weeks of frantic effort. The weekend before last, Steph had also been busy; our only break had been a 'memory lane' Saturday evening for me – a performance of *Don Giovanni* at the Royal Opera House, which had been well timed to provide a talking point in Madrid. Just before I went there with George Armstrong, I had posted a draft of the paper to Terry McAvitt in Leeds. In the course of an hour's telephone meeting with him soon after my return, he had put several questions which he knew that other directors would raise, concerning possible threats to their autonomy. Work on answering these questions had occupied me right through the last weekend and to last evening.

Steph's meeting in Rotterdam was to discuss the final settlement arrangements for the oil trading fund. Paul was doubtless at the same meeting, which was scheduled to continue the next morning. So I had been expecting the message from Pat's office that summoned me, along with George and Paul, to a meeting late the next afternoon. We would review the arrangements, and also the outcome of the visit to Madrid.

At five o'clock I was down at reception, to greet Carol. She had been at an afternoon meeting in Camden Town Hall, so it was convenient for her to join me there.

"Wow, you do look smart. You're dressed to impress. Do you want help with that bag?"

"No, it's fine. Steph told me about the shop she uses. I decided to splash out. I collected this yesterday."

"I've bought my ticket, from St Paul's Station. It'll be easier to go down there. The queues for the escalators at Bank will be horrendous today."

I knew that Carol and Paul usually travelled in on the Northern Line, and had season tickets. Our journey began well enough. We crammed on to a Central Line train to go the one stop to Bank, where we could reach the Northern Line platforms quite easily. However, as we pulled into a crowded platform, I realised my mistake. The doors opened on the opposite side of the train to that on which we had boarded, and tightly packed people blocked our way. Unless I made an effort, we were going to end up in Leytonstone, or South Woodford. After twice saying 'excuse me' to no avail, I shoved across the train as hard as possible.

The effect was spectacular. There must have been a near balance between people on the platform trying to get on and those on the train trying to avoid being even more squashed. My shove gave the latter a momentary advantage. Within seconds, some thirty people between us and the doors had spilled out on to the platform, pushing those there aside. Carol and I stepped out at our leisure.

"Just shows, let passengers get off first," I murmured.

We in turn squeezed on to a Northern Line train and headed for Morden. There, I knew where to catch a bus which stopped nearby, rather than join the queue outside the station. We were with Roberta soon after half past six.

A few days after I posted my anonymous envelope, Roberta had called me, to describe a circular from the Bishop's Park Residents' Association. I followed shock and sympathy with practical suggestions. They should call a residents' meeting. They should ask Frank to look at the legal position. They should write to Tamfield Investments, their Borough councillors, the Council offices, the GLC, the local newspapers, and their MP; and also to other parliamentary candidates, including Carol whom she had met in July. Most of this had been already in hand. On Sunday, Roberta had called again, to say that the meeting was set for eight o'clock today. She also said that the Labour Party office hadn't replied about their candidate coming along, so I promised to bring Carol myself.

Roberta was grateful to see us, but agitated.

"What *have* we done? You'll need the answers, my dear, particularly about *this*."

She handed Carol that day's *Bellinghame Record*, with its headline:

'SNOBS' TAUNT IN HOMES ROW

The lead article stated that the local Labour Party had described the Bishop's Park residents as 'greedy, uncaring snobs' for objecting to living next to an overspill council estate. Carol's grimace at being addressed as 'my dear' turned to grim silence as she read through the article. Frank Booth's arrival spared her from responding straightaway.

"I've spoken to the *Advertiser*. They're sending a reporter, and a photographer. They won't want the *Record* to make the running on this."

Over dinner, I engaged with Roberta and Frank. I realised that Carol would want to listen and think.

At five to eight, we arrived at a nearby church hall, and Frank introduced Carol to the organisers. Once she had emptied her bag, to add to the stacks of papers on a side table, they both took seats on the platform. Roberta and I sat a little back in the audience, which by five past eight numbered about sixty. In cold and drab surroundings, the meeting got under way.

The chairman was a middle-aged man who knew it all, because he worked for the housing department of another London borough. He began by thanking his wife, who was the secretary, for circulating a note to residents so quickly and for booking this hall. He explained fairly clearly (and correctly, as Carol said afterwards) the powers of the GLC. He then introduced Frank, who many of them knew already through their recent purchases. The committee was very grateful for his advice, given without charge.

Frank confirmed that there was no legal remedy the residents could seek, and referred to his discussions with two local estate agents. They both considered that having the overspill estate nearby would make it very difficult to sell properties for some time, and would reduce values by some 10%, or more if there were difficulties with many of the tenants. Therefore, anyone who had a mortgage of 90% or more, and these were now fairly common, was facing – a new phrase then – 'negative equity'. Frank also said that it was an open secret that almost all prospective purchasers who had not exchanged contracts had withdrawn.

By now it was half past eight, and the audience had expanded to well over a hundred. One of the late arrivals was a tallish man in his fifties, who was sitting next to Carol. The chairman looked at the reporters and continued.

"We now have represented here over half of the households presently at Bishop's Park, and more are arriving. On an evening when travelling has been such an ordeal, this shows how concerned we all are. Whatever the exact legal position, Tamfield Investments has let us down, and shown contempt for its customers. Let future buyers beware. Tamfield Investments and the GLC have confirmed that discussions have taken place, but neither has accepted our invitation to send representatives to this meeting. Bellinghame Borough Council has also declined our invitation, though it has sent us a letter, a copy of which you can pick up from the side table. The letter states that the Council has asked the GLC for information as to what tenants it would intend to place in the properties, so that an evaluation of the demand for local services can be made. The GLC has yet to respond."

"We have also contacted Sir Reginald Emerson MP and the prospective parliamentary candidates of the other main parties. Sir Reginald has expressed concern and sympathy for our position, but says that he's sure we understand that as a minister he cannot comment further. He can't be with us tonight, owing to parliamentary commitments. However, we are pleased to welcome Mr Cyril Horsley, who has contested this constituency for the Liberal Party, and Mrs Carol Milverton, who has recently been adopted as the candidate of the Labour Party. I believe they've agreed that Mr Horsley should comment first."

He motioned towards the tallish man. I could guess why Carol wanted to defer to age, position in the last election, or whatever. Cyril Horsley began, to some smiles and waves in the audience.

"First, I must apologise for being late. Like many of you, I was delayed in my return here from Central London. However, your chairman visited me last Saturday, so I think I am au fait with the issue. The unacceptable faces of capitalism and socialism have met, and you are all trapped in between. If this sale goes through, and of course that is not definite yet, you need clear assurances, *very* clear assurances, that the quality of tenant will be appropriate to this area. Regrettably, Bellinghame has not elected a Liberal Greater London councillor. However, Sutton has done so, and I will be working with her, to ensure that these assurances are obtained."

He went on like this for some minutes, sounding good whilst saying nothing. Then he sat, and Carol stood. Before she could say anything, there was a shout from someone sitting a few places along from me.

"Are we greedy, uncaring snobs then?"

The chairman frowned at the interruption, but a plant couldn't have been better.

"No, you are not. That stupid remark, which I heard about only today, does not reflect Labour Party policy. You are quite right to be concerned about your position. You've paid a great deal of money for your houses and flats – twice as much as you would have paid two years ago, when building here started. That suggests a jolly good profit for someone, to quote Ian Carmichael."[46]

She paused for a murmur of amusement, before continuing.

"Now, when things get difficult, you feel that the response is to solve the problem at your expense. I'm very glad to be here tonight, because what you need is a constructive solution which protects your position *and* allows people who are currently very badly housed to progress to something better. I've put on the side table some pictures of the way some people live now in London. Please look at them.

"Let me tell you what I've done so far towards such a solution. I'm in touch with the Greater London councillors who actually take the decisions on matters like this. I've pressed for the kind of assurance which Cyril has described. More precisely, I've said that a GLC estate here could be acceptable only if it was clear that all tenants regarded moving here as an opportunity to better themselves. There's no place here for layabouts or

---

46 In the film, *I'm all right Jack* which then would have been familiar to all.

troublemakers. The response I've had is positive. I've said that I expect to see in writing the selection procedures and rules of conduct that the GLC would propose. That's a start. There's more to be done, but it's a start."

"Will there be Pakis?"

This shout was followed by some murmurs of 'shush'. It was more manna from heaven for Carol. There weren't so many black and brown faces at the meeting as there would be now, but there were a few.

"With respect, I don't like the tone of that question, and I don't think most of you like it, either. There could be immigrants, if they are here to better themselves."

Another voice was more measured.

"I welcome the effort you're making, and I'm sure others here welcome it too, but you've only just been adopted as a candidate. How do you think you can make a difference, when others can't?"

"I'll make a difference by trying a bit harder and using what and who I know. I have housing in my blood. My father is a Manchester City councillor, and chair of the housing committee. My present job in the Labour Party means I know who to contact. I would say also that whilst this isn't the time for political points, I'm surprised that Sir Reg Emerson isn't here because of parliamentary business. Tonight's main debate is on the Defence Estimates, with no division expected, and accordingly there is a one-line whip. As a minister in another department, he won't be speaking."

The meeting was warming to Carol. She got away with the party line on ASLEF. There were a few more questions, and then some discussion which was quite emotional but did not throw up any practical proposals.

The chairman brought the meeting to an end by thanking Frank, Cyril Horsley and Carol, and saying that he would write again to Tamfield Investments, the GLC, the borough council, and Sir Reg, recording the views so strongly expressed. He hoped too that the press representatives would continue to report the residents' case.

Afterwards, a group developed round Carol and Frank, to which the press gave attention. Roberta and I kept in the background. Eventually it was time to leave, and the four of us came outside. A flashbulb went off, and a young woman reporter addressed me, breathlessly.

"Mr Milverton, what does it *feel* like to be married to a parliamentary candidate? Does it take up *all* your time?"

"I don't know, because I'm not Mr Milverton. I've known Carol, and her husband Paul, since we were all at Cambridge a few years back. Currently, he's abroad on business, for the same company as I work for, in fact. I'm here because Mrs Strutt, my aunt, has recently moved to Bishop's Park."

"Yes, Pete is so supportive at this worrying time; and you've heard how much Frank Booth and Carol Milverton are doing for us."

Roberta's best 'dear old lady' manner seemed to satisfy them, and soon we were drinking coffee back at her bungalow. Frank gave Carol his card.

"You did well, young lady. To keep in touch, call me. As you spotted, the chairman is a strong Liberal supporter. He's trying to raise something for dear old Cyril out of Reg not giving a damn, but dear old Cyril has been around here for years and years, getting nowhere. You on the other hand are a refreshing change from your predecessor, who couldn't put three words together coherently."

Carol contained herself at Frank's mode of addressing her, and passed him her card.

"Thanks. I thought it would work, letting Cyril go first. Make sure the follow-up letters go out quickly, openly copied to Reg, Cyril and me, and send me copies straightaway."

I went off to my room, to pack a few things that I was taking up with me. A few minutes later, Carol came in, took off her jacket and began to unbutton her blouse. I smiled at her.

"Hey, what's all this?"

"I told them I would see if you needed any help with packing. Actually, I must get this bra off. It's really chafing me, and the clip is stuck."

"Ah, yes I see, it's the same as Steph's, not the standard type."

"There speaks a man experienced in removing bras."

"Until Steph, not that experienced, actually. You never wore one. Liz and Jenny usually undressed themselves."

"Ana gave you some experience, I gather."

"Mmm. Ah, here goes."

"Ooh, that's better. A quick rub would make it better still."

"Never miss a move, that's the Carol I know. It *is* a bit red there."

For a minute or so there were sighs of satisfaction as we faced the wardrobe mirror and I stroked her chest gently. Then she got dressed again. With her jacket buttoned, she didn't look noticeably different from before.

"Great, Pete, you've not lost the touch. I knew that anyway, from talking to Steph down in Brighton. I won't take her shop's advice on bras again, though."

"Don't worry about putting on that extra weight. It's filled you out very nicely."

Soon we were saying our farewells. On the way to Tooting, we had a chance to catch up.

"You've made quite an impact, but you've set yourself up to deliver, Carol. What are your plans?"

"As I said a fortnight ago, I want to move it on towards a housing association solution. The timing depends on what happens to Tamfield and the banks, as well as on any election. Gosh, if that had been a real meeting I would have had Cyril on the ropes. He had the nerve to talk about the unacceptable face of capitalism, when his leader, Jeremy Thorpe, is a director of

London and County Securities! It was definitely 'be nice to dear old Cyril' day. What a phrase of Frank's. Cyril looks about the same age as him."

"Frank and Roberta are both mentally younger, since they've been together."

"Oooh yes, that's nice to think of for them." She shifted her legs.

"Frank is a very useful ally for you, Carol. Through the Rotary Club, he's well known around here in circles that matter. Now, how are things going with Robin?"

"We sent someone suitable along and he had a great time. He said he'd been tipped off by Reg, and noticed the response. Then we brought in the *Clarion*, whom we trust, and the money got talked. The upshot is a big story. In July, Reg was provided with this guy by Tamfield. He's been having very full and regular services ever since."

"By Tamfield, do you mean Harry personally, or Tamfield Investments?"

"His charges are paid by Tamfield Investments."

"So, all shareholders are forking out for Robin."

"Yes. Now, the problem is keeping the lid on until we want the story out. You never told me how you got on to him, Pete. Turn left here, then second right."

I had my cover story ready for this.

"When I visited the Tamfield offices back in July, I noticed a club nearby which offered massage and other services. It occurred to me that some of the hosts at Harry's party might work there. That day we had lunch, I called in before coming on to the pub. The start was encouraging. Gloria, on reception, was the women's winner who looked so good in a swimsuit. I recalled the party, and said I would be interested in a massage from one of the men. It turned out that the one called Andy, not the one we wanted remember, worked at the club and could do me straightaway. I took all the trimmings for the experience and because Steph was away. That left me quite exhausted, as I told you later. Afterwards, I said to Gloria that I'd liked it with Andy, but I'd been even more attracted by the look of one of the other men. Of course, she had cards handy in her desk."

"From what our man said, I can guess what you went through, Pete. We're nearly there, now. Turn left here, and be careful. There are a lot of parked cars. Once you've passed them, pull in."

"Andy wasn't too bad. He delivered rather the equivalent for a bloke of how you like it. I gather Robin's technique is less gentle, and perhaps more suitable for a man who's fully homosexual."

We pulled up outside a block of maisonettes. Her right hand moved over to feel me, and she shifted her legs more.

"Here we are. Pete, you're not exhausted now, are you? We've done darn well together today. There's no point in us both being alone tonight. Mmm, yes, you would like, wouldn't you?"

For the second time that evening, I was surprised at what she had said, though not for the most obvious reason.

"Carol, of course I'd like, if you and Paul have decided to be open. Not tonight though, for three reasons which are all good, though temporary. First, Paul still reports to me on some business. Secondly, if you're going to demolish Reg Emerson, the last thing you want is any suggestion of hanky-panky by you, with me or with anyone else! Third, and most important, someone is watching us."

"What do you mean?"

"Three behind us is a car with someone inside. That same car was parked in the road we walked along from the meeting to Roberta's house. There's no reason I can think of why someone from around here should be at the meeting."

"Are you sure it's the same car?"

"Yes. Once you're a mathematician, you're always a mathematician. I thought the registration was interesting when I noticed it earlier – ACG 137K."

"What's so interesting about that?"

"The first three letters are the first, third and seventh of the alphabet. Thus, they match the numbers. So, Carol, I'll walk you to your front door. You'll go in and lock up. I'll drive off. Don't look back at the car behind us, or peep out of the window. I know what to do. I'll call later."

9. THURSDAY, 13ᵀᴴ DECEMBER, 1973

Carol answered my call very quickly.

"Pete, where are you? Are you all right?"

"I'm back at the Barbican, and fine though rather tired. Your observer must have left about forty minutes after me."

"I peeked half an hour ago, and he wasn't there. How do you know?"

"It was just Harry's form to send someone to the meeting. There were lots of people there, and they don't know each other well, so no one would have spotted someone who hadn't signed the attendance list. After the meeting, his man hung around outside. Perhaps he overheard my telling the reporter that Paul was away. So, he went to the nearest call box, and used the fact that Milverton isn't a common name to look up Paul's home address in the telephone directories, which cover all of south London. He nipped over to wait outside your place and see if anything happened. What would he do, when nothing did? First answer, stick around for a while. In the films, the man says good night all proper like, and comes back quietly later. What next, when I didn't come back? I thought again of Harry's form. At Cambridge, he wasn't a man for early nights. After concerts, he would keep everyone up, yarning on about what had gone right and what could go better. I guessed that he would want a report straightaway. I had his home address in Islington from three years ago, and I'd read that he'd not moved. So, I came back here, found the address, and headed off there. By about half an hour later than if I'd travelled directly, I was snugly parked where I could see and my car registration couldn't be seen. Ten minutes later, ACG 137K turned up, the driver got out and went in. There was no point in hanging around any longer."

"So, Harry Tamfield is having us watched."

"Or, once again, someone over-enthusiastic is trying to do what he thinks his boss wants."

"But now Harry has spotted that I'm after him, and you're involved too."

"Harry might suspect that I was involved in the leakage of the plan to sell Phase Two to the GLC. That doesn't link to you, though. We had separate reasons for being there tonight, and ASLEF gave me a good reason for taking you home."

"Will Harry realise that we know about Reg?"

"No, for the reasons we went over two weeks ago."

"It is rather frightening, to think of these hidden eyes."

"Harry isn't frightening. He's ruthless, and rather paranoiac. Actually, Steph and I will be seeing him later today. We've invited him to a concert in the City, featuring Bill Latham, who was the leader of the Baroque Orchestra. We're giving him dinner afterwards. If anything comes up, I'll call you."

Carol replied after a short pause.

"Gosh, you're going into the enemy's camp. That's risky, Pete."

"Harry is coming to our camp, and he's not my enemy, Carol. He was a friend of mine at Cambridge. But for Paul, he would still be in musical administration. Without him, Steph and I wouldn't be together. In five years, he's built up a big company. Now, it has serious problems, which are worsened by the secondary banking crisis. I hope you can broker a deal that keeps him in business *and* suits Roberta and other people at Bishop's Park."

"That's quite a challenge."

"If you can bring it off, you'll have a big local achievement, to show against a discredited Conservative and a dud Liberal.

That's for whenever. For now, the message for you is very clear, Carol. As I said earlier, stay in line, this side of the election. That's with me, or with anyone else."

"Oooh, that's a tricky one; you know me, Pete."

"I certainly know you, Carol. I know your priorities, too, because they're the same as mine. Results first, fun second – a good second, but second."

"Right enough, but I'm aching just now. Your hands felt so good earlier."

"Are you in bed?"

"Yes."

"So am I. Are you wearing pyjamas?"

"Yes, the blue striped ones; remember them? It's cold here."

"I'm not. Steph likes it warm. Take the jacket off, like you did earlier. What a good excuse you had, then. Stroke your chest, as I did earlier… How are your nipples? Are they getting really hard?"

"Mmmmm, yes…"

"Now take the trousers off, and move your hand down. That's where my hand's going. I'm thinking of you using yours…"

"Ooooh, I've a finger inside, and now two… I'm thinking of you – *ooooh* – are you hard?"

"Yes, it won't be long. I know what you do next, bottom girl. You've another finger greased. Legs up…"

We were both very contented when we wished each other goodnight a few minutes later. I drifted off to sleep, without worrying overmuch about the surprises of the evening.

I was in the office by eight o'clock, and finished off correcting my paper while others trickled in, grumbling and relating their experiences. One of the first to arrive was the secretary who had done most of the typing for me. She lived in Cheam, and yesterday had cycled the few miles to Morden. However, in those days there was no interchangeability of tickets between surface rail and Underground, so she would have had to buy a ticket there. The queue to do so was already over a hundred yards long. So, she had continued cycling, and was surprised to arrive at the office only a few minutes later than she usually arrived. She had found that in congested traffic, it was safer to go straight down the middle rather than up the inside, advice which people still ignore to their cost. The weather remained fair, so she had cycled in again today, though feeling rather stiff. The next evening, she would buy a weekly ticket from Morden.

Once she had her breath back, she set to with gusto. My paper was finalised and handed in to Pat's office well before the immutable deadline of noon, set to allow Board members to receive them by post before the weekend.

When I arrived at the pub opposite St James's Park Station, I was still wondering what to say to Greg. I couldn't really add to what I had said to Liz. He had the facts. He had to make the decision for himself. However, things did not turn out as I expected.

Greg, usually so punctilious, was over ten minutes late. He was usually quite abstemious, but now he asked for a double Scotch, downed it and asked for another. I was anticipating a heartfelt decision one way or the other, but I wasn't anticipating his outburst.

"This has been the worst morning of my life, Pete. You'll know why, soon enough. Just be aware that I and a few others were given twenty minutes – *twenty minutes* – to work out what to do. It makes me sick. People like me have qualifications and training. We know how to do our jobs. Then, a gang of ignorant twerps think they can come and tell us how to do them."

I was limited to sympathetic murmurs while he continued in this vein for some time. I persuaded him to stop drinking and eat something, for doubtless he would have more to do this afternoon. Indeed, soon he was saying that he needed to get back. Then he concluded.

"This *has* made up my mind, Pete. God knows how we'll get out of the mess we're all now in. What Liz wants to do might just help us to get out, eventually. So, I'll tell her tonight that I'll go along with it."

"Greg, I'm glad to hear that, for both of you. You're better for Liz than any of us has been."

"I knew about Dick, Brian, you and that there have been other men. Now, she's told me about Morag – *Morag!* That was a shock. Have there been any others like her?"

"No. Morag was important to Liz when she was so let down by Geoff, and then Liz was important to Morag who had come to London on her own. They've been close enough to know when the other needs physical support."

"What about the lesbian orgy before Jenny married Dick? Liz thought I'd better hear about it from her, before anyone else told me."

"Jenny's friends and relatives blessed her body, and showed their support of her decision to take on Dick, despite his history. In your terms, that decision was absolutely right and has been fruitful. There was no repeat of the party before Susie or Carol married, because there wasn't such a decision for either of them. There won't be a repeat before Liz marries you, because there isn't such a decision for her."

"Liz's friends are so close to her. This man's plan will get around."

"No, it won't. Like Steph, Sheila and Susie you've joined a circle of close friends, who value and support each other. It was a good idea of Steph's to call us 'The Creators'. The state this country is in makes it important that people like us achieve, create and make a difference. Most of us are very determined to do all of that, but each in our own way. So, there are things we don't share, as well as things we do share. We don't pry into each other's affairs. You can be sure that I won't tell anybody else about what Liz has told me. I'm sure that her man knows how to be discreet, too."

Greg went back to his work, and I set off for the Barbican flat, whilst reflecting on what I had said. Liz, Greg and I now had a secret, which had joined many other secrets amongst Creators. Carol and I had the story on Reg Emerson; probably she had told Paul how that was to be used. Steph, Jenny and I knew about what I had done to thwart Harry's renewed interest in Dick. Steph, Paul and I were in on 'Crafty'; I hoped that nobody else knew of it, though I had some questions to ask about that. The full story of what Paul had done in Cambridge those years before was known to Liz, Carol and me. Carol, I and probably Susie knew how Brian had saved Paul that June night. Steph, Jenny and Liz knew that Paul had shared Carol with me for so long. Were there other secrets, kept from me?

On my way, I called in at various shops in Covent Garden for what was needed for tonight's meal, a flavoursome casserole that I had learnt to cook in Spain. The flat was equipped with a timer oven, then a rare luxury. I put the casserole in and was back at the office by a quarter to three. There, I finished off my note about Tony's computer, whilst keeping an eye on the time.

Greg too knew how to be discreet. In the pub, he had not given anything away, despite being under great stress. Only because I knew his job did I realise that his outburst suggested that some major, and unexpected, government announcement was imminent. That would be by Oral Parliamentary Statement, at half past three.

I had met the leader of the team of civil servants which had been set up to promote UK industrial involvement in the North Sea. He was based in the government department responsible for energy supplies. Shortly after half past three, I telephoned him. Fortunately, he was there. I said that I had heard a rumour of a major announcement. I knew it would not be anything to do with him, but I had a meeting with IE's Chief Executive at half past four, and it would be very good to have details. Could he or one of his staff collect a copy from the press office, and meet me in the department's entrance lobby, at four o'clock or soon afterwards?

He knew nothing of any announcement and thought I would be wasting my time, but agreed. I jumped into a taxi, and asked the driver to wait outside the department. At ten past four, my contact came almost running into the lobby. He said nothing, but the expression on his face showed it all. It was matched on mine as I read text which had evidently been prepared in extreme haste, indeed in panic.

There were huge ambiguities and uncertainties of detail, doubtless reflecting the short time people like Greg had been given to work something out, but the overall intent was clear. Mr Heath had announced that to save fuel, all of industry was to be put on to a three-day week. It looked as if from the start of 1974 half our factories and offices could use electricity only on Monday to Wednesday, and the other half only on Thursday to Saturday. It was just mind-boggling that such a drastic and damaging decision should be announced out of the blue.

Back at the office, I just had time to make three photocopies before Pat's meeting began. I handed them round.

For three or four minutes, there was total silence. Then, Pat pressed the buzzer for his audio secretary and dictated a note to all factory managers, copied to divisional Directors, asking them to enquire immediately of their local electricity board what this announcement meant, and to let me know the result by 10 am the next day. I would forward whatever information I could obtain, but doubtless they would find out more themselves, from the newspapers and TV.

After the secretary had gone out, Pat turned to me, with the hint of a smile.

"You won't be on a three-day week, Pete. You do know how to find things out, fast. See what you can find out about Heath's sanity."

Paul, who had been looking quite cocky, seemed rather crestfallen. He was supposed to be the man with contacts, but had known nothing about this. He had been back for a couple of hours, so if Carol had known she would have called him.

Whilst the note was typed, we talked briefly about how I could produce a coherent plan for operating the company, to be set out in an emergency paper for the next week's Board meeting. Pat signed the typed note, which was to be circulated using another of IE's latest products – a facsimile scanner which could transmit short notes to similar machines on as many as five telephone lines simultaneously, taking less than five minutes per page.[47] Then, he continued in a calm tone.

"Now, what have you for us, Paul?"

Pat was showing one of the most important qualities of a great leader. He could do what was needed on an issue and then switch off from it, however serious it was, until he needed to act further. As a West Country boy, I knew the story of Drake continuing his game of bowls when the approach of the Spanish Armada was signalled. His ships were ready, but could not sail before the ebb. Montgomery turning in early on the eve of Alamein is a more recent example.[48]

Paul handed round some near final accounts prepared by New Hampshire's people in Rotterdam. With oil prices hitting $17/barrel, over five times higher than three months before, the expected return to IE España was 2.84 billion pesetas, about £19 million. He also handed Pat a personal note which Tom Sambrook had asked him to deliver. Pat opened it, and then passed it back to Paul.

"Do you mind if I read this out? My answer is yes and I'll match."

---

47 Thus, it was a predecessor of the FAX machine which became common in the early 1980s, only to be itself rendered obsolete from the mid-1990s by the ability to email word processed documents.

48 'There was nothing I could do and I knew I would be needed later. There is always a crisis in every battle where the issue hangs in the balance, and I reckoned I would get what rest I could, while I could.' Montgomery of Alamein, *Memoirs*, p. 128.

"Many thanks, and please go ahead."

"Dear Pat, I'm writing to put on record the significant contribution Paul Milverton has made to our operations during the last few months. The tactics he proposed have very materially increased the benefits. Subject to your agreement, New Hampshire Realty wishes to offer him a gratuity of $5,000. Don Pedro Guzman has confirmed to me that Banco Navarrese wishes to make a similar payment."

Paul, usually so impassive, was showing about the proper level of embarrassment. I was wondering, what about me? Then I reflected that I was already being paid very well indeed for my age, and doubtless would receive a bonus in April. Also, I was to profit handsomely on money of my own. I had never spoken to Paul about his salary, but I suspected that it was around the average for someone with his qualifications. There were now more graduates than good jobs, and terms recognised that. He was not entitled to a car, and he hadn't been able to put any money into 'Crafty'.

Next, George and I reported on our meeting in Madrid. Carlos had come up with the goods, by applying his experience in South America of what would now be called money laundering. £7 million could be reinvested in Spain straightaway, and would therefore be exempt for all taxation. Another £2 million could be held for possible investment there, which would at least defer any tax liability. The other £10 million could be recorded as an unspecified capital gain and pay Spanish company tax. However, various reliefs were available, the right people would be sympathetic, and Spanish accounting practices were flexible. So almost all of it could transfer to a Swiss bank, and need not appear in the accounts of IE España or of the consolidated IE Group. Later, the money could reappear in IE España and be transferred into other parts of IE as tax paid profits arising from use of their technology. By that time, the turnover of IE España would be much higher, and the sums would stand out less.

George concluded, with less doubt in his voice than I had thought he might show.

"So, Pat, I'm satisfied that this is just about legal, though it wouldn't reflect well on the company if it became public knowledge."

"It had better not become public knowledge, then. The four of us know, fully. Doug Gilbert knows just enough to know when to keep quiet. Does anyone else need to know?"

"No. I'll take personal responsibility for the international section of Group accounts. Our auditors know that numbers from Spain can be almost meaningless and subject to huge revisions. Also, in any spare moments I might have, which look to be few in the near future, I'll think about how we could if necessary bring back the Swiss money quickly to strengthen our balance sheet. You know I'm worried that our decentralised structure could make us vulnerable to a hostile takeover and break-up. Perhaps more hopefully, events could give us opportunities to acquire good companies in cash trouble. Also, we may need to commit resources fast to stay in areas where the technology is developing rapidly."

I asked for and was allowed two minutes to give an example of George's last point. I referred to Tony Higgins' demonstration before concluding.

"So, portable computers for individual use will arrive, but not for several years. There's no point in committing big money now. Several large American companies which were spending in the area have quit for the moment. What we might make will be developed by individuals like Tony. We need to have them use our components as much as possible, and find out how these components could be improved, particularly through reduced size and electricity consumption. To begin with, I would like to ask Tony to repeat his demo down at Staines, and to ask people there to assess what we should be making. A few hundred pounds' worth of free sample bits would be money very well spent."

I had taken a chance on raising this when there were such important immediate issues, but it was nodded through, subject to circulating the information note I was already preparing. The research laboratories now reported to George, rather than having a rather unclear independent status.

Just after half past five I emerged from the meeting, to find the cyclist secretary seated at my desk, adding to a stack of messages. Pat's note had begun to be read at about five o'clock, and since then she had been taking calls. As soon as she put the phone down, it rang again.

One message was from Steph. She guessed I could be delayed, but she could be at the concert in time to welcome Harry before the start. The other messages were somewhat repetitive, in asking what the hell this was all about. All I could say in response and to further calls was that I wish I knew; please tell me your immediate questions, and I'll try to find out the answers if you don't find out otherwise. At least I was showing factory managers that HQ was as much on the ball as was practicable.

By half past six, it began to quieten down. A few minutes later, Paul came by.

"I talked to a CBI[49] economist on his direct line. Unsurprisingly, Pat's office is finding their enquiries number to be continuously engaged. They're organising a meeting at half past ten tomorrow, at which some officials will be able to answer questions."

"Good. Tell your contact I'll go unless Pat wants to go himself, and let his office know that. God, I'm supposed to be in Chelmsford tomorrow afternoon. I can make it later, and be around here until two o'clock. I've my work cut out in what I'd been hoping would be a quieter time up to Christmas. I guess you'll have your work cut out, too."

"George has already given me a list of questions on the financial implications, starting with what will happen to the sterling exchange rate."

---

49 Confederation of British Industry.

"That, at least, is easy for you to answer. You'll have to be around Bellinghame, too. An election can't be far off. Sorry, I'm sure you've had all this from your dad already."

"Yes, but thanks for helping Carol last night. I spoke to her just now. She said you got her out of something rather frightening. She also said that Wilson knew about Heath's announcement only an hour before it was made."

"Heath didn't know much earlier than that. Carol did darn well at the meeting, and she'll tell you about what happened afterwards. Now the phone isn't ringing, I must dash. Congratulations on your three bonuses. All you have to do now is find a way to tell Carol about them, *without explaining the reasons, of course.*"

I put some emphasis on those last words. Paul looked more defensive than at any time since we had met again in July.

The concert was only five minutes' brisk walk away. I made it just as the leader came on. Steph and Harry had had no problems about holding me a good seat, because the combination of transport problems and people being kept by the announcement meant that the forty-or-so-strong orchestra initially outnumbered the audience. More came in after the all-Beethoven programme, marking his 203rd birthday,[50] had begun with the *Fidelio* overture. That was played for all possible drama, perhaps reflecting the feeling of crisis that permeated everyone present.

In the Concerto, Bill Latham restored classical calm, keeping to a restrained cadenza by Joachim. I was taken back to the last time I heard him play. That had been at the Baroque Society concert in Waterhouse College Hall, before it was smashed up by thugs organised by Paul and paid for by Sir Archibald Frampton. Then, my mind was in turmoil because I had just heard that the first attempt to elect me to a Fellowship of Waterhouse had failed. Now, my mind was in turmoil in

---

50 He was baptised on 17th December 1770 and was, it is thought, born a day or so before then.

reaction to the news of the day. Just what was Heath trying to do?

Once again, I remembered Paul comparing the government's economic policies to trying to fly an airliner with only the engines on one side running. In principle, that was possible in calm weather, though not for any length of time. Now, the buffetings from outside definitely had the British economy on a flight to destruction.

We waved to Bill as he took applause, and went to find him at the interval. I had made enough casserole for four and had hoped that he could join us, since that would certainly take some pressure out of the evening. However, the next evening his quartet was to play in Manchester. Rather than risk being late or under rehearsed, they were taking the last train tonight, which British Rail was saying 'they would make every effort to run'. He also mentioned a telephone call from his agent in West Germany, about a short tour they were making in January.

"He says that people will come along out of pity for us. The UK is a laughing stock over there. What *did* over a million of our best die for? They included both my grandfathers in the First, and two uncles in the Second. My father got away with leaving his right arm in Normandy, though that did rather finish his musical career."

We returned for the Seventh Symphony, my favourite of the nine since at the age of twelve I listened to 78s of the 1936 recording conducted by Toscanini. Tonight's performance had something of the ferocious drive of that recording, and suited the occasion. As we left, Harry agreed with my comment to that effect.

"Yes, to hear it gives one some hope. The Seventh was written when Austria was a French satellite and Beethoven was in debt. By the time it was performed, Wellington's victory at Vittoria had prompted Austria to join the coalition which finished Bonaparte off. Beethoven cashed in with a piece that though musical rubbish was lucrative, and had people playing his music again. Next, he revised *Leonora* into *Fidelio* for the Congress of Vienna. Though Beethoven had admired Bonaparte, by then he was celebrating release from tyranny."

"I'm glad you still keep up an interest in music, Harry."

"I've not touched the violin for a long time. What about you, Pete?"

"It's rather the same, I'm afraid. My cello's been at my parents' house since I went to Spain. I'll take it to Aberdeen, where I expect to be from next month. Hopefully, I'll find a band there. Dick has done better. Violas are always needed, of course."

This breezy conversation brought us back to the Barbican just after nine. Harry seemed less tense than he had been at the start of the concert, and doubtless I was much the same. He hadn't troubled to open a large envelope given to him by someone waiting outside the church.

Steph had heard that Mr Heath was to broadcast. So as Harry relaxed over a drink, and Steph and I finished preparing the meal, we watched the TV news. Statements about how the three-day week would work reinforced the impression that they were making this up as they went along. The ministerial broadcast followed.

It is difficult to convey in words the depressing impression that Ted Heath gave. This was partly caused by his delivery. He had adopted a serious approach, so as to portray as lightweight Harold Wilson's skill at snappy repartee. Seriousness had passed through ponderousness to caricature. However, no delivery could have saved the content. Having helpfully observed that 'We shall have a harder Christmas than we have known since the War', he moved to a memorable peroration.

"At times like these, there is deep in all of us an instinct which tells us we must abandon disputes amongst ourselves. We must close our ranks so that we can deal together with the difficulties which come to us, whether from within or from beyond our own shores. That has been the way in the past, and it is a good way."

Once we were eating, Steph gave an outsider's view.

"So, is he fighting the miners or not?"

"How should *I* know?" I replied, rather irritably. "Because of the increase in the price of oil we need more coal, for the moment at least. Therefore, we need miners to dig it. Therefore, this dispute must be settled. The longer it goes on, the more expensive it will be to settle and the more it will become a political matter rather than an industrial dispute. There's no point in trying to spin it out. As of this afternoon, I'm responsible for producing a plan for operating a large company and fulfilling its contracts, including exports, on a three-day week. By the time I left the office, I had over thirty questions from factory managers. What I heard on the news just now answered a few of them. Those answers have been worked out during the last few hours. Maybe by tomorrow there'll be more answers, and maybe not."

"We must fight the unions," said Harry. "We can't let them take the country over. Their leaders are a threat to democracy. Look at some of the things McGahey has been saying about getting this elected government out. It's a pity Heath didn't make that clearer. He needs to say that the only people who can throw the government out are the electorate. He needs to give the electorate a chance to stand up and be counted. Let them look at what Labour has already said. If Heath's Government can't sort this out, we need a new team who can. Perhaps we need a team from right outside current politics."

"I hope that Heath calls an election soon, because tonight he's lost it. Now, we must stop the damage as soon as possible. How will your company cope, Harry?"

"At first sight, construction isn't affected too much, though we'll be hit if shortages of materials develop. Our main current issue is marketing, as I think you know, Pete."

Steph came in quickly, before I could be expected to say anything.

"There'll be lots of damage that can't be stopped. Earlier today, on the plane back from a business trip to Holland, I was looking at how Stage 3 of Incomes Policy actually works. The details go on for about fifty pages, but the key point is that as soon as inflation goes over 7%, people are entitled to extra rises. Remember that this was dreamed up before the oil price hikes. They didn't think that this feature would be triggered, so it looked like a cost-free sweetener. But now, it will be triggered. Heath has stumbled into an inflationary spiral."

"What's it like in Holland?" asked Harry. "They were the first to be hit by the Arab embargo."

"I've only been there during the week. It seems perfectly normal then. They've banned driving on Sundays, and are trying to pretend that's good for you. The embargo is coming to an end, though. They'll just pay more, like the rest of us."

"They're silly fools, speaking up for the Jews, who take you apart, and enjoy it. To change the subject, that was a very good casserole, and Rioja to go with it. Did you learn the recipe in Spain, Pete?"

"Yes, it's served in colder weather at places in north Castile. At weekends, I managed to get out to some of those."

"That's why I missed it during my trip round Spain. It was hot, then. To explain, Steph, when I was at Cambridge, there was a fad for bumming down to Greece during the summer vacation – this was before the colonels took over.[51] I wanted to try something different. I had done Spanish at school, and found I could cope. It was very cheap, and you were welcome provided you behaved yourself. For that reason, I didn't suggest to Dick that he came with me."

"Pete told me you and Dick did go on a trip with him."

---

51 Greece was a military dictatorship between 1967 and 1974.

"That was the next year, to Austria, Hungary and Czechoslovakia."

I produced the bottle of good Spanish brandy that I had bought at Madrid Airport 'last week, on my way back after sorting out a few loose ends from my time there'. The picture on its label prompted Harry to ask what I thought of bullfights.

"They're an interesting experience, but not one I much want to repeat, though those I saw, at the festivals in Seville and Pamplona, are reputed to be the best in Spain."

"I went to several small-town bullfights, in the cheap seats in the sun. You get what you pay for, I suppose, but to be in that yelling crowd, watching people taking real risks, was hugely exciting to me. In fact, it brought me on in ways I won't say in front of Steph. I wasn't the only one, either. Did you go on the bull run in Pamplona?"

"Not me! I saw it from the house of a business colleague, who'd invited me there."

Harry and I carried on for a while about places we had visited in Spain, and developments there. He shared my optimism that the Franco regime would give way to democracy. About eleven o'clock, we rang for a taxi. As he thanked us, and said how good it had been to keep up, I felt that the evening had gone well.

I saw Harry out. In the lift, he opened the envelope he had been given, and passed me a copy of the next day's *Bellinghame Advertiser*, with the headline:

LABOUR LASS WOWS ESTATE

Below was a picture of Carol and me, taken when we emerged from the residents' meeting. Roberta and Frank were left out. I was described as 'a friend', but somehow, I had been smiling at Carol. Text praised Carol's efforts 'on a difficult evening'.

"Thanks for showing this to me, Harry. As I told their reporter, I was there to support my aunt. You can't be surprised that Bishop's Park residents are worried about the proposed sale to the GLC. Your company turned down an invitation to send a representative to the meeting."

"Come off it, Pete. I know you're working with this woman, and with her husband. I don't know why. You let their gang do for me at Cambridge. Then they tried to do for you, so why are you such chums with them now? You're up to something. Just let me tell you that if whatever it is hits me, I'll hit back. You'll be very sorry *indeed*."

Before I could say anything, he was off into the taxi, with the vicious, hunted expression on his face that I had seen before. As I started back to the flat, worries raced through my mind, but a little thought reassured me.

Once we had finished tidying up, Steph and I settled on the sofa. After a minute or so, Steph broke the pleasurable silence.

"We've lots to talk about."

"Yes, we have. I must call Carol before long, though."

I showed her the newspaper, and explained what had happened the night before. That led to a replay.

"Mmmm, there are no problems with the clip on *your* bra. Her problem was genuine, but it gave us a nice minute or so."

"And a nice bit longer than that for us now. Oooh, my sweeties feel really good. Do they taste good, too?"

"Mmmm, very good indeed... So, Harry was left with nothing to use, and a bill from whoever he employed to stalk us. I wasn't surprised that Carol made a pass at me, but I was surprised that she knew you were away. I'm wondering whether Paul has told her about 'Crafty'. When I reminded him not to tell Carol how he won these bonuses, he looked pretty defensive. I was also surprised that Carol knew that Ana liked me to remove her bra. Apart from you, I've only ever told Liz and Jenny about Ana. One of them must have talked to Carol during the Brighton weekend."

"Are you sure you've not told Paul?"

"I'm quite sure. Paul has met Ana as Don Pedro's daughter and Carlos's fiancée. He knows that I went on some photo trips with her, including passing through Santo Domingo on the way to Pamplona. In September, we were very careful not to give any different impression. Paul might have noticed that Ana was quite friendly to me, and maybe he guessed something, but he wouldn't have any detail."

"Harry was interested in your time in Spain."

"At the party in July, he said he wanted to hear how Spain had changed since he was there."

"Is there any way he could have found out about 'Crafty'? Careful with that zip…"

"I don't see how. I referred only to a business colleague. Harry didn't ask any more about him, or about Pamplona. I wonder why he made that nasty remark about Jews. Have National Amalgamated been squeezing him?"

"The loan agreements provide for interest at 2% above base, going to 3% above if base goes over 10%. Base is 13% now. Mmmm, just a little bit further up…"

"I'd better call Carol."

"Don't be long. I'll get cold. I could turn the heating up, but Mr Heath says we shouldn't."

"I'll be watching you keep yourself warm."

Carol was only just back from an evening session at Transport House, working out tomorrow's response to Heath's statement, and lines for the two-day debate to take place the next week. Her reaction to my news was blunt.

"Fuck that constituency office. They've not alerted me to this, just as they didn't to the snobs story, or the letter from the residents' association."

"So, though Harry has it in for you, he's done you a good turn. You have the *Advertiser* on your side. Remember what Frank said about rivalry with the *Record*?"

"Could Harry Tamfield know about our times together?"

"That could explain the activities of the man in ACG 137K, but it seems very unlikely. Dick knew about our first few times, and he was with Harry then, but he knew not to talk about you, just as I knew not to talk about them. Liz knew not to tell anyone, and in any case, she hardly knew Harry. Did you ever meet Harry then?"

"No. Could he know of what you found out about Paul? Who else knows about that?"

"Since I know only by chance, I don't see how. The only others who know are Liz, Arthur Gulliver, and at least two Framptons. Everybody in Waterhouse knew about Paul having a go at me, so Harry may have picked that up. If ACG 137K man overheard what I said to the reporter, Harry may also know that Paul now works for IE. I think he has some rather simplistic views about the left. He groups you all together as a 'gang.'"

"Could he know about your rescuing me after Harold Wilson's visit to Cambridge? Reg Emerson could make big use of that."

"Liz is the only person I ever told. It's a good thing I did, remember. So, the answer is again no. Has Wilson recognised you, by the way?"

"Maybe, but that doesn't matter. Everyone was in demos then."

I returned to the sofa, where Steph was definitely warm to my hands. I was quite surprised, though certainly relieved, that she didn't ask any questions about my conversation with Carol, in which I had tried to avoid saying too much myself. After a little while, I gave her a compliment.

"You seem very lively, after a busy couple of days."

"Mmmm, yes, they were a nice change, but it's nice to be back."

"And what do you mean by that?"

"Oh, nothing."

There was a hint in her voice of either defensiveness or enticement. I didn't know which, but I had noticed her change of subject when I talked about Paul and Ana.

"Paul is obviously well thought of by you all at New Hampshire."

"He's a star. Tom and Mart are both *very* impressed. What's more, Gail is moving to our office in Minneapolis. She comes from round there and is homesick. Everyone to their own taste, I say. New York can be too hot or too cold, but it's worse in Minneapolis, and the *bugs*... So, there'll be a vacancy here in London from March. Because of that, I'm staying here until the summer, so there'll be no problems about Ana's wedding. It suits the man who's slotted to take over from me. He's currently in LA and his wife has just had their second child. Mart knows I'll need to stand out of the selection to replace Gail, but I know the result. Oooh, you're tickling. *Oooooh! Pete, no... ooooooooh!*"

"I'll stop if you tell me the rest, Steph."

"Just move your finger down a bit, and keep going gently, oooh that's great. I guess it's time for me to fess up. You understand me, Pete. That's what's made being together these last four months so special. In five years, I've not been with anyone for so long. I like variety, though. You've shown me that younger men are worth it. When I first met Paul back in July, I liked the look of him. Then Paul came up with ideas which convinced our experts. That showed me just how bright he is. Bright men turn me right on. You did, that first time *we* met, and you still do.

"In Brighton I found a chance to be with Carol. I gave her some tips on clothes, though I didn't mention bras. Talking about you led to, shall we say, a girls' technical conversation. She remembers the great times you had together, and there sure was that look in her eye. You still give her the hots, Pete. I said it was up to her. I wouldn't stand in the way, as I'll be off back to the States before long. I also said I was grateful to her for showing you what definitely gets that extra for me. That made her wistful. Paul doesn't like doing it. He's very straight in his approach. Sometimes she thought to herself that things might be better if someone brought him on.

"Well, for me, message received. Two weeks ago, in Rotterdam, we had a good meeting, with some drinks in the evening. I pretended to be a bit over the odds, he helped me back to my room, and then I said he'd better undress me. It was standard, corny stuff, you see. He sounded duly doubtful, but he was showing what he wanted only too well by the time I said how I liked you undressing me. That's when I said about Ana, too. He did it straight, but very nicely, and I was appreciative. He said how much he admired me, and then went back to his room.

"Last night he made the first move. He said he was rather tired. His back hurt from being in a cramped seat on the plane. I said I knew how to deal with that, came to his room, and gave him the full Andy treatment, using Vaseline that just happened to be in my handbag. But before it went too far I asked whether he was enjoying it, and he said yes. I said I was turned on, so he should undress me and do it how Carol likes. He went in real hard, fingering pretty well, and I made damn clear I was enjoying it. Mart was in the room next door, so I had no option but to fess up to him today. He said no problem if it doesn't cause any fuss. There's not much else he could say. His current wife was his secretary. Before her, he had me twice. That was back in New York, when I was still with J. P. Morgan. I guess it smoothed my way into New Hampshire. Going back to Paul, we did it again more quietly this morning. He said that now he would get more out of doing it Carol's way. So, there we are, guilty my Lord but no regrets, ready for sentence."

I paused before replying to all this, my finger still working gently.

"You said you were a hustler when I first met you, Steph. I know that once I'm not here much you'll want someone else, though I hope we can still go on together when we can, including Pamplona at Easter. You think you've a green light from Carol, and maybe you have. How are you going to continue?"

"We'll need to wait a bit, as there aren't any more 'Crafty' meetings. Once he's at New Hampshire, and you're in Aberdeen, we'll find ways to go on."

"I told Carol that she must stay in line this side of the election. So must Paul."

"Don't worry, we'll keep this quiet. Just Mart and you know."

"Won't people know when you aren't on the panel for Gail's replacement?"

"Mart will make sure the only time the panel can convene is when I'm not here."

"Have you thought about whether you'll improve Paul's marriage, or destroy it? Years ago, I may have helped Carol's relationship with Paul. Carol said she was improving mine with Jenny, but there was no time to find out whether she was right, because Jenny thought she was helping Dick, and found she couldn't stop. That was the right ending, of course, but it wasn't what she was expecting. Whatever encouragement Carol may have given you, she doesn't know about or even suspect this, or she'd have told me last night."

"Paul said he wasn't going to tell her before the election."

"Paul and Carol aren't the swinging couple they sometimes pretend to be. They came together mainly because it was convenient. They were the boy and girl next door, they had common interests, and their parents had no objection. Paul has never had anyone else, as far as I know. Carol had that bad time when she was eighteen. Then she had me, with Paul's agreement or at least understanding. That stopped, well before they got married. Now she likes flirting with me, and teasing. I join in the fun, as I did last night and early this morning. If I went further, she wouldn't stop me, and she would enjoy it, but underneath she would be sorry she started the game."

"Once she knows, you'll have a great time with her."

"Carol is the outgoing one in that partnership. Paul is the very bright, quiet fixer. That's the way she expects it, and it's why they're absolutely right for each other. It will be a terrible shock to find that he's been the first to 'go extramarital', as they say in Hollywood. She'll feel let down, like at the end of her bad time, but she'll be blaming herself. She'll be realising how you took what she said."

"With your help, she'll get over it."

"I hope you're right, Steph, but I think you're being rather callous and selfish. So, *turn over!*"

"Yes, Headmaster – ow – *ow* – OW – *OW* – *OW* – *OW*."

"Ow," I contributed, as a flailing leg caught me.

"OW – OW – OW – OW – *OW* – *OW!!!*"

"And now, I'm going to show you what a 'Carol' done really hard is like."

Her reddened bottom brought me right on, and I slammed in. Her first few yells were of pain, but then they turned to whoops of pleasure. She tightened round me as I retook possession.

In silence, we settled in bed. After a few minutes, I put my arm round her. That was welcomed. For a few minutes, we kissed, quietly.

"I'm sorry I was carried away, Steph. I meant what I said about going on together."

"No worries, Pete. I'm pleased you've done me over a bit. I'm just a little sore, inside and out, front and back, but very *nicely* sore. It's nothing like I was after Vic found out about Beth. Luckily, that was on a Friday. I was just OK to go to the office on Monday, saying I'd tripped. My dentist's bill was $550. You've shown you still want me, though I'm a two-timer. That message is received, as much as Carol's. We can go on together. That will help stop Carol from finding out, too. You're right to care about her."

"Yes, I do. We had a long time together, on and off."

"Mmm, I know, the girls' technical conversation roamed. Didn't your second round start with something like just now?"

"It started with her climbing back into my bed as her price for something I wanted. That turned out to be a fake. When I found out that she'd known it was a fake, I said that we could go on if she wanted, but the next time would be something like just now. She went on."

"She likes your hand on and in her butt, but for the present, Paul and I will cool it, and I'll remind him to keep quiet about 'Crafty.'"

Soon I was nearly asleep, but then there was a new sound.

Steph – worldly, experienced Steph – was crying, for the first time I had ever known. I took her in my arms again.

"Pete, there's something I've meant to say for weeks, but haven't been able to. I must say it now. It's not what I'd thought, and not what I told you when we met. *I want kids.*"

"I noticed how you liked playing with David and holding little Katie."

"I've done that before. I've two sisters and I've been a good aunt. It wasn't so much that as seeing how Jenny will have a family *and* a career. It's shaken me up inside. I'm envious of her. I want both too, and I'm running out of time. Now I've met a man who fits me, and I fit him. That's you, Pete. Tonight has finally convinced me. You're caring, but when I misbehave you don't just take it. You're tough enough to keep me under control. You act up, with me as well as with others. I'm ready to stop looking. *I want your kids.* Call that a proposal, if you like."

I held her hard for a while before replying.

"I've really liked being with you, Steph, and I still do, but how would this work? We could live well enough on what I'm earning, but you would have to come to Aberdeen. Brokers are setting up there. They employ analysts, though not at your level. The times you were working, you would face a big drop in salary."

"That's not my idea, Pete, and today's the day to say it. Britain is finished. It's tragic, but true. People like you, who want to get on, have to face up to that. For hundreds of years, this was the place to go and get. Even when your best struck off on their own in America, the rest of you led the Industrial Revolution and gained another empire in quick order. Then, you stopped the Germans twice before we came in and finished the job. But people here don't go and get any more. The place is stuffed with losers, not winners. Heath is certainly a loser. Wilson is little better. Don't stay and be more and more frustrated. Get out, with me. Come over as my spouse, so with no visa problems. You can find a good job in the States, fast. They appreciate guys like you over there, and I know people who can help. You can double your pay straightaway, and then the sky's the limit. Don't say anything now. You're very committed to the new office in Aberdeen, like you're very committed to everything you do. So, go to Aberdeen and see how it works out. Live your own life for a while, but come here when you can. Whoever else I have around, until the summer *I'll be waiting for you*. Once I have you, there won't be anyone else, ever."

She cried again. After some minutes, I got out of bed and returned with a well-thumbed book, the basis of many long discussions with Ana. I showed it to her, and read.

"Yet all were nevertheless, consciously or unconsciously, aware that their country had once been the greatest nation in the world, that at that time the country had at least seemed to be united, and that these continual disputes were unworthy of so great a history. This partly at least caused them to think that there was something undignified in any compromise of their ideals (even if this meant that they could never become practical political programmes). At the same time, also, a very large number of people wanted 'a new nation' (which might mean a hundred different things) which would be grateful of their great past and indeed of the continuing qualities of her superb people."

Then I continued.

"What you say is very tempting, Steph, and I feel very honoured that you've said it. I know I could live with you. But equally I know what I should do here. That passage is about Spain, on the eve of their Civil War.[52] It could be about this country, now. Harry isn't the only one saying that maybe we need a new kind of government. That would set us back over three hundred years, to our Civil War. We need to find a way out. To do that needs people here who can make a difference – people like me, and the others you've styled The Creators. So, can I just pack up and go? As you say, we needn't and shouldn't decide now."

After that, there was little more to say. Steph drifted off to sleep. I lay back myself.

It was dark now, and not because of the emergency. The City wasn't 24/7 then. I could only imagine Steph's body beside me, but could feel its warmth. I had never lived with a woman before. I had become used to that comforting feeling. So had she, whatever she got up to outside.

We liked doing things together, all kinds of things. I had assumed that when she returned to the USA, our relationship would be another that continued as a deep friendship, albeit at long distance. Now, I was challenged with an alternative. But did I *want* an alternative?

What I had read out to Steph had reminded me that the 1936-39 conflict was only the most recent of several civil wars that had marked the decline of Spain. I recalled long evenings with Ana, discussing the reasons for that decline and what the lessons were for the UK in its current predicament. In the 1620s Spain was in its 'Golden Age'; though challenged it was holding its own as the greatest European power and the ruler of the first

---

52 Hugh Thomas, *The Spanish Civil War*, first edition (1961) p.160. At the time of which I relate, this was the standard historical text and was freely available in Spain. It is less unfavourable to Franco and the Nationalist cause than more recent texts, for example that by Antony Beevor (1982, revised 2006 as *The Battle for Spain*) or Thomas's later edition.

empire on which the sun never set. Forty years later it was a pawn in European politics, and on the verge of falling apart completely. The change in the status of the UK since the 1930s seemed alarmingly similar, even if being on the winning side in the War gave it a rosier hue.

Ana was an observant Catholic but agreed that excessive religiosity had been bad for Spain, through its promise of a better afterlife leading to lack of interest in improving the present life. I had compared this with the desire for a quiet life that was holding the UK back. I had also compared the dominance of the military, knightly caste in Spain with the disdain for 'trade' shown by so many 'public school men' in the UK. I wanted to be part of a change in attitudes, here and now.

That was really part of my desire to help others to sort out their lives. I had helped some friends to sort out their lives. But was it time to sort out my own? Here was the chance to make my way with someone who suited me so well. Could I turn it down?

I had changed direction when I left Cambridge, but I had kept the friends I had made there. They formed an important part of my life. In particular, there was one friend, and a little more, whom I had not seen for three years before last July.

Ever since the massage session two weeks before, images of Jenny had flooded into my mind. I had seen her feeding Katie. I had imagined her doing what Steph suggested she might have done immediately afterwards. I had imagined the hen party; not now so much her 'hazing' as what happened later. Jenny had been displeased at Amanda saying so much about what had happened at the sunbaths, just as the year before she had been displeased with Dick for doing the same. She had shown her displeasure through almost impassively taking Amanda's total submission and then licking her lips in relish as with one finger she brought about the loudest orgasm of the day in a woman who worshipped her. The picture in my mind was of a classical goddess, who relished being able to combine beauty, intellect, and power – power exercised in the loveliest sort of way, but power nevertheless. I knew that I had helped her to become what I pictured.

My time with Jenny had been shorter than any of my times with Liz, Carol, Ana, or now with Steph, but its memory seemed to grow in intensity. It was one thing to say that Jenny and I should not meet often, quite another to say that we would never, or hardly ever, meet again.

The crisis had broken on my country, on my friends, and on me.

BOOK V
THE CRISIS RECKONED

10. SUNDAY, 17TH FEBRUARY, 1974

"It's good to see so many of you here. Others couldn't make it today, but will be with us during the next twelve days, the twelve days in which Carol is going to shake the world of Bellinghame South. On Thursday, the view from Transport House changed. They called me that evening, and began by going over the prospects my side of Manchester. I said everything was under control, and we should pick up a couple out into Derbyshire. Fine, they said. You've seen the papers. We're going in big for Carol. Go and take over. So here I am. Much thanks to Brian for calling all of you, and much thanks to Roberta for inviting us here. Hear that, Roberta?" A cheerful gurgle broke the silence, and brought the house down.

Over thirty of us were crammed into Roberta's lounge, listening to Fred Milverton, Paul's father and now Carol's agent. Jenny and I were standing near the door. We had just arrived, with Steph, who was in the kitchen with Roberta, helping to dispense coffee and look after Katie.

"To business, then; hands up, Labour Party members." Morag, Sheila, and two or three others responded. "The rest of you are very welcome to join, and I have forms, but that's not the point. You, and people like you, are the Common Sense Party. Right now, Common Sense means Labour. That's the message we want you to give. See this map? Unlike most of you, I went to a school where no one learnt Latin, but Carol tells me that geezer Caesar said Gaul is divided into three parts. Bellinghame South is like Gaul. The big council estate delivers most of the regular Labour vote. That's where the local party organisation is, and from now on that's where it will stay. They'll give the Party line absolutely straight, and make sure everybody comes out on polling day. Over there is where the Liberals are strongest. That's where we're bringing people in from Sutton. They're used to dealing with Libs. Round here is the solidly Tory area which has noticed what Carol can do and has been shaken on Thursday and even more today. This will be your area. Here's your own leaflet. Make sure to read Friday's *Advertiser* as well as the nationals. Over to you, Brian."

We looked at the leaflet, which was full of quotes such as:

'I've never voted Labour before, but I'm going to this time. Carol has already shown how she can help us at Bishop's Park.' – *Roberta Strutt, local resident for 28 years.*

And, though not adjacent:

'Voting Labour is new to me. I don't agree with everything in their manifesto, but there's no practical alternative now. Conservative policies have failed. They need time to rethink. We need the country back at work.' – *Frank Booth DFC, solicitor based here for 15 years, Vice-President of the Bellinghame and District Rotary Club.*

Brian pointed to a larger street map of our third or so, decorated with numbers 1 to 100. Alongside the map was a large sheet, on which people could sign alongside these numbers. On Roberta's dining table were sheets numbered 1 to 100, on each of which about sixty addresses were listed, with space for comments.

"Our job is to cover every address between now and polling day. By then, we need lists of yeses, noes, and people needing transport to their polling station. That means an average of two calls per address, to cover people who aren't there first time, and people who are wavering and need another call. There are about 6,000 addresses. You can average about twenty calls an hour, so we're looking at 600 hours of work. That's four or five three-hour sessions for each of us, and for those not here today. You need to be out each day you're not working in your jobs. Pick up today as many of these sheets as you think you can cover realistically, and sign for them. If you find you can do more, or unavoidably can't cover what you've taken, call here as soon as possible. Jack Unwin will be here on Mondays to Wednesdays, and I'll be here on Thursdays to Saturdays. Roberta can take messages."

It was amazing to see Brian transformed from the happy-go-lucky man I had known at Cambridge into someone who could organise and deliver. He had had rather longer to prepare than most knew that morning, but he had repaid the trust placed in him, and stepped up to the job.

On New Year's Eve, I had set off for Manchester with Steph in a loaded car. It was a tedious drive, on account of the 50 mph limit imposed to save energy. However, the 'embargo' created by the oil companies was coming to an end, so petrol was easier to find. Paul's and Carol's families lived a few doors apart, and were having their usual joint New Year celebration. I was invited to break my journey to Aberdeen.

Mary and Bert Gibson were pleased to see me again, with my new partner. I was reminded that Carol and her older sister had inherited much of their vivacity. I had met Fred Milverton only once before, whilst Paul was unconscious in hospital during my last week in Cambridge. As then, Fred was forceful but calm, and rather reserved. His wife knew her place.

Halfway through the evening, Paul tapped me on the shoulder and I found myself literally in a smoke-filled room, to hear Fred and Bert explain the plan agreed at top level. Soon after an election was called, Reg Emerson would be exposed, and Fred would travel south. Who could help to flood the constituency with supporters? Carol, Paul and I said the name together. He was right outside, though he and Susie would have to leave soon, to head back up the M62 and see 1974 in with his own people.

The next day I carried on north, and Steph returned to London with Carol in the car Paul was now driving courtesy of 'an unexpected bonus'. The party ended a festive season that hadn't been as gloomy as Mr Heath had predicted.

The three-day week had established a pattern of frantic activity when permitted, reflection or enjoyment when it was not. My father said that it was rather like the War. That observation was towards the end of the first Christmas lunch I cooked, and before we watched the Queen, following whom Steph and Frank had to put up with a barrage of criticism from four 'locals' of the inaccuracies in *Far from the Madding Crowd*.[53] The family Christmas had been a tight squeeze, but fun.

Other brief encounters had painted the same picture. On the Saturday before Christmas, we went east to partake of a buffet prepared by women currently resident at the Pankhurst Centre. This was not a secret refuge; those who needed that were sent on. Rather, it was a reception centre, where women who needed a break and mutual support could stay for a while. It was rather like 'going back to mother' for those who had not that option. There was a police station a hundred yards down the road, whose staff both referred new 'clients' and kept an eye. If errant partners visited, as often they did, they had little scope to cause trouble;

---

53 The 1967 version starring Julie Christie.

that wouldn't be 'just a domestic' any more. Instead, they were confronted and given a good talking to. Quite often, this led to reconciliation and improved behaviour. It was hit and miss by present-day standards, but much better than nothing.

Morag's interest in the work was evidently important to her relationship with Sheila. Steph was particularly impressed by the evident capability of some of the residents, and the efforts being made to find them jobs which would allow them to support themselves and their children if necessary. She could empathise with other women who had outrun their partners. Brian remarked on how in his home community of mining families, so many women suffered in silence. That was the way it was.

We all left suitable cheques, as did many other guests. Sheila's notes of thanks told us that these assured funding through 1974 of a full-time social worker, and of visiting experts on issues such as literacy.

The next day, we entertained the Sinclairs with a light lunch, to break their journey between Brighton and Cambridge. They were in cheerful pre-Christmas mood: Dick's research continued to go well, and whilst in Cambridge he was to meet with Geoff Frampton about it.

Steph and I booked an international call in time to wish Don Pedro and Ana well. From their country house outside Pamplona, they expressed sympathy in our troubles. Ana would be remaining there; her work for 'Crafty' was done, and work on the photo book would move ahead.

Steph chose times I was out to make news calls to her chums back home, doubtless so as to be able to give some graphic descriptions of our life together. She did remark that she wanted her friends to know about me. She told me that Beth now had a pleasant but rather hesitant boyfriend. She encouraged offering a 'Carol', and a few days later had an appreciative call back.

The power engineers' overtime ban had been called off, so Liz and Greg were both working all hours in 'essential' jobs, but they found time to come to dinner. Pressure was deepening their relationship, again rather as happened during the War. Greg had moved in with Liz, 'to be closer to his office'.

During the run up to Christmas, Carol and Paul were much in Bellinghame South. Frank had them invited to the Rotary Club Ball, at which Paul had worn a dinner jacket for the first time. Steph said again that Paul and she were 'cooling it' until after the election, and his move to working for her. I knew that I would hear very quickly if Carol found out about them.

Certainly, I was reassured by attending New Hampshire Bank's lavish Christmas party. In the gentlemen's toilet, Mart Steinberg gave his 'public' view, by congratulating me for holding on to Steph for longer than anyone else had done recently. As a result, she had been more settled in the office. My impending move north was regarded with foreboding.

IE's Christmas celebration was, as usual, restrained by Pat's view that it was not for the company to organise the leisure activities of its employees. Before then, I had obtained Board agreement to my North Sea project, though two of the divisional Directors were clearly less than happy at the way it would cut into their autonomy. So, once I had delivered an operating plan for the company under the power restrictions, I had been most of the time on the phone, frantically confirming arrangements to set up an office in Aberdeen. I had already made a provisional booking of serviced office space, and a few of the prospective staff I had identified were ready to move there at short notice. Most staff would not move, at least for a while, and would provide an essential network of contacts and progress chasers at the main IE sites. We could all keep in touch using the IE telephone conferencing and document transmission systems. I had not failed to point out to the doubters that this arrangement replicated in miniature the organisation of the whole of IE.

I arrived in Aberdeen late on New Year's Day, and settled in during the following day, which was a Scottish Bank Holiday.

After that it was a Thursday, and 'eyes down', since the office could be fully open for business on Thursdays to Saturdays only. On Mondays to Wednesdays, one could attend and use electricity for office equipment, but not for heating or lighting. In Aberdeen in January, that allowed only a short day. However, on those days there were companies whose offices were open and we could visit; equally, people from those companies took to dropping in when my office was open. Also, the lights stayed on in homes, including the bedsitter I had taken whilst my flat was completed. Fortunately, I had been able to find a place that already had a telephone; otherwise, it would have taken months to have one installed, in those days of the Post Office monopoly and Treasury restrictions on its expenditure. So I was able to work a six-day week. I upgraded my outdoor kit, and on Sundays was out to the hills whenever the weather permitted.

News came through from the South as if from a different world. The IRA terrorists (who never operated in Scotland) killed twelve in a spectacular bombing of a coach carrying off-duty troops and their families along the M62, and thus showed what they thought of the government's attempts to broker a settlement in Northern Ireland. The political temperature was raised by statements that the victims had been travelling by coach only because of industrial action on the railways. The government rejected attempts by representatives of industry and the TUC to end the miners' dispute. Opinion amongst the miners hardened, and a strike ballot yielded a huge majority.

Speculation had raged about a general election, despite Enoch Powell describing it as 'an act of total immorality' and declaring that he would not stand. However, it was only as the miners came out that Heath called the election for 28th February, on the theme 'Who governs Britain?' He had a useful lead in opinion polls, despite total uncertainty as to what an election might achieve. Of more interest in Aberdeen was how far the

Scottish National Party would go, on the slogan 'It's Scotland's Oil.'

Various phone calls told me how plans were unfolding. Just as the election was called, the Westbury Housing Association announced its purchase of Bishop's Park Phase Two. Some tenants would come off the GLC waiting list, whilst others would be local. All would be people with a genuine interest or need to work in the area, and by implication not layabouts. The next day's *Bellinghame Advertiser* led with an account of how Carol had worked behind the scenes to bring this about, and looked forward to her election campaign. The finance columns said that the sale should keep Tamfield Investments and its bankers, particularly National Amalgamated, out of immediate trouble. Some also mentioned Carol's part as a welcome sign of a new approach by Labour.

On the evening of 13th February, Carol's call was brief, and somewhat coded, but to the point. I warned Steph and Dick. Most papers marked St Valentine's Day by taking a break from the election, and leading on the deportation of Alexander Solzhenitsyn from the USSR. The *Clarion* ran its exclusive scoop. Even its Scottish edition was full of how Sir Reg Emerson had enjoyed himself after the spectacle of naked cavorting at Harry's party. It gave as much detail from Robin as was then printable, and local interest was provided through some elder of the Kirk saying that this showed how immoral life was down South.

Later that day, Pat O'Donnell called from his home, because IE HQ had heat and light only on Mondays to Wednesdays.

"Pete, I need you here next week. I've been asked to appear on a live TV programme, late on Tuesday. I'm one of three non-politicians who have been giving strong views about the election. The other two show that it's a small world. One is James Harman. I think I met him that evening I first met you – windbag, no problem. The other is also from Waterhouse College – Harry

Tamfield. His party is in the news today – didn't you meet Steph there? I hope *you* don't find your name in the papers. Handling Tamfield will be tricky. I need to be very well prepared. Our press department is fine for announcing contracts and profits, but no good for this. Paul could have done it, but George and I agreed that before he starts at New Hampshire next month, he could go off to support his wife. So, come to a meeting at my house at four o'clock on Sunday, and stay around until Thursday for follow-up."

In a tone which made clear that I meant it but deterred further questions, I reassured him that I wasn't expecting any publicity for me, or for International Electronics. A frantic day and a half at the office followed, and then a dash for an afternoon plane to Gatwick. Forty minutes after I landed, Steph was waving from a window as her train pulled in, and I joined her to continue south. That was once again possible, since ASLEF had suspended its industrial action, in response to an appeal by Harold Wilson. Miraculously, trains without speedometers were once again safe to drive.

Jenny collected us at Preston Park. The chance for a meet-up wasn't to be missed, and we needed to discuss the arrangements for Katie's christening. That was only a fortnight away, and Liz and I were to be godparents. Jenny suggested that Steph and I might take our time 'unpacking' whilst they looked after the children. We did so, and talked more about our future, though with no decision and none expected. Over dinner, I said that Carol had tipped me off that there would be more in the Sunday papers, though I did not mention the timing of the tip-off.

So there was no surprise when I returned from the newsagent with pages of material about Reg Emerson's continued entertainment at the expense of Tamfield Investments, just as that company was trying to sell Bishop's Park to the GLC. This was 'the second torpedo' that Fred had described on New Year's

Eve. The loyal Conservative response to Thursday's coverage had been predictable: Sir Reg had been led astray at the rather exuberant party, whilst still under stress following the break-up of his marriage. The *Sunday Clarion* smashed that line to smithereens, and also gave a further national airing for Carol's success in securing a better solution for the residents of Bishop's Park.

Roberta had needed little prompting to allow her bungalow to be used as a base for the campaigning that Brian was organising. Jenny wanted to do what she could for Carol, Steph was interested to see the action, and here we were.

Once plans for the next few days were sorted out, Fred looked at his watch.

"Well done, Brian. You're made for this."

"My company has over a thousand salesmen. Computer programs I've written help to schedule their work."

"In twenty minutes, Carol hits the local shopping centre. Fan out in the crowd, all of you. Use these copies of the *Advertiser*."

Thursday had been selected for national coverage, so as to feed into Friday's *Advertiser*, and also to wrong-foot the *Record*. On Wednesday, that newspaper had welcomed Emerson's formal nomination, and had speculated that following the convincing Conservative victory so essential for the nation, his ministerial career might progress. The *Advertiser* headed copious local reactions with one word.

DISGUSTED

We set off, and after passing where Roberta's house had stood, took the footpath. For some of us, that brought back memories of our escapade of the previous July. I commented that then, we had been in a different world.

That was demonstrated when we arrived at the shopping centre, to find it quite busy rather than deserted. A positive legacy of the three-day week was that *one can do things on a Sunday*. Before that time, 'everybody' had said that a 'Continental Sunday' would be quite inappropriate here. Now, football matches were being played on Sundays, so that those working on Saturday could attend them. Also, some shops were opening on Sunday, since there were no restrictions on their electricity use on that day. There were fewer objections to this than 'everybody' had expected. We started towards the present day, when the unwary traveller abroad can find that 'Continental Sunday' has the opposite meaning to that of the past.

A loudspeaker van pulled up and announced that Carol would arrive in five minutes. Whilst a platform and microphone were set up, we handed out leaflets and car stickers. By the time Carol got out of Paul's car, there were over a hundred people gathered around. It was unusual then for parliamentary candidates to be personable young women. Since December, Carol had had a lot of publicity, and events since Thursday had stepped that up. As well as the local papers, two national press cars arrived, one from the *Clarion*, the other from a more serious newspaper which would discover 'the Bellinghame effect'.

Soon Carol's voice was echoing along the street, and the crowd was growing.

"First, I will say how honoured I am, to have the chance to represent you all in Parliament. As the *Advertiser* put it so well two months ago, I'm the Labour Lass from Up North. But Paul and I live not far away, and next month we expect to move into a new flat, on the Bishop's Park Estate. Whatever happens a week on Thursday, we'll help bring together all the people living there, into a new community. We share your aspirations and concerns. I know what these are, because I've talked to so many of you over the last week. You're concerned about inflation. Prices have risen 2% *in a month*. That's an annual rate of 25%, which we have never seen in this country in peacetime. You're concerned about jobs, and about the damage being done to us all by the three-day week. Above all, you're concerned about what would actually happen were the Tories to win. How would that get the miners back to work, producing the coal we need? How would it mean there were enough drivers to run your train service? The Tories have run out of ideas. They need a rest. On the twenty-eighth, give them one."

"Good on yer, girl. Our *member* certainly needs a rest."

The shout brought laughter. Carol grinned at Paul, who was standing nearby. He was the sign of a happy, stable marriage. However, people had to believe that she would be able to do the job, and therefore that they wouldn't be starting a family just yet. Saying that they were moving into a new *flat* gave some assurance. The first question was predictable.

"Should the unions run the country?"

"No. It's never been and isn't now Labour Party policy that they should run the country. It's not the policy of the unions, either. The unions' job is to look after their members. They want to be able to do that, and negotiate effectively with managements. That's what most people in management want, too. They don't want to be stopped from making sensible deals, which deliver higher pay for higher productivity. They don't want trouble caused by some bumbling court out of anyone's control.[54] They don't want to be told they can run their companies for only three days a week. *And nor do you!*"

That got good applause. After a few more questions, nearly two hundred people went on their way as Carol spoke to the nationals and the *Advertiser*. I kept well back, canvassing views. I didn't want to be noticed by the people who had snapped me before. On the way back to Roberta's house, I found myself talking to Jenny.

"I'm glad I could stay for a little while, but I must go now. We've an invitation to a late lunch with a friend of Dick's. Do you think you'll be here again?"

---

54 A reference to the National Industrial Relations Court, a Heath experiment by then totally discredited.

"Until Wednesday, I'll have my time cut out on briefing Pat for the TV programme, and following that up. I'm also fitting in some meetings with London based oil company people. Pat asked me to stay over until Thursday, though. I'll be down here then, unless something crops up."

"It's great that Steph could look after Katie. She is good with children. You both seem very close, Pete. Is there any chance of it being permanent?"

"Just for you, Steph wants me to go back to New York with her and find a job there. I'm not sure I can do that, though I've more time to decide, because she's now to be here until the summer."

"It's your decision, Pete, though you'll be missed over here if you do go. I do hope you find someone. Being with Dick is much better again now that Katie is beginning to take food, and so I'm more in the mood. And he's more in the mood because his work is going well."

"Last night, he did seem very upbeat about it. I'm glad he's found the funding to see these people at Geneva University. He needs input from someone besides Geoff."

"It's probably a coincidence, but his research looked up just after he was over that business with Andy."

"Perhaps getting Andy out of his mind left him with more room to think."

"Perhaps. I'm glad you were able to reassure us that Dick won't be mentioned in the papers. You seemed very confident. I guess you knew something. Did you spot Reg Emerson at that party?"

"No. Carol told me they were delving around. I said that because the only way she knew of the party was through Steph and me, she must make sure that we, Dick, and the other people there from Steph's bank were kept right out of it."

"I hope you've stopped Dick worrying. He was put out by the jibes at Reg Emerson's homosexuality. He's also concerned about what this will mean for Harry Tamfield – more so than I'd expected after what happened to that girl Gloria."

"The GLC will advance Tamfield Investments up to 90% of its share of the Westbury deal. No-one wants Tamfield to run out of cash. Tell Dick that the deal has saved Harry. I'm pleased about that. Harry is an outstanding man, though he's cut corners. This should have taught him a few lessons. I hope that he'll behave more sensibly in future. The trouble Paul got himself into six years ago taught *him* a few lessons, and now he's a Creator. I know you don't like Harry, but he could be a Creator, too. He doesn't have proper friends. He needs to value people."

"I hope you're right, Pete, about Paul as well as about Harry. Paul has changed since he tried to pull you down, thank God. Carol has done him a power of good. I admire her tremendously, which is why I'm here now, but I still don't really trust Paul, and nor does Liz. She hinted that she knows more about him than most. I don't know how. She never went with Paul, did she?"

"No, she didn't. As far as I know, whilst she was in Cambridge they met only twice. The first time was a few days after Paul arrived, at the reception for new students. The second time was when we saw Paul being carried into hospital. I wouldn't always trust Paul, but he's very capable. In this country we need more people you can't always trust. One of the reasons why we're in such a mess is that there's been far too much of being British and keeping a straight bat. Some people think that inspires respect. It doesn't. It inspires derision."

"Gosh, you sound like Corelli Barnett."[55]

"I mean to. I don't think he's right that we should have supported Japan against the USA, though."

"Two years ago I met him in Cambridge, at a party of Dad's. He can certainly talk. Gosh, he did rather finish Amanda off. She *is* a strong supporter of the Liberals."

---

55 His *The Collapse of British Power* had appeared in 1972.

"How are she and John?"

"They're formally engaged at last, with the wedding set for June."

"So she'll be right in the family, at last. Well done, Jenny."

As we approached Roberta's bungalow, I smiled in a brotherly way and licked my lips. She smiled in a sisterly way, and licked hers.

It was heartening to chat, as close friends and honorary siblings. I still called up images of Jenny in my mind, but the distractions of the last two months had made these into an enjoyable diversion, rather than an obsession. That of her licking her lips as she took Amanda had been very helpful in relieving my frustration at being alone. One night, I had called up even more helpful images of how she might have gone on. A memory from just before I left Cambridge made these images very plausible.

Clearly, then, *I* was not causing any difficulties in her relationship with Dick. We were making our own ways, and related best on that basis.

Roberta had provided good sandwiches and campaigning would pause until three o'clock, to allow time for the electorate to fall asleep after roast beef and Yorkshire pudding. Brian's skilful bonhomie had allowed him to assemble a good crowd, with new faces as well as Cambridge friends. The only definite absentees from the campaign would be Liz and Greg, who were not on three-day weeks. I swapped news with various old Waterhouse people. Many of them appeared to be getting on, purposefully. Perhaps that reflected the message of my last evening in Cambridge, but if so only because they had translated it into effort.

A happy trio called in after visiting the party office. With Carol and Paul was Bert Gibson, who had joined the campaign the day before. As Carol worked the room, she was full of confidence and poise. She had the knack of making people feel wanted and important. She looked intelligent, but not overpowering; such a change from the strident but nervous girl whom I had met over six years before. I was proud of my quiet part in that change. There was no sign of any problem with Steph.

Brian called us to order, for a first quick check on intentions. Of the small sample of people we had talked to that morning, the definite Labour vote was 20%, compared to the last election's 11% constituency-wide and less in this area. Fred summed up.

"Thank you all. We're moving up, fast. The local Tories don't know what week they're in. In principle, Reg Emerson could still pull out and another candidate be adopted. The final date for nominations is tomorrow. In practice, they've no time to find someone new. I've not seen a Liberal. They're all in Sutton, trying to keep Graham Tope in. So, the sky's the limit. There's a chance – an outside chance, but a real chance – of the biggest upset of the election. I know the Tories are ahead nationally in the published polls, but I can tell you that our own returns aren't in line with that. Anything can happen between now and polling day. Mr Heath could well have some nasty surprises."

Soon afterwards, I needed to leave. Fred offered to run Steph and me over to East Croydon, since even the normal service from the local station was pretty wayward on Sundays. As I suspected, he had something to say.

"Pete, you'll want to tell Pat O'Donnell that instalment three comes out in the *Clarion* on Tuesday morning. It's not about Reg. That night in July, Sir Ambrose Dugdale of National Amalgamated and his wife Martha had a girl *each*. Both girls have sold their stories."

"How will that help Carol, or the Labour campaign generally?"

"It won't, directly, but it will keep the whole story on the boil, and remind voters of other stories about senior Tories. Also, our private polling is picking up that Labour is still regarded as too pro-Israeli, though the petrol problems are past. We'll come to no harm from dirt on someone from a big Zionist family, who've not given us a penny."

Steph glanced at me and came in.

"This is bad news for Harry."

"Why's that?" I asked.

"All the loans to Tamfield carry the provision that the bank can call them in at any time. It's standard practice in a high risk situation. If a company is going over the edge, you grab your money before the other man."

"Tamfield isn't going over the edge, now the Westbury deal is in place."

"On Tuesday, Martha will be very angry, very angry indeed. So will be Ambrose. They'll blame Harry for showing them up. You told me about Ambrose saying he was sure Harry would ensure that the party remained a wholly private event."

"They should blame themselves. It's one thing to be very angry with Harry. It's quite another to force Tamfield Investments over the edge and lose their bank millions."

"You're right in logic, Pete. Of course you're right. But logic can go out of the window. I've known it happen on Wall Street, and it could happen here, especially if it just means that National Amalgamated get a bigger bailout. It's all over the City that they're overstretched, and could be in the lifeboat before long.[56] Ambrose Dugdale is a front man. He goes down well in the City club, but he's a weak guy, over-promoted. Martha will call the shots. The big house and the pictures are hers, and won't be affected by anything that happens to the bank. She has all her family's ruthlessness, with a touch of sadism too. I've felt it. When I was on that line, she was just loving having us stripped and in her power. She'll be furious, and so will be her father. Reuben Levi is eighty-six, but he's still one of the people in London you *never* cross. Fred, if instalment three appears,

---

56 The name of the Bank of England's rescue scheme for secondary banks. It had been brought into existence hurriedly, during the Christmas period.

there'll be big trouble – *very* big trouble. Can you get the story pulled, even now? You've done enough for Carol. At the least, keep the dirt to Ambrose. Then Martha can tell her family how badly she's been treated, and dump him if she wants. Otherwise, it's curtains for Harry, and a big shortfall in donations to Labour from others of the Faith."

Steph had seemed mightily amused by the first two instalments of the unfolding story, once reassured that it wouldn't involve New Hampshire Realty. Now, she was speaking very vehemently. Rightly, she felt that no one had properly analysed the merits of going on. I added a point.

"There's also Harry's public image as an opponent of Labour, which doubtless he'll put out on TV. Wrecking his company would be seen as an attempt to silence him. That wouldn't suit your aim at all."

"Well, instalment three is going to happen," said Fred, defensively. "It's a pay-off for the paper, too. There'll still be absolutely nothing about Mart Steinberg, about either of you, or about your friend Dick, Pete."

"I went back to town with Mart and his wife. There wasn't any offer of services to them," said Steph, curtly.

"I hope it won't affect the deal over Bishop's Park," I said.

The rest of the car journey was in silence. Steph and I found a quiet corner on the train to Victoria. I was reflecting that this was not an intended consequence of my decision to tell Carol about Reg Emerson. After a minute or two, I continued.

"You're a lady who can stand up to sadists, Steph."

"Sure, yes, I *liked* it on that line, I told you."

"So did Gail, and Dick, and so I think did the ladies' winner, Gloria, whom I guess we'll read about on Tuesday. I told you I met her when Dick and I visited Harry's club. You're quite right, though. Instalment three hasn't been thought through. Before lunch, I was saying to Jenny that the Westbury deal had saved

Harry. I hope Fred does act on what you said. Later on, I'll try to speak to Carol about it."

"I don't know why she should pay much attention to you. Or perhaps I do… Mmm, Pete, I think it's you who has some explaining to do, later on. Perhaps then, *you'll* be across *my* knee." She gave me a little peck on the ear.

I had told Steph as much as I had told Dick about what had happened at Harry's club. Fred had said nothing that definitely conveyed that I had put Carol on to the story about Reg Emerson, and now about Ambrose and Martha Dugdale, but the implication was clear enough to her. My efforts to sound unknowledgeable had not been very convincing.

"Perhaps you should speak to Paul."

"I don't know when, *this* month. Very lonesome, I've been. It's nice you're back for a few nights, and again next week."

"Yes, Pat wants me here for the day after the election. I'll try to arrive in time to help at the end of voting, and stay over at Roberta's for the result. The timing fits with our being in Cambridge over the weekend, too. We're staying over Saturday night in the Master's Lodge, and can travel there with her and Greg."

"I'm looking forward to visiting the real Pembroke College, as well as your Waterhouse, and to seeing you as a godfather. It ain't gonna be like the film, is it?"

"No one will be massacred at the same time, so far as I know."

"Wow, ain't this train quiet?"

"People aren't yet used to being able to use trains on Sundays again."

"Perhaps. It's sure different from two weeks back. I had to go see a company in Haywards Heath. They told me not to worry, because the trains to there have speedos, so they're sort of running. I arrived only twenty minutes late. Then I made my big mistake. I got on the back end of the return train. After waiting outside Victoria for half an hour, it came into a packed platform. I could hardly get off, and then I had to shove my way through to the gate. Hordes of people were fighting to get aboard the train and another opposite, and more were pushing onto the platform. It was like pictures you see of trains in India, except that no one was climbing onto the roof. Charles Darwin would have thought it great – a struggle for existence, which would lead to improvement. Nowadays, I don't meet so many Brits as I used to who say that they can just coast along, because life here is really quite nice, and it doesn't matter if they're not doing quite so well as some others."

"That's a benefit, at least. You still hear people talking about 'managed decline'. There's no such thing. If people see themselves doing badly compared to others, they look for someone to blame. A lot of the trouble in Northern Ireland must stem from industrial decline and dispute about who gets what decent jobs are available, though the collections allowed in your home city for 'the struggle' don't help, Steph."

"There are more Irish in New York than in Dublin, Pete. You don't win elections without their support."

"People have also been shaken up by what Heath's mess on credit deregulation has done to house prices. To win the race, watch out, and act sharp. Don't just coast along, waiting for your turn at the head of the mortgage queue."

"Wasn't it Nietzsche who said that it was the duty of governments to make their people uncomfortable? Heath has certainly done that."

"He's certainly making people realise that a quiet life is no longer an option."

"My experience at Victoria may have caused some benefit straightaway. Two days later, New Hampshire had a couple of middle to senior Labour people to lunch. I jumped the gun in a respectable way by bringing Paul along. We had quite a go at them. If they wanted to win anything around London, if they wanted candidates like Carol to keep their deposits, they *had* to get the ASLEF action called off. I guess lots of people were saying so besides us, but we did our bit."

At Victoria we parted, and I made my first visit to Sir Pat's house in Hampstead. He worked long hours in the office, and did not expect to be bothered at home. His wife of over thirty years never appeared at corporate events. None of his three grown-up children had wanted to join the company. However, as with much else the three-day week meant changes in practice.

Plenty of big industrialists were saying that Heath's policies would lead nowhere. Pat had had more publicity than most, because he put things more forthrightly, and because IE had a history of confrontations with unions and poor industrial relations. He had supported the efforts of young managers like me to move on from that, but his public image had stuck, so he had been invited to appear on the TV programme.

James Harman, Waterhouse College's Fellow in Literary Studies, had long been a well-known media figure. Now, he was following the Liberal Party's manifesto, to the effect that we couldn't continue as we were and would all have to live differently. He didn't actually say that we were all doomed, though that was the implication. This message can be and is served up again and again, with adjustments for the latest perceived problem. I recalled whispers of 'James, say something apocalyptic' when some argument on High Table was bogged down in technicalities. Pat knew he could deal with James, so he moved quickly to the main issue.

"I want us to pool our knowledge of Harry Tamfield. You knew him at Cambridge, Pete, and you've seen him once or twice recently, including at his party, of course. What do you think makes him tick? All for this room only."

For the last year, Harry had been praised in terms such as 'one of the tough new younger breed of businessman, who isn't afraid to say what we need'. One exuberant reporter had described him as 'The Arthur Scargill of business'. There was some justification for all this. At the age of twenty-six, he was running a company which had been worth nearly £100 million just after the takeover of Cardinal. It all seemed like magic. The political commentators still had that image of him, though their business colleagues could tell them that Harry wasn't doing so well just now.

In several recent press interviews, Harry had stated that the unions were a threat to democracy, and that the rest of the nation must unite to resist them. This line was similar to those of various retired army officers who fancied themselves at running some kind of militia, but it was more effective through being taken by someone who wasn't a has-been. Thursday's and today's revelations had raised Harry's profile.

"He's a loner," I said. "Ten years ago, his parents divorced. His father quickly remarried, and Harry doesn't like his stepmother. His mother died just before he went to Cambridge. He's very determined. I don't think I've met anyone who is so obsessed with achievement. He's prepared to take a great deal of trouble to get exactly what he wants. He wants to show that anyone who tries to thwart him will be crushed. That can lead him to do unwise things, in both his business and his personal life."

I told of 'Tamfieldgate', and of Harry's efforts to win Dick back.

"It's a small world again, Pete. You knew Tamfield already, and then you had two different reasons for being in touch with him. Paul's wife did well in brokering the Westbury deal, and now she stands to benefit from Reg Emerson's discomfiture, the story of which began at Tamfield's party. I've not met her, but she deserves to benefit. She's certainly keen to achieve, though in a healthy way, like you and me. In my time, I've met two or three Harry Tamfields. They always come to grief. Obsession replaces judgement and ambition replaces profit. They may in the end quite consciously destroy themselves and anything they've created, in pursuit of some final effect. To digress for a moment, their ultimate model is Adolf Hitler. People ask why even when the Germans were going down to defeat they put a lot of resources into killing millions of Jews who would probably have been ready to help them as an alternative. To me, the answer is obvious. *They killed the Jews because they knew they were going to be defeated. At least, they would have done something irreversible first.* There's a speech by Himmler, hearing which has been regarded as proof of culpability, which says as much.[57] To return, thanks Pete. Now, George, what have you found out?"

Since the start of 1974, George Armstrong had been styled as Director, Finance and Corporate Services. That move towards making IE a more integrated operation was not wholly to the liking of some divisional Directors, but it was very much the way ahead suggested by my work in Spain and now in Aberdeen. He was the man for the job, since before going in for accountancy he had taken a law degree. He had been uniquely able to take care of the accounting and legal aspects of 'Crafty'.

"There's no doubt that Tamfield Investments acquired Cardinal on bargain terms. On the other hand, with the

---

57 Made at a meeting in Poznan (then Posen) on 6th (!) October, 1943. Part of Albert Speer's defence at the Nuremberg Trial was his claim that he had left the meeting beforehand, and therefore didn't know. This is an appropriate place to point out that the attitudes displayed in this narrative to the UK's interest in the Middle East War, and to possible influences on Harold Wilson, were widespread at the time; however, these attitudes did *not* reflect any ignorance of the mass murder of Jews and others under Nazi German rule. That may be a statement of the obvious, but I heard it suggested on the radio recently that before the mid-1970s, people were 'unaware of the Holocaust'. Such a description of events came into use around then, but that is terminology. The facts had been revealed in 1945 and had been fully in the public consciousness since then. There was a belief that the crimes were almost wholly (rather than partially) committed within 'death camps', and so were largely unknown to members of the regular German armed forces and the civilian population, including to many who remained in senior management posts during the 'Economic Miracle'. Some encouragement of that false belief was perhaps understandable given the need for West German participation in NATO, and it continued for long enough to be the basis of Robert Harris's 1992 novel *Fatherland*. The facts are clearly set out by Adam Tooze in *The Wages of Destruction* (2006).

acquisition came a lot of risk, which recent events have turned into loss. The Westbury deal came in the nick of time, and somehow there's enough cash to keep the confidence of suppliers. There are two points of interest to me. The first point is that before the acquisition, National Amalgamated was Cardinal's lead banker. It's clear that it pushed Cardinal into Tamfield."

"That's right," I said. "But I'm told the terms of its loans are pretty tough. Tamfield will currently be paying 15½%.[58] Also, National can take its pound of flesh at any time."

I went on to recount my conversation with Fred and Steph. Then George responded.

"Certainly, it would seem very stupid of National Amalgamated to pull the plug on Tamfield, especially as last November it increased its stake. However, its balance sheet, such as it is, is pretty unusual. Last year, an undisclosed asset of over £2 million made it look less shaky. I guess that's part of Lady Dugdale's personal fortune."

"So, the Dugdales won't want to do anything stupid," said Pat.

"Yes, and no. Despite the rumours, so far National Amalgamated has avoided needing help. That may well be because its balance sheet has been sustained by further infusions of Dugdale capital, or rather of Levi capital. As Pete says, the Bishop's Park sale should allow Tamfield to get through. However, that keeps the Dugdales locked in. Reuben and Martha may decide that they've had enough. If they pull the plug, Tamfield would be bankrupt and probably wouldn't be able to pay more than 50 pence in the pound. National Amalgamated would face a loss of anything up to £10 million. They would be a lifeboat case. However, the Dugdale capital is likely to be in there on the same kind of terms as the loans from National Amalgamated to Tamfield. It could be pulled out intact. Imagine a fast getaway launch for the first-class

---

58 Base rate had fallen to 12.5% on 4th February.

passengers, whilst the steerage passengers are kept below decks."

"That's smart thinking, George. Once again, it's good to have you here." George beamed. He did like to be appreciated.

"Moving to the second point of interest, last April's flotation brought Harry Tamfield over £600,000 from the sale of half of his shareholding. That was normal enough. What was less normal is that as soon as the stock went away at a premium he sold most of the rest of his holding, for another £500,000 or so. He has only a very small shareholding in the company now."

"It doesn't stop him calling the shots, and it shouldn't do so," said Pat. "I now own less than 2% of IE. I get your drift, though. Harry Tamfield is wealthy, whatever happens to Tamfield Investments. He's contributed towards revamping his local swimming pool, but that will have left him plenty in the bank. Thanks George, and thanks Bill, for this pile of cuttings, which gives the same kind of picture of Harry Tamfield. Pete, what I want you to provide in the next two days, using your contacts, is lines on all the questions I'm likely to be asked – by the presenter, by James Harman, and particularly by Harry Tamfield. Draw on what I've already said, and fill the gaps. I'm supporting Labour, but not of Labour. I'm for Common Sense, not the crazy stuff in their manifesto."

"I can use how Carol put it at a rally today. I'm hoping to speak to her later this evening or tomorrow morning about the risks of pushing Tamfield Investments into bankruptcy, though I won't mention your information, George."

Bill Anstruther, IE's Chief Press Officer, now made his only contribution to the discussion.

"If the *Clarion* is already set for Tuesday, there'll be no scope for change."

"Like Harry Tamfield, we'll have to take that as it comes," said Pat. "He'll be thanking his stars he sold his shares. George and Bill, thanks for coming in this afternoon. You know I don't like to break into home lives more than absolutely essential, but this was absolutely essential. Pete, if you can spare a few minutes more, tell me how things are looking in Aberdeen."

Pat poured two large whiskeys. I gave an account of the last six weeks, before concluding.

"Being there makes a huge difference. There are a lot of senior oil people there on single status postings, with evenings to fill. They want to meet people who if not local have at least some idea of what's going on in the UK. I'm already regarded as an authority on what might happen to government policy after the election. One thing leads to another, and soon they, or members of their staff, are in our showroom having bits of gear demonstrated. We've logged over £100,000 of sales already, and a couple of people are going back to Texas convinced that we're better than their usual suppliers there. Once I'm in my flat, I'll be able to entertain with views right across the Granite City. That's when things will really get going."

"So your own profits from 'Crafty' are being well invested for the company, as well as for you."

"The way values are moving there, I'm not doing badly."

"Good. Now, I've one more thing to tell you about Harry Tamfield. I met him once, soon after you joined IE. I'd said that I might put some money into his company. My office tracked him down. I gave him ten minutes, was impressed, and put £10,000 in. Incidentally, last year I made the same decision as he did. Two weeks after the flotation, I sold for £85,000. That was a good move. My shares would be worth under £30,000 now and God knows what next week. Anyway, Tamfield was pleased to have my money, but asked also where Andrew Grover had gone to die. He'd been one of the few people at Waterhouse College who thought well of Andrew, and so he wanted to visit. I gave the address to him on the strict understanding that he wouldn't pass it to anyone else. Andrew had made clear that he didn't want anyone from Waterhouse to visit him. Three weeks afterwards, I went to see Andrew again. He told me that Tamfield had already visited him twice. They'd talked a lot about what had happened in Waterhouse. Tamfield had been particularly interested in what Paul Milverton had been doing. I understand that there were more visits before Andrew passed away in September."

"This explains something that's been bothering me. Two months ago, Steph and I gave Harry dinner. He was mostly quite friendly, but right at the end he suddenly became very angry about the way I was on better terms with Paul and Carol. I thought he knew a lot about them. I see now how he found out. I wonder if Andrew told Harry why Dick Sinclair had tried to kill himself."

Pat opened a desk drawer and took out a notebook. "Do you remember this?"

"No."

"It's Andrew's diary. I read out a few extracts to you and Arthur. Here's an entry which I didn't read out, because it wasn't relevant to what we were talking about."

He passed the notebook to me, and I read.

'Friday, 24th May.[59] I've found out how Pete Bridford knows that it was Milverton who reported three undergraduates to Bertrand for what they did to Woodruff. Last evening, I went briefly to the staff party, and overheard a conversation between Mrs Simmonds and Mrs Bailey, the bedmaker for Gilbert House. Mrs Simmonds recalled Bridford's time with Liz Partington, and asked about his current girl, whom her husband has noticed as being very attractive. Mrs Bailey said that the two of them were doing very nicely together. She also remarked that Bridford had had a different girl during the last autumn and winter. She had never seen her, but had noticed a name on a discarded envelope: Carol Gibson. That is the name of Milverton's girl. I said nothing at the party, and will keep this information to myself. This morning, I asked Simmonds to ensure that his wife is more discreet, particularly in regard to Fellows and Fellows elect.'

---

59 1968.

"Goodness, is there any more about this?"

"No. I take it that it's true."

"Yes. It's an old Cambridge saying that your bedmaker knows everything. In fact, Carol and I were on and off for some time. We began again a week before the staff party, but fortunately Mrs Bailey hadn't spotted that. It came to a definite end before I went to Spain, and two years before Carol married Paul. He knew about it, from the start."

"I accept that. It's none of my business, provided it doesn't react on IE, and it hasn't done so far. The point is, though, that Andrew could well have passed this information to Tamfield. That would explain why he thinks you're in cahoots with Carol Milverton, and by implication with Paul."

"He would be building a lot on very little. He would know only that six years ago, Carol was my girlfriend for a short time. He can't use that to do much damage."

"I agree, but it does show once again how Tamfield works to find out things that might be useful to him. Bear that in mind in what you prepare for me, Pete. Provide safe answers to questions he oughtn't to be asking, but might. He's coming out with a million, so he's not actually in a corner, but he may be so obsessed that he thinks he is, and has nothing to lose. He could try to cause maximum damage, just as Hitler did, and I suppose as Andrew Grover did. That's for all of us to remember, including you. You've got across him. Beware of his hitting back in ways which might be quite irrational, and therefore unpredictable, but very destructive."

THIS SCRIPT WAS TYPED FROM A RECORDING, NOT COPIED FROM AN ORIGINAL SCRIPT. BECAUSE OF THE RISK OF MISHEARING AND THE DIFFICULTY IN SOME CASES OF IDENTIFYING INDIVIDUAL SPEAKERS THE BBC CANNOT VOUCH FOR ITS COMPLETE ACCURACY.

TOPIC: "ELECTION ROUND-UP", BBC2, 10.35 – 11.15 pm TUESDAY, 19th FEBRUARY, 1974

CLIVE TOLHURST (presenter): Welcome again to Election Round-up. One of the most remarkable things about this remarkable election is the level of public participation. Usually at election time people who are not politicians leave it to the politicians to make the running, and then cast their vote. Not this time, though. All sorts of people who would normally remain silent have joined in the debate. Perhaps it reflects the way the issues affect us – all of us – directly through the three-day week. Tonight, we have in the studio three well-known people who are not politicians but have made their views clear. Considering what they've said before, their views can be surprising. First, we have Sir Pat O'Donnell, founder and Chief Executive of International Electronics. Seven years ago, he didn't seem to be a friend of Labour.

PAT O'DONNELL (recorded in April 1967): The workforce at Ham Lane have priced themselves out of their jobs. They can have work only if they can deliver the goods better than people can and want to do on the Continent, and increasingly in the Far East. That's a fact of life, not something I've made up. We've given them, and their unions, every chance. We've warned them what would happen if they didn't respond. They haven't responded, so that's it, finish.

MAN ON PICKET LINE (recorded in May 1967): Smash O'Donnell, class enemy, traitor.

CLIVE TOLHURST: But a fortnight ago, Sir Pat had a different view.

SIR PAT O'DONNELL (recorded on 5th February): The sooner Heath calls an election, the sooner we can get rid of him. He's messed up completely. His policies are wrecking our industry and wrecking the country.

CLIVE TOLHURST: Sir Pat is one of our most senior industrialists. He's built his company up over the last thirty-five years. A younger generation is coming on. Just over six years ago, Harry Tamfield was still at Cambridge. Last year, his property company, Tamfield Investments, took over a much larger company, which was beset by industrial disputes.

HARRY TAMFIELD (recorded in April 1973): We want to make a fresh start at Cardinal. Tomorrow, I'll be meeting all the unions involved, with the aim of getting work going again, fast. That's in all our interests.

CLIVE TOLHURST: And he did get work going again, fast. But recently, he also has made his views clear.

HARRY TAMFIELD (recorded on 23rd January): We are faced with a choice. Democracy, or dictatorship. Government by people we all elect fairly, or government by union bosses who get where they are without even the members of their unions having much say. Each and every one of us will have to stand up and be counted.

CLIVE TOLHURST: Of course, Labour isn't friendly to property companies. Only yesterday we heard their view.

DENIS HEALEY (recorded on 18th February): We will squeeze the property speculators till the pips squeak.

CLIVE TOLHURST: Now, we've heard of the connections between Tamfield Investments, its main banker, National Amalgamated, and Sir Reg Emerson. He is Parliamentary Under-Secretary for Works and member for Bellinghame South, where Tamfield Investments has its biggest project, Bishop's Park.

That's enlivening the campaign there (flashes of press coverage). Finally, we have another figure from Cambridge University. James Harman is well known to viewers of 'Artsnight'.

JAMES HARMAN (recorded in October 1972): The author has made a brave attempt to conceptualise the structural and materialistic aspects of his subject matter, but has ignored the vital work of Noam Chomsky.

CLIVE TOLHURST: Recently, he's been promoting the Liberal Party.

JAMES HARMAN (recorded on 12th February): The capitalistic, competitive world in which we have all grown up and which has caused so much destruction is now coming to an end. It is time for all of us to look to a better way of life, based on co-operation and respect for the environment. I am pleased that the Liberal Party has realised the importance of this.

CLIVE TOLHURST: So, here we are. Three changed minds, and three new points of view. We'll start by letting each of them explain, and then we'll debate.

SIR PAT O'DONNELL: I haven't changed my mind. The government has changed its mind. Company managements need to manage. That includes deciding how much to pay their employees, in the light of negotiations with unions. What they can pay depends on how much the company's products can be sold for, and how cheaply, fast and well the products are made. Isn't that quite obvious? It's why in 1967 International Electronics took the decision to close Ham Lane. It's what the Conservatives said in 1970, when IE contributed to their funds. Now we have this fantastic bureaucracy of controls, drawn up by people who can't know what's best for individual companies to do. It was bad enough before last October. Now, it's the madhouse. We need more people to dig coal, and drive trains, not fewer as we thought a few years ago. There's only one way to get them. Next week, there's only one party to offer that way.

HARRY TAMFIELD: Over the last few months the threat to British democracy posed by the trades unions has become only too clear. Last spring, I was prepared to give them the benefit of the doubt. Now, they're taking advantage of a national crisis to blackmail the rest of us. We all know that giving in to blackmail never succeeds. It's getting worse. The communist Vice-President of the NUM, Mick McGahey, has suggested that troops should disobey orders. That's treason. He was quickly disavowed, but he's still Vice-President. Some of the unions' behaviour is just sadistic fun, for example the ASLEF men pretending their trains aren't safe to drive and drawing full pay for doing nothing. They've temporarily changed their minds, but they'll be back. They want the rest of us to be conditioned into knowing who is boss. Heath hasn't been as tough as he should have been, but a clear mandate next Thursday will allow him to be tough.

JAMES HARMAN: You're both speaking the language of competition and confrontation. Today, we need a new language, or rather an old one. That's what the Liberal Party offers today. The capitalist model, of grabbing as much as you can for yourselves, was invented only a few hundred years ago. All the peoples of the world lived happily for many thousands of years without it, and most of them still do. We need to take only what we need. We must develop resources carefully, for the benefit of all. We must adopt an alternative lifestyle, in which respect for others replaces greed, avarice and pride. We must look carefully at what the other great cultures of the world can show us. We must look at what the great philosophers of the past can tell us, like Rousseau.

HARRY TAMFIELD: With respect, Dr Harman, you're talking rubbish. Capitalism is as old as humanity. It happened in ancient Sumeria, it happened under the Greeks and Romans, and certainly it happened under the Jews. Two things have changed. Technology has improved, allowing more things to be made and better communications. That's good. Also, there's more care for the less successful people, who in the past you never heard about. That's good too, provided it doesn't hold back the winners who drive on progress. What care you can provide for the rest depends on their success.

JAMES HARMAN: How can you adopt such a simplistic attitude? You're speaking like a combination of Hegel and Nietzsche.

HARRY TAMFIELD: I prefer Hume and Locke myself.

CLIVE TOLHURST: Ha, I can see the makings of a good argument over the port in the Combination Room here.

HARRY TAMFIELD: Hardly. When I was at Cambridge, I only met Dr Harman once. He's a Fellow. I left without a degree, because I wanted to get on with my life.

CLIVE TOLHURST: Which you certainly have done, during the last six years. Sir Pat, you evidently believe that universities are important, because you've given generous support to several of them, but I don't believe you went to university yourself.

SIR PAT O'DONNELL: No, I didn't. When I

started selling radios, I went to night school to find out how they worked. But I do know about living happily, as James Harman imagines it. I grew up in the Irish countryside in the 1920s. People were happy there, I suppose. They didn't have time not to be. They worked all hours to scrape a subsistence living, and when they couldn't do that anymore they usually starved. Capitalism has lifted most of us out of that, so I won't argue any more about its virtues. I'll concentrate on the important issue for now. I'll ask Harry Tamfield this. Last April, you took over Cardinal Properties, and met the unions. What pay increase did you offer to get the men back to work?

HARRY TAMFIELD: Er, 17%, with conditions about productivity.

SIR PAT O'DONNELL: Gosh, that's quite an inflation buster. Inflation was only 9% then. Your unions did well. Isn't it rather unusual for building workers to be in unions, and how did this relate to the Stage 2 Pay Policy of the time, which limited weekly wage increases to £1 plus 4%?

HARRY TAMFIELD: We inherited the unions from Cardinal, but as usual in the trade the men are all self-employed.

SIR PAT O'DONNELL: Last April, house prices

were still rising, but you could see a peak coming. You had to finish houses and sell them, fast. You had to pay what was needed to do that, and you could afford to, given the profit you would make from the price rise that had already happened. Because your workforce was self-employed, Stage 2 didn't apply. You were able to make the right commercial decision, without interference, and you made it. Good for you. I should declare an interest to viewers, by the way. I was an early investor in your company. I've done very well out of it.

JAMES HARMAN: You're both talking about how to make money, and how to get round the rules. The Liberals believe in sensible rules that people believe to be fair and don't try to get round. There would be free collective bargaining, but if this led to higher wage increases than the country could afford, both employer and employee would pay an additional tax on them. This is all aimed at narrowing the gulf between the classes. It has worked in the past. It can work again.

SIR PAT O'DONNELL: It's never worked in the past, though it's been tried. We've heard about capitalism under the Romans. One of their later emperors, Diocletian, tried to control inflation through incomes policy. He also tried to stop anyone doing a different job from what their father had done, so he certainly didn't narrow the gulf between the classes. His policies were a total failure, and hastened the decline of the Roman Empire. Later, the Black Death killed a third to a half of the population of Europe. The survivors were in demand and wanted more pay. In England, the government tried to prevent pay increases. The result was the Peasants' Revolt.

JAMES HARMAN: We must try harder. We can advance from the past. We can discard the old values that have led to so much conflict. There are more modern role models. I would recommend you both to read the writings of Herbert Marcuse. In his book 'One-Dimensional Man' he shows how consumerism is a form of social control. It is even more irrational in the sense that the creation of new products, calling for the disposal of old products, fuels the economy and encourages the need to work more to buy more. An individual loses his or her humanity and becomes a tool in the industrial machine and a cog in the consumer machine. Additionally, advertising sustains consumerism, which disintegrates societal demeanour, delivered in bulk and informing the masses that happiness can be bought, an idea that is psychologically damaging. True liberation must go beyond consumerism.

SIR PAT O'DONNELL: Yes, yes, yes.

CLIVE TOLHURST: Viewers may be more familiar with the name of Ralph Nader, who has expressed some similar views.

SIR PAT O'DONNELL: Nader concentrates on safety and pollution issues, and of course he's right to raise them. You can always improve safety and reduce pollution, and fortunately we do. Where I grew up, the better off people still used horses to get around. The horses frequently bolted, or threw their riders. They made the roads, such as they were, filthy for the rest of us, who walked. The earliest cars were far safer and cleaner. Present-day cars are safer and cleaner still, and that trend will continue. New products have a great benefit. But we're straying from the immediate point. I was going to say something about International Electronics, something which our workforce, and their union officers, know already. We believe in effective trades unions, and want to negotiate with them. Over the last few years, we've generally done well on this. The closure of Ham Lane showed people that their jobs depend on contributing to a profitable business. I'm pleased to say that it's not had to be repeated. Throughout the firm, there's been higher productivity, and prices and quality have stayed competitive. Therefore, higher sales, home and export, have led to higher profits and have allowed higher pay. In the last three years, days lost through disputes have been well below the engineering industry average.

HARRY TAMFIELD: That sounds good, but haven't you allowed the unions to dictate to your managers? At your factory near Sunderland, I believe there's a Works Council which has a say in the setting of production targets. How do you think that union officers can run your factory?

SIR PAT O'DONNELL: The Works Council is of staff, not of union officers, and it doesn't run our semiconductor assembly plant. I'm glad you've mentioned that site though, for it shows well the two problems we face now, neither of which has been created by management or unions. The plant was built ten years ago, with some assistance from government grants for investment in areas of high unemployment. It's been well managed, the workforce is good, and industrial relations are good. It's been extended once, and another block is on the way, this time financed 100% by IE, with no grant. The semiconductor business is very rapidly expanding, and very competitive. It's a key IE objective to build our share. That needs rapid growth in productivity, and reduced costs, to compete with huge new plants being built in Taiwan and Singapore. At Sunderland, we currently employ 2000 people in two shifts. We want to move to three shifts and take on another 500 very soon, and still another 700 next year, when the new block commissions. The Works Council has helped management to find ways of moving current employees around, so they can show new recruits the ropes.

CLIVE TOLHURST: So, what are your two problems?

SIR PAT O'DONNELL: The first is that because of incomes policies, we can't pay what we're ready and willing to pay, to make sure we have the skilled staff who can deliver the products to cost, time and quality. People keep leaving for other jobs. We could recruit, if we paid more than we pay existing employees, but what would that be saying to them? Staff shortages are costing us nearly 10% of production. The second problem is that because of the three-day week we're losing another 15% – not 40%, thanks to the efforts everyone is putting in, but making the total loss up to one quarter of our production. This is all stuff we could sell, at a profit. Management, unions and the workforce at the factory just feel helpless. Customers here and overseas aren't getting what they want. There's no sight of an end, as long as Heath stays. You can imagine what our competitors are saying, gleefully. Kind people overseas regard us with bewilderment. Most people overseas regard us with derision. It's quite pathetic.

JAMES HARMAN: The Liberals' proposal for taxation of excessive pay or profit increases would allow you to pay more, if you really need to.

SIR PAT O'DONNELL: Why should International Electronics be subjected to that? Why is our management judged incapable of working out what we can afford to pay, and need to pay to develop our market? Why are our unions judged incapable of working out what is in the best interests of their members – balancing short-term gain against long-term prospects? Why is our workforce judged to be too stupid to think about what it wants? I'm sure the same applies to your firm, Harry. You and your team knew you needed that deal with your unions, so you went for it and got it – good for you, as I've said. You didn't need someone who knew nothing about your business to tell you that you couldn't do that.

HARRY TAMFIELD: We're both in businesses where there's competition. The miners and the engine drivers have a monopoly. They can't be allowed to take what they want.

SIR PAT O'DONNELL: Some of them may think they have a monopoly, but plenty of them know that's not so, I'm sure. Until last October the aim of all political parties was to run down the coal mines and railways. Both were seen as old-fashioned and uncompetitive in the age of oil and the car. Now, for the moment, oil is much more expensive. So, for the moment, there's a demand for more coal, and more trains. Since we can't increase productivity instantly, we want more miners and engine drivers – now. The only way to have them is to pay them more. This isn't 1944, when that good socialist and union leader Ernest Bevin conscripted young men into the mines. However, the increased demand, and so the extra jobs, will continue only if management, unions and workforce take the opportunity to build industries that can genuinely compete, long-term, rather than just thinking that this is an opportunity to go on like they have been for another few years. There's not a shortage of oil. The price rise will encourage people to go out and find more. There's plenty of coal around the world, too. Not to mention gas, and nuclear power.

JAMES HARMAN: This – this – is remarkable, astonishing. We are faced with the end of the era of industry, of growth, of dominance of the West, that began with the invention of the steam engine. Yet all you can both talk about is competition. You're stuck in the past. We all have to develop a completely new way of life, and realise that the world is not here to serve us. As Claude Lévi-Strauss said many years ago 'The world began without the human race and will certainly end without it.' We are not significant. I must ask Harry Tamfield, don't you accept that? Surely you learnt as much during your time at Waterhouse College?

HARRY TAMFIELD: I learnt several things during my time at Waterhouse College, but for now let's get back to realities. Sir Pat, let me read from the manifesto of the party you suggest we should vote for next Thursday. 'We shall also take over profitable sections or individual firms in those industries where a public holding is essential to enable the government to control prices, stimulate investment, encourage exports, create employment, protect workers and consumers from the activities of irresponsible multinational companies, and to plan the national economy in the national interest. We shall therefore include in this operation, sections of pharmaceuticals, road haulage, construction, and machine tools, in addition to our proposals for North Sea and Celtic Sea oil and gas.' Are you, as the leader of a big company, really in favour of that?

SIR PAT O'DONNELL: No, I'm not, but it won't happen. There's no way any government could raise the money to do a tenth of that. I've been through quite a few elections, and know that one thing not to believe is any of the manifestos, however splendid or otherwise they sound. For example, in 1970 the Conservatives said: 'We utterly reject the philosophy of compulsory wage control. We want instead to get production up and encourage everyone to give of their best.' Very good stuff, but here we are.

HARRY TAMFIELD: What about the 'Industrial Democracy Act, as agreed in our discussions with the TUC, to increase the control of industry by the people'? It's a proposal to establish a union dictatorship. Do you assume that won't happen, either?

SIR PAT O'DONNELL: I don't assume, I know it won't happen. The unions don't want to control industry, whether for themselves or for the people. They do want to be able to negotiate effectively for their members. Presently, they can't do that. There's no negotiation, just a standard increase for everyone, irrespective of the performance of their company. Union officers have to be seen to be doing something to justify their members' dues, otherwise they'll be cut out by local agitators. So they start behaving like local agitators, and pretending to be politicians. I'm not a religious man, but at school a nun taught me one thing that's right. 'The Devil makes work for idle hands to do.'

JAMES HARMAN: We must take a new attitude to life, in which everyone realises their responsibilities to each other, to the wider community, and to the world environment, and behaves accordingly.

CLIVE TOLHURST: We have just over ten minutes left. Sir Pat O'Donnell and Harry Tamfield, so far you've talked only about the situation here in the UK, which you both feel is the main issue in this election. Can you all tell us where you stand on our relationship with Europe, and with OPEC? James Harman, you've drawn our attention to wider issues, but in fairly general terms. Perhaps you can say more, first.

JAMES HARMAN: The multiple crises that face us offer the opportunity to put the past behind us and embark on a new era of reconstruction. The Liberal Party supported joining the EEC, long before either of the other two parties. We must now press for reform of institutions which are a bar to closer union within Europe. The development of closer links between regions of the larger countries and Europe is an important part of this, and also reflects our policies of maximum decentralisation. We must also press for policies concerning relationships between Europe and the rest of the world which place the formation of the EEC as a first step towards a more rational order in world affairs, one in which co-operation replaces the competition for resources which has so often led to destructive war. There need to be positive international agreements, to bring about a new radical world monetary framework and save the world from damaging economic recession and exacerbated racial tension. Many of the great thinkers on the continent of Europe have already set out the agendas for this. It is very disappointing that neither the Conservative nor the Labour Party has given it any thought at all.

SIR PAT O'DONNELL: After years of vacillation we've ended up joining the EEC on their terms, in particular French terms which involve paying out a fortune to subsidise their farmers. Now, we must make the best of it. That means playing it as dirty at Brussels as the rest of them, realising that they're all out for maximum national advantage, whatever fine words they say. We can't afford to be any different ourselves. On one specific point, I would be interested to know from James Harman whether he or the Liberal Party favour the plan for full economic and monetary union by 1980. That means the EEC having a single currency and finance ministry, which apparently some thinkers over there want. I've even heard that they've given the currency a name, the euro, and they want it 'to look the dollar in the eye'. Maybe that's a mistranslation from French, but it doesn't sound like co-operation replacing competition.

JAMES HARMAN: The new Europe should be built on democratic lines. It should offer the world a way of moving on from the sterile confrontation between the USA and the USSR.

SIR PAT O'DONNELL: I'll believe that when it happens. Moving on myself, before Harry Tamfield asks me, I'll say that another thing in the Labour manifesto I don't agree with is the establishment of an International Energy Commission, designed to establish a rational allocation of available oil resources. However, the chances of everyone agreeing to do that are precisely nil. On OPEC, we must remember that absolutely the only thing that unites them is the desire to maximise oil revenues. The Middle East War touched off the price rises, but countries like Iran and Venezuela which had nothing to do with the war climbed aboard gleefully. We must also remember that North Sea oil is the unexpected ace in our hand. If we can get its development right, then within ten years we can break out of the mess we're in now. The costs and technical challenges will be comparable to those of putting a man on the Moon, but to rather more practical purpose. We need to provide enough, but only just enough, incentive that there is a full-scale effort from all the oil companies, financed by their bankers. We don't need any fancy schemes for public ownership. UK industry must move fast to build its share of the huge new market for the gear the companies need, here and elsewhere. I would add that my firm is one of very few with North Sea sales offices in Aberdeen. That's already paying off. Wake up, everybody.

HARRY TAMFIELD: Is there anything in the Labour manifesto that you do support?

SIR PAT O'DONNELL: Getting the country back to work as quickly as possible. That's quite enough to go on with. The policies of the Heath Government are so confused, that it's like trying to fly an airliner with only the engines on one side running. It's possible for a while in calm weather, but in rough weather like we're having now, it's a flight to destruction. The next government must restart all engines. Once that's done, a course can be worked out.

HARRY TAMFIELD: The fact is, however, that a vote for Labour is a vote to allow Britain to be run by all sorts of people who have not been elected, and whom you don't know. I'm not just talking about union leaders.

CLIVE TOLHURST: Who are you talking about, then?

HARRY TAMFIELD: There are others who fund the Labour Party substantially. Only some of their names are published. There are others again who appear to have a close relationship with its leader. Their influence appears to underlie actions which are otherwise inexplicable and are clearly contrary to the national interest.

CLIVE TOLHURST: Could you explain further?

HARRY TAMFIELD: You'll recall that last October, following the outbreak of hostilities in the Middle East, there was initially a sensible and even-handed collective response by members of the EEC. Arms deliveries to all parties involved were suspended and they were encouraged to reach a solution in accord with UN Resolution 242. That appeared to be sufficient to prevent any embargo on oil deliveries from the Arab producers from applying to EEC members. It was just the kind of collective and independent European action that James Harman appears to favour. Then, the Dutch Government broke ranks and resumed deliveries to Israel, with consequences that impacted on us in ways we all recall. Now, what did the leader of the Labour Party say about this? In Parliament on the 30th October, he proposed that things would be much better if we backed the Israelis and the French backed the Arabs. He suggested that that had happened in 1967, when he was Prime Minister. He never explained how this would add usefully to American and Soviet efforts to resolve a situation which was already difficult and dangerous enough. No one has really asked why he behaved in this way. Why not? I think it's because people whose views might carry weight know that if they did ask, they would be in trouble. I'm in trouble already, and I have nothing more to lose, so I'm asking, and I'm saying that a vote for Labour is a vote for decisions in favour of a foreign power, contrary to the national interest. Therefore, it's a vote for treason.

JAMES HARMAN: These are astonishing and unpleasant allegations, which I am amazed to hear made by someone who studied at Cambridge. Let me say now that I believe that a common European foreign policy should be based on high moral considerations, rather than on narrow self-interest.

HARRY TAMFIELD: You're making my point, Dr Harman. Your career depends on many people whom you can't afford to offend. Let me say now that twenty-four hours ago, I, like you, needed to watch what I said. However, today the lead bankers to my company have taken gratuitous and unnecessary action to destroy it. I can assume only that this is a reaction to this morning's press coverage concerning their Chairman, Sir Ambrose Dugdale, and his wife, Lady Martha Dugdale, formerly Martha Levi. So now I have nothing further to lose by speaking out and breaking the conspiracy of silence about the malign influences at the heart of the Labour Party. I say to all viewing this programme, don't give them a chance!

CLIVE TOLHURST: We must come to an end now. Sir Pat, do you have any last thoughts?

SIR PAT O'DONNELL: Only that things have moved on a great deal even since last October, and we all need to take decisions on the basis of what faces us now. Also, Harry, I am sorry to hear of what has happened to your company, in which I invested. These things are very upsetting at the time, but they do happen. In 1937, when I was a little younger than you are now, I was made bankrupt, quite unnecessarily. I wish you luck in further ventures, and I'm sure that you'll overcome this reverse.

HARRY TAMFIELD: Yes, I overcame a reverse to get where I am now, as Dr Harman will recall. In fact, I see some of the same people involved this time as before. I'm sure one of them is watching this programme. Two months ago I warned him that I knew he was up to something, and if he hit me, he would be very sorry. Now he has hit me very hard, and he will be very sorry indeed... (transmission faded out.)

Tamfield crash after TV row

Receivers went in at Tamfield Investments yesterday morning after National Amalgamated called in loans of £20 million. National Amalgamated may face a loss of up to £10 million. Shares in Tamfield Investments had been suspended from the start of trading, after an extraordinary outburst by Chief Executive Harry Tamfield late on Tuesday evening, during the broadcast of BBC2's *Election Round-up*.

Like other property companies, especially those that expanded rapidly, Tamfield Investments had faced cash flow difficulties following the downturn in the homes market last autumn. However, two weeks ago these seemed overcome, at least for the present, by the £8 million sale of 462 properties on the Bishop's Park Estate to the Westbury Housing Trust. The decision by the National Amalgamated Bank to call in its loans therefore came as a surprise, particularly as in November it had extended its commitment, by taking over a loan made by New Hampshire Realty. Yesterday their spokesman referred simply to a reassessment of prospects.

The decision followed Tuesday's revelation that Sir Ambrose Dugdale, Chairman of National Amalgamated, and his wife had separately consorted with female prostitutes, who had earlier posed naked in a 'beauty contest' held at a party given by Tamfield Investments. However, personal anger cannot have underlain the decision to call in the loans, because the impact on National Amalgamated's balance sheet will certainly make it into a 'lifeboat case'.

Mr Tamfield's announcement on air drew particular attention to Lady Martha Dugdale being the daughter of Sir Reuben Levi. This followed allegations that some of Mr Harold Wilson's recent statements, in particular those he made during the Debate on the Address on 30th October, reflected the influence of associates. In a brief statement yesterday, Mr Wilson strongly denied these allegations and drew attention to the full context of his statements; in 1967 the UK and France had played a constructive role in the peacemaking process, which was now absent. He also confirmed that he was taking legal advice concerning Mr Tamfield's statements, but was not considering action against the BBC. His office stated that he had never met Mr Tamfield, and had encountered Sir Ambrose and Lady Dugdale only at large social events.

Other participants in *Election Round-up* were quick to disassociate themselves from Mr Tamfield's allegations. Sir Pat O'Donnell, Chief Executive of International Electronics, who had repeated his earlier recommendation to vote Labour, said "Harry Tamfield was under great stress, having suddenly been faced with the loss of his company. He's made the wise decision to take a short holiday."

Mr Tamfield, who is an expert ski-er, flew to Switzerland yesterday morning. His absence is not expected to hinder the work of the receivers, Messrs Cork Gully. They have confirmed that the Westbury sale will proceed on unaltered terms, as will all other property sales in progress, and work to complete properties sold will continue. The National Association of Building Societies confirmed that accordingly its members were likely to honour mortgage arrangements already made for such properties.

The failure of Tamfield Investments added intensity yesterday to campaigning in the Bellinghame South constituency, in which the Bishop's Park development is situated (our political correspondent writes). Sir Reg Emerson, the sitting Conservative MP, whose association with Tamfield Investments has been revealed over the last few days, said that a Labour inspired witch-hunt had now begun in the press; electors should recognise the panic tactics of a party that knew it could not win in any other way. Mr Cyril Horsley, the Liberal candidate, said that the continuing revelations showed the need to bring decency back into public life. Mrs Carol Milverton, the Labour candidate, welcomed the news that the Westbury sale was to proceed, following her work to bring it about as an alternative to the GLC taking over the Bishop's Park properties. She and her husband were looking forward to moving to Bishop's Park themselves in a few weeks' time. She also said that Mr Tamfield's false allegations about Mr Wilson were made under stress and were best forgotten.

11. THURSDAY, 21ˢᵀ FEBRUARY, 1974

"Thanks for inviting me, Fred. I was planning to come down, later on. The IE office is closed today, and Pat reckons that Bill Anstruther can handle any further queries."

"Pete, it's right that you and Brian should be at this meeting, given how much you've both contributed to where we are now. The first question is, how do we convince Transport House that the campaign here should go on? I need to call them at ten o'clock, with our case. I'll do my best, but I'll have to work hard."

"What on earth do you mean? I know that the plan was to review after a week, but surely things have been going well enough?"

My surprised question cut through the mixed aroma of bacon, eggs and cigarette smoke. Brian, who had arrived just before me, looked bewildered. Bert had his hand on Carol's knee and was murmuring fatherly consolation. Paul looked rather detached, as usual, with his head inclined to one side in much the same way as when I had first met him at Waterhouse.

The same group as had met on New Year's Eve was eating breakfast at the hotel where Fred and Bert were staying. Fred continued.

"Yesterday, we had a private poll taken. Intentions split 36% Tory, 34% Lib, 28% us, 2% independent. That compares with 57%, 32%, 11% in 1970 when there was no independent. There's currently a 17% Tory to Labour swing, with the Libs going nowhere. You've done great, Carol, well enough to get you noticed and in line for a much better seat next time. So have you and your team, Brian, and all the other people we've drafted in. It could go further. Nationally, we're closing the gap. Currently the polls put us on average about 4% behind. We reckon the Reg story and its follow-ups have already pulled us up 1%. Not for outside this room, two more things will hit the Tories hard. Later today, the Pay Board[60] won't give quite the message Heath wants about miners' current pay. Then, at the weekend, something or rather someone else will happen. By polling day, we should be neck and neck. With another push here, there's a very real chance."

"So what's the problem?" said Brian.

"It's a problem here, but an opportunity nationally. Yesterday afternoon, someone big in the Libs rang Transport House. They haven't got that poll figure, but it could be read as supporting what they said. Presently, it looks as if our intervention is going to save Reg from Cyril. So, if we cut down effort here, and give them a clear run against Reg, they'll pull out of two constituencies where they could be a threat to our beating the Tory."

"How could they do anything here? We meet no one from the Libs. That's why they've got nowhere."

"They now know they won't hold Sutton and Cheam, Brian. They want to divert their people from there to here. They reckon that if we pull out there's a real chance for them."

"For Cyril? He's a complete no-hoper. That's what everyone tells us."

"Maybe, but thinking at Transport is that if we take two other seats off the Tories and the Libs can take this one, that's better than our setting up in Con-Lib country. There's another bother to the bosses, too."

"What's that?"

---

60 The Pay Board was supposed to provide independent adjudication as to whether special groups of workers merited increases in excess of those allowed under Pay policy.

"On Tuesday, Harry Tamfield came close to playing the Jewish card. It's the ace Heath holds, but hasn't played. Our own polls have made that clear. He may not realise he holds it, or he's so confident that he doesn't think he needs to play it, or he's just too nice to play it. Who knows? He could have called an election in November. He could have said that we were faced with an embargo over something which was nothing to do with us, and that meant we had to give the miners a big increase. He could have asked why Labour appeared to be supporting policies designed to get us into worse trouble with the Arabs. He would have lost a couple of his Cabinet, but he would have won a landslide."

"It was clear then that Labour had to rethink," I said. "Several of us said as much to Carol. However, people have forgotten the petrol shortages now they're faced with the three-day week."

"I agree with you myself, Pete, but Harry Tamfield's performance made quite an impact. People at Transport will do all they can to low-key it, but they're shit scared that Heath will now play the card. He needn't agree with what Tamfield said, so he needn't risk trouble on his own side, but he could suggest that if you're worried, play safe and vote Tory. So, the emerging line at Transport is to close down anything linked to Tamfield. That includes here."

Carol burst in. She was as upset as ever I had known, and I had been with her that night in Cambridge when Paul was attacked.

"How can they close down a growing story? There were four national reporters here yesterday, and there'll be more. What message will appear if we're seen to close down? What will it say about how much we care for the loyalty of our supporters? How can people be expected to vote for a party that pushes for support, and then gives up with the goal in sight? What commitment does that show? I've had so many voters say welcoming things to me. Brian, that's happened to you and your people, too. What impact do you think stopping would have on

Brian and the others who've done so much here? They live all over London, and even down to Brighton. If they're let down, that will get around. When you speak to Transport, Fred, I want to as well."

"I wouldn't recommend doing that in your present state, if you want the next chance, Carol. Just now, everyone at Transport is as edgy as you are. They can see the chance of winning nationally, but everything must be right over the next week. Our vision is local, theirs is national."

Paul came in, quietly.

"Where are the two constituencies that the Libs are offering?"

"Birmingham, Allbright and Stafford, North."

"Someone else will win them both for us, Dad. They're where his hit will be biggest. At the weekend, the Libs will see that coming, and pull out anyway. Their offer isn't worth it."

There was a silence. Brian mouthed the name in all our minds. I was reminded of his drunken yelling of it at some overseas students, back in my last summer at Cambridge.

Fred, Bert, Carol and Brian continued to argue. Paul said a few words, and then he went to use the call box in the hotel lobby. I couldn't contribute much. On Sunday evening I had spoken to Carol to try to stop the third round of revelations, but to say 'I told you so' now would have been even more unhelpful than it usually is.

By a quarter to ten, Fred was noting down the points he would make to Labour headquarters, and saying that he would do his best. Once Paul had returned, I asked to use the phone first. Soon, I was back with news.

"For most of yesterday, Steph was busy with the receivers for Tilford Investments. It wasn't something a senior economic analyst would normally be doing, but New Hampshire's accounts and legal people weren't around as their office was closed. She knows the documentation for the agreement that transferred New Hampshire's loan to National Amalgamated. She was making sure that no bright spark at National Amalgamated found some defect in it. She told me last night that something she overheard had made her think, and suggested that I call her about now. It seems that overnight work has confirmed that £2 million is missing from the Cardinal Properties employees' pension fund. The trail points to Harry Tamfield. If it isn't on the lunchtime news, then it won't be long. Anyone who picks up on Harry's cue will look very, very silly."

A long silence was broken by Brian.

"You – you mean, Harry Tamfield is a crook. He's bunked off, with anything he can lay his hands on."

"It looks like it. For him, just now, Switzerland is the land of secretive banks, not of snow and skis. It's good news here, I guess, but it's tragic. Last year, Harry disposed of most of his shares. That gave him a totally legitimate million. Now, he's got three million, but he'll be a hunted man, and will end up in prison, eventually."

After about ten seconds, Bert continued, cheerfully.

"Well, Fred, you can reassure Transport House that Harry Tamfield has discredited the Jewish card. Why has he done it, Pete? He must be *mad*."

"I know him better than any of you. I think that after what happened to the Baroque Society, the failure of his company has sent him right over the edge. This was boiling up in him. On the night of Heath's three-day announcement, Steph and I had him to dinner. He was very stressed then, and made a nasty remark about Jews. As I was seeing him off home, he said that he knew I was up to something with Carol and Paul. I told you about that the same evening, Carol. He knew that you and I had been at the meeting in Bellinghame the night before, and he might well have known that Paul worked for IE. On Tuesday, just before they faded him out, he used much the same words as before. He was referring to me. It was quite unnerving to watch, because the camera crew had him close up. He may have guessed that I was behind the story about his party. However, this latest news means that his scope for making any of us sorry is somewhat reduced. There's nothing to worry about."

Fred pointed to the *Clarion*, open at its inner page photograph of Harry at Heathrow Airport under the headline:

BROKEN TYCOON QUITS TOWN
goes skiing as company crashes. No clue to Mystery Man.

"Is anyone nosing around you?"

"Not to my knowledge, and there's no reason why they should. I hope it stays that way. Brian, just in case, put me somewhere today where I'll be well away from reporters. I'm returning to Aberdeen early tomorrow, and I won't be here again until late on election day."

"Jack told me that yesterday several of us were asked whether they were the Mystery Man who Harry had accused of plotting his downfall," said Brian. "The line is that it's Dr Fu Manchu."[61]

"So, Fred, we've a good case to go for a win. Thanks, Pete," said Carol.

"It's thanks Steph, really."

I nearly also said 'and thanks, Paul, too' for his point about the two Liberal seats, but decided not to annoy his father, who should have spotted it himself. Carol looked at me in a way that both Paul and I knew. It was clear what she would want when she found out about Steph.

For a few minutes, we talked about lines on Harry. Then Fred went to phone Transport House, whilst Carol wanted her father's help on some questions on housing that she had promised to answer. Paul wanted to call at Frank Booth's office with papers about their new flat, so Brian ran us both over to Roberta's house. He was cheerful at the ending of the threat to his campaign, and reminded us of another cheerful event of the week.

---

61 A fictional villain whose name was familiar at the time.

"I'm not surprised that Martha Dugdale wanted Gloria, the girls' winner. In Tuesday's *Clarion*, she looks a real smasher. Her face did remind me of Jenny."

I made a small qualification. "In life she looked best in the swimsuit round. In Round Three, she was exposed as not a natural blonde. If Jenny had been able and willing, she would have joined Dick in sweeping the board."

"'Twas a very smartly done picture of her top half. It showed just enough to hint she were wearing nowt below. *Very* tasty."

Paul, who had been giving an impression of slightly pained boredom, came in.

"You're obviously an expert, Brian. How much do you think she was paid for posing?"

"For her story and the photo, at least five hundred. She'll get good business from it, too. You're saying move on, aren't you Paul, so tell Pete what you said when I told you about Tony Higgins' computer."

"You know that I did my PhD research on the history of the oil market. If there's a big change in the oil price, up or down, people who bet on it happening make a lot of money in the futures market. Or they lose a lot, if they get it wrong."

I replied vacantly. Fortunately, I was sitting at the back. Brian could not see my face.

"Yes, every gain must be someone else's loss."

"Despite what's happened recently, big changes aren't part of the normal market. There's no reason to suppose that they'll be part of the normal market in the future. The normal behaviour is more like a random walk."[62]

"So, betting on the fluctuations is like betting on the tossing of a coin. On average, it will be fruitless."

"It will be fruitless if traders have no information about what other traders are doing. If they do have such information,

---

62 In other words, the price moves in small steps and it is quite unpredictable whether the next move will be up or down.

they can use it. For example, the best way to corner the market in some commodity is to build up a large stock quietly, and then to engineer a fall in the price by suddenly selling part of it. That attracts the people who sell short, hoping that by the time they need to meet their commitment the price will have fallen further. They're the bears. When they need to buy, there'll be only your stock available, and you clean them out. That's the bear raid."

"It won't work for oil, will it? No one can stock enough."

"No, it won't, but the short-term fluctuations, which appear to be a random walk, are actually influencing each other. If you knew what other traders were doing, you could on average make a profit."

"You don't know what other traders are doing, and not everyone can make a profit. Isn't all this still like betting on a tossed coin – self-defeating, a zero sum game?"

"If you knew faster than anyone else, you could act before them and on average make a profit. That's called arbitrage. If computers in different parts of the world could link together to share information, the trader with the fastest computers and links would get in first and win. That applies to any commodity, and to foreign exchange assuming we stay with floating rates. It needs lots of small computers, linked together."

"How could they link together?"

Brian had the answer to that. "There's already something called the Arpanet in California. It will develop."

"Probably," I replied. "It all sounds way ahead to me, not an immediate challenge like getting North Sea oil on stream."

"I agree," said Paul. "But I've talked to Steph about it. New Hampshire has a big oil trading operation, based in Rotterdam. She thinks they should be taking an interest in people like Tony Higgins. They may make him a small grant for expenses."

"That's no problem for IE. Tony isn't signed up to us in any way. We're keeping in touch with him, and providing free samples of various components for him to test. Maybe the two of you, and Tony, could meet with Sydney Felhurst, who's the section head involved at our Staines research labs. You could form a little committee to support Tony. I'll give you both Sydney's contact details."

"Thanks. We'll try to bring Morag in, to help with the maths. I've tried looking at a few of the published papers myself, but with only first-year maths I haven't a hope."

"This is nearer Sheila's research subject. I wouldn't mind staying in touch, but I won't be around very much."

We had to park some way from Roberta's house, because several volunteers had arrived already. Her lounge was littered with toys, around which two lively toddlers were racing. She was happy enough.

"It's all part of the service. Later on, I'll be busier. Jenny Sinclair called just now. She'll be here at lunchtime, with both her children."

The phone rang in the front hall. Paul answered, and turned to us cheerfully.

"Dad has sorted Transport House."

He made off to see Frank Booth. I called the IE offices, where a few staff were working near windows and wearing their overcoats, to warn them to listen to the one o'clock news and brief Pat. They had a message for me, to call Sir Arthur Gulliver urgently. After a short conversation with a Waterhouse College porter, I was put through to him.

"Pete, I've not spoken to you for years, not since you stayed at the Lodge for Dick Sinclair's wedding, I believe. Pat told me recently that you've done a good job in Spain, and are now based in Aberdeen. Today you're electioneering, though."

"That's right. I'm speaking from my aunt's house, which is in the constituency where Carol Milverton is standing. Others from Waterhouse are helping, too. The three-day week gives us time to do so."

"Lots of you are down to dine on Saturday week, I see."

"Yes. It's a combination of people taking MAs and the christening of the Sinclairs' second child, which is the next morning."

"Right now, that seems a long way off. Once again that ass James Harman has landed us with a problem. Maybe Pat told you about it."

"He said that after the TV programme on Tuesday, Harry Tamfield just rushed off. Over the unwind drink, Clive Tolhurst said he'd noticed that Harry and James were both from Waterhouse. That prompted James to say that there were more connections. He brought up that Pat had nearly given the College a lot of money, and also that Carol Milverton's husband had been there."

"Yes. The upshot is that *Election Round-Up* is now scheduling 'The Waterhouse Connection' for Sunday night. They want to combine some interviews here with footage of everything going on that involves old Waterhouse people."

"What's the problem with that?"

"Tom Farley says that the College is a private place and must stay that way. He's not Senior Tutor any more, but he has a lot of influence and has assembled some unlikely allies including Francis Bracebridge, Bertrand Ledbury, Charles Oldham, and also Alec Wiles, who's now a Tutor. I would agree with them if the programme were to give James more time to open his mouth, but by luck he's going off to some beano in Italy over the weekend. What will be the picture of the College if we refuse?"

"You'll be seen as pretty stick-in-the-mud, and perhaps with something to hide. You should *boast* that your people are involved in events. Putting Waterhouse on the map will mean more good applications, and more good results. However, you'll need to take into account one piece of breaking news. By lunchtime, you're likely to have heard it for sure. Decide then." I explained about the missing £2 million.

"Jeeze, the man must be right off his head. I can remember Peter Sancroft saying that he was unbalanced."

"Yes, I can remember that, too," I said, rather icily.

"Perversely, I think that settles it. We're just going to have to take this on the chin. We've nothing to hide, and the man did leave early."

"Like me, you mean."

"No, *not* like you, Pete. You, and your friends, will be very welcome here on Saturday week, especially if you have something to celebrate. I never thought I might vote Labour, but I'm totally with Pat this time. His performance on Tuesday was magnificent. I expect you had a hand in that. However, all this shows a danger area. We don't want the BBC to probe around exactly why you left, or what happened then involving Paul Milverton, though that turned out to have done him a power of good."

"I'll warn people down here of what's up. Paul will be here at lunchtime."

Brian allocated me a road of forty houses. I obtained eighteen answers, five of which were definitely for Carol, and two were possible. On my return to Roberta's house, I was just beaten to the door by three Sinclairs.

Jenny greeted me pleasantly enough, but quietly. This wasn't just because she was carrying carefully the car seat in which Katie was fast asleep. She was clearly worried about something. She had the nervous, droopy look that I remembered from the time I first met her.

Inside, Roberta quickly engaged her in passing sandwiches around. At one o'clock, Brian turned on the radio news. Jenny listened intently. After speculation about the Pay Board report due later, the reader went on.

"Cork Gully, receivers for Tamfield Investments, have announced that a sum of just over £2 million is missing from the assets of the pension fund of Cardinal Properties, which

Tamfield Investments took over last April. They have asked Harry Tamfield, the Chief Executive and one of the trustees of the fund, to return from a skiing holiday in Switzerland, so as to help them to locate this sum. Our financial correspondent..."

Jenny seemed relieved, but still nervous. The buzz of comment was broken by Brian.

"Right, the line on this is that it shows that gambling on property prices leads nowhere. We need real enterprise, generating real business, profits and jobs. The sale of Bishop's Park Phase Two which Carol brought about is safe. People around here, including Carol and Paul who are moving in shortly, can be reassured about their neighbours."

I followed this with the news from Waterhouse. We exchanged contacts so we could all keep in touch about what to say if interviewed. I took Paul aside.

"We'll have to keep in touch about what we say. *If* anything comes up about old controversies, they're all in the past and we've all learnt. That's what growing up is about."

I gave the same message separately to Brian, for him to pass to anyone else who needed it. None of them need know more than they already knew.

The phone rang. I could see Jenny in the kitchen, giving Katie some prepared food. She mouthed me a message to answer. After a brief conversation, unheard by others amidst the hubbub, I went over to her.

"Dick says to tell you that everything is fine. He's returned the car and is now at the university. He'll be back late tomorrow, as planned."

"Oh, thank God, he's safe for now, then. Pete, let's work together this afternoon. I need to talk. I knew you would be here today, and Roberta is so good at looking after the children."

"It gives her a chance to be a granny. The arrival of Frank in her life has led to some falling out with her son and his family. I need to finish by five o'clock. Steph has returns for

Solti at the Festival Hall tonight. I guess you need to finish by then, too."

It was usual enough for women canvassers to work with a man. They could take alternate houses, and any rudeness in response could be handled better. Not that I could imagine any man, at least, being rude when answering the door to Jenny.

We set off once Katie was changed and settled, and I had checked that there were no urgent problems up in Aberdeen. The weather had been mild for the last week, and the last few days drier than before. Today had strong hints of spring, with some real warmth in the sun. From the diminishing stock of unallocated roads, I had selected one which after about an hour's work took us past a small park. We found a seat. Jenny pressed up close to me and began.

"I'll tell it as it happened, Pete. On Sunday, when I got home, Dick told me he'd called Harry, to offer sympathy for the press coverage. Harry said he suspected that it hadn't finished yet, but it would finish him, and he might ring on Tuesday. Dick said it would have to be early, because that day he was off to Geneva. Early on Tuesday the phone rang, while I was looking after Katie. Afterwards, Dick said that Harry was planning to come out to Switzerland for a few days, mainly for a holiday. He was flying to Zurich the next day, doing some business there, and then catching a train to Geneva. The next day, that's today, Harry needed to call on some people along the lake from Geneva. Could Dick hire a car, with a ski rack, for half a day? He could take the morning out from visiting the university, and see some of the local scenery. Then in the afternoon Harry would go off to Zermatt. As we have a joint American Express card, Dick could hire a car, and he'd agreed to do so. Dick didn't say whether Harry would come to Geneva yesterday evening or this morning, but I could guess. I could also guess what would happen then. Dick knew how I felt, but there was no time to talk. I was to drive him to Preston Park, to catch a train up to Gatwick for his flight, and the children would be in the back. All I could do was to kiss him goodbye and ask him to be careful. In the evening I saw the TV programme. Well done, Pete."

"You mean, well done Sir Pat."

"Yes, but I could see your hand in some of what he said. Then at the end, there was Harry. There's something in what he said about Wilson, but he looked completely bonkers. Then it almost sounded as if he was talking about *you*."

"He was."

"Yesterday, I heard that Tamfield Investments was in receivership. I was really shocked. What kind of man would just make off when his company was failing? What kind of responsibility did he have to his staff? If he was behaving like that, what was he trying to do to Dick?"

"His calls in Zurich and near Geneva were doubtless to do with making the three million he now has accessible from elsewhere. He wanted Dick to hire the car so that his name wasn't on record. My bet is that far from going to Zermatt, Harry is now on a plane out of Geneva, on the way to somewhere in South America. He can speak Spanish fairly well. Alternatively, he's already been nabbed by an attentive Swiss at passport control following an urgent message from the Fraud Squad. Either way he won't see Dick again, Jenny."

"You haven't heard it all, Pete. Early this morning, Dick rang. He wanted to say that he loved me, just in case anything went wrong. They weren't using the hire car to drive along the lake. Instead, Dick was about to drive south into France, as if heading for one of the resorts there. Harry's skis would be on top, and Harry would be curled up in the boot. Harry had said that people would be after him. He wanted help to have another chance. He'd flown to Zurich. No one would be looking for him in France, at least for a while. He could stay in a quiet hotel in Savoy, the kind of place where the proprietors don't keep records of people paying in cash. Dick could return to Switzerland around lunchtime with skis still on top, as if after a morning on the slopes. All I could think to say was that I would come up here to help take my mind off things. I asked him to call when he was safely back."

I put my arm around Jenny and gave her the kiss of the person she turned to when really troubled. If I was right about what happened sometimes now, it was more of a kiss than John gave her, and certainly more than what Amanda gave her.

"Dick is back, safe and sound. I wonder what Harry will do. He's a resourceful chap. Perhaps he'll go to Lyons, fly to Madrid and catch a plane to South America from there. Or maybe he'll head for Marseilles. I've read that's the kind of place where if you have money you can get on a boat with no questions asked. He's a better chance of getting away from France than he would have had from Switzerland, but I reckon he'll be picked up in the end. Dick may have had the fling with Harry that there was something inside urging him to try, but it's over now, for good."

"He could have been in serious trouble, for that man."

"You have to think, and decide, fast if necessary. I'm sure that the risk was quite small. The frontier controls around Geneva will be fairly lax, and Dick would have looked the part. Years ago, I took a risk and rescued Carol from the police. If I hadn't done that, she would have a criminal record and we wouldn't be here today."

"You are reassuring, Pete. You've always been able to think things through and decide what to do, calmly. That's why I wanted to be with you this afternoon, whatever happened. Last night I couldn't sleep. I was thinking of Dick being with Harry. Eventually, I rubbed myself and thought of you."

She kissed me back, and for a few minutes we said nothing. If there had been somewhere to go, we would have gone there. Fortunately, there wasn't anywhere to go. Consoling Carol would be manageable enjoyment. Consoling Jenny could lead only one way.

Eventually, I spoke.

"What's happened now may be for the best, Jenny. Dick showed nerve and took a risk, out of loyalty to Harry. He acted decisively, on his own. That makes him more confident, and less frustrated, like when he won the Body Beautiful contest and showed himself off with Gail, and like after he visited Harry's club. On Sunday you were right. That visit helped him to get his research going, so it's why he's in Geneva now. When you see him, don't be too hard. Then, he should be readier to accept what you've done and might do."

Jenny smiled. "Pete, are you talking about – more than my work?"

"Mmmm, yes." I licked my lips.

"So you know?"

"Only what I heard a while back. Dick talked after Liz had got us into that lake, and others talked about your hen party. I've put that together with what you told me about John long ago, when we were getting ready for your uncle's party."

"Amanda's crush on me made sure she and John stayed together. It came to a head at the hen party –"

"Where you made very clear who was in charge."

"Yes, and afterwards Amanda *was* sorry she had said too much. But she was sure she needed to tell John what we had done, before he heard it from Angela. I agreed, because I was fairly sure what he would say. I suppose you've guessed what he said, Pete."

"He looked forward to joining in a repeat."

"Mmmm, yes. It's great for us all. John and I feel there's a bit of each other in us, and Amanda feels she's having it from us both. These days it can't happen often, but we had a *very* nice Boxing Day at Amanda's place, when Dick was talking to Geoff and Mum was looking after David. After I had Amanda well going, she rubbed herself on while I gave John some of the Andy treatment. Then with one hand I gave John sisterly pats on the bottom as he took Amanda, Carol's way, and with the other hand I gave myself a little rub. Wow, Amanda yelled louder than at the hen party, and I came quite loud, too. Fortunately, Katie slept through it all!"

"Does Dick know?"

"He knows I'm close to John, and how Amanda feels towards me. He doesn't need to know more. Neither of them *touches* me. Only Dick touches me. He's my husband."

"You could use his escapade with Harry as an opportunity to tell him. It could make it easier to arrange repeats, but that's up to you. Anyway, I'm glad you've told me. I won't tell anyone else."

"Thank you, Pete. You're the only person who knows, but I trust you, I always will."

"Famous last words. Talking of those, we'd better get on."

By five o'clock, we were back for a cup of tea, with another fairly encouraging result: fifty-eight calls answered, with seventeen definite for Carol and seven possible. We had sighted both Conservative and Liberal canvassers, and others had too. The Conservatives weren't going to give up without a fight. There were plenty of safe seats nearby from which their supporters could be redeployed. Cyril Horsley's 'decency, not Socialist nuttery' line had its attractions for some, and the Liberals were moving in, despite the lack of any local pact.

Brian was out on the road, but Fred had looked in. Though he had good news, he looked worried. Perhaps party agents are always worried.

"Transport House is *right* on, now. If we're going for it, we'll go hard. The local party did do one good thing before I arrived. They booked the Memorial Hall for Tuesday night. We'll have a *very* big name speaking there, then. We can handle the Libs' decency line, too. We know about dear Jeremy.[63] I talked to the *Advertiser* earlier. Tomorrow should run well. Yesterday's *Record*

---

63 There had been some speculation about Jeremy Thorpe's personal life, though his sensational arrest and trial following the shooting of Norman Scott's dog were well into the future. It had already been pointed out that he had been a director of London and County Securities.

has again been totally wrong-footed. They ran a story that but for Harry Tamfield we wouldn't have the Bishop's Park development at all, so let he who casts the first stone, et cetera. Now, this TV programme, Pete. How can we use it?"

"We can put over the message that there's been no conspiracy to destroy Harry Tamfield. He's destroyed himself. I've a few ideas on that."

"How can we counter the line that the Labour campaign is being taken over by a gang of Cambridge toffs? It won't help to say that Reg is Harrow and Sandhurst, whilst Cyril is Winchester and New College."

"We're not all from Cambridge, and we're not toffs. We don't have plummy accents. Very few of us went to fee-paying schools. We want to get on in our lives, but are giving up our time because we see that there's only one way out of the mess the country is in now. In the 1964 election Harold Wilson did well out of selling Labour as the classless party, and the party of the future, not of the past. Perhaps that can be run a bit more."

"You'll be talking about 'the New Britain, forged in the white heat of the technological revolution' next, Pete."[64]

"I was taken by that then, but not now. Technical advances can't be planned. They arrive out of feasibility and market coming together. We need clear thinking, clear decisions, and no more mistakes. That's what our group here believe. The fact that some of us were at Cambridge is just incidental."

"I remember Steph calling your particular friends 'The Creators'. We must keep that name right off air. It sounds like some gang of Jesuits or Freemasons out to control the world, especially as there are twelve of you."

"Half of the people whom she called The Creators didn't go to Cambridge. Two, including her, have joined the group during

---

64 As mentioned in Harold Wilson's address to the 1963 Labour Party Conference.

the last six months. We all have our own aims, but we like talking to and helping each other."

Jenny dropped me at Purley, which had a better service than the local station, and by half past six, I was with Steph in a small Italian restaurant near Charing Cross[65] Underground Station. She arrived a few minutes after me, having visited the Pay Board's offices so as to collect a copy of their press release. As Fred had trailed earlier, it suggested a different way of interpreting the miners' pay statistics, which undermined the government's contention that miners were the highest paid industrial workers. By the time we ordered, I had read it through.

"It's a pity they didn't produce this before. It shows what flexibility there could have been earlier."

"Wouldn't Mr Gormley have picked up anything offered, and then asked for more?"

"Yes, if it had all been offered at once, but this would have given plenty of scope for dribbling it out and allowing him to claim that he's won."

"That all depends on what the objective of your Coal Board actually is."

"True enough. Meanwhile, thanks for your information this morning."

I described my day, apart from my conversation with Jenny. Our lasagne arrived, and it was Steph's turn. We spoke quietly amidst the hubbub of the restaurant.

"I've turned into a kind of unpaid consultant. From the point of view of New Hampshire, my job is done. The lawyers showed up today, and it's sure that we're right out. So now I'm someone with no interest who knows their way around the loan agreements – what they mean, not the exact legal detail. That's no end of help to the Cork Gully team. It's not my job, but hell it's interesting, will probably generate a nice letter from Kenneth Cork for my personal file, and though my office is open there's

---

65 Now Embankment.

damn all happening this side of the election. Mart is fine with it."

"Is anything else emerging?"

"Yeah. Some while back, Harry began to make his dispositions to flit. Cardinal was one of these old-fashioned companies, of course. They had a nice office in Berkeley Square, and a nice pension fund. The fund is on the edge of legality as far as independence of its trustees is concerned. The Chief Exec of Cardinal was a trustee by right. So, when Harry took over, he found he was a trustee, amidst a bunch who had grand-sounding names but did nothing for their fees. At the beginning of December, the trustees signed documents which were seemingly aimed at placing some liquid assets where they were safe against further falls in the pound, but which actually put the dosh where he could get at it via some nominee banks in Switzerland."

"So when we gave him dinner, he was already making contingency plans."

"It seems so. He must have guessed that National Amalgamated might pull the plug even if a sale of Bishop's Park Phase Two came about, indeed once it did come about, because it would provide more for the creditors. Remember what he said about Jews, then?"

"Yes. I still don't understand why National Amalgamated took over your loan."

"Their year ends on 31st December. They were able to show it then for more than they paid for it. Given compliant auditors, they'll still be able to make a profit for 1973."

"What benefit is that, if they rather than you have lost a packet on it now?"

"It made it easier for the Dugdales to have their own personal lifeboat, the way George Armstrong spotted. George *is* smart. IE is lucky to have him."

"Pat knows that very well. What beats me, though, is why Harry has done this. He had his own personal lifeboat. He'd taken his own money out of the company while the going was good. That was sharp, but quite legal. So he had the capital to go into business again, as Pat was encouraging him to do. Now, instead of being an honest man with a million, he's a crook with three million. He'll probably be picked up within days."

"Yup, the Swiss are pretty efficient at keeping track of who's in their nice country."

"Even if somehow Harry gets away to somewhere that has no extradition treaty with the UK, what will he *do*? He'll find himself in hock to all sorts of dubious types, who'll end up taking all his money. It's so tragic. Somehow I feel I could have stopped it, and put him back on the rails."

"You couldn't, Pete. The figures I've now seen make clear that Tamfield Investments couldn't have survived, even with the Westbury sale. The management accounts were wishful thinking. Back in November, Joe Aspinall must have seen that. Eventually, the Dugdales and National Amalgamated would have done what they did on Tuesday. Perhaps the publicity brought it forward, that's all. Harry must have known that Martha was enjoying dangling him on a string. Things have gone completely wrong for property companies and secondary banks. The good news today is that they haven't gone wrong for Carol."

"You and Paul made the difference on that, though I'm still quite surprised by how quickly Transport House dropped the idea of pulling out, after contemplating it seriously. Carol has done fantastically well, but she's still a few points down on Reg."

Steph paused briefly before replying.

"Enough of that. Since Sunday we've hardly seen each other, what with you working non-stop on briefing Pat and then all that happened yesterday. I'm looking forward to the Mahler. I've heard all the symphonies conducted by Leonard Bernstein. I wonder how Solti will compare. I wonder what the London Philharmonic will make of it, too. It's used to Bernard Haitink.

Nowadays, Solti is used to the Vienna Philharmonic or the Chicago Symphony for Mahler, though he used to conduct the London Symphony."

"That was before he read in the papers that the LSO had for the first time appointed a permanent conductor, a little oik from Hollywood called André Previn. I think Solti will find that the LPO has plenty of Mahler in its blood, thanks to Haitink. When I was here for three months before going to Spain, I fitted in quite a few concerts, including my first live Third with him. I've not heard the Sixth live before, though I know it from Bernstein's recording. I first heard that in Cambridge, with Dick and Harry in fact. Those were the days when to have a good stereo system in your room gave a lot of cachet. Dick had one, a twenty-first birthday present from his parents. Harry was, as you might expect, on the committee of the College Record Library. So when the library acquired Bernstein's recording, we were the first to hear it."

"Oh dear, Pete, you can't get away from Harry, can you?"

"Music is music. Once I'm listening, I'll concentrate on that."

We talked on as we crossed the footbridge to the Festival Hall, and were in place in good time for the Mozart piano concerto that began the concert.

When I went to Cambridge I had barely known of Mahler, and certainly had never heard any of his symphonies. The appearance of good-quality stereo recordings changed all that, but even into the 1970s concert performances of most of them were rare. The Sixth became my favourite, as it still is. Apart from overall size and grimness, its main feature is the huge finale with its three 'hammer-blows of fate,' supposedly representing a hero three times cut down. The first time he gets up and goes on nearly as strongly as before, if more nervously. The second time he is still determined to press on as best he can. The third time he does not get up. There continues debate as to whether Mahler's final intention was to include the third blow. Bernstein included it, but that day's programme told us that Solti preferred to omit it, instead presenting a final collapse to nothing.

I was indeed able to concentrate on the Mozart and the first three movements of the Mahler, but as the finale got under way, pictures of which contemporary hero it might represent crowded into my mind.

Perhaps it could be Ted Heath, a man who would have made a better career by using his musical talents to the full. He had begun the election campaign confidently, and in the lead. The revelations about Sir Reg Emerson had impacted on this, but he had shrugged them off. Another blow was the Pay Board's undermining of the government's position on miners' pay, but doubtless he would press on from that. However, as Fred had warned, a third blow was coming. There was no doubt what, or rather who, would deliver that. Enoch Powell regarded joining the EEC as a betrayal of the nation. He regarded incomes policies as misguided. All that remained was for him to come out with an explicit endorsement of Labour.[66]

Audiences for this symphony have the interest of seeing how the hammer-blows are delivered. This time, it was by dropping a large baulk of wood on to a hollow platform. As the first blow arrived, my thoughts turned to hearing the work for the first time, and thus to Harry. The first blow to him had been engineered by Paul. The wrecking of the Baroque Society concert had ended Harry's hopes of a musical career. He had recovered spectacularly, but now the Dugdales had delivered a second blow, which had felled him for good. No third blow could arise. For Harry, Solti seemed to have it right.

Or did he?

There were no domestic videotape recorders then, let alone HD recorders, so I had not been able to do what I would certainly have done now; play through Harry's televised outburst again and again, wondering what to make of it. I could have asked

66 Which he did two days later, in Birmingham on Saturday, 23rd February.

to see the BBC's own recording, but that would have drawn undesirable attention to me. Very wisely, Pat had not asked me to accompany him to the studio. I had watched the programme with Steph.

Earlier in the day, I had taken the outburst lightly, because I thought I knew what Harry had been talking about. The dying Andrew Grover could have told him of the animosities of my last weeks at Waterhouse, and also something about Carol and me. That could have prompted Harry to have the two of us watched. Yet his actual information would be limited to what Andrew could have known. He could not have known that I had rescued Carol from the police. It would hardly be sensational to reveal that she and I had had a brief student affair. I had not troubled her with the possibility.

Now, Harry had crossed into France. He might be at large for longer. He might get clean away. Could he have something else up his sleeve?

In December, reflecting on Harry's face to face outburst had put again into my mind the possibility that Arthur might have told Pat of Paul's role in the wrecking of the Baroque Society concert. Pat might then have told Harry, though there was no reason for him to have done so. Now, that was definitely ruled out. If Pat had known of Paul's role, he would certainly have referred to it at the same time as he showed me Andrew's diary. Nor could Andrew have told Harry about it; he had never known. As I had reminded Carol, I had found out what Paul had done only by chance. If by some other chance Harry had also found out, then by now he would have made it public, with devastating effect. Instead, he had run away with the stolen money. So he couldn't have anything else up his sleeve. For Harry, Solti *was* right.

My chance discovery about Paul, and about Sir Archibald Frampton, had followed the breakdown of my train back to Cambridge, after Pat had offered me a job. On the train, I had been thinking of this finale. Over the three days before, I had surmounted two huge blows, but a third seemed to have felled me. However, by the end of the day, I had turned the tables, and then I had moved on fast at IE. For me, there had been no finality; rather a new and better road. Perhaps it would turn out that way for Harry, too.

Mahler's Sixth Symphony ends with a *fortissimo* chord, which makes one leap off one's seat as much as do the hammer-blows. That evening, there were several seconds of silence before the applause began. Audiences were better behaved then than often they are now.[67]

Some minutes later, we were amongst the crowd streaming out of the hall. It was beginning to rain.

"Well, Pete, did you manage to concentrate on the music?" asked Steph.

"Yes, for most of the time. I'll tell you more, later."

"I prefer Bernstein's interpretation."

"I think I do too, though I've heard it only on record. Solti is fairly classical. Bernstein gets more hysteria in, which is part of Mahler to my taste."

There was a tap on my shoulder. "Pete, thank goodness I've found you." I turned to face Bill Anstruther. I had told Pat's office where I would be.

"What's up, Bill – something urgent for Pat?"

"No, he'll keep right out of *this*. It's on sale now, across in Fleet Street."

He handed over the first edition of the *Messenger*, which was supporting the Conservatives. One corner of the front

---

67 I continue to wince at the memory of what happened at a Promenade Concert that I attended in 2016. Haitink conducted the LSO in another performance of Mahler's immense Third Symphony, to mark the fiftieth anniversary of his first appearance at the Proms. He remarked beforehand that in 1970 the audience had been quite sparse; this time, the Albert Hall was packed. The performance was distinguished in several ways, including superb control of dynamics. However, the effect of the conclusion was marred by a supporter shouting '*Yeah*' or some similar word, at literally the moment the music stopped.

page noted a 'Headache for Heath as Pay Board reports, see page 6', but much of the page was covered by a banner headline.

As Swiss police seek
runaway, we ask –
IS THIS THE
MYSTERY MAN?

Beside was the *Bellinghame Advertiser* photo from December, described as portraying 'Carol Milverton, Labour candidate for Bellinghame South, with a friend'. There was a small amount of text on the front page, and more inside. It speculated that this 'friend' had been at Cambridge with Carol and her husband, and that now he was working with Carol on her campaign.

If this really was all that Harry had come up with to hit me, I was right to be relaxed about it. I saw too how we could turn it to advantage.

"Well, well, information put in the post somewhere between Islington and Heathrow yesterday morning, received at their news desk this morning, I guess. I'm surprised they're making so much of it."

"It's gone round the Street. Everyone is after more. There's been a tip-off that you live in Cromwell Tower. There are already reporters camped outside."

"Harry did visit us there. Is there any sign that they know I work for IE?"

"No."

"Harry must have left that out of what he passed them. He didn't want more from Pat, I guess. They could find out, though. In December I told the *Advertiser* that Paul worked for the same company as I did."

Steph laughed. "You're giving the hacks too much credit for intelligence, Pete."

"So let's give them a run for their money, starting with a cold night. They won't recognise you, Steph. Can you pack my case, and bring it to King's Cross? Meet me near the gate to Platform 8, as soon as possible. The *Night Scotsman* leaves in seventy minutes' time. I'll be on it, hopefully in a sleeper. Bill, hang on while I nip into that call box to try for Carol, and for my aunt who will need to warn people about this. Then I'll tell you my plan. You'll need to speak to Pat first thing tomorrow, and then to the Beeb."

THIS SCRIPT WAS TYPED FROM A RECORDING, NOT COPIED FROM AN ORIGINAL SCRIPT. BECAUSE OF THE RISK OF MISHEARING AND THE DIFFICULTY IN SOME CASES OF IDENTIFYING INDIVIDUAL SPEAKERS THE BBC CANNOT VOUCH FOR ITS COMPLETE ACCURACY.

TOPIC: "ELECTION ROUND-UP", BBC2, 10.35 – 11.15 pm SUNDAY, 24th FEBRUARY, 1974

CLIVE TOLHURST (presenter, recorded in Cambridge earlier that day to background views of Colleges mentioned): Welcome again to Election Round-up. Sundays are traditionally a quieter day for campaigning, a day to take stock. So today, we're following up last Tuesday's programme. Until then, Cambridge was best known for its grander Colleges, like King's, with its superb chapel, or Trinity, home to Isaac Newton, and this century to more Nobel Prize winners than most countries. It wasn't known for Waterhouse College, whose Victorian buildings are squeezed in just round the corner. People from Waterhouse, like James Harman, made little of being there.

JAMES HARMAN (recorded in October 1972): The author has made a brave attempt to conceptualise the materialistic aspects of his subject matter, but has ignored the vital work of Noam Chomsky concerning neo-structuralisation.

CLIVE TOLHURST: Now, all this has suddenly changed. We have discovered (display heading):

THE WATERHOUSE CONNECTION

The first news of this was on Tuesday.

HARRY TAMFIELD (recorded on 19th February): I learnt several things during my time at Waterhouse College… I overcame a reverse to get where I am now, as Dr Harman will recall. In fact, I see some of the same people involved this time as before.

CLIVE TOLHURST (in studio): That was after Harry Tamfield had announced the failure of his company, and made allegations which we won't repeat here. The next day, he left for Switzerland.

REPORTER (recorded at Heathrow Airport on 20th February): Mr Tamfield, don't you think you should remain here, to deal with the receivers on behalf of your employees and shareholders?

HARRY TAMFIELD: There is no more I can do here, good morning.

CLIVE TOLHURST: Then on Thursday, the receivers found that over £2 million was missing from a pension fund. On Friday, a formal request to the Swiss authorities for Mr Tamfield's arrest and extradition was made. His whereabouts are currently not known, but there is confidence that he will soon be found and returned to the UK. Meanwhile, all this has drawn more attention to the quite sensational three-way contest that has developed in the Bellinghame South constituency. We sent our reporter, Arthur Harnett, down there yesterday.

ARTHUR HARNETT (recorded on 23rd February): Ten days ago, this was just another constituency in the leafy suburbs. Sir Reg Emerson (picture), who's been the local MP since 1955, seemed to be safe. Cyril Horsley (picture), the Liberal candidate, seemed to be destined for another respectable second, with no chance of repeating what Eric Lubbock did in Orpington or Graham Tope did in Sutton and Cheam. For Labour, a lively new arrival, twenty-five-year-old Carol Milverton (picture), hoped to improve her vote enough to keep her deposit and to be noticed, so as to have a chance of a better seat next time. She'd made a good start by brokering a deal for the Westbury Housing Association to buy a large part of Tamfield Investments' Bishop's Park development, which you see behind me. That was a much less unpopular prospect around here than the previously proposed sale to the GLC, and one which two weeks ago, seemed to have cleared away the financial troubles of Tamfield Investments (sight of article in Financial Times for 8 February). Despite this, no one was expecting a great change on the 1970 result (table: Conservative 57%, Liberal 32%, Labour 11%).

And then it happened (sight of newspaper headlines concerning Sir Reg Emerson and Tamfield Investments). Carol Milverton moved fast, and Labour piled in support, sending her father-in-law, who's a senior party agent, down from Manchester. For the next week, she made the running.

CAROL MILVERTON (recorded on 20th February): This election is about what's best for all of you. It's about being able to do a proper week's work for a proper week's pay. It's about not being at the mercy of banks and property speculators. It's about knowing that your lights will stay on, and that your trains will run. Vote to get this country moving again.

ARTHUR HARNETT: Over the last few days, Conservatives and Liberals have fought back.

SIR REG EMERSON (recorded on 22nd February): You know my record for this constituency. Vote for me, or vote for someone with no record, perhaps for someone quite unknown to you. My party is facing up to the difficulties of the last few months, rather than hoping that somehow they will go away. Vote for me, or vote for a party which failed only a few years ago, or for a party which has no chance of success at all.

CYRIL HORSLEY (recorded on 23rd February): People are fed up with politics by scandal, by innuendo. You can laugh at the cartoon in yesterday's Times, showing one voter asking another 'Are you voting Liberal to get rid of Mr Heath or Mr Wilson?' – I certainly did. But the answer is that you're voting Liberal to get rid of both of them. On Thursday, the signal from here, from Sutton and Cheam, and from all over the country will be just that.

CLIVE TOLHURST (in studio): Nor should we forget the Independent, Finola Donoghue, with her strong support for the women's liberation movement. Bellinghame is unusual in having two local newspapers. They have joined in with gusto. The Bellinghame Record is giving its usual support to the Conservatives, whilst the Bellinghame Advertiser, normally independent, is backing Labour (sight of front pages).

The message this programme can give to them all today is, keep trying hard. It looks to be a real cliffhanger. We commissioned our own poll which covered about a thousand electors during yesterday, and this is the quite remarkable result (table displayed: 77% of voters definitely intending to vote and committed to a candidate, split Conservative 34%, Liberal 33%, Labour 31%, Independent 2%).

I repeat that this is quite remarkable. One would have expected the press revelations about Sir Reg to have benefitted Cyril Horsley as the established second runner. Instead, the big winner so far has been Carol Milverton. The 20% swing from Conservative to Labour is way off any 'swingometer' I've ever seen. Don't forget too, that this poll was before Enoch Powell's speech last night. Uncertainty in the poll is about 3%. Taking account of that, and also that some votes are uncommitted, any of the three main parties could win the seat.

They're all going for it. Jeremy Thorpe has a tough battle in his own constituency, but yesterday his foray out included support for Cyril Horsley. Tomorrow, Michael Heseltine appears for Sir Reg Emerson, and we've just heard that on Tuesday, Harold Wilson will look in on Carol Milverton's final rally.

This is all very exciting, but you may be asking, what's it to do with Waterhouse College? You know part of the answer already. Harry Tamfield studied there before he went into property. But also studying there was Carol Milverton's husband, Paul. He was a leader of the moderate student left, and became President of the Junior Combination Room or JCR – that is, he was the undergraduates' main spokesman. Carol Gibson, as she then was, could often be seen around Waterhouse. She was also active in student politics. Many friends they made in Cambridge have been working for her in Bellinghame South. Yesterday, they were amongst those taking a break at a bungalow on the Bishop's Park Estate.

ARTHUR HARNETT: Clearly, you weren't all at Waterhouse College. It's still men only, though I believe it's to go mixed in 1976. Did you all know Carol Milverton from your time there?

BRIAN SMITHAM: Some of us, yes, mostly though knowing Paul first. Others, like Gerry and Steve here, have joined in because they know they're needed.

ARTHUR HARNETT: I'm told that you're all spending day after day of your time here. Clearly you're very committed to her.

STEVE FOSTER: I went to Liverpool University, and Gerry to East Anglia. Like the people here from Cambridge, we have plenty of free time, because of Mr Heath's three-day week. Only Labour can bring that to an end. That's why those of us who aren't generally supporters of Labour are working so hard for Carol.

MORAG NEWLANDS: Speak for yourself, Steve! When I was a child, my grandfather told me of the giants he had met as a child, including Keir Hardie, and James Maxton.

JIM SMYTHE: If you went round asking everyone why they're here, you would have many different answers. One thing we've learnt is that there's no one answer to most questions. You should listen to others' points of view. What everyone here wants to do is to make a difference with our lives. Mr Heath's Government isn't allowing us that chance. It's got this country into a mess, so we don't support it.

ARTHUR HARNETT: Those of you who were at Waterhouse College must have met Harry Tamfield. How did he strike you then, compared to what you've heard of him now?

BRIAN SMITHAM: Few of us knew him well. He was very tied up with the orchestra he ran.

ARTHUR HARNETT: Wasn't it after his orchestra's concert was wrecked by left-wing demonstrators that he left Cambridge without a degree?

BRIAN SMITHAM: That's right, it cut him up a lot. I was one of those who tried to keep the demonstrators out, but some got in another way. Their leader was from a loony left group. He was sent to prison.

ARTHUR HARNETT: So, at Cambridge, you weren't part of the student left, but now you're backing Carol Milverton, who was.

BRIAN SMITHAM: Just to be clear, Carol and Paul were nothing at all to do with the people who smashed up that concert.

ARTHUR HARNETT: But they were part of the student left.

BRIAN SMITHAM: Yes, they were, and I wasn't, though my dad's a miner and now a NUM branch secretary - hello, Dad (wave). I was darn pleased I'd got to Cambridge. The first time I met Paul, I said I didn't understand why he wanted to change the place, when he'd only just got there. We went on having arguments. We still do. You don't have to agree with someone on everything, to work together with them.

ARTHUR HARNETT: Do you support the miners now?

BRIAN SMITHAM: Even if my family weren't miners, I'd see that if we want more coal, miners must be paid more. Maybe Heath sees that now, after the Pay Board report.

CLIVE TOLHURST (in studio): I was struck by what these young people are saying. They're highly motivated, they've thought about what the key issues are, and they're trying to make a difference. Many of them were at Waterhouse College, and clearly they benefitted from their time there. Earlier today, I showed what you've just seen to people who are there now (switch to recording). I'm now with some of the Fellows, in the Master's Dining Room. It's very fine if you like Victorian interiors (pan around). Sir Arthur Gulliver, a physicist who became a senior scientific advisor in the Ministry of Defence, is the Vice-Master of the College. Colin Mackay is the Senior Tutor. He has overall responsibility for the College's students. In 1971, he took this job over from Tom Farley, who was doing it when the people we've seen were there. Nick Castle is in charge of maths teaching, and is also responsible for the College's rowing club.

COLIN MACKAY: An upward trend in the College's performance began about six years ago, while some of the men you've seen were here. In 1966, we were near the bottom of the inter-college league table for degree results. Last year, we were sixth. That's making my job of selecting applicants harder, but once again, thank you Tom for getting this trend going.

TOM FARLEY: Six years ago the College had a difficult time, particularly following the bad business of the concert, which I recall only too well as I was sitting in the front row of the audience. But out of it came a realisation that having differences, strong differences, and arguing about them didn't preclude constructive effort and action – individually and together. That's benefitted Waterhouse, and also the people we educate, as you've seen. I hope that in the future it will benefit the country.

CLIVE TOLHURST: It hasn't benefitted Harry Tamfield.

TOM FARLEY: I can't comment on his present position, but less than a year ago he was admired as one of the best of his generation for enterprise and thrust. His time at Waterhouse contributed to that. After the reverse of the wrecked concert, he decided to seek new opportunities and seemed to have made the most of them. Nick can give you another example of how determination and effort shone through after a reverse.

NICK CASTLE: At the time we've been talking about, our College First Boat achieved a really astonishing result in one of the summer races, beating another College to move up three places. Then that College raised a complaint, and the result was disallowed. Our men could have sulked, but instead they trained hard and applied themselves. That didn't affect their academic work, as Tom has pointed out. Indeed, it didn't stop them from enjoying life here. In the next lot of races, all boats, not just the First Boat, started to move up. Any boat of the College which had complained had particularly short shrift. Improvement has continued as new men arrive and others leave. Incidentally, Jim Smythe, the shortest of the men you saw in Bellinghame, was Captain of Boats and the cox of the boat which did so well. He went on to get a good degree, and also became the Secretary of the JCR while Paul Milverton was President. As I recall, Tom, they worked together very well.

TOM FARLEY: Yes, they did, and so there was a much better involvement of the undergraduates in the affairs of the College than had been possible when things were factionalised.

CLIVE TOLHURST: There's another Waterhouse connection with last Tuesday's programme, dating from that time. James Harman, who can't be here today owing to a commitment to speak at the International Philosophical Conference in Rome, told me that Sir Pat O'Donnell was to have made the College a substantial donation, but that fell through.

SIR ARTHUR GULLIVER: Yes, another College put up a better scheme, and had the money. Actually, it was the same College as pipped us on the river. That was another reverse, but again we got over it. We've overtaken them in the results league, as well as on the river. We're going to stay in front.

CLIVE TOLHURST: Turning you down hasn't stopped Sir Pat from recruiting your students for his company, International Electronics.

SIR ARTHUR GULLIVER: No, it hasn't stopped him. Why should it have done? IE or any other good employer wants the best.

CLIVE TOLHURST: Now, it's time to hear from some of Waterhouse's present-day students. I've moved to their common room. It's just after one o'clock. You can hear the News in the background, and I can see twenty or so people catching up on the election. John Birkbeck is the current President of the JCR.

JOHN BIRKBECK: Before last Tuesday, it was easy to just ignore what was happening outside Cambridge. Educational institutions are exempt from the three-day week. People watched your programme on Tuesday because James Harman was on it. Before then, no one knew that Harry Tamfield had been here. Now, everyone is interested. There's a lot of discussion and argument here, and downstairs in the bar.

CLIVE TOLHURST: Who are people backing?

JOHN BIRKBECK: Mostly Labour.

CLIVE TOLHURST: So, the student left is still in charge?

JOHN BIRKBECK: No. People see Labour as the only choice now for getting the country back to work.

CLIVE TOLHURST: Does Carol Milverton being a candidate contribute to this?

JOHN BIRKBECK: It hasn't so far, because again most people didn't know about her connection with the College. There's no way that we can know directly about people who were here several years ago. Ray here has something to say on that.

RAY PEARSON: Most people stay here for three years. I came up in 1972. I heard about past events here from people then in their third year, who came up in 1970. They could have heard about them from people who came up in October 1968. So, anything I've heard about people who left before then, such as Harry Tamfield, is fourth hand. Not surprisingly, there are all sorts of different stories, passed on through generations by word of mouth, and embellished on the way. They're like the myths and legends I study in my course on anthropology, for example Beowulf, or The Iliad.

ANOTHER STUDENT: There's a story about a man here six years ago. Apparently he came top of the University in the maths degree examinations, proved an important theorem in his first year of research, was elected to a Fellowship, and then left suddenly. You hear different versions of what happened to him. One is that he was incurably ill and went off to die.

RAY PEARSON: Wasn't that what happened to the man who was Bursar before Graham Harcroft?

THE OTHER STUDENT: Another is that he had a huge offer from a university in America, and yet another that he was a secret communist and is now in Russia.

CLIVE TOLHURST: I think you'll find out the real story if you watch tonight.

THE OTHER STUDENT: I know the answer; I asked Dr Castle.

CLIVE TOLHURST: Well, don't spoil it for viewers. This is fascinating. You don't know much about these legendary people, but it seems that their example inspires people to try harder and get more out of being here now.

JOHN BIRKBECK: No one is trying to emulate some hero, but it's certainly right that there's been passed on a culture of trying hard, and of making the most of the big opportunity we've been given. We don't slack around. Not that Waterhouse is a dull place. We have plenty of fun.

CLIVE TOLHURST (in studio): I returned here this afternoon, feeling that I was beginning to understand the picture, but I knew that there was one piece of the jigsaw needed to complete it. To remind you, our programme last Tuesday ended with Harry Tamfield's dramatic announcement of the failure of his company, and then…

HARRY TAMFIELD (recorded on 19th February): Yes, I overcame a reverse to get where I am now, as Dr Harman will recall. In fact, I see some of the same people involved this time as before. I'm sure one of them is watching this programme. Two months ago I warned him that I knew he was up to something, and if he hit me, he would be very sorry. Now he has hit me very hard, and he will be very sorry indeed.

CLIVE TOLHURST: He appeared to be suggesting that he was again up against people who had been involved in his previous reverse, presumably in the wrecking of his concert, and that he had warned one of them off. The Clarion ran the story that a 'Mystery Man', who had been at Waterhouse, was plotting to destroy Harry Tamfield. On Friday, the Messenger joined the party, by connecting the 'Mystery Man' with Carol Milverton. (sight of front page). The pack thought they knew where he lived, in the Barbican's prestigious Cromwell Tower (picture) but there was no sign of him there (scene of wet and bedraggled reporters breaking camp on Friday morning). They went after Carol Milverton. She explained that the picture had been taken in December, when she attended a meeting of Bishop's Park residents. The man in the picture was the nephew of one of them. She diverted the story to a further rerun of how she had brokered the sale to the Westbury Housing Trust, and how that was going ahead as planned (sight of various articles in weekend papers). Yesterday, the 'Mystery Man' seemed to have faded away. However, this morning a brief statement by Sir Pat O'Donnell's company, International Electronics, identified him as Peter Bridford, head of their North Sea sales office in Aberdeen. Arthur Harnett caught the next plane up. We go over to our studio there – BBC exclusive, live.

ARTHUR HARNETT: So, Peter Bridford, you're the Mystery Man.

PETER BRIDFORD: There's no mystery about me, and I've certainly not been plotting to destroy Harry Tamfield. At Waterhouse College, I knew him quite well. He and I played in a string quartet. I went on a musical trip to Eastern Europe with him. His big ambition then was to get into the administration of an orchestra or opera company. To show what he could do, he'd built up a fairly obscure outfit into one of Cambridge's top bands. It was a big shock to him when the concert was wrecked. I tried to persuade him to stay, but he felt that he couldn't continue. He wanted to do something else. He turned out to have a big aptitude for property.

ARTHUR HARNETT: Have you seen him since he left Cambridge?

PETER BRIDFORD: A few times. To answer your next question, he invited me to the party we've heard so much about.

ARTHUR HARNETT: Did you take part in the contest?

PETER BRIDFORD: Hardly. It was fun to watch, though, and Harry asked me to count the votes.

ARTHUR HARNETT: Did you meet or recognise any of the people who've been reported as having had extra services after the party?

PETER BRIDFORD: I talked to the Dugdales about business in Spain, where I spent two and a half years up to last summer. I didn't notice Sir Reg Emerson, though he has been my MP. I've already used my postal vote.

ARTHUR HARNETT: Oh, how is that?

PETER BRIDFORD: After returning from Spain, I was attached to IE's London HQ for a while, though I was dashing around a bit. An aunt of mine recently moved into a nice bungalow on the Bishop's Park Estate. I stayed with her sometimes, including on the qualification date for the new electoral register. She was pretty worried at the prospect of living next to a GLC overspill estate. In December, she wanted my support at a protest meeting. Sir Reg was invited to that, but didn't come. Carol Milverton, and Cyril Horsley, did come.

ARTHUR HARNETT: Is that when the Messenger's photograph of you and Carol Milverton was taken?

PETER BRIDFORD: Yes. When Paul Milverton came up to Waterhouse, I was just starting research. Research students help with College teaching of undergraduates, and I found myself teaching Paul. Thus I came to know him, and I met Carol. Naturally, I thanked her for coming along to help at the meeting. The photograph first appeared two days later, in the Bellinghame Advertiser.

ARTHUR HARNETT: So, that's your involvement with Bellinghame South?

PETER BRIDFORD: Yes. You, and viewers, have seen my aunt's bungalow. It's where you filmed yesterday. My aunt is not a natural Labour supporter, but, like others on the Bishop's Park Estate, she's very pleased with the help Carol gave in fixing the Westbury deal.

ARTHUR HARNETT: Your aunt bought a bungalow on the estate that Harry Tamfield's firm was developing. Carol Milverton, whom you had met, secured the Labour nomination for the constituency which includes the estate. She has helped to sort out its future. You're telling me that Harry Tamfield has put these separate matters together, to make a plot to destroy him.

PETER BRIDFORD: Exactly. It's coincidence. Those do happen. I can say that as someone who specialised in statistics at Cambridge. If you tile your bathroom in different colours, picking each tile at random, the result is likely to look odd. There'll be too many clumps of the same colour. You have to even the colours out to make it look random. Harry has misinterpreted a clump. That's a great pity, but given the stresses he's been under, it's understandable.

ARTHUR HARNETT: You mentioned your time at Cambridge. I'm told that you got a very good degree indeed, were elected a Fellow of Waterhouse very soon after, and produced some important research within less than a year. Then, you suddenly left. Why?

PETER BRIDFORD: Sir Pat O'Donnell offered me an extremely good job. I'd completed the work you mentioned, and could move on. It's turned out well, so far. For a while, I was in the management team at the Sunderland factory Sir Pat told you about last week. That was very hard work and I had a lot to learn. Some viewers will remember how I caused a strike within six months of arriving. We all recovered, and moved on. Next, I was developing business in Spain. You'll have heard of Ford's plans for a huge car factory near Valencia. IE owned or licensed suppliers stand to be big in the supply chain for that. Now I'm here, building IE's share of the greatest business opportunity this country has had for very many years – North Sea oil. If we use that opportunity right, it could get us out of the mess we're in now.

ARTHUR HARNETT: You sound very determined that we should use it right. Thank you.

CLIVE TOLHURST (in studio): So, the Waterhouse connection is fully explained. There's no mystery and no plot. Rather, coincidences have reunited determined people whose time in Cambridge was clearly formative and who have left a tradition behind them there.

We've just time to whet your appetite for tomorrow's programme. Arthur Harnett isn't returning directly to London. He will report from Shipley in Yorkshire, where Enoch Powell is to speak. I need hardly remind you that in Birmingham yesterday, Enoch Powell restated his view that the government had had no electoral mandate to take Britain into the EEC, and concluded that:

'The national duty must be to replace the man who has deprived Parliament of its sole right to make the laws and impose the taxes of the country. If you want to do it, you can.'

We will be bringing you full coverage of the meeting and of reactions to it, only two hours after it takes place.[68]

---

68 Viewers were well rewarded. A heckler shouted 'Judas' at the end of Enoch Powell's speech. His immediate response was 'Judas was paid. *Judas was paid.* I am making a sacrifice.'

ADDRESS BY CAROL MILVERTON

Given in the Bellinghame Memorial Hall,
Tuesday, 26th February, 1974

I'm told that Harold Wilson will arrive in about fifteen minutes. In the meantime, you'll have to put up with me.

We're nearly at the end of the campaign. It's my first campaign for election to Parliament, and I will admit to beginning it with less expectation of success than I have now. Three things have changed over the past few weeks.

First, here as right across the country, more and more people have come to realise that there is no realistic alternative to Labour. Only Labour can sort out the mess the Heath Government has made, and get this country working again.

Secondly, here in Bellinghame South we have learnt of the shocking, exploitative behaviour of the sitting Conservative MP, and of his links to a man who has fled abroad following the collapse of his company, and is now sought by the police. Just before he fled, that man made, on television, the absurd suggestion that there was some kind of plot against him. Many of you will have seen or read about Sunday's television programme, which set the record straight.

Third, and this really follows from the first two, I have had huge support from people who are prepared to make an effort to make a difference. I'm pleased to see so many of them on the stage behind me. I invited them up here, along with Labour Party members, so as to give more room in the hall.

These people come from all walks of life. Many are local people. Some are from not far away. Some have come long distances to help. Some are people I have known for some time. Others are people I'm pleased to have met recently. All have devoted much time to supporting me. Some have pointed out that Mr Heath's three-day week has given them the time to do this. But we all know it isn't just a question of time. There are always other things to do. It takes commitment, and motivation, to tramp the streets, to put over the message. All the people behind me have shown these. I have no doubt that on Thursday night I shall be able to thank them officially, as your elected MP. But space at the count is limited, and most of them won't be there. So, I am going to turn and thank them, face to face, now. I hope you will all join me (*standing applause*).

Why have I gone into politics? I come of a political family, as does my husband. His father and mine have travelled from Manchester to be with us. But there are plenty of other rewarding jobs I could have done after I left university. For example, my sister, two years older than me, is already a head of department at a new comprehensive school in Bolton. (*Interruption – "who paid for that, then?"*) I'm sure you wouldn't have asked that question if you hadn't guessed the answer. It's been built as part of a programme authorised by the present Secretary of State for Education, Maggie Thatcher the milk snatcher (*laughter*).[69] Not everything the Tory Government has done is wrong, but on the key economic and industrial relations issues, they are totally and disastrously wrong. The latest example of that is January's record balance of payments deficit of nearly £400 million. To continue, why have I chosen to take this hard and risky course? Because I want to make a real difference to as many people as possible. Manchester used to be the workshop of the world. It isn't any more, and for most of this century it has been coping with the problems of decline. My father has told me what it was like in the 1930s, of the poverty, the sense of hopelessness. Since then the efforts of Labour local government, supported by Labour – and Conservative – national governments, have cleared away the worst of the poverty and hopelessness, but they haven't reversed the decline.

Many of you in Bellinghame are reasonably well off, but I've seen some real deprivation here. The poor will always be with us, you may say, and you're right. Some people are better off, and some worse off, than others. That's a fact, true everywhere, whatever official statements you may read. The vital thing is that people should be able

---

69 A reference to her abolition of free milk for primary school children.

to become better off through their own efforts and abilities, and that they should contribute to society as well as to themselves. That is the basis of the pragmatic, practical socialism that we have in this country. What I've heard from so many of you is worry about where we're going. Less than thirty years ago, much of the continent of Europe lay devastated by war. Now many of our continental neighbours are better off than we are. The Japanese are catching us up, and others are on their way. Why? Where is this taking us? (*Interruption – "It's the unions."*) I'm not saying that anyone is entirely to blame for this, nor that anyone is free from blame, and that includes the unions. I would say that the Tories' attempts to make industrial relations subject to a legal framework are now recognised as a disaster by all, including by the Secretary General of the CBI.[70] (*Interruption – "What did Babs do then?"*) I think you're talking about Barbara Castle's proposals under the last Labour Government.[71] As you might guess, she has been a role model for me for some time. She was absolutely right to open a debate. But it was also absolutely right that that debate did not include anything like what the Tories have tried since. They could have learnt from us. They chose not to, and the country is paying the price.

The next government must turn this country round, out of decline, away from being a laughing stock. As I've said, the first step is to get the country working again. Only a Labour Government can do that. That's only the first step, though. Then, there are two priorities.

The first priority is to renegotiate our terms of entry to the EEC, and to put the result to the electorate in a referendum. Only Labour will do that. Without it, we will go on paying a huge price for Mr Heath's lifetime obsession with Europe. As one of my supporters has said, the other members saw him coming, and skinned him alive. Being in has many advantages and personally I hope we can stay in, but not at anything like Mr Heath's price. Now France is, on its government's own boasting, better off than us there is no reason why we should pay a vast subsidy to their farmers. (*Interruption – "Enoch's right again."*) Yes, he is right again (*short pause*). He was right when I

---

70 Earlier that day, Campbell Adamson, thinking he was off the record, said that any new government should repeal the 1972 Industrial Relations Act.
71 These included compulsory ballots before strikes, as eventually enacted in 1987, but no Industrial Relations Court.

first heard of him, when I was eleven years old – where I lived, we were exposed to politics at an early age. Then, he was protesting at the mistreatment of detainees in Kenya. In between then and now, though, he's been wrong – spectacularly and dangerously wrong. Heath did do something right, when in 1968 he sacked Enoch Powell from the Shadow Cabinet.[72]

The second priority is the development of North Sea oil. With the oil price as it is now, the prize is huge. To survive, we simply must win it, but the costs and technical challenges are huge, too. It's for the seventies like putting a man on the Moon was for the sixties. To succeed, we need the oil companies to do the work, and the banks to finance it. The government must set rules for development and operation which are seen to be fair and which give the oil companies, the banks and the nation a good return. The Conservatives have failed to set such rules. Labour will do so. We need British industry to supply equipment and services. Some companies are already doing that, but many are not. Labour will ensure that British industry has every opportunity to compete fairly for business.

Those are national priorities. As your MP I will have local priorities, too. I've made a start already with the Westbury deal, and in trying to help anyone who has faced problems or been treated unfairly, usually for no fault of their own. My office tells me that during the last two weeks I have written fifty-four letters and made seventy-two telephone calls on behalf of people here. It's probably too early to have a response to any of them (*Interruption – "You've sorted my rent – good on you" followed by applause*) – oh, not quite too early, I'm pleased to hear. Rather selfishly, perhaps, I have another local priority. My swimmer's hair has already been noticed. The Hills Road Baths are a good size, but everyone agrees that they need renovation. We need to find a way of getting that done, rather than just going on talking about it.

(*Harold Wilson has been standing by a side entrance for two minutes, having waved Carol Milverton to continue.*) And now it is time for me to hand over to the leader of the Labour Party, Prime Minister for six years and to be Prime Minister again after Thursday – HAROLD WILSON! (*Prolonged applause.*)

---

72 That followed the 'rivers of blood' speech.

12. FRIDAY, 1ST MARCH, 1974

My mouth opened in alarm as I picked my way through the crowd in Roberta's darkened lounge. Her 21-inch colour TV was showing the 1930s interior of Bellinghame Town Hall. The Town Clerk had drawn himself up to his full height to declaim. Behind him, people wearing blue rosettes were already cheerful. I was quickly reassured, though.

"... and accordingly, I declare the aforesaid Charles Donald McFadden to be elected for the constituency of Bellinghame North."

'CON HOLD' flashed across the screen, and the familiar voice of Arthur Harnett followed. It was twenty past one.

"No surprises, there. A swing of 5% from Conservative to Liberal leaves a Conservative majority of over 7,000. The Labour vote is slightly down as people switch to Liberal, but candidate Dick Phillips just keeps his deposit. It's typical of other results coming in across Outer London, and it's not good enough news for the Liberals. That swing on 1970 won't keep Graham Tope in Sutton and Cheam, where the result is expected in about an hour. Nor does it give any clue as to what will happen in Bellinghame South, where they started recounting ten minutes ago. Albert Dickson, whom you've just seen announcing the result, told me earlier that he's determined to be on stage again tonight. He reckons they can do at least three recounts. Now that the North count is finished, those counters will take a break, and then do a second recount on South if it is needed. After that, the teams will alternate. Over there, you can see counting in hand. It will be about fifty minutes before there *may* be a result. Conservative, or Labour, or Liberal, we just don't know. You certainly can't tell anything from the size of the piles of votes on the tables, except that Finola Donoghue, the Independent, hasn't done very well. We do have some information, though. The voter turnout in Bellinghame North is 78%, which is up on 1970, but not as much up as we've been seeing elsewhere, perhaps because really there's been no campaign there. In Bellinghame South it's over 87%, 87.6% in fact. I repeat, *eighty-seven point six per cent*. That's a quite extraordinary figure for a freezing and unpleasant day. It reflects the quite extraordinary contest. I don't know whether Albert Dickson expected the sheer volume of votes, which will make the counts take longer. Now, back to the studio."

Morag lifted her head from the pad of paper before her.

"That turnout figure makes total votes cast about 57,300."

On screen, Clive Tolhurst carried on.

"Yes, I'm told that in Bellinghame South today, one could hardly move for canvassers. Perhaps the most telling contrast was in this straight residential road. The boundary between the North and South constituencies runs down the middle. On one side, there's nothing at all. On the other side, almost every house has a poster, and there are three canvassers trying to avoid each other. Well, we'll be back with Arthur for a result, or not, in about three-quarters of an hour. Meanwhile, we've no more clue to the national result. The computers are forecasting a small Labour lead over the Conservatives, but almost certainly no overall majority, a hung Parliament. So, much will depend on regional issues – how the Liberals do in the West Country, how far the Scottish National Party advances, and how many more constituencies in the West Midlands heed Enoch Powell's advice. Now over to…"

"Pete, we'd given up on you," said Brian.

"I'd more or less given up on myself. It had seemed simple. I had an important meeting in the afternoon, but it would finish by five o'clock , so I could catch the 6.20 plane down. I might even have been here in time for the last round-up of voters. Then at lunchtime my office heard the flight was cancelled, because of an unofficial strike by BEA ground staff at Heathrow.[73] They made a snappy job of rebooking me on to the 6.25 Air Anglia to Norwich, since I could come on by train from there. However, that flight was delayed, and we didn't land till ten past nine. I knew the last decent train left Norwich Thorpe at 9.30. I was first through the terminal, and bagged the only taxi. The driver said he couldn't make Thorpe, but he could get me to the first stop out, Diss, in time to pick the train up there. He did – just. It was due into Liverpool Street at 11.40, but wasn't there until ten past twelve. I ran to Bank Underground and arrived on the platform as the last Morden train came in. Fortunately, buses always meet that train. So now, it's something to eat and a large Scotch, I think. Where's Roberta?"

"She's to be called when things happen. She was dead beat, providing sandwiches and tea all day. As is Susie, who took the day off to help her, aren't you, Susie? In fact, we're all shagged out here. We've done our best for Carol, though."

Susie murmured assent, her head on Brian's shoulder.

"I'm sorry I couldn't be with you today."

"We know how you've helped, Pete. The programme on Sunday turned out great. Fred reckons it was worth 250 votes to us."

"You were very smart to cue Steve and Gerry in up front, so as to make clear this wasn't just a Cambridge effort. It was all worth my phone bill. I spent most of Friday and Saturday nights speaking to you, Fred, and Arthur Gulliver in rotation about what everyone should say."

A few minutes later, I brought in a tray and squeezed in beside Brian. Over twenty people, singles and couples, were

---

73 British European Airways – the strike was about the terms of their merger into British Airways, to take effect from 1st April.

perched on chairs, draped over the sofa, or propped on the floor with what cushions could be found. Some of them had waved as they noticed me, but most were not noticing anything.

Liz and Greg were awake, but had no time for anyone else as they kissed gently, and Greg ran a hand through her hair or around the place on her belly where she became tense. It was deeply satisfying to see that after all these years, Liz had found her man. She had told me that they would both be out here on election day, since then nothing would be happening in their jobs. Clearly, they had done their all. They would deserve a good long honeymoon in May, before Liz started at the NUM.

I leafed through the *Advertiser*'s Election Special, which had appeared on Wednesday afternoon so as to trump the *Record*. The front page was mainly occupied by a good picture of Carol, under the headline:

IT'S LABOUR FOR ACTION
Back to work, then EEC renegotiation and North Sea oil are the priorities – and the Hills Road Baths. Leader visits to support

Pages two and three featured extracts from the address Carol had given on Tuesday evening, under headlines including *Maggie's schools programme praised.* Harold Wilson's follow-up was on pages four and five. Brian agreed that it had come over well.

"She's been working speeches out with her dad as audience. She has the knack of using notes and sounding spontaneous. She didn't know beforehand how long she had to speak. Paul did a lot of the notes."

"I know. I had several calls from him about the North Sea. It's good that the *Advertiser*'s reporter took down what Carol said."

Brian passed me a copy of the full address.

"The *Advertiser* didn't take it down. Their reporter didn't have shorthand. Luckily, Jenny was here. She had a carrycot with her, and settled Katie just in time to get over to the hall. Our printer was keen to run it off. Frank babysat. He's been great support, but he wasn't so keen on being on the platform for Harold Wilson."

"Ah, it's nice to know that men can babysit."

"Yeah, it won't be too long before I'm on that job. Jenny did loads, at the weekend and twice this week. She knew what she wanted to do. On Tuesday, Jack heard her phoning Dick to say she would be late. She took no nonsense. Forget your plans, cope with David. She wears the trousers in *that* house. You had a lucky escape, Pete."

"Maybe, Brian. Where's Frank now, by the way?"

"At the Rotary Club's election party. He said, best if he weren't here if the press turned up, and he ought to show at the party anyway."

Some firmness in Jenny's handling of Dick was unsurprising. During a long call on Monday, congratulations on Sunday night's TV programme and a few final details for the christening had been followed by news. Dick was unrepentant about what he had done, though he now knew what Harry had done. He was sitting uncomfortably, because on the Wednesday night, Harry was 'wound up' and had given him 'a pretty rough time'. The next day, he had left Harry in a quiet village not far from Megève, and Harry's skis with a colleague at the university who knew little about skiing and wouldn't realise that they weren't Dick's size. Harry would lie low for a few days before deciding what to do next, and would never reveal how he had left Switzerland. I had encouraged Jenny to remember why Dick phoned her, but otherwise to forget what had happened. That was easier said than done.

I had not mentioned John or Amanda, but I hoped that Jenny had taken the opportunity to tell Dick that they were still occasionally part of her life. That would make fixtures easier to arrange. Pleasurable images drifted into my mind…

At ten past two, Clive Tolhurst passed us back to Arthur Harnett.

"Yes, and it's going to a second recount in Bellinghame South. You can see the counters who did Bellinghame North beginning work, and those who've already counted twice going for a break. They won't go home, for they could be needed again. This is turning into the cliffhanger of the night. Nothing we can see gives us any clue to who might be in the lead. There's Sir Reg Emerson, putting a good face on a result that will be very bad for him, even if he scrapes home. There's Cyril Horsley, who fought a serious campaign, and is looking serious now, as usual. And there's Carol Milverton, talking to her father-in-law, Fred Milverton, whom Labour have brought down from Manchester to be her agent. She's looking cheerful, but then she usually does. That's one of her strengths. She's plenty to be cheerful about. Win or not, this will be a sensational result for her, and for Labour. In 1970, Labour had 11% of the vote. Now, it's certainly over 30%."

Clive Tolhurst came back in. "We're now moving a few miles along the road, for the result from Sutton and Cheam…"

As expected, this was a disappointment for the Liberals. A new Conservative candidate reversed the by-election loss. We settled down for another wait. The flurry of on-screen activity had woken Brian up. He passed me some typed sheets.

"Early on Saturday, I met Tony Higgins. He lives not far away, near Wimbledon. He doesn't like little committees. He has too many of them at King's. He wants some of us to join him in forming a company. At lunch break on Sunday we talked. Sheila and Paul are both interested. Jenny offered to draw up some Articles of Association. It's all in her text books, she said."

Rather vacantly, I read through what he passed me. It specified that a company should be formed for the purpose of developing portable computing systems, links between such systems, and software to allow their scientific or commercial application. Authorised capital would be £25,000, of which half would be paid up by five shareholders and directors: Tony, Brian, Paul, Sheila, and I would provide £2,500 each. Jenny would act as company secretary.

"Jenny mentioned this when she called me on Monday. I'll look at it again when I'm more awake, but in principle, I'm game. I'll have the money next month. Are you OK for your share? You could easily lose the lot."

"I'll be OK if Universal pay me a decent bonus, which could depend on what incomes policy we have, and hence what the result is tonight. Meanwhile, Tony is drawing up a business plan for the first year, and Jenny will look at it. Basically, it's to develop an improved version of his design, which customers are willing to try as a prototype. Vacation students would do the assembly work."

"I'll call Sydney Felhurst at Staines, and say that you and Tony will see him later this month. IE likes staff to be involved in their own business ventures, provided there's no conflict. Hopefully your firm is the same. What's the name of the company to be?"

"Jenny suggested 'Creators Technology'."

"Back to the present, what's your father's mood?"

"They're on top. Joe has played it superbly. All the National Executive agree, left or right. He's the reasonable man, but he's getting what they want."

Again we drifted into sleepy silence as the screen before us showed swingometers, and patterns of Liberal and Nationalist troops nibbling away at the edges of red and blue territory. At twenty past three, we were again with Arthur Harnett.

"It's a third recount, here at Bellinghame South. This really is a cliffhanger. Nothing we can see gives us any clue as to who may be in the lead. Maybe that's already settled, and the recount is for second place. All three parties have gone for this so hard, especially over the last week, that none of them will give up until the end. The strain on the candidates, particularly on Carol Milverton, is huge. She's done so well anyway, but when you get to this stage, you just want to win. She's bearing up, and looks as cheerful and positive as ever. She's had huge support from her family. You can see her now talking with her husband, and with her father, Councillor Bert Gibson, who is well known in Manchester politics. Over here, her father-in-law and agent, Fred Milverton, is talking to Albert Dickson. Whoever wins, it will be Albert Dickson's night. He's determined to be the man people stayed up for, rather than someone announcing the result in the middle of the afternoon. He must be hoping this count is the decider, though. So, hopefully I'll see you in about an hour with a result. It could be any of the six possible orders of the three main candidates."

Clive Tolhurst continued. The rush of early results was over, and he needed to fill in whilst waiting for the next one.

"I'll second Arthur about Carol Milverton. Whatever happens, she's fought a quite incredible campaign. Three weeks or even two weeks ago, who could have thought we would be here, now? I'm told that Harold Wilson liked his visit on Tuesday. There were nearly four hundred people packed into a fairly small hall, and well warmed up for him. Then he went on to the Fairfield Halls in Croydon for his final rally, before heading back to Huyton.[74] He saw an encouragingly large crowd outside, but they turned out to be waiting to see a film. His audience was about the same as in Bellinghame, looked lost in the large hall, and was totally unresponsive. Every seat counts, now. Look at the latest swingometer predictions. With over half of results in, Labour are predicted to be ahead of the Tories by about ten, but the regional variations in results we're seeing leave such uncertainty that the Conservatives could still pull into the lead. What is clear is that neither main party will have an overall

---

74 Harold Wilson's constituency.

majority. The limelight will be on the Liberals, the Scottish and Welsh Nationalists, and the Ulster parties."

By now, the tension had most people wakeful, talking of what they had done, or what might happen.

"Heath is finished," said Morag. "He went for a positive mandate to resist the unions. He hasn't received one. He can't carry on with his policies, even if he does end up in the lead."

"Before the last few days, Harold Wilson was pretty crap," said Jack Unwin. "He didn't look to be trying to win."

"Perhaps he didn't think he could win," said Liz. "I can tell you, he didn't expect the Pay Board to interpret the figures the way they did. That, and Enoch, and Campbell Adamson, to say nothing of dear Reg and Harry, are what's swung the votes. All the surprises have been for Labour, or at least against the Tories."

"I'm just a simple engineer," said Greg, "but I wonder if either Heath or Wilson *wants* to win. The best result for each is that the other wins with a small majority. In two or three years, we'll be in an even worse mess than now, and the benefits of North Sea oil will still be way off. A shaky government might collapse then, leading to an election in which whoever loses now wins handsomely and takes the benefits."

"However, we're heading for neither winning. I don't know whether *that* was anyone's plan," I commented.

Greg had the knack for very perceptive remarks, and he had come in before anyone could be tactless enough to ask Liz anything more about the Pay Board. They couldn't have delivered their report without expert input on the miners' hideously complicated pay structure. It was clear who had made that input, and why. Everyone had their unsaid motives. Back in July, Pat O'Donnell had declared his to Paul and me.

The argument ran on in a desultory way. Sometimes we listened to Clive Tolhurst, but he was running out of things to say, and becoming repetitive as a result. Various party notables gave their comments, which added little.

At ten to four, Roberta made us jump when she appeared in her dressing gown.

"I'm surprised that I've not been disturbed for so long. Goodness, you all look tense."

"Not half as tense as Carol must be," Brian replied.

Roberta was certainly the freshest of us, now. We found her a chair, and sat or lay in silence again, half attentive to the screen.

Just before half past four, we were back with Arthur Harnett, for a shock as the cameras panned around.

"We have a result coming, at last. Albert Dickson is showing the spoilt papers to the candidates' agents, to make sure there's no dispute about them. That's a sign of how close it is. We've no clue, except that it doesn't look good for Carol Milverton. She was out of sight for a while, and came back in only a couple of minutes ago. She's not looking her usual cheerful self. In fact, she's almost in tears. Neither Sir Reg Emerson nor Cyril Horsley look much happier, though. If Emerson is just in, that's hardly a good result for him, and if Horsley wins, it will be by default. The happiest looking candidate is Finola Donoghue, who is positively giggling. Remember that she too has an opportunity to make a speech. Perhaps we shouldn't read too much into how Carol Milverton looks. The stress of the last few hours would make anyone snappy. She's speaking to Fred Milverton, her father-in-law and agent. It doesn't look as if she's saying nice things, and nor does her father look happy. Her husband isn't here; ah yes, he's joining the group. He's not looking very happy, either. Well, we'll know the answer soon enough."

In silence, we saw the candidates line up, each with a little group of supporters behind them. Albert Dickson had been strict on numbers. All the places in Carol's party had been filled by the official party organisation, rather than by us irregulars. Looking round the room, I could see that all except me thought Carol had missed it, doubtless by a hairsbreadth. I knew that there was an alternative explanation of Carol's demeanour. I didn't know which explanation I wanted to be the truth.

Finally, Albert Dickson began. This was his moment. He was determined to make the most of it.

"I, Albert Victor Dickson, being appointed the acting Returning Officer for the constituency of Bellinghame South for the Parliamentary election held on 28th February, 1974, hereby give notice that the votes cast in the election for each candidate were as follows."

"Donoghue, Finola Mary."

He paused, to allow Arthur Harnett to murmur "Independent" into his microphone. Party affiliations were not then on ballot papers or given at the declaration.

"Two hundred and sixty-three."

Against the background of sporadic cheers, Morag had her comment.

"Between 56,950 and 57,000 votes to go, allowing for spoilt papers."

"Emerson, Sir Reginald St John George William."

"Conservative."

"Eighteen thousand, nine hundred and ninety-seven."

There were cheers of encouragement from his group, and grim concentration in our group. That vote was probably just over one third of the total remaining. It could win, if the other two were very close together.

"Horsley, Cyril James."

"Liberal."

"Eighteen thousand, nine hundred and seventy-six."

There were louder cheers from the Conservatives. With what they had seen of Carol, they thought they had it in the bag.

"She's ahead of that," said Morag. But by how much was she ahead?

"Quiet, please. Milverton, Caroline Frances."

"Labour."

Albert Dickson paused, and lifted his head slightly. Brian realised what that meant.

"*YES.*"

"*NINE —*"

The bedlam at the count was matched by bedlam in Roberta's lounge. Morag threw her arms around Brian and kissed him, without annoying Sheila.

"You wonderful man, you did it."

"No, we all did it. Creators and friends did it."

"Nineteen thousand and five. Spoilt papers, fifty-two. Accordingly, I hereby declare that the said Caroline Frances Milverton is elected to serve as Member of Parliament for this constituency."[75]

Arthur Harnett seemed as much carried away as 'LAB GAIN' and a still of a grinning Carol flashed onto the screen.

"So, Carol Milverton has won after all, despite the signs just now that she hadn't. Those were understandable reactions to the level of stress she's been under. People fighting their first election at the age of twenty-five don't usually finish this way. What a race. Eight votes in it, and less than thirty separating first and third. This one will be in the record books for a *very* long time, as the culmination of one of the most remarkable constituency campaigns for a generation. I think, though, that in the future I'll remember tonight as when, to quote rather a cliché, 'a Star is born.' Perhaps one day you viewers will be able to tell your children, and your grandchildren, that you stayed up to see that happen. Now, we'll hear her speak."

I helped Roberta bring in the champagne that had been kept unobtrusively cool outside the back door, so I missed the first part of Carol's speech, in which as usual she thanked Albert Dickson and everyone involved in the running of the election.

---

75 So 57,293 votes were cast, of which 56,978 were valid and for a main candidate. The split was: Emerson, 33.34%; Horsley, 33.30%; Milverton, 33.36%.

By the time I was settled with glass in hand, the stress had melted out of Carol's face, and any tears were of happiness.

"…and now I must thank some special people who have helped me. My father, Councillor Bert Gibson, from whom I learnt what practical politics means. My father-in-law, Fred Milverton, who decided that his place was here rather than in Manchester. My husband Paul, who has been with me so much during these last weeks. And many old and new friends, who have united to support common sense. They have seen, as the whole country is seeing, that only Labour can get the country out of the mess the Tories have made. It will be a proud moment when I take my seat in the House of Commons as the representative of everyone in this constituency, however they voted. I am sure that I will be doing so as one of the party in government."

"You look thoughtful, Pete," said Morag. "What's up?"

"Oh, I was thinking about why Carol looked so unhappy just before the declaration. Release of tension can hit you that way, particularly if you're tired out. Wellington said it after Waterloo. 'There is nothing worse than a battle won except a battle lost.' After my final exams at Cambridge, I was totally exhausted. When I first knew I'd topped the list, I was very irritable." This was a good story to put around, at least for the moment.

"Hey, look at him, what a prat."

Brian's shout interrupted my thoughts. Sir Reg was speaking now. He wasn't being a good loser, despite his impeccable education.

"The electors here and across the country will quickly realise that they have been told lies, and that they've been conned by a gang of tricksters out for their own personal advantage. You will be hearing from me again about this, very soon."

"Speak for yourself, queer – loveaboy. Sorry, but he was sounding like Harry Tamfield."

Brian corrected himself quickly as Sheila turned sharply towards him. He had brought another name to mind. Perhaps a star had been born, but in the films of that name one dies to allow that.

I heard the telephone ring, and went to answer it.

"Pete, it's Arthur Gulliver. I'm glad you gave me this number. What a night, eh?"

"How has it gone down at Waterhouse?"

"I'm at home, but am told that the cheer for Carol Milverton was heard all over the College. I don't want to cut into your celebrations, but I bet you've quite a few of 'the Waterhouse connection' there with you right now. I've a message for you all, indeed for Carol Milverton herself. Yesterday, Graham Harcroft and I visited New Hall. We made some contingency plans for the weekend, which we'll now put into operation. A celebration is called for. New Hall is only too pleased for us to host it, though they would like the Milvertons to stay there. So on Saturday, the President and some Fellows of New Hall will be dining with us, as I expect will be some of their students. The message for your friends is that if anyone hasn't already booked to stay, let Graham's office know by noon today. We'll fit them in somehow."

"That sounds great, but can the College afford to celebrate?"

"The College can't afford *not* to celebrate, Pete. You were right about our going with that TV programme, as well as superb on it yourself. It's put us on the map. Three top schools called Colin Mackay on Monday, and two more since then."

"Don't make it a triumph. Carol will be totally exhausted."

"Good point. Also, is there any chance of you staying over Sunday night, and talking to the College Maths Society before dinner?"

"Yes, that fits well. I don't need to be back in Aberdeen until Monday afternoon. I came down via Norwich because of the BEA strike. There's a plane back from there at noon."

"I'll see you tomorrow, then. Get some sleep in between."

I had hardly put the phone down when it rang again.

"Bert Gibson. Glad it's you, Pete. Tell everyone that Carol is just finishing first press interviews. We need to go to the party office, then we'll be with you by six, I guess."

"Great. Bacon and eggs for two?"

"Yes, thanks. Pete, she needs a few minutes with you, on your own."

"I know why. No one else here does, and it will stay like that. I've put round already that she's clearly exhausted."

"Right she is. Just to say, I don't blame you, but I hope you can help – in any way."

Again, as soon as I put the phone down it rang.

"Hey, Brit boy, everyone wants to talk to you. All our table raised their glasses to Carol – ain't it jest great?" Steph had been on the New Hampshire table at a City election night party.

"Were you watching Carol just before the declaration?"

"No, but we heard it. That returning officer sounded *very* pleased with himself."

"She was in a state. Paul must have told her. Her father wants me to help."

"Gee, sorry Pete. That shouldn't have happened so soon."

"Well, it did."

"Actually, I was meaning to say, Paul and I are having an introductory lunch, as he starts with us on Monday. We might come back to the flat after. Best if you're not there."

"Best in the circs if I *am* there, I think."

"Now look, Pete, it's my flat."

"I'm contributing to expenses, Steph. I'll need a rest. I'll be there, before lunch in fact, assuming Pat's meeting doesn't go on very long."

These conversations had certainly not been overheard. In fact, it had been difficult to conduct them against the shouts and laughter that had burst out in the lounge. Now, I heard a familiar voice on the TV.

"There's no mystery about me…"

In those days, these were dead hours in election coverage. Overnight counts were finished, and politicians were unavailable during their journeys to London. To fill in, we were seeing extracts from the last three weeks of *Election Round-up*.

I gave people the news, and then Susie and I helped Roberta cook breakfasts. We were all munching away when Carol and Bert arrived by taxi, with an explanation that Paul had some things to sort out with Fred. There was a friendly and satisfied welcome rather than wild acclaim. We were all too tired for more.

The lounge was stuffy, because there had been several smokers overnight. Before long, Carol nudged me to come and see their new flat. We stepped outside into the cool and dark. Once we were by the nearly completed block, the cheerful mask dropped. For a couple of minutes she cried on my shoulder.

"I don't know whether I should be loving or hating you, Pete. Without you, I wouldn't have been elected, but you've brought Steph into our lives. Don't get me wrong, I half knew there was something between them. I had the hint from some of the way they talked at New Year, when we were coming back from Manchester. Paul is doing better with me, maybe because of Steph, so that's not so serious provided it's kept quiet. It's what's happened now that's so awful."

"Steph's excuse is that she was helping you both, after a chat you and she had in Brighton. It's not much of an excuse, but she's like that. She said that Paul would tell you about it after the election. I hadn't expected that to mean during the count."

"That was half *my* fault, I suppose. The first count had me ahead of Reg by eleven. The second had him three up. The third, I was seven up. Would the fourth confirm that? You can guess how I was feeling. To distract myself, I started talking to Paul about his new job. He said that they would want him to move to America later this year, and he and I needed to think about our future accordingly. I asked who 'they' really were and it came out. He's lunching with Steph today, and there may be afters."

"The afters will be a talk with me, unless you say just keep out, which you're perfectly entitled to do. I'll ask you a question, Carol. What do you think is going to happen now?"

"Heath will resign, and Harold will form a government."

"He'll have no majority. He'll be looking for the first chance – as he did in 1966, but quicker. There'll be another election later this year, perhaps within three months. There'll be a new Conservative candidate here. Getting this seat back will be a top priority for them. Dear old Cyril will be for the chop, too. I'm sure our gang will support you as much as possible, but with no three-day week they won't have so much time. You've no chance of holding the seat, though you'll stay well up on the 1970 Labour vote. Have you any chance of moving to a winnable seat, straightaway?"

"No."

"You can speak, and you can write. You're temporarily famous. Newspapers will want your name, immediately. Get into journalism here. After the next election, carry on over there. There'll be loads happening. Nixon can't last, so what then? As an ex-MP, you'll have access to all sorts of people in Congress. So, insist that Paul and you don't move to the States until after the next election, and that you both come back after two years there. That will be when to look for a winnable seat."

"You're suggesting that I tag along with Paul and Steph, then."

"It won't be like that for long, Carol. Meeting Jenny has made Steph realise that what she really wants is a permanent relationship, with children. Paul isn't the family type, is he?"

That remark clearly touched another sensitive area. There were more tears before Carol replied.

"That's something we're to talk about, more."

"Over there, she'll be looking out. I think her Mr Right will be in his forties, loaded and seeking his third wife, the first having been serious but limited and the second glamorous but dim. I don't think she would mind a couple of stepchildren. Therefore, she'll want to be discreet with Paul. She'll want the two of you to be clearly together. I'll say it again. Paul is right for you, and you for him. You're both your fathers' children. You go out front, and he's quietly effective in the background. Remember that meeting last week, when things were wobbling?"

"Yes, you saved me then."

"By luck, I had something useful to say, but what really saved you was that with Powell coming up, the Libs weren't offering anything of value. Fred, and Transport House, had missed that. Paul pointed it out. You wouldn't be here without him. Think it over. We can talk again in Cambridge, later tomorrow. I've some news about that."

I passed on what Arthur had told me, and made a fairly obvious suggestion as to what 'later tomorrow' might mean. That had a fairly obvious response.

"Mmm, it sounds like a chance, Pete, and back on our first-time ground, too."

"That's the bottom girl I know."

We kissed, and I reached under her skirt, for a good feel around. A few minutes later, she reached under her skirt, to pull her pants back up. We returned to Roberta's bungalow, with plans made. She was much more relaxed, and I felt pretty good, too. Brian ran her and Bert to their next call.

The phone rang again. Jenny regretted that she had missed Carol, and then was quickly to the point.

"Pete, we listened to the radio in bed and after Carol's result I dropped off quickly. Then I heard the phone ring and Dick go down to answer. When he came back he was reluctant at first to say who it was, but then admitted that it was Harry Tamfield, who had wanted to know the result, that's all."

"Did he say where he was?"

"No, and Dick didn't ask."

"Sensible man. It's pretty odd that Harry should get you up. Hopefully it means that he's so far away that he's forgotten what time it is here. Now, it looks as if dinner in Waterhouse tomorrow will be quite a do. You can both come, on Dick's dining rights. Have him call the Bursar's office."

"Mother's fine in charge of the children for a while, but we can't stay long after."

"Thanks for the draft Articles. I'll look at them later today. You're doing the work, but not putting anything in."

"I've nothing to put in right now, Pete. There's scope for me to subscribe when I can."

After washing up was done, the party dispersed, most of them still bemused by their achievement, and some looking forward to the next evening. I set my alarm for nine o'clock. There was a short moment before I went to sleep. Why was Harry still interested? Where was he?

Before leaving for Pat's wash-up meeting, I took a cup of tea to Roberta, who had said that it would take her about a week to catch up on *her* sleep.

"Pete, I suppose I won't be seeing so much of you now."

"I'll try to look you up when I'm in London. To second what Carol and Brian said, so much thanks for the help you've given."

"It's for me to thank you, Pete. Since last July, you've helped to change my life in so many ways. You've given it some meaning. You've shown that I can make a difference. I'm not just a useless old woman any more. You'll always be welcome here. You, and whoever you choose to bring with you. Don't ever say this to your mother, but – I wish you were *my* son."

Pat's meeting was short, since there was as yet little to wash up. The predicted Labour lead over the Conservatives was now in single figures, but the position was exactly as *The Times* headline summarised.

Mr Heath's general election gamble fails.

However, the Conservatives appeared to have slightly more votes cast than Labour, and Ted Heath was quoting this as a reason for not resigning. It was being suggested, without much substance, that he was hoping to assemble an anti-Labour coalition with the Liberals and some Ulster MPs.

As the others left, Pat motioned me to stay.

"Heath is definitely flying on half his engines. It's just a matter of time. Things are going as I hoped for back in July. Before long, we'll be on a proper working week again. Well done, Pete. I know too that without you we wouldn't be £19 million to the good through 'Crafty'. At the end of this month, you'll have some more tangible reward. What's up?"

We were sitting in our overcoats in his office, in the dim natural light of a bleak day. We had interpreted 'office equipment' as including the TV set, since we were using it for the business purpose of keeping up with what was going on. Something, or rather someone, had caught my eye.

"Behind the commentator outside Conservative Central Office, Sir Reg Emerson has gone in. I'm positive it's him. What's he there for?"

"God knows. If we wait, perhaps we'll see him being kicked down the steps."

We watched for a few minutes, but saw nothing of the sort. Eventually, Pat continued.

"Whether that was Emerson or not, you've reminded me to say that I've a hunch. Harry Tamfield is up to something. Why else would he have stolen two million when he had a million of his own? I suppose he'll be caught before long, though I'm surprised the Swiss police haven't found him already."

Back at my desk, I just sat for a while, reflecting on the consequences of the decision I made in November. I had had a real influence on national events. Perhaps I had changed the course of history. Others had joined in, but I had created the opportunity to make a difference. I had taken forward IE policy as defined by Pat, who clearly knew that I had something to do with Emerson's fate. I had made things happen, and most had turned out as planned. That was what being a Creator was about.

Now, I could relax into and over the weekend. The next evening at Waterhouse looked to be quite something, and its conclusion would be enjoyable as well as therapeutic. This would be my first real return to the College that I had left so suddenly in 1968. The Sinclairs' wedding had been well out of term, and I had stayed with Liz in the Master's Lodge. Then, she had been Maid of Honour and I had been Best Man. On Sunday, we would be the Godparents.

I asked my office in Aberdeen to book me on to Monday's flight. It was quiet there, while most potential clients awaited developments. They did mention, in an amused way, that a woman had tried to contact me and they had said I was down here. I cleared a few bits of mail and drafted a short memo about the computer company. It was a pity that Jenny couldn't put anything in. Her financial skills would be very valuable. Perhaps we should pay her for her work.

I was packing up to leave when reception called me, in a tone of scarcely veiled disapproval.

"There's a *woman* here, asking to see you. She looks rather *strange.*"

Downstairs was a tallish blonde. It took me a moment to recognise her. She was very different from when I had met her before, and from a more recent photograph. Her face was covered with bruises, she had several teeth broken, and she stood with obvious discomfort.

"Gloria, what's happened to you?"

"Come to tell, but not 'ere. Not the type for 'ere, I'm nawt."
The receptionist was pleased to see us leave hurriedly for the flat.

Steph was just about to go out, but one look was enough for her to ask the restaurant to tell her guest that she would be a little late. Gloria was quickly fortified with a gin and tonic. She looked for a soft chair, sat down uncomfortably, and began to talk.

"I cin't sleep, I'd turned on the telly to find out wot was 'appening, an' afer a time I sees yer, Pete. They sez yer works for Int'national Electronics in Aberdeen. I thought, how nice yer'd been before. I could tell me trouble. I gets yer number and calls. They sez yer at the London orfice today, so I goes there."

"So what happened to you?" Steph asked.

"It was a week last Toosday – late, 'bout midnight. I'd 'ad a good day with blokes spottin' me in the *Clarion*. Booked a coupla' extra jobs straight off. I was jest back and there's a knock. I opens carefully like and there 'e is."

"Who?"

"'Arry Tamfield – the bloke wot threw the par-ee. He looks pretty odd, but sez he wants me, for a change. So I lets him in, pours him a drink, and strips. He strips too, looks well up. It all looked good for a big fee and it was nice thinkin' I made him wanna do it proper. Then he knocks me down, puts his shoes on again and starts kicking me. 'This is for blabbing about Robin' he shouts. I sez I'd not blabbed anything about Robin. 'You put the *Clarion* on to him', he yells, and kicks me more. I sez, ain't told them anything 'bout Robin, only 'bout me night with Martha Dugdale. 'He was the one who talked first', he shouts. I screams, but where I live no one cares. Then he stops kicking me, goes all quiet, grabs me 'air, pushes me down and does me like he does boys. I was shrieking in agony, shouting at 'im to stop. He sez he likes hurting me 'cos I look like the girl wot cost him his boy, the girl he reall wants to do over like this. Then he kicks me more and goes away."

"You mean – he raped you – up the butt?"

"Yuh, I was bleeding for days and it's still sore. But that's going, risk of the job. Not likes me face, and mouth. Can't work

381

in a parlour like this. I got to see me dentist yesterday. He sez, have to take the bits out, youse need dentures. 'Ow cin I doos me job with dentures? I'll 'ave to takes the rough stuff. And with the *Clarion* money I'd 'nough saved to start a place of me own."

She began to cry. Steph put an arm round her.

"Have you told the police, or the *Clarion*?"

"What's the point? Soon as the cops hear what I do, no dice. 'Arry ran orf straight after this, dinne? I called the *Clarion*. Not on it any more, story finished. I hate this place now. I wanna get out of London and start agin. I've no people I get on with here. But how cin I?"

"I've an idea, Gloria. I go to a dentist, not far from here. He's an expert. I like my teeth to look good. He's crowned some of them. He could sort out your teeth and make them lovely again. He's not usually very busy on Friday afternoons. I must go out now, but I'll be back by three o'clock. I'll call his surgery now."

She was quickly off the phone. "Yes, he can see you at half past three. I'll take you round there. Until then, Pete can look after you here."

"Won'ee be expensive?"

"Yes, but you're not to worry, isn't that right, Pete?"

"That's absolutely right."

Steph motioned me out into the entrance hall and closed the door.

"I guess we owe her something. She could have guessed that you put the *Clarion* on to Robin. After your performance on TV, that mustn't come out."

"Right. I'm sorry if this messes up your afternoon, but tomorrow night will suit us all." I described the plan that I had worked out with Carol.

"Wow, Pete, you're getting as much of a hustler as me."

"I was taught by Liz."

Steph set off, and I returned to Gloria. She had another gin, and I made a couple of sandwiches. She told me of her wretched childhood in the East End with her mother, now dead 'thank Gawd' and a series of 'uncles'; then life in the superior part of 'the trade', and her ambitions to become a 'madam'. She would run a 'class place' – clean, safe, no drugs. Many of her clients had said she had the personality to do that, and I could believe them. She seemed to have plenty of business sense. The germ of an idea formed in my mind.

Talking with her at least took my mind off the horror of what Harry had done. On TV, he had said that the train drivers were having sadistic fun. An hour later, he had had his own sadistic fun. He raped Gloria brutally, because she looked like Jenny. He said that he wanted to rape Jenny brutally, because she had taken Dick away from him, though in actual fact, his casual rejection of Dick had given Jenny the idea that brought her and Dick together. The next night, he took Dick back – not by renewing a caring relationship, but by giving Dick the same 'pretty rough time' as he gave to the men he paid. Evidently, he was quite deranged. In a way, that was reassuring. He might be up to something, but he could hardly do any more damage.

After a while, Gloria yawned and took off her shoes.

"Kinn I kip down on the sofa till it's time to go to the fang man? Yer and Steph are just great. Not many like you bother with the likes of me. Any'ow you're lots nicer than 'Arry Tamfield. I should have slammed the door on him after wot happened that night you was at the club and got the intro to Robin – hopes yer likes him."

"As it turned out, I didn't get to him before I went off to work in Aberdeen. I guess he'll be much more expensive, now."

"Cor, that 'Arry, he woz funny then, too. First he takes the change room locker pass key. Dunno why he wanned it. Shouldn'a given it 'im, he'd no reason 'avin' it. Then he brings it back, and slaps me up…"

She dozed off and was soon snoring, and whistling through the gaps in her teeth. The phone was on a long lead, so I moved it into the bedroom to make sure she wasn't disturbed. I lay on the bed myself, to have some quiet.

I looked again at Jenny's draft Articles, and jotted down a few suggestions. Then I made some notes for the talk on Sunday evening. *A Mathematician at large* was my title, and I would give examples of how my training helped me in my present work. I wouldn't include anything about car numbers, but I would put questions such as one that had come up the week before, when I had taken to lunch the man who was so helpful in getting me the three-day week announcement. He had referred to a plan for developing an oilfield, in two phases. Phase 1 had an estimated cost of £457 million, whilst Phase 2 had an estimated cost of £543 million. What could you tell about the accuracy of at least one of these figures?

I couldn't concentrate, though. How responsible was I for what had happened to Gloria? Either she hadn't cottoned on to my part, or she didn't hold it against me. I had brought her fame and fortune, despite what had happened later.

My mind moved on. I was tired, but things were whirling round in it – all sorts of things that people had said, all sorts of questions, and possible answers.

Suddenly, for the second time in my life, the questions and answers lined up, like lemons on a fruit machine. The first time had been on a hot June day, nearly six years before.

In November, I had visited what Harry had described as his club. He had become paranoid about Jenny. He could have been looking for evidence that she had put me up to keeping Dick away from him, such as a letter asking me to come along to the club with Dick. Only a few of the changing room lockers were in use. He could have found mine easily enough. Whilst Andy looked after us, Harry could have searched my clothes. It sounded crazy, but Harry had done all sorts of crazy things.

He wouldn't have found what he was looking for, but he would have seen Ana's note. He would have seen that I was up to something lucrative with people in Pamplona, and that Steph and Paul were involved.

That would explain what he had said to me two weeks later, and then on TV. A look at the New Hampshire and IE Reports and Accounts would have shown him that both had links with the Banco Navarrese, whose HQ was in Pamplona. So:

Where was Harry now? Why had he wanted to know the Bellinghame result? Why was Reg Emerson visiting Central Office? What did his speech in defeat actually mean? And why was Heath hanging on?

I grabbed the phone and asked for the international operator. Five long minutes later, I was through to Don Pedro's house outside Pamplona, and was using my Spanish, unpractised for months.

"It is Peter Bridford, the English friend of the lady Ana who visited you just before her betrothal. I must speak to her very urgently, please."

"She is out riding, but will return for lunch."

"Please ask her to telephone me at this number as soon as she returns, before lunch, even before she changes. It is very urgent and important."

It was nearly two o'clock – three o'clock in Spain. Though Ana would surely be back soon, I took the risk of making another call.

"Jenny, can you call the international operator and see if they have any record of from where Harry's call came this morning. I know that's the opposite of what we said earlier, but something is up. I'll tell you more, later."

The phone rang and I answered, hurriedly.

"Pete, it's Bert Gibson. I just wanted to say what a great job you did for Carol. You've got her through half a dozen press and TV interviews. Watch the six o'clock news. She's told me what you've said. It makes sense, though her mum will be tearful about her going away."

"Good. I'm glad I've been able to help."

"And, you'll console her," he chuckled. "This does makes me wonder again, could things have worked out between you?"

"It's good of you to say that, Bert, but things wouldn't have worked out. Would Carol have wanted to be with me in Franco's Spain? Where would I have been the last three weeks? She *has* got the right man. He'll be with her in public. This will pass over. Meanwhile, I've a favour to ask. About half past eleven, I was watching TV and was surprised to see Reg Emerson sneak unnoticed into Central Office. I'm sure there's someone at Transport who keeps an eye on comings and goings across the square.[76] Can you ask whether there have been more sightings of Reg?"

Five minutes later, once again the phone rang and I answered hurriedly. I hadn't expected Jenny to be so prompt.

"I persuaded the supervisor to bend the rules. I said the call was from a friend whose birthday was coming up, and we wanted to send him a surprise present. We knew his itinerary, but weren't sure how far he was along it. The operator who dealt with the call will be back in at 7.30. She'll call me then. Fortunately, Dick will be at an orchestra rehearsal."

Another ten minutes went by. In Spain, it was half past three. That was late for lunch in winter, even there. Perhaps there were delays on the lines. Had the maid who answered taken the number down right? I was about to try calling again when the phone rang. At least the wait had allowed me to work out what to say.

"Pete, it is wonderful to hear from you, and thank you for the gracious acceptance of our invitation. I hope nothing is now wrong about that. Your message was urgent, and I have telephoned as soon as I returned."

"Nothing is wrong for your wedding, but you need to have enquiries made and be on your guard. I told you about Harry Tamfield."

---

76 Then, the two party headquarters were very close to each other, in Smith Square.

"He is the homosexual who was with your friend Dick, and who is doing well in the property business."

"That was right, but his property company has now failed, and he has fled to Switzerland. The police are seeking him there. He thinks that Paul and I have plotted to ruin him, and he has threatened revenge on us."

"I am sorry to hear that, Pete. How does this affect me? Switzerland is far away from here."

"There have been signs that Harry wants to renew his relationship with Dick. A few weeks ago, Dick was invited to a bathing club where Harry is well known. It was clear that Harry was responsible for the invitation, so I accompanied Dick."

"I understand, Pete. Jenny felt that you would keep it safe for Dick. To help her, you will do much."

"Dick was safe, though we did meet Harry there. I have found out today that whilst we were in the club, Harry could have searched our clothes, to look for information about Jenny. By mischance, I had in a pocket your note, which had reached me earlier the same day. He may be trying to find out what we and Paul have done that is so profitable. He has much money, so he could buy information. He may have left Switzerland before their border guards were alerted. He would not have been sought at the Spanish border. I hope that this is what we call a wild goose chase, but you must check whether he is in Pamplona."

"Thank you for the warning, Pete. When might Harry Tamfield have arrived here?"

"At the weekend, or perhaps on Monday."

"There were crowds then, for festivity, not bulls. Tuesday was the day before Lent, when your people run around tossing pancakes. What is it called in English?"

"Shrove, or Pancake Tuesday. There has not been much festivity in England, because of our fuel shortages. We have been having our general election. Paul's wife Carol is elected, by just a few votes."

"I am pleased for her. I believe your warning is fanciful, Pete, but I will do as you ask. It is quiet here, particularly now that Lent has begun. I have not seen Carlos for three weeks. He is presently in Sevilla. Father has been in Rome, but returns this evening. Can you describe Harry Tamfield, please?"

"He is slim, has shortish blond hair, and is of height 1.7 metres. He speaks some Spanish. A few years ago he travelled in Spain, though I don't think he visited Pamplona. Have the *Guardia Civile* check the bars that people like him use. I'm sure they know where those are."

"You can be assured that even if he is here, he will find out nothing. Everyone who knows of our business can be trusted absolutely."

As Ana rang off, I heard the front door of the flat open, and a laugh as Steph saw Gloria. The two of them left for the dentist's once Gloria had been fortified with a strong coffee. Paul stayed for a little while. I passed on Bert's message about the six o'clock news.

"I had better be back in good time to watch it. Carol should be back already. I do want her, Pete. Does she want me, anymore?"

"I know you do, and I'm sure she does."

"She's a wonderful woman. At the count, we were both stressed up."

"She knows that's why it happened then."

"Steph is a wonderful woman, too. You know that."

"Welcome to the world of more than one woman, Paul. You need to make them friends, rather than jealous rivals. You need to make them all feel important, and cared for. Make sure you do that tonight, if Carol isn't too tired. Steph's excuse for seducing you isn't so different from the excuses Carol made for going with me. We can all enjoy tomorrow night."

I described the arrangements for that, and soon afterwards

Paul left. I returned to notes for my talk, trying to keep out of mind what might or might not be happening in Pamplona, and what might be the consequences of Ana's and my unwitting breach of security. For a while, I dozed.

The return of Steph and Gloria made me jump. It was five past six. I dashed to turn the TV on, but Steph interrupted me with a grin. Gloria grinned too, and opened her mouth. The jagged, broken bits were now under temporary crowns which though ungainly already looked much better.

"He worked on to complete the first part of the job. The finished crowns will be ready to go in next Thursday. Then, you'll be as good as new."

"Yeah, great, real great. My mouth's all fruz up, but later I'll der yer both real good, that's if you wants. Yer've been great to me. I wanna to be great back."

The news went on at length. The predicted Labour majority over the Conservatives was now four or five. At twenty to seven, there was a flashback to the Bellinghame South declaration, which had contributed half of that majority. Gloria, though 'fruz up', was perceptive.

"Gor, I saw this before seein' yer sayin' she wuz yer chum, Pete. She was dead scared jest before, wan't she?"

I could see why Bert was pleased with the interview with Carol which followed. The most memorable exchange was:

CLIVE TOLHURST: One last question – when do you think there'll first be a woman Prime Minister?

CAROL MILVERTON: Who knows? Before you ask me whether I might be the first, I'll say that I hope and believe that there'll be one long before there's the remotest chance that it could be me.

I heard the phone ringing, and went to the bedroom, where I had left it. It was Ana.

"Pete, I have two pieces of good news for you. Your warning was not fanciful, but there is nothing to worry about."

"Wow, you've worked fast."

"In Spain, there is no *mañana* when people like us speak to the *Guardia Civile*. I must confess that when you told me Carol was elected, I wondered if you had been celebrating too much, despite the season. Last Saturday, Harry Tamfield arrived in Pamplona. However, he departed on Tuesday. We do not know where he is now. None of the few employees of the bank who are aware of our transactions was approached by him or knew that he was here. He discovered *nothing*."

"That's a relief. He may have thought of coming to Pamplona to nose around, but it was also a good place to stay while perhaps he booked a flight out of Madrid to somewhere in South America."

"I am glad we have been able to check this, Pete. When my father returns, I shall tell him of what we have found out. I shall not mention my note, and I expect you will not do so, either. I shall say that you had remembered something Harry Tamfield said, which suggested that he might come here. We will not check with Madrid Airport. We do not wish to hear any more of Harry Tamfield."

"That's right. Thanks, Ana. You've taken something off my mind."

"Good. I will let you continue your celebrations."

I kept talking, though I was being distracted. Gloria and Steph had followed me into the bedroom, and were transforming themselves into Numbers 6 and 7.

"There is a different celebration this weekend, the christening of the second child of Jenny and Dick Sinclair. It is in Cambridge, and I am visiting Waterhouse College for the first time since I left."

"My felicitations to parents and child."

"I will pass those on, and leave you to preparations for your happy day."

"Before that day, when will you and Steph be arriving in Pamplona?"

"We will arrive on Holy Thursday. The chance to view the Easter processions is too good to miss. We can see you as much, or as little, as you like before the day."

By the time I finished with the usual salutations, Gloria had gone into the bathroom, and Steph's look of anticipation had turned to alarm at what she had heard. Indeed, she looked suddenly very bare and vulnerable.

"What was all that about, with Ana?"

"Pat O'Donnell had a hunch that Harry Tamfield is up to something, and his hunches are often worth attention. Back in December, Harry was interested in my time in Spain, and particularly in Pamplona. So, when I called Ana to give the news about Carol, I asked her to look out for him, just in case he had managed to sneak out of Switzerland."

I repeated what Steph had partly overheard, and she recovered her composure.

"That's smart work, both of you. Ana is a tough young cookie. You set her quite a task. She's not meant to know about homo bars. Thanks to you she does, I guess. Now, I'm completely bushed. After the party, I went straight into the office. I was only just back here to freshen up when you arrived. Then I went back to the office while Gloria was at the dentist. I've had a big breakfast and a big lunch, and I need some more office time tomorrow morning. When do we have to leave for Cambridge?"

"Greg will pick us up at half past three."

There was a shout from the bathroom.

"Water's real 'ot now, Steph."

"So now, Brit boy, I'm having a nice shower with Gloria. She's 'unfruz' enough that then she can help me relax, for a nice long sleep. I'm sure you'd like to watch, before you and she eat. In the fridge, there's a pork casserole to reheat. You two won't disturb me. Where we bought the massage oil, we bought what you'll need, too. *Coming.*"

I gave Steph a friendly smack as she went into the bathroom. To the sound of laughter, I put the casserole in the oven and prepared vegetables. Then I poured myself a drink, and knocked politely at the bedroom door. Steph's voice sounded very contented.

"Come in."

Gloria was a fit woman, and lived up to her name. In the dim light from the bedside lamp, her muscles rippled and her bruises were less noticeable. Steph looked as handsome as ever as Gloria's fingers worked over and into her and she thrashed around, moaning with pleasure.

After a few minutes, Steph moved her legs off the bed, and spread them. Gloria was clearly enjoying her work, but signalled to me that she could enjoy it more with a little help. To lick Steph off, she crouched with bottom raised and legs apart. I slid a finger in, gently. With encouragement, I found her spot and fingered harder. She and Steph climaxed together, to a chorus of yells.

Steph was dozing off when Gloria and I left her, taking the telephone with us. We were about to eat when Jenny phoned.

"The operator called me just now, Pete, but didn't have that much information. The lady who put the call through was speaking Spanish, but not normal Spanish. She said she was speaking from Chackor, or Chackar, or some name like that. I wonder if actually she was speaking from South America. They speak Spanish there differently from in Spain. Dad once wrote a paper about the Gran Chaco, which is mostly in Paraguay."

This seemed to be further reassurance. If Harry had flown out of Madrid on Tuesday, he could have reached Paraguay by the time he called Dick, though he would have been very tired and possibly confused about the time. I knew little about the country, other than that it was said to be a refuge for various undesirables.

We checked the arrangements for Sunday. There would be a musical surprise, she said cryptically. I passed her my comments on the Articles. Then it was back to Gloria.

"Yer doos have lotsa calls round 'ere. What's yer bill like?"

"There shouldn't be any more calls. Some business is now sorted."

Gloria tucked in heartily for a while, before continuing conversation.

"This is great. Who cooked it?"

"Steph. She'll be pleased you're enjoying it. You did just right for her."

"You don' mind Steph goin' with girls?"

"No. She's gone mostly with men, but likes both."

"She looks and feels good. An' you'se a nice touch and knows where to go. That was real great for me."

"I enjoyed it lots, too."

"'Part from what you've both done for me, it's nice to 'ave clients wot brings me off."

"I can't enjoy unless I know the other is enjoying, too. Steph is the same. She's had bad times with people who think differently."

"Likes 'Arry Tamfield. An' old Martha. She was 'orrid, too."

Over the rest of the meal, Gloria launched into a fuller description of her night with Lady Dugdale than the *Clarion* had been able to print. Then she got up, opened her borrowed wrap, kissed and felt me.

"Now, it's us time, Pete."

"We'll enjoy it more when the food and drink have gone down, Gloria. Meanwhile, I've an idea about how you could move and start again."

"Ooh, 'ave yer? Let's cut out the Gloria. I'm Jane – Jane Sandford. Yer cin see why I change it."

"You're certainly not a plain Jane! Listen, I'm working in Aberdeen because it's the centre for the huge new industry we're developing, North Sea oil."

"Yeah, sounds like it'll be great."

"It will be. It's only just getting going. There are platforms floating in the sea, drilling for oil. Soon there'll be platforms standing on the seabed, artificial islands really, producing oil which will be loaded into tankers, or piped ashore."

"Wot's in it for me?"

"Men work on these platforms, for two weeks at a time, twelve hours on, twelve hours off. While you work, another man sleeps in your bunk. There's absolutely no drink allowed. Then you have a fortnight ashore while someone else goes out there. Now, some of these men are married, but a lot aren't. So what do you think they want as soon as they get back to shore, usually at Aberdeen?"

"Ter get smashed, and 'ave a girl."

"Yes, usually in that order though not always. Aberdeen is a big fishing port, so though it's a very respectable place, all that is already available. But, something you could provide isn't already available."

"Wot's that?"

"I've met a lot of the more senior oil people. Some work offshore, others are based at offices in the town. Many of them are single or away from their families. They work all hours, and outside work they're lonely. Already, I've had two or three of them ask me how they can relax and enjoy themselves. When I described the club in Islington, they were interested in putting money in to start one like it. Just outside Aberdeen, there's a rather run-down indoor swimming pool, which is up for sale. So, how much does all the gear cost?"

Jane confirmed her grasp of money. After an hour, we had the bones of a business plan for a rest and recreation centre. I could see why in November Harry had said that he and his associates weren't losing. In Aberdeen, some costs would be lower than in London. Since there would be no local competition, charges could be higher. It did sound like what the people in Aberdeen would call a 'gold mine'.

"I'll talk to my contacts. If it looks possible, we'll bring you up to look at the site."

"Great. No need for a hotel room."

"There probably is a need, if I'm still living where I am now. In June, I'm moving to a new flat. Now, Jane, we've earned our play. Let's do it here, so as not to wake Steph."

She grinned, and stepped out of the wrap. Once I was undressed, she felt and sucked.

"Yer feel real good, an' yer taste real good. This is gonna be real nice. Your pick." She passed me a pack of condoms.

"I want it to be nice, Jane. I won't enjoy it if it isn't nice for you. To start, let's see what I can do about those bruises."

"Yup, I curled in a ball when 'Arry Tamfield started kicking me. 'Least 'e don't get me up the crotch. Gor, that bastard. If ever I catch up with 'im, I'll gets even. But he's gorn, and for the slammer if they find him, ain't he?"

"Yes, we can forget Harry. A woman I still know well was as covered with bruises as you are, after her engagement ended in a fight. I was able to help her. I'll be back in a moment."

I slipped into the bathroom without disturbing Steph, returned with oil and witch hazel, and spread Jane's wrap over some cushions on the floor. She lay on her front for me to work round and over the bruises. The yelps of pain as I strayed turned into sighs of content. Once she was relaxed I began to finger her, until she was very aroused.

"It's my turn to lie down, now."

A few minutes later, we were exhausted, but both very satisfied. By leaning well forward, she had been able to avoid coming down on any bruises.

"Yer does like the cowgirl."

"I like it lots of ways. We've done a 'Liz'. That's the favourite of the woman I mentioned. She was my first girl. Then she met a man who turned out to be Mr Wrong. Now, she's engaged again, and definitely to Mr Right."

"Ye're great, Pete. Yer gets me off, no fake, two times in a day."

"It was great to see and hear you enjoying it, Jane. I could feel you weren't faking. That really satisfied me. I hope my idea works out. I want to go on seeing you."

"Gor, I've not 'ad a bloke since I started. Coupla' girlfriends, but blokes just wanna take a cut."

"I won't be your bloke. I hope I can be your business partner. Business can mix with pleasure. Meanwhile, I've two ideas for you. You're a redhead. That's beginning to show on top, because you haven't been out to have your hair done during the last week. Be the real you. Let it show. Also, we'll need to do something about your speech."

"Yer not the first wot sez that. I cants spik Cimbridge."

"We must keep your East End accent. A lot of your clients will be Scottish or American. They'll like it. It's the literacy education that you've missed. I've an idea about helping you with that. "

Soon we were squeezed into bed, in a dim light left on because Jane said that her job made her a little afraid of the dark. She was most comfortable face down, a sight which brought back memories of feasting my eyes on Jenny as she slept. But looking across her to Steph, who lay face up, moved me on quickly, to imagining more recent events. Maybe John had a similar view of Jenny and Amanda, when the three relaxed after an energetic time together. I would be able to imagine that more clearly after meeting John and Amanda again on Sunday.

A week before, Jenny and I had done each other good turns. I had helped her to face up to what Dick had done. She had been frank about what she needed to complement her relationship with Dick. We had both moved on, from stifled regrets and desire to the comradeship and trust of special friends and honorary siblings. We could both enjoy imagining each other on that basis.

That would make it easier for us to meet more often, as would happen if Creators Technology went ahead. And another thought came into my mind, tired though I was. If I took profit from the rest and recreation centre as income, most of it would be taxed away. There might be another way. If there were, a good creative accountant could find it. Perhaps Jenny could earn a shareholding in Creators Technology. There wouldn't be time to talk this weekend, but in a few days I could call her.

The afternoon had not been the quiet time I was expecting, but it had been satisfying. I had learnt how security breaches could arise in the most unlikely ways. I had reacted fast, and so had Ana. She was indeed a tough young cookie, worthy of her operatic namesake. I had learnt again the lesson that apparently worthless people like Gloria could actually be very worthwhile, like Jane.

I wondered what Sunday's musical surprise could be, and also why Reg Emerson was apparently welcome at Central Office. Doubtless there was a good explanation…

13. SATURDAY, 2ND MARCH, 1974

The ringing of the telephone awoke me, but I was distracted by what I could see in the dim light, and the murmurings I could hear.

"Go on, that's real nice, suck my sweeties too. Mmm, that's just the right spot, oooh. *Ooooh*, harder. *Aah – aaah – aaaa – aaaaa – aaaaaaahhh!*"

Jane was certainly a professional, capable of hard work. I couldn't resist the temptation to join in.

"No-Pete-no, you're tickling! ... No! ... *Oh, no!!*"

Steph slid out from under Jane and curled up pleadingly, allowing me to deliver some friendly smacks. We were quickly heading for a 'Carol', despite my need to save something for said lady that evening. Jane was rubbing herself as she enjoyed the spectacle. Then the phone rang again. I stumbled through to answer. It was Ana.

"Pete, I am sorry to call you so early, but I have spoken with father and he has said I must. On his return last evening he was told that a cashier has not reported for duty since Tuesday and has given no reason. No money is missing. The cashier is not senior and was not in any way involved with 'Crafty', but we were told that he lives on his own, and is said not to be interested in women. Because Harry Tamfield also left on Tuesday, I asked for further enquiries at the hotel where he stayed, and also for information about friends and relatives of our cashier. I have now learnt that someone resembling our cashier was seen with Harry Tamfield at his hotel on Monday evening. I have also learnt that our cashier's brother, who has a similar reputation, is a waiter. He used to work in Jaca, where he lives, but since December, he has worked at the Hotel Excelsior in Formigal, where we met last September."

A light flashed in my mind. After a moment, I replied.

"In September, on our way to Formigal, Steph and I had time to stop in Jaca, to see the Romanesque capitals in the cathedral. I read that when most of Spain was occupied by the Moors, it was the first capital of the kingdom of Aragón."

"That is right."

"You pronounced it 'Harka' which is the official, Castilian way, but I know that Aragonese Spanish is different. What is their pronunciation?"

"'Chaca'... Pete, are you still there?"

"Harry Tamfield was in Jaca early yesterday morning."

I explained about Harry's telephone call to Dick. It was her turn to pause.

"I will speak to father about that."

"Harry could have got to know about our meeting at the Hotel Excelsior. We all checked in under our own names, so this brother could have found out who was there. So, Harry would know that there was something going on, but he would be no nearer to finding out what it actually was. We talked in English, were careful not to be overheard, and left absolutely nothing lying around."

"That is right, Pete. We shall have the brother's house watched, and check at the Hotel Excelsior. No doubt he stays there overnight, if he works late."

"Can you find out what international telephone calls have been made from the house since yesterday morning, if possible to what numbers, and monitor any more that are made."

"I do not know how easy that will be, but I shall ask. We shall also alert the frontier guards, in case Harry Tamfield attempts to travel into France."

"Which passes are open, now?"

"The direct way to France from Formigal, over the Pourtalet pass, is closed in winter. The main road through Jaca, over the Somport pass, should be open to vehicles with snow tyres or chains. They work hard to keep it open, now that the railway is closed.[77] The checkpoint is at Canfranc Station, below the summit on our side."

"You need also to know that Harry is an expert skier."

"He will have to be *very* expert to cross the Pyrenees in winter. There is no reason for him to try, provided that he is not warned. He can be detained when he tries to cross normally. The *Guardia* know that. Fortunately, I told them only to locate relatives of the cashier, not to contact them. I will keep you informed, Pete. Father and I will go to the bank's offices, where it will be easier for us to be in touch."

As I rang off, I was grasped from behind and a fat kiss or two was planted.

"Who's ringing *you* up so early, Brit boy? Is someone missing you in Aberdeen already? She's distracted you, just when Gloria had gotten me real hot. You left two frustrated girls in there. Say, or I'll squeeze harder."

"It's Ana again. Let go and I'll tell you."

I explained, and Steph's face assumed the same look of alarm as the night before.

"Pete, I must brief Mart. You must tell Pat O'Donnell. We must stay in touch with Pedro and Ana, and with Tom Sambrook. We can use the new gear in your office."

I began to wonder about Steph's reaction, so I played it cool.

"I'm not sure that's ever been tried on international calls. Pat will be working from home today, and we would need someone from his office to set it up."

"You can make it happen, if you want to, Pete. This started with Pat's hunch."

---

77 A rail route had closed in 1970 following an accident, and never reopened. The present-day road tunnel opened in 2003.

"Steph, I know we were very concerned to keep this quiet while the trades were going on, but they're all closed off now. There could be some tricky public relations handling for all of us if it came out that we've made a lot of money out of the crisis, though I daresay others have, too. That's why I called Ana in the first place. It wouldn't be a complete disaster, though. Anyway, even if Harry is bumbling around Jaca and Formigal with his new friends, he's very unlikely to pick up anything."

"Just let me say, Pete, it *would* be a complete disaster, beyond anything you've dreamed of. You call Pat as soon as you dare. I'll go find Mart."

Steph dashed off to explain to Jane that a business crisis had come up. We all dressed and made a quick breakfast. I talked of our conversation over dinner. At least, that distracted Steph.

"Wow, it sounds a great scheme. Show me more details and I might be a sleeping partner, back in the States. Meanwhile, Jane and I can be sleeping partners here!"

"Yup, great, whens yer want. There's that big bill for me ter work off. Half price, as youse both so nice. 'Ere's me card; jest call."

"So you live in Stratford," I said.

"How ders yer know?"

"The exchange code is the same as that of friends of ours, who live above a place for women there, the Pankhurst Centre. It's handy that you're not far away. My idea about your speech is to ask if the Centre's literacy worker can help you."

"They're great. Not for likes of me, but I knows women they've 'elped. I gave 'em ten quid at Chrissmas."

By eight o'clock they were both off, with a date in Steph's diary on Thursday to follow Jane's dental appointment. I called Pat at home, to explain how I had followed up his hunch. Like me, he was surprised at the strength of Steph's reaction. We decided to set up a conference for 10.30. I called Steph and asked her to warn others.

I turned on the TV to catch up on the latest developments, but there weren't any. David Dimbleby was still feeling cold outside No. 10.[78] No one was clear what Heath was waiting for – a miracle, perhaps? There was more news from the USA. A grand jury had indicted seven former aides of President Nixon, and by implication Nixon himself, in regard to the Watergate cover-up.

Just after nine o'clock, Carol rang. She sounded very cheerful.

"Hi, you alone? I can't be overheard. I'm thinking of you tonight, lots and lots. I'm at Transport, with three press interviews to do before Paul drives me and our dads to Cambridge. I've had a note that's made me even more chuffed. I won't say more now than that it's from across the road. On something different across the road, you were asking Dad about Reg Emerson. He was there again early this morning. He was seen leaving about half an hour ago. That is rather odd."

By a quarter past ten, I was with Pat, Mart Steinberg, and Steph in the conference room at IE HQ. We were sitting in our overcoats, and looking out at the City on a dull, raw, late winter's day. Shortly, we hoped to be in touch with Don Pedro and Ana, and with Tom Sambrook at his home near Rotterdam. Pat thanked me for following up his hunch. Then Mart spoke, grimly.

"I think that before your people connect us up, you need to know why this is so serious, Pat. You've seen advantage in Labour taking over for a while, and so have we. New Hampshire Realty has been over here for only a few years. We want to expand, but the City gents don't like us. We've got in only with second-rate outfits like National Amalgamated. A grateful government will help us to muscle in properly. Thanks first to Pete and Ana, and then to Paul, we've lots of winnings, which won't appear in our accounts. The last three months, some have gotten diverted to help Labour. A Labour government will be duly grateful."

---

78 This vigil was recalled during the even longer wait before a coalition was formed in 2010.

"Political parties have to disclose their funding. IE's funding has been public, last time and this. Aren't there limits on what parties can accept?"

"We've not walked in with a big cheque," said Steph. "It's gone over by lots of ways which won't attract notice, such as individual donations and loans from apparently private nominees. Some of these needn't be counted towards the limits. There are signs the Tories are suspicious, but they haven't picked up anything definite, yet. If the story about our winnings were to come out, some of the people we've used to funnel the money in wouldn't like it. They would talk, fast."

Pat paused for a moment before replying, his face hard.

"So, if this came out while Heath is still in Downing Street, he could say that the Labour campaign has been financed, perhaps illegally, by vested interests who have made a lot of money out of the problems the country has faced. Therefore, he could say that the electorate has been deceived, and that he didn't accept the election result as a mandate to depart, particularly as the Conservatives have a slight majority of votes cast. Labour might not have enough support from other parties to force a vote of no confidence. If they did, they would either have to form a government themselves and be under immediate attack, or ask for another election straightaway."

"Yup, your Queen would be in a real spot. No back to the Aussie sun," said Steph.[79]

"She wouldn't be the only one in a real spot. There would be no government. The miners would still be on strike. No one could do anything. By the time all this was sorted out, the economy would have collapsed."

"That's just about right, Pat," said Mart, ruefully. "I need to say too that while you were still paying Paul Milverton, he wasn't just spending time supporting his wife. He was the link

---

[79] The Queen had interrupted a visit to Australia, to be ready to 'kiss hands' with a new Prime Minister.

man between us and Transport House. He helped to identify nominees."

"So we would be tarred with this brush, too, especially in the light of my public position. In your language, Mart, I've been taken for a ride."

"I must apologise, Pat. It's what we face now, having seemingly achieved our common objective. We won't mention it over the phone. Tom doesn't know of it, though our Corporate President is right in the picture."

Pat had been speaking calmly and quietly, but I knew the signs. He was angrier than I had ever known. Steph's flippancy had not helped. I added some information which at least diverted the discussion.

"Pat, we were puzzled to see Reg Emerson show up at Conservative Central Office yesterday. I'm told that earlier this morning, he was back there. He could be in touch with Harry. That would also explain what he said after the declaration. Heath could be hanging on in the hope that he'll get some hard information he can use."

We fell silent as the expert from Pat's office set the equipment up. This was far worse than I had thought – far, far worse. I remembered wondering if some Creators had a secret from me. Steph and Paul had had a secret, which went far beyond their affair. I had little doubt which of them had come up with the funding scheme. This was the Paul I had known in the past, the Paul whose first victim was Harry. In a sense it would be amusing if Harry now exposed him. However, the damage caused would be just as Pat had said.

Harry had known that Paul, Steph and I were involved in something lucrative. Sir Reg Emerson could have told him of Tory suspicions about Labour funding. I recalled Harry's appearance on TV, which had ended with his threat to the 'Mystery Man'. He had referred to unrecorded funding, and to Harold Wilson's circle of friends, before telling of the malign influences at the heart of the Labour Party. I realised now why he had referred to influences in the plural, though all the shocked public comment had been about his remarks concerning the Dugdales, and his allegations about what Wilson had said in October. Harry had said that he had nothing to lose, because his company was destroyed. He had been prepared to act on that. He had stolen the pension fund money so as to have access to as much as he might possibly need to buy the information he wanted.

What train of events had been set off by my telling Carol about Reg Emerson? *What had I created*?

Fortunately, the equipment did work on international lines, and soon we were in private with our three callers, two of whom were on separate phones in the same room in Pamplona. After greetings and checks that everyone could hear everyone else, Pat began.

"Pete has briefed us this end. What have you found out, Pedro?"

"More than we wanted. The Pamplona *Guardia Civile* asked the Jaca force to mount an out of uniform watch of the house of our cashier's brother. The house appeared to be empty. Then, at about ten hours, that is nine hours your time, a car arrived. Three men went inside. The *Guardia* recognised the brother, who had been driving the car. The two others matched the descriptions of our cashier and of Harry Tamfield. Nothing happened for half an hour. Then, an hour ago, the brother and Harry Tamfield came outside, with a suitcase. As they were getting into the car, the brother recognised one of the *Guardia*. They were challenged to stop, but drove off quickly."

"Shit," said Steph. "Now they know you're on to them. You can't just pick Harry up when he tries to leave Spain."

"Yes, I am sorry that has happened. The Jaca force was careless. The cashier is being brought here and should arrive in about an hour. I will interview him myself. *Guardia* and traffic police throughout the area have particulars of the car."

"They ran when challenged, which suggests they have something," said Pat. "What are their options for getting out of Spain, Pedro?"

"The frontier guards at Canfranc are alerted. They will check every car, carefully."

"What other ways are there?"

"The nearest is Ibañeta – in French, Roncesvalles. That is three hours' drive. The guards there, and along to Irun, have been warned. At this season you may cross the frontier further east only by first going south to Huesca. Harry Tamfield will not leave Spain overland. Nor will he leave by air or sea."

"Now Harry is warned, I reckon he'll try to ski out," I said. "He went off to Switzerland with his ski kit, but I expect he left that behind somewhere. If he were taken to Formigal, he could buy skis there. Then it's less than ten kilometres, and three or four hundred metres of climb, to the Pourtalet. Alert all the ski shops in Formigal, straightaway."

Don Pedro asked Ana to call Jaca with that message, and as Pat moved us on we heard her speaking Spanish on another phone.

"It sounds as if your police are doing all they can to catch Tamfield, but what can he have, and why has he been to Jaca to get it? Your cashier's brother wasn't working at the Excelsior when we met there, so it must be something that he had heard about since, and was for sale. Pedro, could the room we met in have been bugged?"

"That is not a possibility, Pat. I had it checked by the bank's head of security, early on the day we met there."

"Then the only hard evidence of our agreement is the note of our meeting. We took special care with that. Pete, you typed it yourself, making two carbons, and Ana typed a Spanish version, one copy only. Those are the four numbered copies."

"That's right," I said. "We worked together to verify that the two versions were consistent. We let nothing out of our sight before giving the copies to you, Pedro, Mart and Tom. The annexes were already prepared, but only the copies we needed were brought to the meeting. We burnt all other notes afterwards."

"I kept IE's copy with me all the time, until I was back here. Since then it's been in the private safe in my office, to which only I have a key. It's been out once, to brief George Armstrong, who is the only IE employee not at the meeting to be in on the plan. What's happened to the other copies?"

"I brought mine back, same way. Only Steph and I have ever seen it," said Mart.

We heard Tom Sambrook's voice from Rotterdam. "I kept mine on me, too. The only people who have seen it are the three traders involved."

"Ana, Carlos and I stayed another day, with Steph and Pete," said Don Pedro. "I did not keep the note with me when we went out, but it was in the safe in my suite at the hotel. That had a lock without key, how do you say it?"

"A combination lock," said Pat.

"That is right. A good Swiss lock, with eight numbers. I set them myself, and not to my birthday."

"So if some dishonest employee of the hotel had tampered with the lock, then while you were out he could have opened the safe and made a copy of the note."

"That is absurd, Pat."

"It may be, Pedro, but it seems to me the only possibility."

Some thoughts clicked together in my mind.

"It might explain why Harry has been in Jaca since Tuesday. You stayed in the Presidential Suite, which is presumably where any notable guest is accommodated. Suppose that someone at the hotel has fixed the safe in that suite, and copies anything left there that might be saleable. Perhaps the brother had heard that there was something to be bought, but Harry found that he couldn't buy it straightaway. Pending anything the cashier has to say, I suggest a fast check on who of the Hotel Excelsior staff has been away this week."

Tom Sambrook sounded doubtful.

"If last September someone had a copy of our meeting note, wouldn't they have used it then, to make lots of money of their own?"

Ana was back with us. Evidently she had kept an ear for what we were saying.

"Tom, do not forget my mistake, which Pete politely did not mention earlier. I left the Spanish versions of the annexes here in Pamplona. They were not in the safe with Father's copy. I do not think that someone looking at the note without them could have made much profit from it. It mentions no actual event, or date."

"Thanks, Ana," I said. "In retrospect, though, the meaning of the note is clear. Harry Tamfield knows enough Spanish to understand it."

"I have asked that Formigal be alerted. Your thinking was good, Pete. The brother's car has been found, abandoned, about ten kilometres out of Jaca on the Huesca road. That is a few kilometres before the road to Formigal turns off, and about thirty kilometres from Formigal. Perhaps another car is taking Harry Tamfield to Formigal. It is not likely that he has arrived there yet. Also, Pete, I now have the information you requested about telephone calls. Early yesterday morning there was a call to your number 27340691."

"That's the call we know about, to Dick Sinclair."

"Also, over the last three days, most recently at ten hours fifteen this morning, just before Harry Tamfield and the brother left the house, there have been calls to a London number, 15417654."

"Ask your telephone people to check for any further calls to that number, from anywhere."

"Pedro, shall we break now?" said Pat. "You need to speak to the cashier, and make more enquiries at the hotel. We need to check up on that number."

"We should have fuller information here by fourteen hours. Can you contact us again, then? Meanwhile, be assured that we know how important it is to stop Harry Tamfield from disclosing any information about 'Crafty.'"

Whilst we were being disconnected, I thumbed through a London E-K Telephone Directory. That gave me a further suggestion to make, once we were alone again.

"Mayfair addresses have the same exchange code as this number. Reg Emerson lives in Mayfair, though his directory phone is the constituency office in Bellinghame. Perhaps it's his private number. Steph, he's never heard your voice."

Steph dialled the number. There was no answer. I continued.

"Emerson was seen leaving Central Office at about half past eight, so he could have taken a call at home at 9.15 our time. I wonder if he's back at Central Office now. If so, he'll have given them an encouraging message. Unless Harry has called again, which I don't think he'll risk now he knows he's blown, they'll be thinking he's over the Somport and in France by now. They'll be working out how to bring him back here as quickly as possible today, and sorting with the Home Office how he can dish the dirt before he's arrested. We have, at least, caused some further delay."

Mart looked at Steph. "It's 6.20 in New York. We'd better go back to our office and make some calls."

Pat turned to our guests, with an acid note in his voice. "A moment with you on your own, first, please, Mart."

Steph and I were left in the conference room. We didn't say much. When Mart emerged from Pat's office, he looked quite shaken. He and Steph made off, quickly. After a few minutes Pat emerged, and asked me to come in.

I entered with some trepidation. I wasn't sure how much of Pat's anger would rub off on me. He would be pleased that by following his hunch I had put people on to Harry's trail, but he had seen Harry live rather than on screen, and might well feel that a fixation on me and Paul had caused all this.

To my relief, his first move was to turn on the TV. Mr Heath had just made a defiant statement. He had suggested that the non-Socialist parties, which had been supported by two-thirds of the electorate, should now combine in a government of national unity. The commentator said that he seemed to be playing for time, and was hoping that something would turn up. Pat's mood changed for the better.

"Thanks to you, Pete, we know why he's hoping. That gives the best chance of it not turning up. I'm sure you had no idea what Steph was about with Paul."

"Certainly I knew nothing about New Hampshire funding Labour. Since I moved to Aberdeen, I've not seen much of Steph."

"You're both going off to Cambridge later, aren't you?"

"I was meant to go, for dinner tonight, and tomorrow for a christening. I can cut out of tonight."

"Go, and take Steph with you. In a crisis, the first rule is to behave as normally as possible. As Chief Executive, *I* have to make sure that Mart and Pedro sort this out, more because of the possible damage to the country than because of problems directly for IE. George is in Leeds until lunchtime, but I spoke to him just now. He's quite clear there's nothing illegal in what *we've* done to date, though it would be very tricky in public relations terms, and annoying to have to take the whole windfall in this year's Accounts. There's one thing I didn't remind Pedro about. Various Spanish grandees got in on the profits, though we've been told that they didn't have any of the detail. Could any of them have talked?"

"Not to Harry. They're all in Madrid. If this comes out, though, they'll not be pleased. Some notable absences from Ana's wedding could be expected."

"That's good. Pedro has more reason to make sure it doesn't come out. I must say, he and Ana can get their police moving. That's the advantage of a dictatorship, I guess. Well, I'm going to deal with some other pressing business. I suggest you do the same."

I tried to do the same, with limited success. It seemed incredible that so much might depend on whether Franco's police caught Harry. I seemed to be cast as one of the villains directing the hunt, as in a novel by John Buchan or Frederick Forsyth.

I called Aberdeen, sorted out a couple of problems there, and had confirmation of my flight back from Norwich on Monday. In those days, nothing was open in the City on a Saturday, so soon after midday I went over to the flat and made sandwiches for Pat, me and the equipment expert. At ten to one, Mart and Steph returned. Steph said she had called the Mayfair number again, twice, but there was still no answer.

Once we were back in the conference room, and reconnected, Don Pedro began rather hesitantly and vacantly, once again to the background of Ana talking in Spanish.

"The casher has confessed. It is very much as you thought, Pete. On Sunday, he was in a bar which apparently people of his type frequent. He was pointed out to an English visitor as an employee of the Banco Navarrese. The visitor, who was Harry Tamfield, already knew that I was to make a fine celebration of Ana's wedding – all in Pamplona know that. He asked how I had so much money to spend. The cashier told of a rumour that I had obtained great benefit from a meeting in Formigal last September, which had been attended by English and American people. I regret that I did not know there was such a rumour. Tamfield was ready to pay twenty thousand pesetas to know who attended the meeting. My cashier telephoned his brother that evening, and on Monday he was able to give our names. Now, Tamfield was very excited. He was ready to pay much more, very much more, to know what happened at the meeting. The brother thought there might be a possibility. So on Tuesday, after Tamfield had obtained more money from Switzerland, they caught a coach to Jaca, and stayed at the brother's house. There was a delay, because the man who might have something for sale was away. Late yesterday, he was back at the hotel. He talked for a very long time with Harry Tamfield, so long that they all stayed overnight and returned to Jaca this morning. Today the brother is not working. He was going to drive Tamfield into France."

"Well, he hasn't done that," said Pat. "I'm astonished that Tamfield could obtain cash from his Swiss account so easily."

"I know which bank was involved. No doubt it was profitable to its staff in Pamplona. They will now regret it."

"It's a miracle too that one of his new chums didn't knock him over the head and take his money. He must have some magnetism."

"The three of them have something in common," I said. "Harry can use that, to put them against the rest of us."

There was no response from Don Pedro to that. However, we could hear Ana finishing her conversation, and she came on to report.

"The Deputy Manager of the Hotel Excelsior was away from Wednesday until yesterday afternoon. He is being questioned now, but two million pesetas in cash has already been found in his room. Late yesterday, three international telephone calls were made from the hotel. One was to the same London number as the others we have detected. The others were to numbers in Switzerland."

She gave the numbers, and this prompted Tom Sambrook to one of his fairly rare interventions.

"Using those numbers and the right passwords, you can move funds instantly."

"Why should Tilford want to do any more of that?" asked Pat. "He had completed his deal, doubtless using the cash he had on him."

"To get clean again, or at least fairly clean," I replied. "Harry stole the pension fund money so as to have as much as possible to hand, and to take with him if in the end he cleared off. Now, he's returned it, because he has the goods, and is trying to come back with them as soon as possible. Sorry Ana, we've stopped you. What other news do you have?"

"Thirty minutes ago someone reported to the *Guardia* in Formigal that near the junction with the Huesca road he had been flagged down by a man who spoke with a foreign accent and wanted a lift. Then as they approached Formigal, the man said he would like to try some cross-country skiing, did not want to wait at a store and wanted to buy the skis on top of the car! This seemed very strange, but the cash offered would cover the cost of a much better replacement, so the driver took it and left the man near Formigal. He then went to buy a replacement, and found the *Guardia* checking on everyone at the shop. So, Harry Tamfield *is* trying to ski over the Pourtalet Pass, Pete."

"Can we call for a helicopter, to go after him?" asked Don Pedro.

"That is not possible, for the same reason as there is no need, Father. The weather is turning bad, much more quickly than was expected this morning. The slopes are being cleared, and the chairlifts have closed. Above one thousand five hundred metres, there will be a full windy snowstorm; what is the word?"

"Blizzard," I interjected.

"Yes, there will be a blizzard, within one hour, and for the rest of the afternoon. Harry Tamfield will not reach France. Either he turns back, or he dies."

"Is there anywhere he could shelter until the weather improves?" I asked.

"He could take refuge in the frontier post at the top of the pass. There are two men there, even in winter. They are alerted by radio. What do you think he will do, Pete?"

"He'll press on. There's nothing for him to live for if he's picked up. He doesn't know the country, and he won't know how bad the weather is to be."

"Well, that's that," said Pat. "Pedro, I presume there'll be search parties as soon as conditions permit, perhaps tomorrow morning."

"Yes, and they will be instructed to return to me, immediately, any documents found with Mr Tamfield."

"Might he have put a copy of the note in the post to England?" I asked.

"There are no collections of post there on Saturday or Sunday," said Ana. "We shall have all collections made in the area on Monday checked for items addressed to England. No letter could be expected to arrive in England until Thursday or Friday."

"Good. Look out for anything addressed to a man called Emerson. E-M-E-R-S-O-N."

With mutual promises to keep in touch if there were further developments, and exchanges of telephone numbers including that of Waterhouse College, Pat closed the meeting. Pedro was still sounding as if he was thinking about something else, though Ana was being much clearer and more decisive.

When Steph dialled again, the answer came very quickly, and audibly.

"Emerson."

"Say, who's that? I'm trying to call my travel agent. This airline strike is causing me a heap of problems. I need to change my flight to Nice."

"You have the wrong number."

"Say, I'm sure I dialled what I was told. What's your number?" He spelt it out. "Now, I'm very busy. Goodbye."

"Aw, shucks, I gotten it wrong. Sorry."

Steph replaced the phone, and Mart guffawed.

"There's a man waiting for an important call. It seems his caller is like your man Oates. He's gone out in a blizzard and may be some time. Well, I'll get back to base and tell the good news. New York will be relieved. So will be our friends. There's a couple of points I want to check with you first, Steph."

Pat and I were left alone. Mart's callous joke had left me rather stunned.

"Cheer up, Pete."

"It's difficult to be cheerful when someone I knew quite well is probably dying, because I made him try to ski out."

"You've not made him do anything, Pete. He's brought all this on himself. Of course it's a pity that his company went bust, but he could have walked away honestly, and started again. Instead, he's broken the law, even if you're right that he's now returned the pension fund money. He had planned to steal that and go right away, but then he had a hunch. I think I can say that he wouldn't have got as far as he did without having hunches. He must have looked at our Accounts, spotted our link with Banco Navarrese, and decided to nose around in Pamplona. Once he knew about our meeting, he called Emerson, to say he was on to something about us all making a lot of money. Central Office saw the chance to blow the funding story open. Emerson would have been detailed to tell Tamfield that he would be looked after if he came back with proof. If the man with the copy for sale hadn't been away, Tamfield would have been back on Wednesday, and the whole story would have been out on polling day. If he made it back now, it would be even worse. There would be no government, rather than a Heath Government. The economic damage would kill thousands, through destitution, medical treatment not being afforded, safety improvements not made, and so on. Now, Tamfield won't be back. Which is less bad, one death or thousands? So don't brood, Pete. Get away to Cambridge. You've earned the rest of the weekend off. You've been at your best – fast, sharp, thinking clearly in a crisis. Ana was the same, very impressive compared to her father, who just now was sounding distracted. I suppose he's shocked to find out what someone in a trusted position had done. I'll call him later on, just to hint that our partner hasn't been straight with either of us."

Steph was waiting in reception. We walked back through the deserted City. Despondently, I repeated to her most of what Pat had said. Once in the flat, she pulled me down on to the sofa, and threw her arm round.

"He's right, Pete. This isn't a maths exam. You can't get 100%. Harry is probably dead. Or rather, someone is dead who wasn't any more the man you knew. Think of what he did to Jane, and why. We've had a lucky escape, and so has Britain. We're to go enjoy ourselves. That's Mart's message to me, too. He's grovelled to Pat, but he knows that if Paul and I hadn't gotten together, there would be no Labour lead now and no break into the City for New Hampshire."

"Your game with Labour began three months ago, at about the same time as you hauled Paul into your bed."

"We worked it out that second night, in December. In the morning, I had more to tell Mart than I told you. Paul knew who Mart should speak to."

"You told some Labour people that Wilson had to get the ASLEF action called off. Last Thursday morning Transport House wanted to cut out of Bellinghame South, until Paul called someone. You both had, shall we say, some authority. It was a pity that you weren't able to stop the third instalment in the *Clarion*."

"Transport came to an agreement with the *Clarion* which allowed the paper to seek related business. That was signed before Paul and I came into the picture."

"When I said to Carol yesterday that Paul, rather than I, had got her elected, I was quite right. Does she know about your game?"

"She knows about 'Crafty', but she doesn't know about the funding. Nor do Bert, Fred, or anyone at Transport outside a very small circle."

I patted Steph's bottom. "Two weeks back, you had your revenge, because I hadn't told you about our plans for Reg Emerson. But you knew about them already, didn't you? That's like the time Carol sold me a pup to climb into my bed. There'll be a suitable time, which isn't now."

"Mmm, I guess I'll deserve that."

"Paul showed you how to support Labour, while you showed him how to satisfy Carol. Talk of pillow plots."

"That's the way for people like us, Pete. We're together in body, and together in mind. The one leads to the other. You and Ana spotted Kraftlein and the Egyptians. You and I helped set up 'Crafty', though we were proper about it. You and Carol dished the dirt on Reg."

"'Together in body, together in mind' sounds like your motto for the Creators, Steph. The real tragedy for Harry was that he was a loner, together with no one. Maybe that was why he was trying to get Dick back."

"Life is still very difficult for homosexuals. It's legal now, but it's not something you admit to. That certainly helped Carol against Reg Emerson."

"The message was that Emerson was being bought," I said, perhaps rather properly.

"Come off it, Pete, you and Carol knew just what the message was. What do you think Brian and his friends, let alone the official party people, said when they were out canvassing, certainly if Morag and Sheila weren't around? If Reg had had a girl he would still have been in trouble, but lots would have said, poor man, he has no one else, because his snooty wife ran off."

"So you, I, Carol and Paul are just about as smart, and as bad, as each other. We all need to accept that, don't we, Steph?"

"We all want to make a difference. So do the rest of your crowd, unlike most Brits in recent years. Why could you all do so much during the last War, but so little after?"

"People thought they'd won and could have a quiet life. Hopefully they'll change their minds, now they see where a quiet life leads them."

"So, we're still friends, Pete?"

"Definitely, Steph – friends plus."

"And no more than friends plus?"

"That's right."

For a while we sat in silence, kissing. Finally, Steph chuckled brightly.

"Greg and Liz will be outside in twenty-five minutes. We must pack for our fun weekend. Carol and Paul have begun theirs already. Come and look at what I'm planning to wear." We moved to the bedroom and looked into the wardrobe.

"It's easy for me. I'll just change to this suit."

"Take that tie for tomorrow. I'll put what you leave to the cleaners. You've told me tonight's not formal, so I'll look smartish in this. I might as well wear it now. Tomorrow I want those who know anything to see I'm the best dressed woman there, but I don't want to show off at Jenny's expense, so what about this one?"

"Spot on, and the hat's right too."

"Good. Just remind me of what you've worked out with Carol for tonight."

"Are you going to tell Paul what's happened today?" I asked, when I had done so.

"I'll leave that until Monday."

We were outside when Greg pulled up. Greg wasn't a talkative driver, and Steph had brought a newspaper, to get up to speed on Watergate. Liz and I had some catching up to do, and time for it during the tiresome journey of pre M11 days. So we travelled as upper class people, with Steph at the front and Liz and me at the back.[80]

Pressure of work had delayed wedding preparations for Liz and Greg. After describing where they were, or rather weren't, Liz concluded rather lamely.

---

80 A joke that says a lot about those times is that one could tell what 'class' people were by how two couples travelled in a car, assumed to be driven by one of the men. If they were 'upper class', the other wife would be at the front. If they were 'middle class', the driver's wife would be at the front. If they were 'working class', the men would be at the front and the women at the back.

"Invitations will be out this week, I promise. We do hope you'll be there, Pete."

"I'll certainly be there. You've booked it too, haven't you Steph? It's only three weeks after we're in Spain for Ana's wedding."

"It's not as grand as that sounds to be, but Father has come up with the goods. I didn't want it to be in Cambridge, so it's at Greg's church. I'll need to attend some services there now, won't I, Greg?"

"Yes, and there are some talks with the Minister, the first after the service tomorrow evening. We also need to speak to the Organist. The church has a good organ."

"What's it to be at the end, then – Widor or Mendelssohn?" I asked.

"Neither, if I can help it," said Liz. "They're so corny."

"There's an organ version of a magnificent march by Meyerbeer. It's really a Coronation march, from an opera called *The Prophet*, which is about Anabaptists. You needn't say all that, but you could ask your man whether he knows it."

"Who the heck are Anabaptists?" asked Steph.

"They're nothing to do with Baptists. The opera is set in the 1500s, and at the end they blow themselves up to escape being captured and burnt at the stake. Now, Liz, we need to talk about tomorrow, before tonight gets going. As I understand it, we have only to say a few words each. That's right, isn't it, Greg?"

"Yes. Look as if you mean it."

Steph put it a different way. "You mean, don't look like Al Pacino, Pete. It's interesting there's no god*mother* in that film."

Greg was interested in film when he had a moment, and Steph's remark led to conversation at the front. This gave Liz a chance for a few words at the back.

"It's afterwards tomorrow that I'm dreading, Pete. This is really Belinda's do. The whole Frampton gang will be there, including Geoff."

"I'm sure that Jenny will look after them. I'll be interested to see whether Angela and Penny have benefitted from the lessons you, Carol and Morag gave them."

"Angela was much friendlier to me as soon as she knew what I'd done to Geoff. She invited me out for a drink, to have all the gen. She was a bit miffed to hear that you'd made off. But neither she nor Penny changed much until we livened them up. Penny went better with her chap, and they married two years ago. Angela learnt lots from Morag, including being fair at tennis. She's pretty steady with a man, though he's away this year. Both men are approved of by Archie and Jane. They're in tenured Cambridge jobs, unlike Dick."

"Dick has fathered the only grandchildren, and his research is looking up."

"Lucky Dick. What does Jenny think? She wants her career to go on. She doesn't want to be trailing around as Dick moves from post to post."

"Talking of jobs, what's happening for you?"

"Assuming the dispute's sorted, it's on for when I return from honeymoon. That's still just for Greg, you and me. I wondered whether to tell Brian, just about the job of course, but there's too big a risk of it going around before it should, through his dad. Meanwhile, I've made some unofficial telephone calls."

"I bet you have. I thought of you, when the Pay Board news broke last week."

We were interrupted by Steph. "Hey, what are you two talking about back there?"

"Cambridge people we've met, and the benefits of Jenny's hen party."

"Tell me and Greg about the Waterhouse Fellows we'll meet."

Liz and I shared that task. Greg doubtless listened, but was having to concentrate hard on driving along the busy and winding road. By contrast, I was relaxing. Thinking of Harry seemed like a bad dream, which was passing from my mind. Pat and Steph were ruthless, but right.

It was getting dark when we entered Bridge Street and passed the main entrance to Waterhouse College. Steph saw it first.

"Oh, my God."

From several windows along the frontage was draped a banner:

WATERHOUSE AND NEW HALL WELCOME THE CREATORS

"Who the hell's put them up to that?" said Liz.

"There's one guess. Let's all say it," I replied.

"*Oh, Brian!*"

We parked in one of the Master's reserved places off Portugal Place. Liz let us into the Lodge, with a shout to her father that was briefly acknowledged. Before showing us upstairs she made a rather sad remark, which reminded me of the ups and downs of Liz's time here.

"Pete, do you realise that I've never before dined on Waterhouse High Table?"

Now, she had escaped, to take her life forward. She showed Steph and me to the spare bedroom. For a moment, it was my turn for memories.

"You're thinking of something," said Steph.

"Yes. My last time with Jenny was here." I sighed.

"So it's good that for most of the night, you'll be somewhere else. In the morning, I'll be on for you. Talking of Jenny, I'm looking forward to meeting Amanda and John. They're clearly part of her life, even if not part of The Creators. She knows what she wants, and how to get it."

"Yes, it will be good to see John again, and have a chance to talk to Amanda, too."

I wondered how much Steph had guessed about Amanda, Jenny, and John. To make it easier for us to remain 'best friends plus', I was trying to give her the impression that we were going no further because of my feelings for Jenny. In fact, Paul had made my decision. He had led Steph into the Labour Party funding scheme. Probably, he had realised that climbing into her bed would make her more receptive to it. She had fallen for him. She had failed to spot the implications. He had shown her up.

I looked at the programme for the evening. At the bottom was a scribbled note from Arthur Gulliver, asking us to call in beforehand.

Before doing so, I showed Steph round the College. We greeted the porters, I pointed out where I had lived as an undergraduate, and so on. Our last call was at the Fellows' cloakroom, to leave our coats.

Once Arthur Gulliver had greeted Steph and filled our glasses, he came to the point quickly.

"The idea of you people as 'The Creators' has gone around."

"Yes," said Steph. "I invented the term. It wasn't meant to be blazed. It makes Carol, Pete and the others seem special in the wrong way. When I catch up with who we're sure spilled it –"

"Fair enough, but it's out now. John Birkbeck wants to propose a toast to 'The Creators' tonight. He's the current JCR President, whom you saw on that programme. The Master is over the moon, as it cuts him out of having to say anything except the graces. Also, these are all over the College."

He passed me a copy of the record Jenny had made of my short speech at the 1968 May Bump Supper, on the evening before I had left Cambridge.[81]

"So, there's a duty which will fall upon me – which has in fact fallen upon me, as a great man said."[82]

"Yes, it would be good if you can reply, Pete. I'll introduce you to John Birkbeck."

My reference prompted Arthur to tell Steph of his only encounter with Winston Churchill. That gave me a moment to

---

81 See the Postscript to *Road to Nowhere*.
82 Churchill, *The Gathering Storm*, p. 529

think of what I would say. After a few minutes, we moved along to the Reception Room.

Steph was impressed. I had seen before that the Room looked rich and sumptuous at night, rather than dingy as it looked in daylight. It was already fairly full of the High Table Party and a selection of students. Brian was holding forth. Steph went to say her piece to him. I met with John Birkbeck, to exchange notes. Then I found myself with Morag and Sheila, who were staying at Newnham, but were here as Nick Castle's guests. Carol's arrival was not noticed immediately. She was on her own, and looked very cheerful as she joined us.

"Paul will be along soon. He's taken our dads to Bletchley, to pick up a train back to Manchester. I'm really rather chuffed to have this, though I don't want it to get out and I guess she doesn't, either."

She showed us the note she had received from 'across the road'.

'Dear Mrs Milverton,
I cannot pretend to be pleased at your election, but I am thrilled. The Commons certainly needs more women members. If you can let me know when you expect to make your maiden speech, I shall make sure to be in place, on whichever side. Many congratulations.
Margaret Thatcher'

"She doesn't sound exactly committed to Heath trying to carry on," said Morag.

"I wonder why not," I observed.

I had just time to explain to Carol what I was planning to say, before the President of New Hall swept her away to be almost mobbed by some of their students. Then Nick Castle took me over to a group of undergraduates who had appeared in the TV programme. I noticed Paul enter, in his normal, unobtrusive manner, and find his way to talk to Tom Farley.

Brian joined us, having escaped from Steph, who was now talking to James Harman. I thought back to my first encounter with Paul and Brian, here in this room, at the Master's reception for new students. There had been plenty of argument then, and there was plenty now, mostly about why Mr Heath hadn't yet resigned.

"There are rumours that Wilson is involved in a dodgy land deal."

"If he has been, it would have come out by now."

"Heath has something on Jeremy Thorpe. Co-operate – or else."

"What do you think, Pete?" asked Nick. I made a quite truthful reply.

"I suppose he's spinning it out, hoping that something will come up. If there were something definite for him to say, he would have said it."

"Something won't come up. We're celebrating here, and my people are celebrating up there. They know they've won," said Brian, confidently.

Nick introduced a portly and cheerful man who had also joined the group.

"Pete, you won't have met Graham Harcroft, our Bursar."

"You look very calm. Setting this up in less than two days was quite a challenge."

"Yes, it has been, but the Kitchen Manager and his team have responded. They know what to do, and they're doing it. The real problem has been finding extra guest rooms. Several Fellows are allowing their day rooms to be used. I don't think guests will have much difficulty in sleeping in them tonight."

Brian and I exchanged grins. Most of these rooms were overlooking Bridge Street, and were regarded as too noisy for permanent occupation overnight. Though he and Susie were staying with her parents, no doubt some of his friends were using the rooms, so the banner had been easy to organise.

A moment later, I was able to introduce four new arrivals to Graham.

"Jenny and Dick Sinclair – Dick was here a year ahead of me. I expect you've met Liz Partington, but you won't have met her fiancé, Greg Woolley."

I knew why the Sinclairs were cutting it fine, and I could guess why Liz and Greg had done so. I warned Jenny and Liz about my speech. The Head Waiter took Graham aside, but soon he was back with us.

"We'll take another five minutes. People are still arriving, and the students here need to enter before us and find their places. Can you move towards the entry lines soon, please, and encourage others to do so?"

He pointed to a large plan on an easel in the centre of the room. We took our positions in two orderly lines, which Graham led into the Hall, passing on each side of the High Table. Once Arthur Gulliver's entry had ended the procession, we were all neatly in place. Graham was as good an organiser as Andrew Grover had been, but avoided Andrew's fussiness.

After the Master's brief contribution, we sat down. I was facing inwards, and could see more people of both sexes crammed on to the benches than I had ever seen when I was at Waterhouse, even on the day when I had mobilised the 'silent majority' to stifle a demonstration that Paul had organised against Andrew Grover.

Steph was between me and Arthur, who was in the end seat and was pleased to go on chatting with someone who certainly suited his liking for 'girls with a bit of spunk'. The latest Watergate developments gave them plenty to say. Arthur maintained that Nixon was 'the best man possible'. In retrospect, that was not an unreasonable view, given the lamentable performance of the next two Presidents. I joined in from time to time, but talked mainly with Nick, Morag, and Sheila, who were opposite me. Morag engaged me on the Nationalist breakthrough along the 'oil coast' of eastern Scotland. Then she had the latest news from the Pankhurst Centre.

"It's frantic there. When we left, twelve were staying. Quite possibly, three or four more will turn up after the pubs close and their hubbies come home roaring. Sheila is going back, after a short rest. She's booked a taxi from Newnham at 12.40 am for the one o'clock train. That goes in via Stratford."

"Is it OK from Stratford Station to the Centre in the middle of the night?"

Sheila responded firmly to that, and certainly looked the part.

"The way passes the police station, and I can look after myself. Pete, I called Jenny to apologise for missing tomorrow, and gave her a couple of suggestions on the draft Articles. Do you think they're right?"

I did, and then Nick purveyed the latest gossip in the Cambridge maths world. As we talked, I looked down the packed table towards Graham, whose lead in the procession had placed him at the far end. He had continued one habit of Andrew Grover – that of sitting near the kitchens entrance. Most of the profiles I saw in between were familiar. The Master was centrally placed, with Liz and Greg to one side of him, and the President of New Hall, Carol and Paul to the other. Opposite Liz was James Harman, who was gabbling away as usual. I wondered how she was finding her first experience of High Table.

By nine o'clock coffee and port were circulating, and Arthur called on John Birkbeck. I had been impressed with him on TV, and I was impressed again, though in a sense he had said it all then. He thanked us for making him a TV star, and finished with the hope that The Creators would visit regularly. Then Arthur introduced me as 'the Mystery Man no longer'. Steph held my chair. I climbed onto it, and began.

"It's really great to be back, with old friends and, I hope by the end of this weekend, some new ones. It's really great too that so many people at Waterhouse – Fellows, graduates, undergraduates and staff – have made such an effort to look after us, together with our visitors from New Hall. Many thanks to you all.

"I want to tell you about three memorable events of my time at Waterhouse, all of which happened right here in this Hall. I'll begin with my very last evening, though I will not call on two Creators to repeat the contribution which made that really memorable. The Hall is far too full for that, and it is March, not June."

I paused for muffled explanations and laughter to go round, and then continued.

"I will repeat one thing I said then, which certainly remains true today. 'Each and every one of us is capable of far more than we might have thought, if we are fired up and determined enough.' Now, I move onto tricky ground, for it was the lady sitting next to me who first called us 'The Creators'. If she doesn't like what I say next, you'll see me crash to the floor. She was saying – weren't you, Steph?"

The chair wobbled, but I maintained my footing, to more laughter.

"She was saying that we're The Creators because we're determined to create something with our lives. So, what I said on my last evening here is that each and every one of us can be a Creator. We're not some exclusive club. We're open to all. You're not toasting us. You're toasting your own futures.

"But, don't think you'll always succeed. That takes me to an earlier time in this Hall. A concert was wrecked by thugs, who have never been called to account. They came in through the window behind where the Vice-Master is sitting. The concert's organiser felt that he couldn't continue at Waterhouse. He left and started again. He was very successful for a while, but now things have again gone wrong for him. You may think that the moral is, don't take chances, have a quiet life. That option isn't open any more. In our lifetimes, too many British people have taken it, and look where we've ended up as a result. Make the future – it's *our* future.

"Finally, I remember a speech made here, by an undergraduate who was under great personal stress because her boyfriend had been attacked and was in hospital. Her listeners had occupied this Hall. She convinced them that their legitimate concerns could and would be met by agreement. She's moved on from there, ain't she half? She's shown what being a Creator is all about. A Star is born, as the TV man said yesterday morning. *Stand up, Carol Milverton MP, let's all see you!* Hold her chair, Paul."

The applause raised the rafters for a good minute, before Arthur thanked me. He looked a little puzzled, as he had every right to be, since he knew the facts about the wrecking of the concert. There were three others at the table who also knew those facts, including Carol. While she took the applause, thoughts came into my mind of Harry's freezing corpse, in the darkness somewhere above Formigal. He was the Star who had died, so that Carol could be the Star that was born.

Back in the Reception Room, Jenny touched my arm. "That was just right, Pete."

"I wanted it to be clear that we're celebrating Carol. I felt I should refer to Harry."

"It looks as if he's faded out of our lives, thank goodness. We must go, now. Here's a revise of the Articles that I did this afternoon, while Dick was talking to Geoff. Let me have any more comments tomorrow."

Sight of Jenny brought back happier memories from my time at Waterhouse – of the Ladies' Night a week after I was elected a Fellow. Later that evening, she had given me the book of photographs, and our friendship had begun to deepen. Tonight was not a full dress event, but Jenny still matched Brian's description of that time, which he had repeated in regard to Jane: 'what a smasher'.

After a while I joined a move to the Crypt bar, led by Brian and including Carol, Greg, Liz and Susie. I waved vaguely at Steph, who was still with Arthur, and now with James Harman. Paul was talking to Colin Mackay. Our plan was working out.

In the bar, I stayed with Brian, at the edge of the crowd around Carol.

"What a great weekend this is, Pete, and what a great time we've had, these last weeks."

"Yes, we'll all remember working together, and so will others. Roberta was saying the same to me. I didn't say she looked ten years younger on it, but that's true."

"She was great. She's a Creator, too."

"It'll be rather tame to go back to normal work, in a normal week, assuming that happens quickly."

"It will, once Heath goes. When I spoke to Dad this morning, he was very clear about that. Mum and Dad saw me take my degree three years back, so they left today's tickets for Susie's people. Thanks for bringing me in to help, Pete. It will be good for my job."

"I'm glad to hear that. I've been linked with International Electronics. You and the others have never said who you work for."

"Before we started the TV interview, we made it clear to Arthur Harnett that we weren't saying. Privately, all our employers have been pleased. It's training for leadership. You met my boss long ago, I mean in July. He's looking to move. Creators Technology, and all this, will give me two pluses on the form."

"I'm glad it's worked out well. Pat O'Donnell isn't unhappy with my contribution."

"The only guy who didn't want to be on the air is Paul. If there's a 'mystery man', it's him. I still don't know what makes him tick."

"He's always been the back-room boy. He didn't want to take the focus off Carol."

I moved on round the bar, which was as noisy as ever. Plenty of people wanted to meet me. Recollections of individual conversations became blurred. It was rather like the evening when I was elected a Fellow, six years before.

By half past ten, Liz and Greg had already disappeared, having announced that they were taking an early run along the towpath, and then Carol spoke out.

"Though the night is young, and it's good to be here, I'm not feeling so young after the last couple of days. It's time for a very long sleep. Tomorrow, I'm speaking to a special meeting of the Labour Club. Three o'clock, at the usual place. Hopefully Heath *will* have jacked it in by then. Bye all."

She left to plaudits and waves. Soon I pleaded much the same excuse to Brian, picked up my coat, and set off along Bridge Street, towards New Hall.

As Brian had said, July did seem a long time ago. Though I had not been idle during any of my time with IE, the last eight months had taught me much about getting results. I had got results that were good for the country, good for IE, and good for The Creators. I had missed what Paul, Steph, and Harry were up to, but once alerted I had led in containment, to use a word from Watergate. Once again I had shown that I could keep calm, think fast, and react to the unexpected. Pat O'Donnell had certainly noticed that. Now, at last, I could relax. My thoughts turned to Carol.

A taxi screeched to a halt and Jenny leaned out.

"Pete – get in. Thank God I spotted you. I need to talk. Where were you going?"

"I wanted a walk before bed. Steph is thrashing through Watergate with Arthur and James. I've had enough of politics for now. What's up, Jenny?"

We returned towards the Wingham house. At the end of their road, she asked the driver to wait, and we stepped out, under a lamp post.

"I had to warn you, Pete, though I don't know what it means. I had just settled Katie down when I heard the phone ring downstairs and Dick answer. I thought it might be Geoff.

Dick had said he was going to call with more information about an idea he had, which could affect me and the children a lot. I nipped smartly round to the small room upstairs which Dad uses as an office, and picked up the extension phone there. I wondered whether Dick would hear me do that, but he didn't because there were a lot of clicks and rings going on as an international call came through. It was Harry Tamfield."

Fortunately, in the dim light Jenny didn't notice the astonishment on my face.

"Goodness, what had he to say?"

"There was a pencil and paper to hand, so I took it down."

She produced a sheet covered with squiggles, and read. Later, she typed it out, as follows.

```
DICK: Gosh, where are you?

HARRY: At the Station Grand Hotel in Bayonne,
south-west France. I've just had a darned good
dinner. You told me you'd be in Cambridge for
one, too. International Directory Enquiries
located Harold Wingham surprisingly fast.
It's lucky you answered. In ten minutes Ramón
and I catch the train to Paris. Fortunately,
we've a sleeper together.

DICK: Who's Ramón?

HARRY: A good friend I've made in Spain. I
wanted you to know about him before anyone
else. I'm bringing him back to England.
BEA is on strike but the hotel desk got
us seats on a Turkish plane that's coming
through Orly Airport. Take off is at noon
tomorrow, due Heathrow same time Greenwich.
```

DICK: Harry, you'll be arrested as soon as you're back here; don't you know that?

HARRY: No I won't be, at any rate not for long. People think I've made off with the pension fund, but yesterday, once I knew I had what I wanted and wouldn't be disappearing, I called my bank. By tomorrow, messrs Cork Gully will find the money has miraculously reappeared, every penny.

DICK: What is it that you wanted?

HARRY: What I promised on TV. I now have proof that the electorate was swindled on Thursday, by the dirty tricks of one Dr Milverton and that girl of his, aided and abetted by Pete and his girl. By tomorrow night, it will all be coming out and they'll be paying. I'd hoped to be back before Thursday, but it took till yesterday to contact the right man. This morning the Spanish police caught up with me, but I escaped. Ramón's brother is in trouble, but he'll slide out of it. He knows about Ramón's time with a nice clean Don who's supposed to be getting married very expensively next month.

DICK: How did you escape the Spanish police?

HARRY: I guessed they would know I could ski. So Ramón, who's about my build and has a knack with foreign accents, laid a decoy to suggest I was trying to ski out

of Spain. Actually, we walked across the
frontier, through a disused railway tunnel.
Ramón knew who to pay, and I had the cash.
They helped Ramón with the decoy, showed us
how to get into the tunnel, and provided a
couple of torches. We were met on the French
side and driven here (warning pips). I must
go now, running out of change. Thanks again,
Dick, for the help last week. Don't tell
your lovely wife that I called. She needn't
worry about you now I've got Ramón, but if
she hadn't worried before, I wouldn't have
been on to any of this, tell you – (end of
call).

"Dick came upstairs a moment later. I said I'd left my gloves
at Waterhouse. They were expensive, and I needed them for
tomorrow. I called a taxi, and here I am. What *is* going on, Pete?"

"These ravings just show how deranged Harry is. He's in a
fantasy world, just as he was on TV. If he does turn up tomorrow,
he'll be marched off to jail quickly enough. No one will listen to
him. It's really tragic. Chaca must be somewhere in Spain, after
all. Bayonne is very close to the frontier."

"I hope we don't see him again. He's been such trouble for
Dick, and now he wants to spoil things for Carol and you."

"Don't worry, Jenny. He won't succeed. Thanks for telling me
tonight. It won't spoil tomorrow. That's your day, and Katie's day
too. I'll take the cab back. Don't worry about the fare."

"It's also my mother's day, and Uncle Archie's day too. That's
a hint about the musical surprise. Goodnight, Pete. You've been
as calm and thoughtful as ever."

The driver could hardly contain his smirks as he imagined
what our conversation had been about. When I asked him to take
me to the Castle Inn, he pointed out that it was closing time.

The Inn was not far from New Hall, and I recalled that there was a call box outside. Fortunately it was working, I had sufficient change, and Pat was at home. I gave most of Harry's news.

"So after all you did, these cretins have let him give them the slip."

"I suggested that he might try to ski out. Then the bad weather was a bit of luck for him, as it stopped people from looking any further. I knew about the rail tunnel, but had assumed that when Don Pedro said the frontier guards at Canfranc were alerted, that included keeping an eye on it. We weren't to know that this Ramón, the brother who's a waiter, was in touch with the right people. Someone at Canfranc will have been paid enough to look the other way."

"Don't kick yourself too hard, Pete. But for you, Tamfield would have been back here by now. Have you any ideas?"

"Just one, which follows from something Harry did just before he left for Switzerland, and which led to some funny looks from the office receptionist yesterday."

I explained sufficiently for Pat, and gave him a telephone number.

"It looks to be the only hope. As you say, keep out of the way yourself, and that goes for the rest of you in Cambridge. Carry on as if none of this is happening. I'll speak to Mart now. Then I'll speak to George. Either he or I will call you at that number later. There's no point in calling Pedro tonight. I called earlier, but young Ana told me he'd gone to Madrid, and won't be back until later tomorrow. That's lucky for him. When I do catch up with him, I'll have words to say. Something took his eye off the ball."

"I think I know what that is. It doesn't concern IE, or New Hampshire. He'll be very put out. Don't press him too hard."

"It's good that he can go off and leave his daughter in charge."

I could follow Pat's instruction for a little while. After making another call, I set off towards New Hall.

At 11.25 I knocked quietly at the door of the President's guest room. There was a short pause before Carol answered. She was wearing the same pair of glasses as that first time after I'd rescued her from the police – and nothing else.

As I undressed, she was doubtful in answer to appreciations.

"I've put on four pounds in the last three weeks. I've had too many late-night fry-ups."

"You look well for it. I've said before that you're meant to be a bit chubby."

"You took your time getting here."

"Sorry, a couple of people buttonholed me and I didn't want it to be seen I was coming this way."

"I've been listening to the late news. Heath is talking to Thorpe, and he's more defiant than ever despite having lost Argyll to the Nats. The final Labour majority over the Tories is five. I hope Harold knows what he's doing. But blow them all. This is our night. Let's start with a nice rub in front of that mirror."

She stood facing it, hands on head, and I stood behind. She squeezed me between her muscular buttocks, my left hand stroked her chest, and right hand fingers worked below and into her. It was good to find again the places which really brought her on. From time to time, she turned her head to kiss.

She turned round, and I removed her glasses. We kissed whilst I caressed her bottom, and then smacked gently.

"Hello, bottom girl. You are naughty, Carol."

"Right I am, very naughty. So, harder… *Harder…*"

Once suitably chastised, she brought out the Vaseline and crouched, facing the mirror, as she had done on our first time. She thrashed up and down on me, using her swimmer's legs to the full. With experience, we kept going for what seemed a blissful age.

"I can't hold it much longer."

"*Now.*"

My Vaselined finger did its work for both of us at once. Then we were into bed.

"It's lovely to celebrate, Pete. You got me here. Thanks again."

"You got yourself here, Carol, with support from Paul. Don't forget that."

"It was good with Paul last night. Steph *is* helping, that way, but he doesn't do it quite like you. You just slide your finger so gently into my arse, and that marvellous feeling shoots through me. It brings me off, straightaway."

"It's the same with me. The feeling of a ring round my finger is the signal. Give Paul the chance to practise, though I warn you that Steph likes it too, so maybe you don't want him too good too soon."

"Paul and I suit each other. We're staying together. I'm hoping to get on to a committee dealing with North Sea oil. That will bring me visits to Aberdeen. I'll rely on you to make me some introductions there, and… *mmmmm*. Steph can have Paul while I'm away."

Soon afterwards, I heard a clock strike midnight.

"Now, Carol, I've a few things to tell you, which you need to pass on to Paul in the morning. Then, I have to go."

14. SUNDAY, 3ᴿᴰ MARCH, 1974

"With God's help, we will."

Liz and I spoke out together, to conclude our contribution to the service. There were yelps of surprise from little Catherine, always to be Katie, as Jenny proudly carried her around Pembroke College Chapel. Then there was a pause, before what was described on the order of service as an anthem.

I had already noticed that the choir was larger than Pembroke College would mount on its own, and included women. My suspicions were confirmed when they formed eight groups of five. The director took centre spot, and brought the groups in one by one, for that masterpiece of Thomas Tallis, the 40-part Motet. After a while, I worked out why it had been included as a 'surprise'. For ten minutes, I was distracted by admiring the interior of the Chapel, one of Wren's earliest commissions, and listening to the variation from sparse to lush sound that the motet embodies.

The normal Matins service resumed, and everything crowded back into my mind. George Armstrong was right to say that the chance of my plan succeeding was about fifty-fifty.

If my plan failed, it wasn't just that Steph and Paul might face prosecution, that Carol's career would be snuffed out as soon as it had begun, and that, realistically, I might well have to be sacked to protect IE's position. It wasn't even the devastating impact on all those who had worked for Carol, and on the enthusiastic students I had met at Waterhouse. It was what might happen to the whole country.

Harry had already said that a vote for Labour was a vote for treason. That message would return, hard. The people would have been deceived.

Heath would be under huge pressure to stand and fight. If he wasn't ready to do so, he would be replaced, in substance if not in title, by someone who was ready to stand and fight. The Queen would be under huge pressure to dissolve Parliament even before it had met, so that the election could be rerun.

The Conservatives would not need to play the 'Jewish card' overtly. Attention would quickly focus on Mart Steinberg's speculation which funded the Labour campaign, and on Martha Dugdale's vengeful wrecking of Tamfield Investments. It would spread to the range of Harold Wilson's associates.

As the miners' strike continued, the economy would collapse, unemployment would shoot up, and shortages would develop. So, there would be more interest in the idea of hitting strikers with the army, or a militia.

There would be those who knew what should be the penalty for treason as Harry had defined it on TV, and who would be ready to carry it out. In the circumstances, such people might be seen as patriots, rather than as criminals.

They would be the amateurs. Lurking behind them would be the professionals. The IRA terrorists would be out for anything they could get.

Words from Hugh Thomas's book rattled through my mind.

'The history of Spain during the two and one half years after the general elections of November 1933 was marked by a steady decline into chaos, violence, murder, and, finally, war.'[83]

Even if that could be avoided, the British people would be scared. We would continue with a quiet life of 'managed decline'.

I had underestimated Harry's resource, and his determination for revenge. He would realise what the consequences would be. As Pat had said two weeks before, people in his position tried to

---

83 *The Spanish Civil War*, p.112

cause maximum damage. Part of me was saying that at least I had not driven Harry to his death. Another part of me was saying, with Pat, that to have done so would have been for the best.

Six Creators now knew wholly or partly what the stakes were. Paul and Steph knew both about 'Crafty' and about New Hampshire Realty's use of some of the profits to fund Labour. Carol, Morag and Sheila knew about 'Crafty' only. All of them knew of the risk that Harry would expose 'Crafty'. Like everyone but Ana, they thought that I had got on to Harry by pursuing Pat's hunch.

I had told Carol enough to give her a restless night before Paul came to her, and was out of New Hall by 12.15 am. Brisk walking brought me to Newnham by 12.35. A taxi was already waiting outside. Two minutes later, Sheila emerged, and very fortunately Morag came outside too, to see her off.

Morag always backed me up. She dealt with Sheila's surprise and doubt by saying that if I needed help, that was good enough for her. We all set off for Stratford, but they wanted the full story.

As the empty train rumbled through the night, I began with 'I never told you that I nearly met Professor Kraftlein last summer...', and continued with the story of 'Crafty'. I had wondered whether Sheila, who was half Jewish, would say that we should have done more to warn of the attack, but she knew that many warnings had been given, to no avail. The greatest problem for them was the involvement of Franco's Spain, but they accepted that most of the winnings were at the expense of the international oil industry. They saw that exposure now would be damaging to Labour, and particularly to Carol.

My call from Cambridge had made Jane ready for us to bring her to the Pankhurst Centre, where several residents and new arrivals were still up. When I returned to the room after Jane had shown them her bruises, there was no doubt about support for my plan. Soon afterwards, George Armstrong phoned.

Plenty had happened whilst I was travelling. Pat, George and Mart had agreed that my plan was better than trying to have Harry held in Paris pending formal extradition. That might not succeed given that Harry was returning of his own accord, and there was a high risk that he would blow the story there, sooner than if he travelled on to London. George had contacted two female lawyers who dealt with violence and abuse cases. They would be at the Centre by eight o'clock, to sort out a statement by Jane of what had happened. Bill Anstruther had been passed 'information received', and had found it quite easy to re-engage the *Clarion*. Their reporter would arrive by ten o'clock, together with a coach to take the party to Heathrow, where a photographer would meet them.

A night cab took Morag and me to Liverpool Street for the newspaper train, which didn't call at Stratford. On the train Morag slept, but I was too tense to do so. I thought of Harry and Ramón, perhaps asleep, perhaps not, as their train swept north through France. I also thought more about why Don Pedro was so distracted, and what I might need to do about that.

We emerged blearily into the darkness of Cambridge Station as the Sunday newspapers were unloaded, full of headlines such as 'HEATH CALLS FOR ALLIANCE – two thirds of voters reject union rule.' I returned to a quiet Waterhouse College at roughly the time I had planned, two days before. Liz and Greg were out on their run, and Paul was making an unobtrusive way to New Hall.

Steph had said that she would be 'on'. Rather to my surprise, I was 'on' too, so we began Jenny's day with Steph's legs hooked over my shoulders in a 'Jenny'. We dozed, until my update rudely awoke Steph. She called Mart before we joined Liz and Greg for a typically quiet breakfast with the Master, and the four of us walked over to Pembroke College, passing some of the main sights of Cambridge. I had been intending that we could take a fuller look later, but I suspected that the opportunity might not now arise. Outside the Chapel, we met Carol and Paul, fresh from their breakfast with the President of New Hall.

Carol had no doubt passed to Paul my news from last night. He had been out of the loop yesterday, and so had much catching up to do. He would have realised the full implications, but had to contain himself until he could speak to Steph alone. Fortunately, Liz and Greg wandered away together, and Morag arrived soon after us. By dint of asking Carol to confirm to her the arrangements for the Labour Club meeting, I achieved the necessary split of five into two and three. Morag and I updated Carol whilst people I had once described as 'Framptons, Winghams and things' assembled around us. Then it had been time to go in for the service.

The organist launched into a Bach fugue for the outgoing voluntary. Greg turned to Liz and me.

"That was a splendid finish, just right for today. And we had my favourite hymn."

"Mine, too," said Liz. "Father told me that one of his surveys during the War put it way in front of any other."

"What, even 'Onward Christian Soldiers'?" I asked, trying to sound flippant.

The last hymn had been 'O God, our Help in Ages Past, our Hope for Years to Come'. The sermon had alluded to the uncertainties of the day, and we had offered prayers for 'those in authority making decisions'.

I glanced at my watch. It was 11.37 am. Harry's plane was due at Heathrow in less than half an hour. There would be two groups to greet him.

Sir Reg Emerson would no doubt be there, probably with the *Messenger*. Harry would have with him a copy of the note of our meeting, and knew enough Spanish to say what it meant. Sir Reg could spell out whatever Central Office knew about how some of the winnings had been used. It could all be on the one o'clock news.

441

But, as soon as Harry appeared, Jane, Sheila and the women from the Pankhurst Centre would rush him, shouting accusations of rape. If, as was likely, some police were there, the lawyers would ask for charges to be pressed. Jane would tell all that the *Clarion* could print, and more. Some good crowd shots could doubtless complement a further 'tasty' picture of her from the *Clarion*'s existing stock.

Jane's story would be completely true. Harry had phoned to say that he was returning, so she had gone to the Pankhurst Centre for help. Anger at her treatment had prompted this demonstration, by people who had no obvious connection with IE, New Hampshire Realty, or any of us – Sheila had studied at the University of Warwick before moving to London. Attempts by Harry and Sir Reg to hit back could rebound on them.

Which story would win? The *Messenger* and the *Clarion* would go head to head. That was the fifty-fifty chance.

Meanwhile, we in Cambridge needed to act unaware, just like Al Pacino. We filed out past Pembroke students, and chatter came to my ear.

"I'm sure that's Carol Milverton."

"She's in Cambridge this afternoon, to talk to the Labour Club."

"How could she be here? There's Harold – Wingham, not Wilson. Gosh, his daughter, the mum, doesn't she look great?"

Steph broke in to my thoughts. She was acting up well, sounding quite natural.

"I am pleased to be here. My alma mater is now part of Brown University, but it was named after this College. Wow, those buildings over there look just like Waterhouse."

"That's because they're his work, though they've been messed around since."

We walked the short distance along Trumpington Street to Carmarthen College, and milled around in the Master's Garden as photographs were taken. Fortunately, the weather was dry, though cold. Steph continued as her natural self.

"I think I've got it right. I'm the best dressed here to those who know, but I'm not overpowering Jenny, or the lady over there who looks important."

"That's Lady Frampton. Yes, thanks for taking the trouble, Steph. You're spot on, and I'm proud to be with you. Let's talk to Linda and Derek."

I took Steph over to Dick's parents. They had driven up from near Guildford, and were looking rather lost amidst the ranks of Cambridge grandees. I had met them before only at the wedding, since Derek's oil job had kept him overseas during most of Dick's time at Cambridge. They had seen me on TV and had a daughter living in Aberdeen, so they were interested in news from there. By the time Jenny joined us and Linda had the chance to hold Katie, I had some useful business contacts as well as the address of the daughter, who could not leave three young children but would be grateful for a slice of christening cake. I noticed Morag talking to the Fellows' Butler, and then going inside the Master's Lodge with him.

Before long, Steph was chatting about New York, where Derek had been posted for a while. This gave me the chance to gesture towards Sir Archibald Frampton, with a question to Jenny.

"When's his sixtieth birthday?"

"Tomorrow. I thought you'd spot the reason for the motet."

"It's said to have been written for Queen Elizabeth's fortieth birthday, and I remember that six years ago your father told me that fifteen years earlier, Archie had been Regius Professor at thirty-nine."

Jenny laughed, and then went on more seriously, lowering her voice.

"I need to talk to you. Can you come back for a cup of tea later on?"

"Yes – Steph is going back to London, but I'm staying in Cambridge tonight. You may hear more about Harry, but don't worry."

"It's not about Harry. By the time I was back last night, Geoff had called. He wants Dick to put in for a Miller Fellowship at the University of California, Berkeley - that's near San Francisco. With his recommendation, Dick should get it."

"What's a Miller Fellowship?"

"It's a top postdoctoral award, worth four times what Dick is paid now."

"How long does it last?"

"Two years, so it doesn't give Dick a permanent job. It's really for people who've just got a PhD, not for people four years on. Geoff says that Dick shouldn't worry, because there'll be the pick of the jobs available for someone returning from one of these fellowships. He doesn't say though, what pick of what jobs?"

"Quite. Another point is, I guess, what about you and the children?"

"Actually, my firm has a big office in San Francisco. Two years there would help my career, as well as our bank balance. It would be best done before the children start school. No, another point is, San Francisco and its reputation. After last week, I really don't want us to be back to square one. Here I am, sweet."

She retrieved Katie, and joined her family as they led the way into the Master's Dining Room. This was where I had met her, some six years before. Memories of that mixed with reflection that Jenny might well not relish two years without John and Amanda. I looked across at them now. John was little changed, still the handsome young man with curly light hair. Amanda looked her part, strong and competent, but a little uneasy at this gathering. Her family was not wealthy. She wasn't a typical wife for a Frampton or Wingham. John would certainly have needed Jenny's help to bring her home.

I added to a growing display Steph's choice of gift, an impressive and collectable teddy bear. I encountered Carol and related what I had heard.

"So, you've been spotted. It's the penalty of fame."

"That slim, bearded, balding guy next to big-shot Frampton was looking at me earlier."

"Geoff Frampton was looking at Paul. You know why."

Carol eyed the buffet. "What a marvellous spread. I'll have to be careful."

"Oh, don't be *too* careful, Carol. Remember what I said. Sort out the Hills Road Baths, and get some more swimming in."

"It's more the drink, right now. I need to be reasonably clear-headed for the Labour Club. Fingers crossed – and thanks again, Pete."

Paul joined us. "The JCR is across the court. I'll go over there for the one o'clock news. Earlier, Whitelaw was suggesting that they would have something important to say this lunchtime. Hopefully, it's that they're giving up."

Morag had been using a telephone in the entrance hall. Now, she also joined us. Steph noticed and moved over, to hear what Morag had to say.

"The Butler was very helpful. I said I had a sick relative, and there might be an urgent call. He's had that phone switched, so it takes incoming calls direct. I called Ruth at the Centre. She's the one in the wheelchair, Pete, who was to have reports from Sheila for us to pick up. She's pleased to be cut out of the loop. Sheila must have rung just after me and taken this number, for I've just had her call. They're in the terminal, placed where they can see arrivals but aren't noticed themselves. There's another group nearer the way out from Customs. They include Emerson, two blokes that the *Clarion* people recognise as on the *Messenger*, and a couple of fellows who could be police."

"So, Reg and maybe Carr[84] have a deal with the cops," said Steph. "Harry can have his say, and then he'll come quietly."

"Maybe, but they've all a wait. The plane is now expected at 12.30."

I tried to look on the bright side. "That's a good start for us. Emerson hasn't arranged for a private reception party. I guess he didn't want to give more of an impression of a plan than he had to."

---

84 Robert Carr, Home Secretary at the time.

Paul also tried to look on the bright side. "They'll miss the one o'clock news."

We dispersed, trying to look natural despite the gnawing tension we all felt. Just as on election night, Morag was showing that she liked to have her finger on the pulse. On balance this was helpful. Any information was better than total uncertainty, though it didn't alter the need for us to keep right out of the way. George Armstrong had told me that IE would react as necessary to what they heard and to press enquiries. If 'Crafty' were exposed, the basic line would be 'We joined in a legal, commercial venture. We made sure that a warning was passed to governments. It's a pity that they didn't act on it.' If the Labour funding issue came out, disapproving noises would include 'Dr Milverton is no longer in our employment.'

Steph and I found ourselves talking to Professor Chris Hunter of the Cavendish. His wife and Jenny's mother Belinda were Sir Archie's sisters. I recalled meeting him in that very room, and there was more talk of New York, as two years before he had taken a sabbatical at Columbia University. Then he turned back to me.

"You've moved on. Someone else who's moved on is Siegmund Kraftlein. Remember all that fuss?"

"Yes, I certainly do." Though Hunter had praised the organisation of the big demonstration against Kraftlein's election, I forbore to mention that the man responsible for it was now about ten feet away.

"There wasn't any more fuss, but he wasn't happy here. He was used to starting work at seven o'clock, but he couldn't have breakfast in Lindsey College until an hour later. He didn't get on with their Fellows, either. He said that he'd been looking forward to meeting you again, and was surprised to find that you'd left. He didn't achieve much here, whilst Carl Obermeyer, who had tried so hard to stop him from coming, secured a chair at Coventry and is having quite an Indian summer."

"Yes, I know that Carl is doing well." I also didn't mention why I knew that – through talk last evening with Nick, and with Sheila, of whom temporarily I had never heard.

"So, for whatever reason, Siegmund resigned two years ago. For us electors, it was back to the drawing board. Eventually, we got Atkinson, from Cardiff."

"I've a job to do," said Steph.

Jenny, with Katie in her arms, was fully engaged with Linda, Derek, Angela, and Penny. Dick was talking to Geoff. Young David was dashing around, clearly bored and probably resentful of the attention being paid to his sister. Steph crouched down.

"Remember me, David? We met when I visited your home. I'm Steph, from a big city called New York, where they have buildings with over a hundred floors. We call them skyscrapers."

Soon she was having fun with David in a corner of the room, building 'skyscrapers' of table mats. I joined Liz and Greg at a table not far from the entrance. Then Geoff Frampton sat down with us.

"Ah, Liz, you're just the person we need to brighten up this singularly dull gathering, and Pete, too."

Liz and I looked at each other. We recalled Geoff using these rather patronising words of greeting, right here in this room, and then going on to introduce 'Jennifer' to us.

"Hello, Geoff. Can I introduce Greg Woolley, my fiancé?"

"I had heard. How did you meet our little Liz then, Greg?"

"We play hockey for the same club in London."

"I'm told that hockey is a dangerous game. I know Liz is good at it. What do you do?"

"I'm an electrical engineer, working for the London Electricity Board."

"Ah, so you go round fixing cookers that have gone wrong."

"No, I don't. Recently I've been dealing with the emergency, but my normal job is to lead a team which looks at the way the peak demand for electricity is increasing in various parts of London, and works out where the local distribution network needs reinforcing. So, we decide where contractors need to dig up the road."

"Fascinating."

"We use quite a lot of maths, to work out what needs to be done to reduce the risk of supply failure to an acceptable level in the most economical way. Pete, I guess you remember some of the concepts."

Greg was reacting politely to Geoff's academic snobbery. He gave a fairly technical exposition, and I chipped in with some references that at least sounded impressive. After a few minutes, Geoff moved on, worsted. Penny Frampton had now settled to play with David, and Steph joined us. Liz kissed Greg quietly.

"Thanks, Greg, for dealing with that bum so well. Thanks for your help, too, Pete. Sorry, Steph, we're talking about a bad time in my past."

"Pete has told me. At least it's gotten you out of *here*. Is this really the Master's Dining Room? It's five times the size of the room we had breakfast in at Waterhouse."

"Yes. Carmarthen is a grand College."

"Your country is falling to bits, but they're just carrying on like it's not happening. I guess it was the same with the monks listening to your man Tallis. They forgot that the King was after their loot."

I pointed out that the 40-part Motet had been written about thirty years after the Dissolution, and we chatted on. Supporting Liz now was a necessary distraction. Geoff had been abroad at the time of Jenny and Dick's wedding. When David was christened, Liz and I had been on our problematic holiday on the Costa del Sol. Jenny and Dick had understood that this was just an unlucky coincidence.

After a while, Susie took over David duty, so Brian joined us for some friendly Yorkshire banter with Greg. The phone rang outside, and Morag, who was with Carol and Paul, went to answer it. I suggested to Steph that we should say hello to

Jenny's parents, who had John and Amanda with them. By the time we had got up, Morag was returning. Her message was short.

"At twenty past twelve, the arrivals board changed to 'Make inquiries at the BEA desk'. Various people including Emerson have been doing just that, but don't look as if they're getting any information. Our people still haven't been noticed. They'll follow Emerson when he moves. Meanwhile, no one knows what's going on."

Steph gulped her drink, and tried to sound relaxed.

"So, someone in BEA isn't on strike. I guess they handle Turkish flights at Heathrow. Well, it's all part of airport life."

After some typically effusive greetings and introductions, Belinda apologised for leaving us, to speak to Jenny. Steph soon had Harold, who was a reader in geography, reminiscing about fieldwork in the Grand Canyon. John and Amanda didn't say much, and nor did I, though I probably looked thoughtful. Were the passengers being taken elsewhere, so that Harry could give a press briefing? In that case, though, wouldn't Reg Emerson's party have moved elsewhere also? Had the plane been diverted, to allow a quieter reception? It was a quarter to one.

I noticed Sir Archibald Frampton standing a few feet away, looking at me. I slipped over to him.

"We meet again, Peter."

"Yes, and Happy Birthday – tomorrow, I understand. I'm sure you enjoyed your present. I certainly did."

"It was a real surprise. The choirs of the two Colleges combined to perform it, along with some friends. This is our first year with women undergraduates at Carmarthen. Compared to the boys at King's, their sound is different, but just as valid."

"I agree. Once again, many thanks for your hospitality. This is a splendid party."

"I have to thank you. Jenny and Dick have made a success of their marriage, and Geoff tells me that Dick has now made a very interesting breakthrough in his research. So you were right to press me to help them carry on."

"I'm very happy for them, and I'm glad you are. Others we discussed are doing well, too. Professor Hunter mentioned Carl Obermeyer's success at Coventry. Brian Smitham is over there, talking to Liz Partington and her fiancé. He's in a good job."

"I've even been fortunate in that investment you advised, though only because last April your Chief, Sir Pat O'Donnell, was at a Feast here and suggested that I sell then. Not all of your friends have done as well as it seemed they might. The world is a very slippery place."

"You helped to teach me that. You completed my Cambridge education."

"I'm interested that the Paul Milverton we spoke about, and whose wife has done so well, is now your friend."

"They're here now because Carol and Jenny are friends. Paul learnt from his experiences, as did I."

"Would I be right in thinking that as well as contributing to last Sunday's television programme, you had a hand in how it was presented?"

"Last weekend, I spent some time on the phone to the people you saw."

Belinda bustled up. "It's time to lead to the buffet, Archie. Speeches are at twenty to two. Harold will speak first, and then Derek, you and Jenny. No more than three minutes each, please."

I held back from the rush and chatted to others I remembered from my time in Cambridge. I was returning to my table, with loaded plate and refilled glass, when Paul came back into the room.

"There's nothing on the TV news. Heath has gone off to lunch with some friends in the country. Ministers are to meet later. There may even be another meeting with Jeremy Thorpe. Something is up, though. At the back of the newsroom, people were passing each other notes and having muttered conversations. There was definitely the air of an imminent big announcement. There's a radio summary at two."

Steph had stayed with the Hunters, and was with them at another table. John and Amanda had joined Liz, Greg, Brian and also Susie, who had relinquished David to Linda Sinclair. I sat down to find Greg and Brian speculating about when the country might actually have a government. I was rather relieved when Amanda joined in before anyone expected me to say anything. For a moment, my mind wandered as I took in her plain, practical face and short but substantial figure.

"In five years' time, national election results will be much less important. There will be a directly elected European Parliament.[85] That will be the democratic control over the European Commission, from which more and more of our legislation will flow."

"How can that possibly be?" asked Liz.

"It's part of the inevitable trend to European integration. For centuries, European nation states have been fighting each other. We must stop fighting, and join up."

"We already have the NATO alliance against the only country we might have to fight – Russia."

"I hope that eventually there'll be a United States of Europe, which includes Russia."

"What, all of Russia, right to the Bering Straits?" asked Greg. "What relations would this combination have with the USA?"

"That's a very long-term aim," said John. As usual, he was trying to smooth things over.

"In the shorter term, are you in favour of a single currency by 1980, Amanda?" I asked.

"We've joined a group of countries whose common aim is ever closer union. We mustn't let technicalities obstruct progress."

---

85 At this time, the European Parliament comprised nominated members of national parliaments, but direct elections were already proposed for 1979.

"Ordinary people here don't think that ever closer union is our aim at all," said Susie.

"You can say that again, dearie," said Brian. "The only thing the rest of these countries have in common is that they lost the War. One of them started it, another changed sides in the middle, and the rest just gave up. They're free now mainly because in 1940 we fought on, rather than join them. That cost us loads. Now Heath has us join them, and he's agreed to pay them loads more."

"Being with them now complements what we did in the War," said John. "It means we can win the peace, as well as the War."

"But we've already lost the peace, spectacularly," said Greg.

"Yup, and the others want to show us we've lost," said Brian. "They want us down."

The talk rattled on. John had a little to say, but Amanda relapsed into a rather sulky silence. I asked her to explain what ever closer union meant, but it was clear that she hadn't thought it through. There was another reason for Jenny to keep these two in a separate box from The Creators. Amongst us, they hadn't a chance.

I continued to try to focus on the conversation, but the suspense was getting to me. What was happening at Heathrow? Which story would come out on top? The two o'clock summary might tell us.

I also tried to take notice of what else was going on in the room. Steph was laughing loudly, though seemingly holding well what she had drunk. Angela had joined Morag, Carol and Paul, and was chatting to her former partner in a relaxed way. Penny and her husband were now with Jenny, Dick and Katie. Earlier, Penny had been crouching to play with David, and I had seen that she was, as Carol had said, a 'bottom girl'. Both sisters looked to be better company than they had been. Now they were older, their faces seemed characterful, rather than meriting them Liz's nicknames of Clorinda and Tisbe.

After a little while, Greg 'needed to go outside before the speeches', as he put it, politely. A stream of people, including Geoff, Morag, and Angela, had been passing us, doubtless for the same reason. So, when I heard the phone ring. I pretended the same reason, and went to answer.

"Is that Pete?"

"Yes, Sheila." She was very clear, though speaking quietly and in a shocked tone. I remember her message, word for word.

"At ten to one, those meeting the plane were invited into a private lounge. Reg Emerson's group led the way, and others followed on. We kept at the back, and were still not noticed. We were told that there'd been an accident, but had no more details. They opened up a bar, and offered free drinks.[86] Then, at about a quarter past, some higher-up guy from BEA came in, and told us that the plane crashed soon after leaving Paris. The wreckage has been found. There are no survivors. They're still trying to get a full passenger list from Orly. Well over a hundred British people boarded there, but there was not room for all who wanted to fly. The news will be released at two. Emerson shouted something about murderers, and stormed out. We let him leave, and then made off ourselves. The *Clarion* team is now covering the crash, as is the *Messenger*. I just got this phone before one of their people."

"So there's no confirmation that Harry was on board?"

"Emerson's behaviour shows it. I expect he had a call from Orly. I must go, there are two reporters waiting outside. We should be back at the Centre by three o'clock."

"To state the obvious, Jane isn't a story anymore. Say nothing to anyone."

"We all know that, including Jane. She tried to avoid looking cheerful."

---

86 As described in the account of those involved – see Eddy *et al.*, *Destination Disaster* (1976), p.12.

I had heard all this to the sounds of a scuffle and raised voices behind me. My look of horrified astonishment matched the scene before me as I turned from the phone.

Geoff was sprawled on the ground outside the cloakroom, his nose bleeding profusely. Greg was standing above him, quivering with anger. The noise had brought Brian and Amanda out, and Morag had emerged from the cloakroom. There was complete silence for what seemed a very long time. It continued as Jenny appeared, and took in the *tableau*.

"Greg, Geoff, all of you, whatever's going on?"

Greg pointed to the cloakroom.

"God, I'm sorry, Jenny. He'd been very unpleasant earlier. In there alone with me, he started talking about Liz. I asked him to stop, but he wouldn't. As we came out, he was laughing, just warning me he said, about how Liz was at least fifth-hand. Besides him, three of her men were here today. I snapped. I said that Liz had told me about the three, and about him. There was a difference. She liked and valued them, and so did I. Then I hit him."

Geoff climbed to his feet, rather shakily. At a glance from Jenny, Amanda moved to steady him as he faced Greg.

"You engineers can't take a joke. You'd better get out of my father's College before he has you thrown out."

Jenny spoke very calmly.

"Oh, no, Geoff. This is *my* party, and Dick's. How *dare* you insult my husband and our friends."

"You keep out of this, Jenny. It's nothing to do with you."

"Oh, yes it is. I'm no longer the little girl you've patronised. Liz gave you what you deserved, and now Greg has done the same. He's ten times the man you are. You may be brilliant, but you're a complete shit."

She slapped his face, very hard.

"Amanda, please deal with Geoff. Brian, please help her. Just up the stairs, there's a bathroom with a medical cupboard. Greg, go back to Liz and tell her she should be proud of you. I certainly am."

Amanda and Brian took Geoff upstairs, none too gently. As Amanda looked back at Jenny, her face was full of admiration, even of worship. Jenny licked her lips.

"At least, Geoff doesn't know about *me*," said Morag.

"Yes, and this has put Geoff just where I want him, now and later."

Jenny went into the cloakroom, to a cousinly pat on the back from Angela, who had emerged in time to see the slap. Meanwhile, I spoke to Morag, quietly.

"Harry's plane has crashed. He's dead. Get to Paul before the speeches. Tell him I'll call Pat O'Donnell. Pat will call others."

Morag nodded, and went back into the Dining Room. Angela turned to me. She sounded very cheerful.

"What were you two whispering about, then, Pete?"

"How we can keep David happy during the speeches. Your sister has done her bit."

"Penny *is* good with kids. Today will encourage her to get on. Donald isn't so keen, though. Pete, you're up to something. You usually are. I remember you at that party of Dad's, just before you left here – talking to Geoff, and then for a long time with Dad. Today I've seen you having *lots* of little chats with people, even with Dad. I'm sure *that* wasn't about David."

"I wished your father many happy returns."

"Did he tell you what he thought about your being on TV?"

"He did mention it."

"Not the same way as he did yesterday, I'm sure. We were looking at the invitation list and I said it would be super to meet Morag, you and Brian again after seeing you all on TV. Oh dear, that wasn't the thing to say, to him or to Mum. Gosh, Pete, stop looking so *shocked*. Whatever caused all that just now, Geoff deserved it. Jenny was great. Did you see the look on her face, and on Amanda's? I'm sure you've heard about the day Morag and I came together."

"Yes, I have."

"What Jenny wants, Amanda does. I hope she's doing Geoff right now. Brian should like helping her, too, after what he tried at Liz and Geoff's party. He stopped me from chatting you up then, but I guess that was a good thing. I would have been in Jenny's bad books. Are you working in London?"

"No, mostly in Aberdeen."

"I'm spending a while in London, drumming up sales and having lots of fun. If you're down, call me and we'll go for a meal. There's this *marvellous* new place in the Brompton Road."

Angela passed me a card which advertised her as a 'ceramic artist'. Jenny returned, they hugged and went off together. I excused myself for a moment, because I had been on my way out when interrupted. To the background of speeches getting under way, I rang Pat at his home. He did not maintain for long his annoyance at being called by someone who was supposed to be keeping away. A few minutes' advance warning was valuable.

Back at my table, I must have looked rather stunned. We were saved, but at what a cost. A disaster had brought tragedy, but had prevented something even worse. Harry's flight to destruction would end that of Edward Heath.

Ten days before, I had thought of Harry whilst listening to the last movement of Mahler's Sixth Symphony. The bankruptcy of Tamfield Investments had seemingly been the second hammer-blow that brought him down for good, but his obsession had led him to another chance. He had nearly succeeded, against the odds, but fate had now struck the third and absolutely final hammer-blow. For Harry, Mahler's original was right.

I can vaguely remember welcomes to the new arrival and tributes to the splendid couple who were her parents. Then it was Jenny's turn to thank us all for coming, and to hope that we had labelled our gifts securely, so that we could be thanked individually later. Apparently, there were two wedding gifts still unattributed. She asked anyone who had never received a thank-you letter to let her know.

There were comings and goings during the speeches. By five to two, the care squad had returned. Brian settled down with a very broad grin on his face, despite walking rather uncomfortably. Amanda was limping slightly as she went to speak to Jenny in undertones before returning to our table. Before Jenny spoke, she had just time for a word with Lady Frampton, who hurried out. A moment later, Paul followed her, but was soon back. Across the room, I saw Carol's grimace as she read Paul's notes. Paul was looking less concerned.

After the speeches, Amanda and John left our table, to help with cutting the cake, and passing pieces around. Angela was now looking after David, perhaps in response to my remarks, so Morag joined us. Steph came back too, looking slightly vacant but not drinking any more. They were all in time to be entertained by Brian.

"Amanda may be nuts on Europe, but she can do her job, and she's strong. She held a cloth round Geoff's nose till the bleeding stopped, and I helped clean him up. Then she had him take off his shirt which was covered in blood, felt him about, and said nothing seemed broken but he might be feverish. So she told him to take his trousers off and bend over a bench, to have his temperature taken. He refused, and she said firmly to do as she said. His mouth was awash, so a normal thermometer wouldn't work, but fortunately there was a rectal thermometer in the cupboard. He still refused, so she took firm hold and asked me to strip him. He kicked out and got both of us on the shins, her worse than me. Right, she said, this is what you get if you hurt your nurse. She sat on the bench herself, pulled him across her and had me hold his legs while she gave twelve of the very best. By gum she put some vim into them. She promised more if he didn't calm down, but he punched her in the belly. I guess that hurt. Right, she said, you've left me no alternative, and she asked me to move his legs

457

apart. I had quite a view. His red arse was across her knee. She held him by the balls with her right and pushed the thermometer in with her left. It was quite a sound he was making, too. I reckon she was squeezing him bloody hard, to remind him of what you did, Liz. The thermometer took quite a while to register, but the temperature was normal and we put him to bed."

This account prompted suitable ribaldry from Liz, Steph and Susie. Greg joined in, too. He was no longer the rather reserved man I had met in July. He had struck out in Liz's name, and defended her honour. Liz and he had given up trying to keep their hands off each other. Morag and I were a little quieter, though I told Brian that Angela had been asking after him and would much appreciate his account.

Dick brought me a small box containing a piece of cake for me to take to his sister. He pulled up a chair for Jenny, who sat facing away from the crowd in the room, unbuttoned, and fed a fractious Katie. Finally, Carol and Paul fitted themselves in, to complete the circle of Creators. Parting of the ways began with Liz.

"Greg and I must be away soon, to be back in time for evening service and a talk with the Minister. We will have the invitations out this week, I promise, but anyway we hope to see you all on 4th May."

Brian gave me a wink. Liz and Greg had plenty of time to return, but clearly had something to do first. Jenny carried on.

"So, directors of Creators Technology, when shall I arrange your first Board meeting?"

"I'm down for an end of financial year meeting on Friday 22nd," I replied. "What about lunchtime on that day, at the IE London offices, subject to you checking with Sheila and Tony. That's assuming the offices are open, of course."

"That should be all right," said Morag. "Terms finish the day before."

Carol tried to avoid sounding too knowing. "There won't be a problem about opening. Heath won't last beyond tomorrow.

We need to leave in ten minutes. Are you coming, Morag? Afterwards, we can take you back to London."

The imposing figure of Jane Frampton loomed over us, to address Carol.

"Oh, my dear, I'm so sorry that neither Archie nor I have been able to congratulate you on your outstanding achievement. Jenny told me that you have to leave quite promptly, to speak to the Labour Club. Now, I wish I hadn't to say this, but I feel I must try to help. During the speeches, I had to go out to see my son, who's not feeling well. He had the radio on in his room, and there was some terrible news."

Before Carol could reply, a nervously cheerful Steph interjected. "What, is Nixon off the hook?"

"No, there's been an air crash, probably the worst ever.[87] A Turkish plane went down, soon after leaving Paris. There are no survivors, and over three hundred dead. Half of them are British people, who were aboard because of the BEA strike. I thought you ought to know before your meeting, so you can say something about it."

Carol replied, in serious tone. "Thank you for thinking of me, Lady Frampton. In fact, I know already. Paul went out to check the news for any political developments. I'll certainly be saying how it puts those into perspective."

"It really is dreadful. There are even suggestions of a bomb on board. What *are* things coming to? What *is* the future, for you young people? I must go along now. I'm having signals from Belinda."

"Oh, how awful," said Susie.

For a moment there was silence. I recalled the good use Carol had made of the assassination of Robert Kennedy, when she had spoken to the people occupying Waterhouse. I was trying not to look at Dick, but now he burst in.

---

87 Regarding the terrorist attacks of 11th September 2001 as an Act of War, it remains the fourth worst air disaster in history, the worst being the collision of two aircraft on the ground at Tenerife in 1977. Air travel is much safer now than it was forty years ago.

"You can say you killed him, Carol, with Paul, Steph, and Pete helping you. You all killed him."

"What on *earth* are you talking about, Dick?" asked Morag.

"Harry Tamfield was on that plane. He rang me last night to say he was coming back, with the story of the dirty tricks those four have been up to in Spain."

Carol showed her political skills in responding to this with a balanced mixture of surprise, anger and sympathy.

"If Harry Tamfield is amongst those killed, that's even more upsetting, but you can't say that any of us has anything to do with it, Dick. I know nowt about any dirty tricks, and I've never been to Spain."

Brian came in, calmly. "I guess no one knows yet what caused the crash. What was said on the news, Paul?"

"Only that inevitably people would be asking whether the plane was sabotaged."

"Of course they'll ask, and I'll bet anyone a fiver that by this time tomorrow at least two Mid East terror gangs will have said they planted a bomb. Whenever there's an unsolved murder, people keep walking into police stations to say they did it."

Brian had no takers,[88] but Dick went on.

"I can't stand this. You're all making excuses, for a horrible and inexcusable crime. This settles it, Jenny. We're getting right away from you lot. I'm putting in for the job at Berkeley."

Liz, who was sitting next to Dick, put her hand on his knee.

"Dick, I know so well how close you were to Harry. If you were speaking to him last night, I can't imagine how bad you feel to hear this now. Yet I know too that the Harry we saw on TV, and who rang you last night, wasn't the Harry you knew at Waterhouse. When his orchestra was wrecked, he was hit harder than we understood."

It was fortunate that both Dick and Jenny were facing away from the rest of the room, for through all this Jenny had been

---

88 And he was right.

looking at me with an expression of total horror. Earlier, I had said that she would hear more about Harry, but she needn't worry. Could she be saying to herself that her telling me of Harry's call had led to the plane being blown out of the air and over three hundred deaths? Did she think of me as the Godfather who had kept out of the way?

I remembered what Pat had said yesterday. What was less bad, one death or thousands? Thinking that way, three hundred deaths were less bad than thousands. However, thinking was one thing, doing quite another. Last night, I had called Pat. He had called Mart. Mart had probably called New York. Could people there have contacted the Mafia or some such organisation, to arrange for a bomb to be put on the plane, and all within a few hours? That was ludicrous, the stuff of thrillers.

As usual, Paul had been expressionless, even when Liz had referred to something he had done. Now, Greg asked him a question.

"Paul, did you hear what kind of plane it was that crashed?"

"A DC-10."

"How long after take-off did the crash occur?"

"About ten minutes."

"That squares with this being a repeat of the June 1972 Windsor incident – the much worse, but predictable repeat."

Brian looked puzzled. "Do you mean the plane coming out of Heathrow which crashed into Staines Reservoir? That cost Universal a pretty penny, but it wasn't a DC-10."

"The incident was a few days earlier than that crash. It happened above Windsor, Ontario, which is just across the border from Detroit. Last summer, I went on a course on safety analysis, which included a talk officially called 'Probabilistic aspects of air safety'. The unofficial title was 'Don't fly by DC-10'. One took off from Detroit with the cargo door not properly locked. It climbed for about ten minutes, and then the door blew open, depressurising the cargo hold. The passenger floor didn't stand the pressure difference and part of it collapsed. Fortunately no-one was sitting on that part, because the plane was less than a quarter full. The collapse broke various control cables and made the plane very difficult to fly, but by a combination of luck and skill the pilots made a successful emergency landing. Investigators made two key recommendations. The locking system should be made foolproof, with a clear sign on the flight deck that doors were properly locked. There should be vents in the passenger floor, so that it wouldn't collapse if the hold did depressurise. The passengers could use oxygen masks if need be. However, the manufacturers persuaded the US authorities not to enforce these recommendations, and they haven't been carried out systematically. Therefore, another accident has been waiting to happen. A full passenger load would worsen the damage caused by floor collapse, and maybe the Turkish crew weren't as experienced as the American crew. A sign will be if some wreckage is found away from the crash site, having been ejected when the door blew out."

Dick stood up and came near to shouting at us. "You're all very clever. If I stay here any longer, I'll be sick. I'll walk back to the house now, Jenny."

He left, to sympathetic goodbyes, and Jenny spoke for the first time since hearing the news. She was now calm.

"Dick has been working very hard. To be frank, we've been arguing about where we might move to next. Now, there's this terrible news. All of you know that before Dick met me, he was with Harry for a long time. That's not known more widely, though, so please be careful. Don't say anything to anyone about Harry calling Dick last night, or about what he said just now. Just forget it. I'll say that Dick suddenly felt unwell. He wasn't the first to feel unwell today, was he? Thanks, Greg. Now, you need a change, my sweet. Wave goodbye to everyone."

"I'll go after Dick," said Morag. "The Centre gives me practice in calming people down. Hopefully I'll get to some of your meeting, Carol."

To Liz and Greg's clear relief, Brian made an offer to Steph. "Susie's people are out today, so we're going straight back, leastways we are when we've said hi to Angela. Do you want a lift?"

I gave Steph a hug. "Bye for now, then."

"Wow, nearly three weeks to come without you, Pete. It's gonna be real hard."

That remark prompted suitable amusement before we stepped a little aside, and she continued quietly, to the accompaniment of hoots of laughter whilst hi and more was said.

"I'm sorry for the clanger. I'm not at my best. If I hadn't butted in, Carol would have headed Jane off."

"I'm sorry there was no chance to pass the news to you after I heard from Sheila. I called Pat, who will have called Mart. Sheila has told everyone to keep quiet, but can you call our Jane later, with the same message? Also, can you call your contact at Cork Gully? Say that you've heard a rumour that the pension fund money has reappeared, and ask if that's true. Then call Waterhouse Porter's Lodge, by a quarter past seven if at all possible. Leave a message – yes or no."

Twenty minutes later, Jenny and I were taking turns to push the pram in which Jenny had once ridden. It was quite hard to push, for Katie was surrounded by presents and there were more on the rack underneath. Ahead were the four grandparents, and David. John and Amanda had gone back to her place, before he returned to Sheffield.

"So, Pete, what did Harry discover about what you were up to in Spain, and how did my worries help him to do that?"

Jenny put that question as if on a tricky audit. Her dispassionate, professional manner expected an answer. I skimmed over 'Crafty' quite briefly, but was full on events at the club in Islington and their consequences.

"Goodness, the forward purchases were quite a coup for you all. They were just about legal, I suppose."

"Our Finance Director, who did law at university, has exactly that view."

"Then, your helping Dick and me led to the exposure of Reg Emerson, and thus to Carol's victory, to the Dugdales bringing Harry's firm down, to Harry raping Jane because she looks rather like me, to his finding out about your oil profits, and to his being on that plane. One thing is clear. As Liz said, Harry was *very* sick."

"None of us is responsible for what's happened to Harry, and to his friend Ramón. He brought that on himself. The story can be that he was coming back to face the music, and start again. That's what it will be, if I have anything to do with it. Tell Dick what you think best, Jenny, but not about the note. Only you know about that, apart from Ana and me. To everyone else, I was following up Pat O'Donnell's hunch."

"Perhaps the moral is that trouble goes with success. You are good at getting out of trouble, Pete. You always have been. Now, I hope Dick is in a state to talk about our future."

"I'll give you as much help as I can, and there's someone *you* may be able to help, Jenny. Last night, Harry referred to Ramón's brother being able to get out of trouble because of what he knew about a nice clean Don who's getting married next month. I told Ana quite a lot about my past, including about us, Dick, and Harry. It was meant to be part of making her informed about subjects that young ladies of quality don't hear about in Spain."

There was a pause, and then Jenny smiled.

"Of course I'll help if I can, Pete. We'd better catch up with the others."

We did so, and as the party approached the Wingham house, Morag emerged and greeted us.

"Dick is feeling much better now. He's organising tea for you all."

"Thank you so much, Morag. How helpful you've been. Won't you stay?" asked Belinda.

"Thanks, but I can hear some of Carol's talk, and then I'm going back with them. Can you walk a little way into town with me, Pete?"

As soon as we were out of earshot, Morag continued.

"I never met Harry Tamfield, but I could empathise with Dick's loss better than any of you. He was already feeling sorry for his outburst. He's such a decent man. He needs looking after, which Jenny does so very well. I said that it's to his credit he's so upset, but it's clear that Harry had this fetish in his mind. Dick said he wanted to move on. He told me how his research is going better, and began to talk about putting in for this post at Berkeley."

"Jenny told me about that. It's not a post. It's a two-year fellowship, really for people starting postdoctoral research. It doesn't move Dick's career on."

"That's right. I can see why Geoff is pushing Dick to apply. He would have his man at Berkeley, keeping him in touch with what's going on there. That would be very useful – for Geoff. But as I told Dick, there's an alternative – for him. He could develop a summer connection there. Several people I know go off to the same place in the States at the end of every June and return in September. Dick should look for the funding to go to Berkeley this summer, including for Jenny and the kids to go for some of the time. Then it would be up to him to make the people there feel that they want him back, enough that they're ready to pay. He's picked that idea up. Jenny is right to be worried about going there for longer. Just as Liz and Angela are basically straight girls, Dick is basically a straight guy. He had two girls before Harry. Now, he's happily married with two kids. He's made his choice, just as Sheila and I have made ours. Was Harry trying to disturb that?"

"He was. You are perceptive, Morag. You always have been, since I first met you."

"Aye – I like watching, listening, and thinking. In Brighton, I knew things were going on. Steph and Paul weren't looking like they hadn't met before, and Carol acted very busy after talking to you. There were more strange little talks in Bellinghame these last weeks. I guess you know more than you've said about how Reg Emerson was discredited, and I think Brian knows more, too."

"You may well be right, though Brian knows nothing about the oil trading."

"So you're in the middle of it all, just as you were here in Cambridge. You helped and supported me then, Pete. When you took me to that film all those years ago, you brought me a social life. I'm supporting you back, and I've helped to bring the right result in the election."

I looked a little up, to her plain, freckled face and dark hair. She had made her life through more difficulty than her calmness suggested. She hadn't changed much from that only time I invited her out. By her account to others, though never to me, we had nearly gone on. I replied accordingly.

"Morag, how can I thank you, for both last night and now? You don't say as much as some of us, but when you do, it's so sensible and helpful. You're such a decent woman, and you look after people. When I'm down in London, you must let me take you out to dinner – only."

Morag pulled out her diary.

"I've a better idea, Pete. On Tuesday, 14th May, I'm to give a seminar in Aberdeen. I've no lectures to give on the Monday, so I'll spend the weekend in Glasgow with Mother and come on to Aberdeen. You can take me out on Monday evening. My friend Laura Westlake can chaperone. Does the name mean anything to you?"

"Erm – she was a research student at Oxford. She came over for a seminar."

"She's now a lecturer at Aberdeen University. She's single, but not a blue stocking, and she's straight. I know that. When we were both at Edinburgh, I tried. Fortunately, she understood the state I was in, and we're still friends. She likes long walks, and good music."

"I'll book something, and let you know. It will be a treat for the day after my birthday. In the meantime, I've an invitation from Angela. Somehow, I don't think that will be dinner only."

"She *was* asking about you, especially once I said that Steph was going back to America."

"You've done Angela good. She's got rid of a lot of her airs."

"She's making her own career, too. Several places here and in London are selling her ceramics, she's receiving commissions, and now she's met people who've taken her advice on interior design."

"Liz told me that she was more or less engaged."

"She is. Jane was always good to me, for example I was welcome at Penny's wedding, but she was obviously very relieved when Angela and I split. Somehow Hugh turned up very quickly, and Angela went along. Then, he announced he was going away for a year – to Harvard, so Jane and Archie couldn't possibly complain. So Angela said she was going away, too. I see her occasionally for dinner, really only dinner. Sheila doesn't want me to do that, or to keep in touch with Gill, but I like to stay friends with my exes, too. Good luck, Pete. Angela likes a good fuck. Sometimes I used a strap-on, Carol's way, hard."

"It could be fun to fuck a Frampton, but I won't try to compete with Harvard man. I certainly don't want to be Geoff's brother-in-law."

We parted the good friends we were, though there was something left unsaid in Morag's face.

I was back at the Wingham house in time for the second round of cups of tea. All seemed to be back to normal. I chatted briefly with Linda and Derek, but soon they left, so that they could make the least familiar part of their journey before dark. An exhausted Katie was in her cot upstairs. Belinda surveyed the scene, and acted.

"You're still fractious, David. You were in your pushchair for too long. You're a big boy now. You'll be three, soon. Come for a walk with Granny and Grandad."

"Shan't."

"Yes, you shall. If you're good, you'll have ice cream for tea."

I was beginning to appreciate the firmness, tact and sensitivity that lay under Belinda's apparent fussiness. Perhaps that was because I was older. Perhaps also, I was seeing how Jenny was growing up as her mother's daughter.

Once they had left, Dick began in a way for which Morag had prepared me.

"I'm really sorry for the scene, but you both know I cared about Harry. Pete, you won't know that I helped him to get out of Switzerland."

"Harry knew you cared," said Jenny. "That's why he rang you. He was under huge pressure. What happened to him at Waterhouse resurfaced in his mind, and made him want to get his own back. Pete tells me that Harry had wind of some business International Electronics and New Hampshire Realty have together in Spain. At least he thought he had a reason to return, rather than to go on running away."

"Yes, he said he'd arranged for the money he'd taken to be paid back."

"So he died an honest man. That will be known."

"Perhaps death was a release, then. Not so for the friend he had with him, though. They wouldn't have been on the plane if I hadn't helped Harry."

"Harry would be under arrest, and facing a prison sentence, and two other people would have died. They're probably still in Paris, celebrating that there wasn't any room for them on the plane."

I forbore to mention that Harry could have faced two sentences. It was up to Jenny what she told Dick about Jane.

"Four o'clock, news summary." Jenny dashed to the radio.

"... Reports from the crash site suggest that the aircraft hit the ground at almost its full speed, and damage was so great that many bodies are unrecognisable. Some items of cargo, and several dead passengers still strapped in their seats, have been found several miles away from the crash site. An official of the French Transport Ministry has said that this could be consistent with an explosion on board. A French newspaper has received a telephone call claiming responsibility from an organisation calling itself the 'Liberal Front'. The Turkish communications minister has said that considering the world situation, he did not rule out sabotage."

"That fits with what Greg was saying,"[89] said Jenny.

"At the end of this bulletin I'll give again the telephone number to call if you have friends or relatives who may have been on the aircraft. Those known to be killed include Jim Conway, General Secretary of the Amalgamated Union of Engineering Workers, and also the fugitive property developer, Harry Tamfield. Sir Reg Emerson, who lost his seat in the general election following reports of his connections with Mr Tamfield, has apologised unreservedly for making the allegation that striking BEA workers were responsible for the deaths of British passengers, through forcing them to use the Turkish aircraft. The workers on unofficial strike include members of the AUEW.

"Hopes are fading that the Conservatives can reach sufficient of an arrangement with the Liberals and other parties to continue in office. It seems almost certain that Ted Heath will resign tomorrow and that Harold Wilson, as leader of the largest party in Parliament, will be asked to form a government. Our political correspondent..."

---

89 As became clear within a few days and was confirmed by detailed investigation – see the final report of the Commission of Inquiry and the full account in *Destination Disaster*. On the Turkish plane, unauthorised modifications 'had made the locking system easier to use', but the key, chilling, points had been set down soon after the Windsor incident, in an unpublished memorandum:

'The fundamental safety of the cargo door latching system has been progressively degraded since the program began in 1968... Since Murphy's Law being what it is, cargo doors will come open sometime during the twenty-plus years of use ahead for the DC-10... I would expect this to usually result in the loss of the airplane.'

I asked to use their phone, and moved into Harold Wingham's upstairs office. I had promised to call Pat again. Unsurprisingly, his line was engaged. Immediately I put the phone down, it rang.

"Pete, it's Arthur. I'm glad I've traced you. Have you heard that Tamfield has been killed in this air crash?"

"Yes."

"There's no obituary set up. The papers want stuff fast – tonight, if possible. We've promised to provide it, in return for reporters keeping away from the College."

"I think you're saying that another duty has fallen on me. Very well, but can you stall them off until tomorrow? I've heard rumours that the Cardinal pensioners will be OK, after all. By tomorrow, that should be definite."

"Right – we don't want to have produced crooks. I'll see you in Hall, then. Colin will say a few words, and leave you to decide whether you want to add anything. Oh, and half an hour ago the porters took an urgent message for you, from a foreign-sounding lady. I don't think they got her name right. It's something like Anna Guthrie. Can you call her as soon as possible? She said you have her number. I've not heard about *this* one, Pete."

I took a chance on dialling Pat again while the international operator placed my call to Spain. This time, I got through.

"I've been talking to Bill about a line. There are already three papers asking. How about this? 'Harry Tamfield's death is just one of over three hundred personal tragedies today. It cuts short the career of one of our most talented young businessmen. He had clearly decided to return and rebuild his career, as he was certainly capable of doing. It is particularly tragic that he has been prevented from carrying out this sensible decision.' There are two uses of 'tragic'. Any suggestions?"

"Read it again... It's a good line, especially if the pension fund money has been repaid. Change 'personal tragedies' to 'terrible losses'?"

"No, but we'll change the second 'tragic' to 'terrible'. Now, who knows you're in Cambridge?"

"Lots of people at Waterhouse, but Arthur is keeping the press out of there. I'm staying overnight, and should be in Aberdeen by two o'clock tomorrow. The office there is closed then, but I'll make sure that any enquiries are referred to Bill."

"Good. We're cutting out as quickly as possible. By Tuesday, Wilson coming in will swamp the story. I've spoken to Mart. After what he said yesterday about Oates, what he said today came as no surprise. Fortunately, there's no reason for anyone to ask him for a line. In my view, he's over promoted. Last night, I had to make a great effort to have him think coherently about your plan. We'll never know whether it would have worked or not, but at least it was a plan. No doubt you've made sure that everyone involved in it keeps quiet, now. If anything is needed for that, speak to George. I've also updated our Spanish friends. Pedro was not long back from Madrid. He sounded to be in quite a state. So I took your advice to go easy on him, and looked forward to plenty of productive work together."

Ana came through about a minute after Pat rang off. She was clearly under stress, but in control of herself. It was much as I had guessed.

After the conference with us finished, her father spent some time on the telephone, and then set off by car for Madrid, without saying why. He reached his house there shortly before Carlos, whom he had summoned from Seville. On their return to Pamplona, Carlos had repeated to Ana his confession of a homosexual relationship with the cashier's brother.

"So, Pete, Father has not challenged Carlos to a duel, but he thinks that I am betrayed and dishonoured. He is leaving the choice to me. I have asked to be alone for a while. What shall I do, Pete? There is no one else I can ask. When Carlos was kneeling before me, half of me was saying that I was seeing my betrothed for the first time in three weeks, and that I love him and want him. The other half of me was saying what Father says."

"When did this affair happen?"

"It was ten years ago, when they were both on military service. It is worse because Carlos was an officer, while the brother of the cashier was a common soldier. Carlos said, and I believe him, that it did not continue, and there has been no other such affair. He has gone with many girls since."

"Ten years ago you were thirteen years old, Ana. Was there any understanding then that you would eventually marry Carlos? Your mother did not die until four years later."

"To my knowledge, there was not."

"The brother of the cashier was with Harry Tamfield on the plane. His name was Ramón, by the way."

There was a silence, as Ana took in the implications of this.

"I will need to tell Carlos that he is dead."

"So your cashier has no evidence for any story he tells. Has your father satisfied himself that there was no attempt to obtain details of 'Crafty' by threatening Carlos?"

"Yes. Perhaps there was no time to do so. Harry Tamfield was in a hurry to obtain information, and Carlos was away."

"It is more likely that the two brothers were to make their own profit."

"I understand you, Pete. Before our wedding day, and after, Carlos would have suffered *el chantage* – what is the English word?"

"Blackmail."

"When the brothers had taken as much money as they could from Carlos, they would expose him, and me. Because Harry Tamfield came to Spain, we are saved from that. There is nothing to force me to reject Carlos. I have a choice. I want him very much, and he wants me. When we meet for a 'rest', it is now difficult for both of us to hold back. At night, we both think of the other, and feel ourselves, sinfully. Yet how can I be sure that Carlos will not go back to his earlier behaviour?"

"Ana, the second child of Jenny and Dick Sinclair was baptised today. Jenny and Dick have succeeded together. They have overcome a much greater threat than you face. As I told you, Dick was with Harry for two years. Six years ago, Jenny wanted Dick, as you want Carlos now. She knew what she needed to do. Recently, Harry was trying hard to get Dick back. That is how he found your note, which led him to Spain. He did not succeed. Jenny and Dick are closer now than they were before."

"Pete, is it possible that Jenny would be ready to speak to me about this?"

"I am at her parents' house. Wait for a moment to let me explain, and I shall bring her to the phone."

Ana had to wait for a little more than a moment, because I went downstairs to hear good news.

"We've been talking about Geoff's idea that Dick should spend some time at Berkeley," said Jenny.

"Morag suggested that I should get over there, but for two or three months in the summer, rather than for two years. I need Geoff's help to fix that," said Dick.

"You need his help to find you a good enough bursary that Jenny and the children can come over for a while, too," I said.

"I think we can persuade him to help," said Jenny, with a smile. "We've time to do that, as we're staying over until Tuesday."

"I'm sorry I was so long. One of the people I was speaking to would like to speak to you, Jenny."

After some more murmured explanation, I put Jenny on the phone to Ana, and returned to Dick. A few minutes later, Jenny was back, to say that I was needed again. Even on the crackly line, I could hear that for Ana, resolution had replaced doubt.

"Pete, it was so helpful to speak to Jenny. She told me how she took Dick to a hotel, and showed him that he could again love a woman. I know I can trust her, and will telephone her again for advice. Today, I will do two things. First, I will ask Father to tell the cashier that his brother Ramón is dead, and warn him that if he ever repeats what he has said about Ramón and Carlos, he will be subject to the full penalties of the law, which are severe."

"Your father could also have the cashier moved to another post, well away from Pamplona."

"That is a good idea, Pete. Second, I will tell Father that I want to be alone with Carlos. We shall go first to Pamplona Cathedral, where we are to be married in six weeks' time. At my mother's tomb, we shall pray together for her, for Ramón, for Harry Tamfield, and for all others killed today. Then we shall go to my family's town house, for a 'rest', and this time we shall not hold back. I feel closer to Carlos than before, and I could see how he felt at the possibility of losing me. It is time to end any hesitation, and to come together fully. If our first child is born sooner than expected, that will be a sign of God's blessing."

As I rang off, I felt really elated. Ana was showing the same qualities of resolve as does her namesake, the most important character in Mozart's opera. I was even more elated when I returned to the lounge, to find Jenny and Dick in each other's arms.

"You were just saying, Dick, that we've a great opportunity now, with David out and Katie asleep. I'm sure you'll excuse us, Pete. Up you go, Dick, I'll just say bye. Gosh, I mustn't be long, must I!"

Dick set off upstairs. Jenny wrote a note to her mother that they would be 'down shortly', and turned to me.

"I think we're sorted. Dick is over Harry, and you saw what he wants now. Though what's happened is so awful, it's made us both realise what we mean to each other."

"So it's well done, Morag. She's a very good friend to us all. And well done, Jenny, for being so helpful to Ana. You're now a very good friend to her. What's happened, and what you said, has made her realise what she and Carlos mean to each other. You've turned her right on for him."

"Talking to her about Dick has turned me right on, too."

"I think you may have already been a bit on."

I licked my lips, and Jenny also licked hers.

"Mmmm, yes, Amanda told me while I was changing Katie. It was lucky that she found the thermometer."

"Geoff was very silly to thump her and Brian."

"I knew he would be silly. He'll know now how silly he was. He won't want Jane to find out what happened. He's still his mother's little boy at heart. I'll have no problem in making sure he helps Dick to get the funding. I just need Angela not to blow the gaff. She heard a bit from Brian, and she and I will have the full story from Amanda tomorrow. The three of us are going to the sauna."

"That will be a nice reward for Amanda, in John's absence."

"It's the public session for women, but as you say, Pete, a nice reward, for me too."

"It was good to see something of Amanda in action, if not all of the action."

"I think we'll all have memories of today."

"Yes, for Creators this will be The Day to Remember. Up you go now, Jenny. My thanks and regards to your parents. I've left money for the calls. I'll ring you in a few days about another idea I've had."

We kissed for just a little longer than either pure friendship or sibling relationship would merit, and I grabbed my coat.

As I walked back to Waterhouse College through the dusk, I had many memories of six years before, but now they were happy rather than wistful. I had seen once again how Jenny organised people in the loveliest sort of way, and dealt with people like Geoff who crossed her. In Steph's terms, Jenny was as smart, and as bad, as the rest of us. She was fully a Creator.

The tragic realities of the day crowded into my mind, as the latest in a series of chance events that had determined so much. I met Ana and her father at the opera. She and I spotted and overheard Kraftlein and the Egyptians. Pat took on Paul. I met the Sinclairs on the ferry back from Spain, and hence I heard about Harry's party. There, I spotted the asterisk by Reg Emerson's name, and also met Steph. So, she became involved in Paul's schemes. Roberta wanted good terms from Tamfield Investments, Harry over-reacted to that, and then he tried to turn Dick. Ana's note arrived on the day that allowed Harry to see it. Carol was adopted for Bellinghame South. Just as had happened during the few weeks before I had left Cambridge, even one different chance could have changed the entire outcome.

For Creators, the desire to make a difference was addictive. Our reactions to events had moved us on. Though we all had our secrets from each other, we formed a real network of friendship and mutual support. Back in July, that had allowed me to help Roberta. In November, Steph had given me the ideas for helping Jenny and Dick, which had also hit the jackpot for Carol. Over the last weeks, Brian had led our successful support of Carol. Last night, Jenny had alerted me to Harry's call. Early today, Morag and Sheila had backed my last ditch plan. Later today, Morag had calmed Dick down, and had him think more clearly, but she would not have succeeded without the help Liz, Greg and Brian had given. Jenny had helped Ana to overcome her doubts, and to be closer to Carlos.

We would all continue to be tested, and to move on.

Carol's star had been born, at the expense of Harry, but it could shine only briefly in the forthcoming Parliament. I hoped that she could carry herself forward with her pen, on both sides of the Atlantic.

Paul had deliberately stayed the schemer, the back-room boy, where he had again made a great impact. Jenny didn't know half of what he had done, but she was right to say that he couldn't always be trusted. Carol didn't know everything about Paul either, but she was right to say that they were a good fit for each other. I was right in what I had said both to Jenny and to Sir Archie. The country needed more people you couldn't always trust.

Brian and Susie were also a good fit for each other. They were becoming a successful man and his supportive wife. As I had remarked earlier, this was quite a move up from where Brian seemed to be going when I left Cambridge.

Liz and Greg had built a very close and intense relationship, which would be tested once Liz started with the NUM. Her plans showed that she too met Steph's standard for Creators.

Morag was settled with Sheila, and the Pankhurst Centre was clearly very important to her. I continued to be worried at Sheila's desire to dominate their relationship. What Morag had said about Angela was another example.

As 'friends plus', Steph and I could have more good times together, whilst she enjoyed Jane as well as Paul. She had not 'made her choice' in Morag's terms. Once she was back in the USA, she would do so. She would come to realise that she had not understood Paul's real agenda. Their relationship would be self-limiting.

For the next few months, I would also have opportunities with Carol, and quite possibly with Angela. In May, I would find out what Laura Westlake was like. I wouldn't say no to Jane, once in a while, though the rest and recreation centre, if it came off, would be business.

In any case, I wouldn't have much time for fun with the ladies. I needed to get on with my day job, within the UK's greatest business opportunity for a very long time. Once my office could open all the week, my work could go into top gear. I needed to justify reaching senior level in IE very quickly. I needed to report to Terry McAvitt, rather than having frequent contacts with Pat. I needed to deliver good profits soon, and thereby satisfy those who were suspicious of my role. Just as when I was elected to a Fellowship at Waterhouse, there was a credibility gap for me to close.

The last three days had been a roller coaster, even more demanding than the three days which had ended my time in Cambridge. Now, I had less than an hour to prepare for my talk.

I hoped I could keep awake for that, and for Hall, and I hoped that I could announce there that Harry wasn't really a crook. The drafting of an obituary could wait until the morning. I was beginning to feel desperately tired.

OBITUARY

Harry Tamfield

Henry Charles Tamfield (always known as Harry), Chief Executive of the collapsed property company, Tamfield Investments, died in the Paris air disaster on 3 March. He was born on 19 March 1947.

He showed early signs of academic promise, but was always regarded as something of a 'loner' during an early life which was on his account not happy, because of the break-up of his parents' marriage. This reputation persisted when he entered Waterhouse College, Cambridge as an exhibitioner, to read natural sciences. However, there he discovered his real bent, for organisation and business, as concert manager of the Cambridge University Baroque Society orchestra. By the start of his third year he had transformed this into a nationally known specialist group, and looked set for a career in musical administration.

Then, a setback led him in a different direction. A demonstration against a planned tour of Portugal led to the wrecking of a concert, injuries to several players, and cancellation of the tour. Responsibility for the violence was established as being that of a small group, whose leader served a prison sentence, rather than of mainstream left-wing movements in Cambridge. However, the experience developed in the previously non-political Harry Tamfield an abiding hatred of the Left.

He departed from Cambridge without completing his degree, and applied his business skills to property development. Starting in a small way, using the proceeds of a legacy, he refurbished for sale previously rented properties, and soon established a reputation as a sharp and ruthless operator. He defended his methods robustly, pointing out that they led to upgrade of basically sound but neglected property near the centre of London.

His company's operations were sufficiently profitable that when credit was decontrolled he was able to raise almost unlimited sums and rapidly expand his business. For a time this remained of the type with which he began. The great and ultimately fatal challenge to him arose early in 1973, when the bankers of the bankrupt Cardinal Properties, a developer of large suburban estates, invited him to take the company over.

He had initial success in ending industrial disputes that had plagued Cardinal's operations, and during the summer of 1973 he was hailed as one of the brightest young entrepreneurs of our time. In retrospect, the high point of his career was the now notorious private party held in July 1973, to celebrate the takeover of Cardinal.

Late in 1973, it became clear that his direct approach to dealing with difficulties did not easily translate into the larger world. This was most demonstrated by the publicity given in February 1974 to his dealings with Sir Reginald Emerson, then Parliamentary Under-Secretary in the Department of Works and MP for the Bellinghame South constituency, in which is located the largest of the developments he had taken over from Cardinal. This publicity was a significant factor in Sir Reginald's narrow defeat by the Labour candidate, Carol Milverton, in the recent general election.

Also late in 1973, Tamfield Investments was hard hit by declining sales and rising interest rates, as were other property companies. A substantial sale to a housing trust, brokered by Carol Milverton, appeared to have enabled Tamfield Investments to surmount these. However, on 20 February 1974 the company's bankers forced it into liquidation.

In the election campaign, Harry Tamfield had already taken a public position strongly supporting the

Conservatives and regarding Labour as a threat. The loss of his company placed him under extreme stress. That explains the remarkable and unsubstantiated allegations, and suggestions of a conspiracy directed against him, that he made on TV on 19 February. He appeared to be reacting to the fact that Carol Milverton's husband had been a leader of the mainstream student left in Waterhouse College, and therefore in his mind was associated with the wrecking of the concert and the ending of his first career.

Harry Tamfield departed for Switzerland, ostensibly on a skiing holiday. It was discovered that substantial amounts were missing from the Cardinal Properties' pension fund. Accordingly, a warrant was issued for his arrest, and his extradition was sought. However, he was not located in Switzerland.

It seems that he crossed unnoticed into France, and perhaps there reflected quietly on his position and prospects. That appears to have decided him to return and face the consequences of his actions. Before he left Paris, the amounts missing had been repaid, so that there will be no loss to Cardinal pensioners.

It would not be appropriate to speculate on what would have happened had Harry Tamfield returned safely to the UK. However, given his previous recovery from a serious reverse, it is very possible that after a while he would have reappeared as a force on the business scene. His death adds to the tragedy of the DC-10 crash.

He was unmarried.